End of August

A Novel

Paige Dinneny

alcove
press

This is a work of fiction. All of the names, characters, organizations, places and events portrayed in this novel are either products of the author's imagination or are used fictitiously. Any resemblance to real or actual events, locales, or persons, living or dead, is entirely coincidental.

Copyright © 2025 by Paige Dinneny

All rights reserved.

Published in the United States by Alcove Press, an imprint of The Quick Brown Fox & Company LLC.

Alcove Press and its logo are trademarks of The Quick Brown Fox & Company LLC.

Library of Congress Catalog-in-Publication data available upon request.

ISBN (hardcover): 979-8-89242-024-2
ISBN (paperback): 979-8-89242-225-3
ISBN (ebook): 979-8-89242-025-9

Cover design by Heather VenHuizen

Printed in the United States.

www.alcovepress.com

Alcove Press
34 West 27th St., 10th Floor
New York, NY 10001

First Edition: February 2025

10 9 8 7 6 5 4 3 2 1

End of August

For Mom: I love you to the moon and back

Prologue

Summer 1979—Monroe, Indiana

It's the end of August when my mother packs her things into cardboard boxes. Carelessly, of course, dumping entire drawers into each, using the bottom of her callused feet to compress the contents, forcing more room. She slides her hands across the vanity, sweeping in bobby pins and lipsticks and aerosol cans of hair products. Each item's fall is broken by the excessive pairs of underwear lining the bottom of a box marked with her name, "LAINE." She's only cautious with her perfume, wrapping it in an old pajama shirt.

"The nightstand," I say, prompting her.

I've always been in charge of final checks during our disappearing acts, making sure nothing important gets left behind.

She looks over as if noticing me for the first time. These past few days she's been worlds away, every conversation an interruption to whatever she's replaying in her mind.

The ashtray on the nightstand is full of late-night cigarettes, the room still thick with the smell. Her smell. I know the smell will stay, even if she won't, forcing me to think of her on the days I don't want to.

She steps over my bare, outstretched legs on the way to the master bathroom. I listen for the sink, and when she returns, the ashtray is washed clean.

"Didn't you make this?" she asks, holding up the misshapen ceramic piece before wrapping it in another T-shirt.

"Seventh grade," I say. "The assignment was a bowl. I got a C–. It didn't pass the cereal test."

I

She laughs, and it startles me.

I stretch forward, bending my torso, my arms too short to reach the end of my legs. My body carries the tension of these last few days, down to my toes. Sometimes, when I'm still for too long, I wonder if I'll break.

There's a letter in the nightstand drawer, exactly where I left it, beside the Bible my mother stole from a motel near Fort Wayne. She examines the name scrawled on the front, like *Laine* is written in a foreign language she can't understand. I wait to see if she places it in the box, but she doesn't. She sets his letter back inside the drawer before shutting it, leaving the dusty Bible behind too. It's too late for the commandments to do her any good.

My mother looks less beautiful than she did at the end of May, before everything started, before things began to fall apart. The years caught up to her over the last three months, leaving her with more fine lines by her eyes and a permanent frown. I watch her move to the closet. With both hands on her hips, she releases a shaky sigh. The shoes form a small mountain. Most are nowhere near their pairs.

We've always traveled light, but this summer she let herself expand. I watched her spend her paychecks on impractical heels and sundresses and new sneakers for me, and all along I thought it was a good sign. How could we leave this place if we had so much to pack? I feel silly now, looking back. I searched for signs we would stay, desperate for them, but I've known her for all my life, and she's never been one to change.

She presses her back against the doorframe and slides to the floor. "I need a cigarette."

The pack is by my feet. She bends to grab it, loosening one and placing it between her lips. Her eyes reflect the glow of the flame. When it lights, she offers it to me. I hold the cigarette between my thumb and forefinger. Supposedly these things are dangerous, but Mom says so are a lot of things.

This is the third cigarette I've smoked in my life, and the second I've smoked with my mother. When I pull it in, it burns my lungs, but I don't cough. She stands, and I watch her use one hand to tug shirts off hangers and drop them in a new, empty box. I won't be there when she unpacks, picking through wrinkled items, searching for the day's outfit. The clothes won't find hangers until well into month two.

"Isn't this yours?" she asks, tossing a summer dress at my feet.

"Yeah, but you wear it more." I fold and set it in the box beside me.

"What about this one?" She presses a red dress against her. "Can I take it?"

The dress is hers, but I don't say that. Instead, I roll my eyes. "Only if you leave behind the denim shorts."

She knows the pair I'm asking for, which is why she bites her lip, considering the trade-off. "Deal, but you drive a hard bargain."

When the shorts land by my feet I pick them up, feeling the fabric. She wore them that afternoon when she made the lemonade, back when Tim was just a mailman, and we were just a house on his route. Our lives were separate then. I guess our lives are separate now too. We continue on like this, exchanging one item for another, dividing our shared life in two.

She's always been better at mindless chatter. I suppose I could accept this. Maybe I've been expecting too much from her. Maybe I was wrong to assume things about motherhood. The only real comparisons I had were moms on TV, and she was nothing like them. We didn't have heart to hearts like they did in *The Afterschool Special*. There were never casseroles. Maybe I'd misunderstood our roles.

The back and forth makes me brave. "Have you decided where you're headed?" I ask.

For a moment, there's silence. "California," she says, in an upbeat, unfamiliar voice. She looks at me and adds, "It's not too late for you to change your mind."

The closet is nearly empty, and the boxes are almost full.

California. The furthest place she could pick without crossing an ocean.

Tomorrow we'll load the back seat with her four cardboard boxes, two more than she started the summer with. She'll make room for me if I ask. She'll lose a box of her belongings to fit mine. I think she'd do anything to keep me in the passenger seat, and sometimes I want to be there.

It's a comforting thought, if I'm being honest. I think staying might be harder than leaving, and maybe that's why she's always going. There are a thousand reasons to go. I make lists late at night in the room that finally feels like mine. But there are a thousand reasons to stay too.

"Gran needs me, though, doesn't she?"

Her back is to me, but I watch as her shoulders slump.

Maybe my mother needs me too.

She says, "It won't be forever."

And I want to tell her to stop there. That I don't need her to continue the monologue that always follows. It's the same speech she's been telling everyone, on loop: me, Gran, Karl, Norma—anyone willing to hear her out. The list of names is short, but the speech is not:

"I never had a chance to find myself.

"I had a kid when I was still a kid.

"I'm hoping to take a break, just for a little while.

"She has school coming up, and Gran and new friends."

Without a hint of irony or regret, in her new, upbeat voice, she tells them:

"There's no reason to turn her life upside down."

And even though every person she tells knows the real story; can see the wood boards covering our shattered front window; heard her screaming when he made his way down our driveway, back to the family across town and the woman he calls his wife, every person she tells just nods like this is a good idea. Like she's running toward something instead of away.

The thought of the distance makes me sick, and I guess the question keeping me up at night is whether or not I should go with. Whether or not I want to. Whether or not she wants me to.

She has things she's running from, and I have things I'm running toward, and for the first time in my fifteen years, we are headed in opposite directions. I don't want to run. She doesn't want to stay. And maybe that's the way it's supposed to be.

End of August

It's the end of August when my mother takes a break from being a mother, waving from the end of our driveway with a cigarette dangling from her ruby lips, hooking a left toward the interstate. It's the end of August when my mother leaves me behind, and even though I won't say it out loud, I think I'm relieved.

1

Our Vega was hard to miss—illegally parked, firetruck red; Mom leaned against the door on the passenger side. In her cutoff shorts and sunshine-yellow tank top, she looked nothing like other moms. If she snuck into a classroom and took a seat, no one would think twice.

The final school bell on Friday always sent everyone into a frenzy. That and the almost-summer smell in the air filled the school with a loud, contagious excitement that spilled outside as we all fled down the steps. The combination of sun and asphalt made Indiana feel like the inside of an oven, but even the almost-summer heat was welcome relief after an afternoon trapped in suffocating classrooms.

"What are you doing here?" I asked nervously, yanking my backpack straps tighter, taking the front steps two at a time.

She worked afternoon shifts at the diner, sometimes picking up the late ones if we needed the money. On those nights I had my pick of the frozen Swanson TV dinners we kept stocked and my choice in TV shows. I had been a bus kid for as long as I could remember. Her picking me up was rare, and it was never a good sign.

A group of boys walked by, nudging one another. Charles, the boy who sat behind me in algebra, mimed big boobs on his chest while the others let out a chorus of cackles. The perks of having a *noticeable* mother.

Mom let out a long sigh. "Jay's dead."

I stopped short on the last step. Jay, I thought, picturing the weathered, white-haired man with thick-rimmed glasses. A murky mix of emotions spun through me. I tried to sort out what I was feeling, a sinking discomfort settling in my gut. He was Gran's husband—the only man she ever truly loved. They'd been married as long as I'd been alive—fifteen years.

But it wasn't like he was a real grandpa to me, like the other kids in my class had, even though he was special to me in his own Jay kind of way. All I really knew of him came from a few trips to their house in Monroe, Indiana. Mom fled from there as a teenager, carrying me, a melon-sized stowaway in her belly. It took more than two hands to count the towns I'd called home since then, but Monroe had never been one of them. Mom kept a distance for the both of us.

"When?" I asked. "*How?* Is she okay?"

"In his sleep," Mom answered, quieting my spiraling thoughts. "Mom woke up and he was gone."

"And Gran? Is she okay?"

Mom shrugged. "I mean she says she's all right."

Gone. I'd never known Gran without Jay, but Mom's stories painted a vivid picture. Jay's presence was quiet and calming—the exact opposite of Gran's, and Mom's, really. I'd pored over enough issues of *Seventeen* magazine to know opposites attract. They were my real-life proof. Mom always said he loved Gran in spite of herself, and she loved him right back. I think Mom was bitter about it.

Even with Jay by her side, Gran was a wild card. It turns out quitting whiskey couldn't cure sass. In all my memories of Monroe, she was bold and bright and constant. Maybe that's why my thoughts of Jay were so muddied—she took up all the space in the room.

What would she do without him?

I approached the car, palms turning sweaty as I recognized the familiar scene. "What's this?" I asked.

Cardboard boxes, three to be exact, were lined up in the back seat. "LAINE" was written in bold, blocked letters on two of them. On my box, "Aurora" was crayoned in a childlike scrawl.

I crossed my arms and my eyes narrowed.

Mom followed my gaze. "We're going to stay with Mom for a while, make sure she's really all right." She opened my door for me. "Come on, let's go."

I made no moves toward her getaway car. "I have a week left in the semester. I'll miss my finals."

Most kids would be thrilled to miss finals, but this was my first full year at the same school, and I was desperate to see it through.

"Come on," she said, "I don't want to be on the road too late."

"Mom." I planted my feet firmly on the asphalt.

All around me, my classmates spilled into the parking lot and piled into cars, oblivious to the life-altering moment taking place. Most were headed to Jimbo's Drive-In, around the corner, for fries and shakes. Some would end up in Danny Mason's basement, or at least that's what I'd gathered from rumors Sharpied on the bathroom stalls.

A wave of sadness hit me. I wished it was for Jay, but it wasn't. It was for myself, which only made me feel worse.

I wasn't naive to this parking-lot routine, and my heart felt the sudden drop. Mom loved a dramatic exit, and my life up until this point was a string of them. Come Monday, when my seat was empty in homeroom, I doubted my classmates would even notice. There was little purpose in making friends beyond lunchroom acquaintances—I secured a place to sit, and that was it.

It hadn't taken me long—maybe three moves, tops—to figure out leaving was less painful when you didn't have to say goodbye.

"Can I at least finish the semester?" I tried, knowing it would be fruitless. "Get my grades in?"

We'd lived in eighteen towns during my fifteen years on earth. Some were before I had the sense to notice, but by the time I was old enough to be aware of Mom's habits, she had little intention of breaking them. I threw a handful of parking-lot fits before realizing Laine always got her way.

Mom rolled her eyes and waved a stack of papers. "I got your grades. Told them we had a death in the family, and they said you were good to go. Turns out I've been raising a little smarty-pants—finals or not, you passed the courses." She opened the door further. "Now come on—get in."

Even with passing grades, I wanted to hear the final bell on that final day. I wanted to see something through to the end. I could have tried to explain this to her, but there'd have been no point. My resistance was rare, and it never made much of a difference. I walked toward the car with lead-filled legs and slumped into the passenger seat, shoving my backpack on the floor. Mom paraded around the front with a pep in her step, her dark curls bouncing, garnering another catcall from Charles and his crew.

The door creaked as she opened it. It took two turns of the key to start the car, like even our old Vega was protesting this new leg of its endless journey. We'd put thousands and thousands of miles on it in pursuit of a place to call home. So far, we'd had no luck.

❦

The drive to Gran's was only two and a half hours, but I waited to start talking until an hour in. Mom didn't mind the silent treatment—she flipped through radio stations until she found one she liked, sang along to a few top forty hits, and started flipping again once she got bored. I think she knew I'd break first. I always did.

"How long are we staying?" I finally asked.

Mom shrugged. "Not long. I just want to check on her."

"Will we go back to Sherwood?"

Mom's eyes were fixed on the outstretch of Highway 24. "Do you want to go back to Sherwood?"

There was nothing special about Sherwood, Indiana, other than the fact that we'd lasted there so long. Mom had refrained from dating up until a few weeks ago. Lloyd from Logansport and his frequent temper tantrums had temporarily cured her need for a man. This independent woman act lasted longer than most. Lloyd was a real doozy. But then, a few weeks ago, she'd brought home Ned, and life began a familiar routine of late nights and awkward mornings.

"I guess not," I said, which was kind of the truth. I went to great lengths to avoid wanting anything. It kept the disappointment at bay. "So, what's the plan?"

Mom reached across the center consul and gave my arm a friendly shake. "Aurora, you and your need for plans." She let go of my arm and flashed her most brilliant smile. "What if the plan is we have no plan? We just see what happens. How about that?"

"Fine."

Mom's smile faded a bit. "We just gotta make sure your Gran is fine, and then we'll find our next spot."

I never knew how long we'd stay—an hour, a day, a week—only that the end would be sudden. Gran and Mom were oil and water, our visits always ending in a fight. Mom never could reconcile Gran now with the mom in her stories. It never took long for her anger to rise back to the surface. Even with the task of burying a dead man, I had no reason to think this time would be any different.

~ ~ ~

I knew the highway to Monroe well enough to know when we were getting close. Even if I was uncertain, Mom's tightened grip on the steering wheel was a dead giveaway. She hated coming back here.

"Too many burned bridges," she'd say. "Some of them still smoking."

We'd been silent for the last three exits, and at some point the radio turned to static. She didn't bother to search for a station. I'm sure her thoughts were loud enough.

The exit to Monroe was sudden—a blink-and-you-might-miss-it sort of town, like most in Indiana. Mom opened the glovebox for a cigarette, hooking a hard left, and rolled straight through the stoplight.

The siren was immediate and deafening, blue and red flashing lights in the rearview mirror.

"Shit," Mom said, pulling over to the side of the road. The tires hit gravel before falling silent on a patch of roadside dirt. "What a welcome home." She angled the rearview mirror down and applied a fresh coat of lipstick, baring her teeth for me. "Anything?"

I shook my head, and she blew me an air kiss. There was a time when everything she did had seemed so glamorous. By fifteen, some of the charm had worn off.

The officer tapped on the window, and she struggled to roll it down. The handle was always getting stuck. She let out a giggle and looked up at the face I couldn't see.

"Ho-ly shit," the man's voice said. "You've got to be kidding me."

"Phil?" she said, the voice she used much more thawed out for him than it'd be for the rest of the town.

He tried the handle, and the door to our shitty Vega swung open. I leaned over the center console, straining to see their embrace. He held her away from him with a hand on each shoulder.

"Still as fine as ever," he said.

She let out a genuine laugh and swatted at his arm.

"Aurora." She bent down to look at me. "Get out. I want you to meet someone."

I obeyed, instinctively reaching to pat down my hair. As hard as I resisted, her habits had become my own.

I circled the car, and she gestured at me like I was a prize on the *Price is Right*. "Phil, this is Aurora. Aurora, this is my oldest friend, Phil."

Phil was an imposing figure in his cop uniform. A thick mustache covered his upper lip, like he was really leaning into the job. But even with the uniform and facial hair, there was something disarmingly kind about him.

I stuck out my hand and he took it. "I've always hoped to meet you."

Most of our visits to Monroe came and went with little fanfare. Mom said she wasn't trying to catch up with the past—she liked to leave it back behind where it belonged.

"It's nice to meet you."

"She's your clone, Laine," he said, speaking as if I weren't there.

His eyelashes were naturally thick, the kind of lashes Mom spent ten minutes trying for each morning. Mom rarely told me stories about her old home. Even from the memories she did share, his name didn't ring any bells.

Mom smiled. "My mom told me you got your badge. Can't believe you used to be making trouble and now you're out here policing it."

"Can't believe you're still running reds."

"This is where I say I won't do it again, Officer." She batted her eyes and jutted out her bottom lip. "Right?"

Phil ran a hand through his hair and smiled. "Only if you let me buy you a drink while you're in town."

The scene felt familiar and predictable, like I'd seen this episode before. No one missed a line, skipped a beat.

"Let me get home to my mom," she said. "Get this one all settled in, and then I'll find you at King's. Unless Monroe's come up with a new watering hole."

Phil shook his head. "Nah, same old haunt."

"Figures." Mom's smile was genuine. "Then I guess I'll see you at King's."

To the surprise of no one, Phil didn't write her a ticket.

⁂

The town was washed orange by the setting sun as we drove through. Downtown looked like most downtowns—a hardware store, a diner, a Rexall Drugs, remnants of a few businesses come and gone. Mom knew her route by heart; there was no need for a map.

Once you passed its center, you had two options: turn right or turn left. Left brought you to the developments, where WWII veterans, for a fair price, claimed a piece of land to call their own. Right brought you to the houses on plots of land that had been there since the start of the town itself. We turned left.

Turning on the street, I was surrounded by a world that felt much more familiar to me than anything we'd seen thus far. My version of Monroe was small—limited to the blue house at the end of the cul-de-sac. Gran's front yard was where I spent most of my visits, making chalk outlines with her, joining her neighbor Karl for his routine watering of the garden. In the afternoon, I'd sit cross-legged on the carpet, watching soap operas I was much too young for.

Mom only hesitated for a second before we pulled into the driveway. The blinds were shut and there was no porch light on for us, but Karl was outside his house, like I'd expected. According to him, dusk was the best time to feed the flowers. It gave them the evening to retain the water before the sun came back out to steal it.

I forced open the passenger door, the car groaning with old age.

"Is that Miss Aurora I see?" Karl yelled, making his way down the driveway with a slower walk than the last time I'd seen him. "You grew up."

"Hi there, Karl," Mom said.

He patted her arm with his weathered hand. "It's a shame about Jay."

Mom nodded. "How's she been?"

Karl stepped back. He was in his pajamas, a striped set with dirt stains at the knees. His wife had died a few summers back, around the time of our last visit. Gran said he was lost without her.

"Katherine is a force to be reckoned with. She's asked that no one bring by casseroles. Poor Norma tried, but she tossed it in the trash, right in front of her face, Pyrex and all." He laughed like he couldn't help it.

Mom bit her lip. "Good to know. Well, I'm sure we'll see you around."

"Yes, at the service tomorrow." Karl used the palms of his hands to dust some of the dirt off his knees. "I'll have to ride with you three—turns out the state isn't too fond of blind bats like me on the road."

Mom laughed.

He reached out a hand and held her elbow like it was something delicate. "How long you plan on staying?"

The million-dollar question. I knew the answer, but I was still desperate for her to say it. There was a comfort in knowing what the coming days held—the coming weeks—the coming months. It was a comfort I rarely had, but I was always looking for clues to what she had in mind.

She looked up at the house, and I watched her smile transform into a frown. "Not too long."

Gran must have been watching from the blinds, because by the time we reached the front door, it swung open. She came out onto the porch and offered me her hand. Her hair was flat without her usual teasing, and her eyelashes were bare. Her cheeks were pale—no rouge to be seen. I suppose without Jay, there was no one to get ready for either.

"Hi there, Aurora," she said, pulling me in for a hug.

Mom slipped past us, setting her boxes in the hallway. I waited for her to offer her condolences. She didn't. "You got any food, Mom?"

Gran shook her head. The room was dark with the lamp switched off. The TV was on, though, a staple at Gran's, making noise in an otherwise silent house.

"Well, we've been driving all day, and I know Aurora's probably hungry." It'd been all of three hours and I wasn't, but I didn't correct her. "Heard you've been turning down casseroles, so I figure the two of us might head to the store."

"Suit yourself. God knows I wasn't planning on parading through IGA while the town gossips told me how sorry they were for my loss." Her face might have looked unfamiliar without her usual glamour, but the edge in her response assured me that Gran in mourning was still Gran. "No thank you, but if you have it in you, be my guest."

"Any special requests?" Mom's tone had an edge, and I didn't know why, but Gran matched it.

"I've got what I need," she said.

"I don't mind staying with Gran." It was the first time in a while I'd used my voice.

"Well, all right then. Suit yourself. I should be back in an hour."

Mom shut the door she'd opened just minutes before, leaving Gran and me in her wake.

When I turned around, Gran collapsed into the recliner that had once belonged to Jay. His P. D. James novel was still on the side table, earmarked two-thirds of the way through. There was a glass on the table too, filled up halfway with a dark liquid.

"I'm sorry about Grandpa Jay," I said, hoping it would count for the both of us.

"Me too." She fixed her eyes on the TV screen, grabbed the glass from the side table, and held it to her lips, pausing before taking a long drink. "Me too."

2

Mom wasn't back in an hour, which wasn't all that surprising. I was used to this. Sometime past midnight, after Gran witnessed my third yawn, she got up from her recliner and showed me to my bed.

"You can take her old room," she said, opening the doorway to the room I'd stayed in for every visit. Yellow floral wallpaper. A dust-covered dresser. "She didn't live in it all that long."

"Mom can sleep here. I don't mind the couch."

Gran shook her head. "No, I'm good out there. Your mom can take the big bed."

There was a set of pajamas at the foot of the bed. "Bought those for you last summer before she canceled the visit. They might flood at the bottoms now that you've grown so tall."

"They'll be perfect," I said.

"Should we be worried?" She glanced down the hallway toward the front door.

I shook my head. "She might come home late, but she always comes home."

"All right then," Gran said. "'Night, Aurora."

She shut the door behind her but left the light on. I slipped into the pajamas. She was right: they would have fit perfectly a summer ago, before my growth spurt. I'd shot up to five feet ten inches seemingly overnight, leaving Mom and Gran (and most of the boys in my grade) in my dust. The non-Taylor genetics were strong.

It took some getting used to, and I'd spent plenty of nights crying into my pillow over it.

"Maybe you should join the basketball team," Mom had said unhelpfully while she ran her hands through my hair.

Mom's room looked like it was picked from a catalogue, like Jay had called in and ordered everything from the page. Floral wallpaper. White wrought iron bed frame. White side tables with a matching dresser. It was perfect for the sixteen-year-old girl who'd left it behind. A time capsule. The drawers were, of course, empty. When Jay and Gran had gotten together, the idea was for Mom to move in here with them, but she'd had other plans.

Maybe if she hadn't made such a big mistake, this room would have been hers for more than a few months.

I, of course, was the mistake. I tried my best not to let it bother me. Mom assured me I was a good mistake, and Gran agreed, but nobody ever said I wasn't one. Gran said I was too smart to lie to. "I can see it in your eyes," she said, tapping her finger on my temple. "You've got a way of understanding the world's truths, and it'd be a shame to try and stop that."

Even before I understood what the word really meant—*mistake*—I think I felt it, and I couldn't change it, as much as I wanted to. I was tiny and pigtailed, but I knew right then I wanted to be the *best* kind of mistake.

I suppose it was a *series* of mistakes, really, starting with Gran and making its way down to me.

Mom met my dad at King's Bar—Monroe's watering hole. Gran spent her afternoons drinking while Mom did homework in a dimly lit back booth—an afternoon routine. It was there, writing in her composition notebook, trying to sort out the complications of high school biology, that everything changed. Gene was tall, which explained my height shooting up past Mom's. His hair was only receding a little.

Gene also had my same toes, the middle one longer than the rest. I remember Mom holding my bare feet in her warm hands. I was five, waiting expectantly for "This Little Piggy." Instead, she took each foot between her palms and stared, concentrating on the too long toe. She pinched it between her fingers and wiggled it around. I laughed because it tickled.

"Good God, can things like this be hereditary?" I must have looked confused because she smiled, kissing each foot before dropping it on her lap. "You've got my eyes, though. His were brown."

I gathered my facts about the man named Gene from moments like that, small tidbits here and there. His height when I shot up past her. The freckles slowly sprinkling my nose. My strange toes a constant reminder. The whole story, the cautionary tale, came later. I was too young for the story, but that never stopped Gran from telling me the things she thought I ought to know.

"Life will come at you fast," she said, her voice rough and fiery. That voice was the anchor to all my memories of Gran. When she spoke, you knew you had to listen. "Might as well prepare for it best you can."

Back then, Gran was too drunk to know what was happening to her daughter, and Mom was too young to know what was happening to herself. He was a little nice and a little cute and a whole lot older. Old enough to know what he was doing, Gran said, adding a finger wag for good measure. Mom let him tell her lies about the places he'd take her and the cities she'd see. Even back then she'd been desperate to leave Monroe.

By the time Gran sobered up for the second time in her life, Mom was four months pregnant and packing up her belongings in a single cardboard box. Just that and her mattress, that was all she was taking. She couldn't stand his mattress. She was barely sixteen then, a few months older than me. Gran had just started seeing Grandpa Jay, the man who made her quit drinking for good. She asked Mom to stay, told her Jay had a home big enough for three more—the two of them and a baby.

Mom had been around for the first sobering up, though. She was sure it wouldn't last. Plus, Gene had promised her a trip to California. It turns out she'd been missing school for months, working shifts at a diner two towns over. He was still looking for work, but when he found some, the two of them were going to save enough to leave Indiana. The baby—me—was something they could live with.

After moving out, Mom lasted nine and a half days in the rented upstairs room he called home. Gran walked out one morning to see Mom and me, the small bump in her belly, curled up on the mattress on the front lawn. She had the same cardboard box.

It happened a few more times after that, the moving to his place and back again. Gran had moved too, into the little blue house at the end of the cul-de-sac. Karl Saunders had all of his hair then, and a wife that was alive. Mom grew bigger while I grew bigger, and Karl would help unload the mattress from the top of Gene's car. Gran would watch from the window and warn Jay so he wouldn't turn on the sprinklers. Most of the time he listened.

And then Mom would sit on the lawn for a while, more stubborn than ever. Sometimes she'd nap in the heat of the Indiana sun, with her hands resting on her belly, her mattress in the middle of Jay's immaculate lawn, Gran watching from the window. She said she watched us both grow, baking in the sun, me the bun in the Indiana oven.

Mom picked up double shifts at her diner job, with swollen feet, insistent that she'd leave as soon as she could. She never unpacked the box or put sheets on the mattress. The sheets Grandpa Jay bought remained in a neat pile on top of the empty dresser. Then one day Gene came for her, with money from the job he'd finally found and a set of bungee cords to strap the mattress on his Plymouth Duster. Gran watched from between the blinds while Karl and Mom hoisted the mattress to the top of the car.

Jay went out for parting words, but Gran stayed in her spot by the window. Before Mom slid into the front seat, she turned around for a final wave, and Gran, invisible, waved back.

Four weeks later Mom was still in Indiana, just at the top instead of the middle. It was the end of August when she gave birth to me in a room full of doctors and nurses and no family. She called Gran after, the both of us crying. Gran said she didn't know which one of us was louder. This time Gran didn't just ask Mom to come home—she begged. But Mom didn't come home. A few months later, she packed up her car again, leaving Gene somewhere near Lakeville. Everyone was left in the rearview mirror.

From then on, it was just the two of us and a traveling mattress. Eventually, we left that behind too. We moved all around Indiana, but never outside of it.

Most of my memories exist in snippets. Afternoons spent in diners, and my toddler years spent napping in their booths or blankets on checkered floors. The schools I left and the same towns with different names. The rented rooms and the men I thought were my dad and the men who wanted to be my dad, the ones she left behind. The phone calls with my gran, who felt worlds away instead of hours. We were always moving. Nothing ever stuck.

⁂

I woke up to Gran at the end of my bed, shaking my foot. She was dressed in a black sheath dress. Her makeup was done—red lips, rouge, black-coated lashes. Her honey-blonde hair was teased, shaped into her typical bouffant style. She looked more like the Gran I'd left all those summers back.

"Get up," she said. "We're leaving in twenty."

I took in her outfit, dazed as I was—the black pumps, the dress, the pearls—and tried to picture what was in our cardboard boxes. "I don't think we packed anything that nice," I said. "I don't think we *have* anything that nice."

Gran released a long, drawn-out sigh. "Your mother and I have established that much. You follow me. You're shopping my closet today."

I followed her down the hall to her and Jay's room. The bed was made and the sheets looked fresh, but I couldn't help thinking he'd died in that bed. I wasn't sure death lingered in the air, but I found myself holding my breath just in case.

Gran sifted through her closet and passed me a black blouse and skirt.

"These are from my skinny days," she said, patting her hips, a ghost smile of Gran past on her lips. Maybe it was nerves about the funeral, but she seemed much more like herself. "I keep those sizes in the wishful-thinking section."

I slipped the shirt over my head and shimmied the skirt over my hips.

"Yep," she said, nodding her head. "Looks much better on you. Fair warning, though: you're about to be hotter than hell. Black in May should be sin. If I'd known he was planning on dying, I'd have asked him to wait till fall."

Mom came out of the master bathroom with her hair up in curlers. She unpinned each and shook the curls free. With her long, dark hair behind her ears, she looked just as much a girl as me. Gran's hair was light, which always led to speculation about mom's paternal side of the family tree. Gran couldn't remember a lot from that time—including who Mom's father was.

"Forties, fifties, sixties, last week—it's all a blur," she'd say anytime someone gave her the chance. But then she'd insist Mom's dad had been tall, dark, and handsome. "Looked just like James Garner." And then her next line, always: "Might've been James Garner. Who knows? Crazier things have happened."

Whatever the combination, and however crazy the circumstance, Mom had the features of a Hollywood star. It wasn't just her looks though; *she* was electric. Like she belonged on the big screen, but had gotten stuck playing the part of the small-town Indiana mother instead.

"You really gotta hike the dress up that short?" Gran asked.

Mom rolled her eyes. "I didn't hike up anything. I'm a good five inches taller than you."

"We're going into a *church*," Gran said, like the service was going to be led by the pope himself. "You'll have the whole town whispering."

"Well, it's this or my cutoffs," Mom said with a shrug. "Your choice."

Gran placed a pointer finger on each temple and closed her eyes. "If you catch on fire in there, there's no putting you out."

"Noted." Mom looked over at me and winked. "But I'd be worried for yourself."

Gran rolled her eyes, but she didn't deny it. We'd never been to church on any of my visits.

"Look at you," Mom said, looking me up and down. "You look nice, Aurora. Mom, doesn't she look so grown up?"

"Maybe we put a little rouge on her cheeks." Gran reached for mine and gave them a pinch. "Just to add to that natural beauty."

"Sure," I said, right as Mom laughed out a "Good luck with that."

Mom turned to me with wide eyes. "I've tried to do your makeup for years. She asks once, and you're ready for a makeover?"

The corner of Gran's mouth turned up in a satisfied smirk. "I'm a grieving widow, Laine. Just be glad she has a good heart. One of us needs one."

Gran hurried to the bathroom before Mom could counter, and came back with her blush and mascara. "A bit of both won't hurt," she said, tapping the brush into a pot of unnatural pink.

Mom hovered over Gran's shoulder, surveying her work. When Gran dipped the brush in for a second coat, I took a step back.

"Don't push it."

Mom ran to the bathroom and returned with a lipstick tube. "It's a natural color," she said, like she was anticipating my resistance. "You'll look silly with blush and mascara and no lip."

The pink that twisted out of the tube felt far from natural, but it didn't seem right to pick fights on the day of a funeral. I'd let them have their fun—I liked seeing them on the same side.

"Perfect," Mom said, reaching her hand up to cup my cheek. "I do hate that you had to turn into a woman on me."

Gran's back was against the doorframe, straight and stiff and determined. "We better go get this over with," she said simply. "Karl's probably outside waiting."

Karl was outside, right beside the Vega. He'd swapped his pajamas for a gray suit that had probably fit better in his younger years. If I was warm in my skirt and blouse, I could only imagine how Karl was feeling.

We piled into the Vega, which would only make us hotter. The more people that got in, the smaller it seemed. Gran and I climbed into the back, Karl taking the passenger seat beside Mom. By the time all four of us were buckled in, we looked like a clown car.

"Roll down the windows," Gran said, tapping Karl's shoulder.

Her voice shook then, and she cleared her throat to mask it. But she'd given herself away. She wasn't as tough as she let on, and I had a feeling it'd be like that for a while. She slipped on her sunglasses, which only added to her glamour, before reaching over to grab my hand.

3

Walking up the church steps, I had the realization I'd never been inside one before. Mom wasn't the most reverent person. Gran wasn't far off when she said Mom should watch for lightning—or whatever it was she said about catching on fire. Did God really use lightning to strike people down? It seemed a bit far-fetched, but what did I know? When Mom wasn't working, she slept in on Sundays. Which meant I slept in on Sundays. The only encounter I'd had with religion was the pastor on channel two.

This church looked like the ones on TV, maybe a bit smaller, but it had what I figured were the essentials. There was a steeple casting a shadow on the front steps. Inside, there were stained glass windows and wooden pews.

"We'll sit in the front," Mom said, hooking her arm in mine and tugging me forward while I kept my eyes glued to the floor.

The place was deathly quiet. Murmuring voices were immediately absorbed by the plush red carpet. My feet sunk with each step—unfortunately for Gran, my feet were too big to fit into any of her shoes. I was painfully aware of my worn-out sneakers as we paraded past the other mourners toward the very first pew.

At the bottom of the pulpit, Jay was front and center in his navy-blue suit. It was nicer than anything I'd ever seen him in. The casket was propped open, and they'd posed him like he was lying down for a midday nap, his hands placed one on top of the other. His face was painted, perhaps to look more lifelike, but I'd never seen anyone look more dead. My stomach dropped, and I forced myself to look away.

"Do we get in line?" Mom whispered. There was a line of visitors stopping to pay their respects.

Gran scooted into the front pew, which felt like enough of an answer. We followed her lead, filing in one after the other. Karl stayed with us, sitting in the front row too. It felt less lonely with him in it. I could hear footsteps while the last mourners made their way down the aisle to their seats. I was desperate to turn around and see the people who loved Jay enough to put on their best clothes on a Saturday, but Gran's eyes stayed fixed ahead, so mine did as well. Neither of us looked at Jay.

The man in the walnut wood box wasn't him. I think Gran knew that too. Jay was gone.

At some point the shuffling of feet stopped, and a man from the front aisle rose from his seat. He left behind a woman with gray hair cropped short, the curls close to her head. There was a boy beside her in black slacks that flooded by his ankles, like he'd outgrown them years before. He didn't look much older than me, his hair a mess of brown curls, his skin tanned like he'd had a head start on summer. When he caught my eye, he gave a closed-mouth smile, and I swear I've never looked away so fast in my life.

The man stopped at the casket, offering a silent prayer over Jay. He moved slowly, the room painfully quiet except for the creak of the stage stairs.

"Welcome," he said, once he'd made his way behind the cross-adorned podium. His eyes seemed fixed on Gran. "Today, we remember the life of Jay Eastman."

Gran reached for my hand, and I had the sinking feeling that this was something she'd never planned on living through. Not that you can plan for death, really, but this was her life taking a hard right when she was hell-bent on it going straight. I didn't know Jay well, but I knew how much he'd loved Gran and how much she'd loved him.

"Before him," she'd said to me one summer, "nothing in my life made sense."

Of course, Mom took that comment personally, and it'd started a fight that ended in us driving back to wherever we were living at the time. I don't remember where that was, but I would always remember the way Mom looked when Gran said it.

The pastor led the congregation in singing "Amazing Grace," and even I knew some of the words. Mom mumbled along when the words failed us both, offering me a rueful smile when she caught my eye.

When they got to the part in the hymn that said, "I once was lost but now am found," I watched Gran cry for the first time in my life. She sobbed the way I thought someone was supposed to when you lost someone you loved with your whole heart. The women in the surrounding pews started crying too, myself included. I looked at Mom. She kept her eyes fixed straight ahead, mouthing along to the words she didn't know, while not a single tear fell.

Jay had found Gran, maybe even saved her. She'd spent her whole life feeling lost, and then one day, she was found. Who was she without him?

On the last note, as suddenly as they had begun, the tears ended. I watched her out of the corner of my eye. It was like someone had simply turned off the faucet. She sniffed hard and wiped beneath her eyes with the back of her sleeve before her face went completely blank.

I was afraid for Gran.

She stayed stiff and still while the pastor talked about Jay.

Resolved? I wondered.

I learned things I'd never known before, like how he was a regular attendee of that very church, sitting three pews up from the back every Sunday. A colleague from the factory he'd worked at before he'd retired told a story about how Jay helped him and his family out when their son was in the hospital.

"He worked doubles when I couldn't be there," he said, his voice cracking. "Made sure my family never missed a paycheck."

Gran's palm was thick with sweat, but I didn't dare let go. I wondered if my hand in hers was the only thing keeping her in that pew.

"Any words from the family?" the pastor asked, looking over at our row.

Mom leaned past me to whisper, "You want to say something?"

Gran shook her head.

"Want me to?" she asked.

She nodded.

Mom stood, tugging her dress down with little success. "I'll say a few words," she said, taking the pastor's hand when he offered her help up the steps. "I'm his stepdaughter," she said nervously, like anyone in the room didn't know who she was.

She wiped her hands on the front of skirt. I'd never seen her so nervous, so off-kilter.

"I guess I'd just like to say thank you," she said, nodding her head like she was proud of herself, like that was a good start to her speech. "Thank you for loving Jay. Thank you for telling those stories today. He was a good man. It seems like that's something we can all agree on. And I guess, if life was fair, he wouldn't be gone." She paused and took in a long breath, like she was searching for something else to say. "I'd like to say thanks on behalf of me and my mom, and my daughter, Aurora." She smiled down on me. The confidence she usually wore well was returning. "Living in a four-stoplight town can be suffocating, but then in moments like this you see what it can mean to a person. Jay was a lucky person to have had all of you in his life, and we were lucky to have had him in ours."

When I looked over at Gran, Gran didn't look lucky at all. It was a devastating sight, and I had to look away. Across the pew, the boy in the too-short pants was looking at me. When I caught his eye again, he looked straight ahead. Mom stepped down the stairs and smiled at the audience she'd managed to charm in a minute, tops. The pastor came up and closed us out in prayer.

He ended the service by saying Jay was in a better place. The way Mom spoke about Monroe, I couldn't help but wonder if he was right.

*

After they planted Jay in the churchyard, a pile of fresh dirt trapping him in the casket, we piled back into the Vega and headed toward

Norma's house. Gran had tossed her casserole in the trash, yet Norma had still offered to host the reception. Mom swore Norma's kindness had no limit. Gran had no comment.

Our ride was silent, and I was glad the drive was short. We parked so far down the street we might as well have parked at Gran's house and walked.

"People love free food," Gran finally offered, her voice hoarse.

Mom laughed. "I highly doubt anyone came for the egg salad, Mom."

"That just tells me you've never had Norma's egg salad," Karl chimed in.

Norma's front door was propped open, and there were fans in all four corners of the living room. It looked like half the town had shown up, and I wondered if Karl was right about the egg salad. I hadn't looked around much at the funeral, but I could swear some of the people on her couch hadn't been at the church.

Gran stepped inside, leading the way. She nearly collided with a bear of a man, his plate piled high with egg salad.

"Katherine," he said, stepping aside to let her pass.

When Mom followed, his brow furrowed. "Laine." Her name was infused with bitterness. "Didn't know God was still making time for resurrections."

"Hi there, Al." Her voice was up an octave, a fake sweetness she reserved for people she truly hated. She scooted past him without a second look.

His eyes landed on me, and they were anything but friendly. If anything, he looked like he was seeing a ghost. Al disappeared out the front door, and I followed Mom and Gran. Clearly, we wouldn't be making time for pleasantries or introductions. I could only assume he was one of those burned bridges.

I was getting the impression there was still a lot to learn about Monroe. Mom leaned close to my ear. "Get ready to have one hundred people tell you they are sorry for your loss, okay?"

"I'll hear the first twenty, and then I'm hiding in the bathroom."

"Good strategy," she whispered.

The two of us settled in the corner with the best view of the room. A lifetime spent in new towns made us good at scoping out our surroundings.

The first to approach was Phil—the only familiar face in the sea of strangers. "You really got up on the stage to tell all these people their town is suffocating?"

Mom reached out to slap his arm. "I said he was lucky!"

Phil chuckled and leaned in real close. "People can read between the lines, Laine."

Phil the Cop was really gunning for the spot of Mom's next beau. He looked at her like I'd seen men look at Mom all my life. If he was successful, we might be in Monroe longer than expected.

I left them behind to go find Gran. On the stairway, the boy from the front row was laughing with a group of teens. His smile was bright—a noticeable row of straight, white teeth. The scene wasn't unfamiliar to me. I'd been in plenty of school hallways and knew these were the kind of kids high school made you notice. They looked like they belonged on the pages of back-to-school catalogues—pristine and glossy.

In an alternate universe, I might've been the kind of girl who introduced myself. But I'd been in those same hallways, watching from the safety of my locker. I kept my head high as I walked past, silently hoping they'd notice me like I noticed them.

Gran was in the kitchen with a group of women who kept touching her arm and speaking to her in hushed voices.

"Aurora," she said, spotting me. "Come here." I could almost hear a *"Thank God"* in her inflection.

She motioned me over to the group, and Gran introduced their ringleader as Norma, the casserole lady. Norma enveloped me in a hug that lasted longer than any hug I'd ever received, so long I nearly relaxed and settled into it. Mom wasn't a hugger. Neither was Gran, now that I was taking inventory of the hugs I'd received in my fifteen years on earth.

"God, you look just like your mother," she said, running her hand through my hair. She turned to Gran. "It's shocking, huh?"

"Spitting image," Gran barked out, before adding, "They have their differences, though."

"I'd hope so," a woman chimed in, earning a chorus of laughter. The woman's eyes lingered on my stained lips, rouged cheeks, and blackened eyelashes a moment too long, and without a shadow of doubt, I knew she had me pegged for Mom's double in more ways than one.

Gran's smile looked forced, and I found myself offering up my own pained version. I knew what they meant—Mom's story wasn't one you wanted to follow, and yet here I was, the living, breathing result of those pages. My smile felt like a betrayal. I was starting to see why Mom had left this town, my cheeks warming as they turned pink. Gran noticed and her face went rigid.

"Aurora, there you are." The voice was unfamiliar. A girl with long blonde hair hooked her arm in mine like we were old friends, tugging me away from the group.

"I see you found the town gossips," she whispered, guiding me through the doorway, away from their assessing eyes.

When we were back in the safety of the living room, she unhooked her arm and took a step back. She looked to be about my age, but it was hard to be certain, with her kohl-rimmed eyes and bright red lip. Her black dress put Mom's to shame. The hem covered the necessary parts, and that's about it. More than a few guests watched our parade out of the kitchen.

"The key is to never end up in the kitchen. It's the golden rule of funerals."

"You come to a lot of funerals?" I asked.

The girl shrugged. "The town's small and people keep dying. Mom's keen on keeping up good appearances. I'm Charlotte, by the way." She stuck her hand out, and the introduction felt formal and sudden.

"Aurora," I offered.

"I know," she said, using the back of her hand to cover a yawn. "We went to Indiana Beach together with Katherine and Jay, like, four summers back."

I remembered that summer perfectly, but the girl at the lakeside amusement park looked nothing like the girl standing in front of me now. Charlotte of 1975 wore her hair in two neat braids down to her waist. She had a handful of freckles across her nose, and her voice was a quiet quiver. Being around her back then had made me feel talkative, and that was saying something.

I searched the girl in front of me for signs of familiarity. Sure enough, the freckles were still there, buried beneath her rouge. Her eyes, beneath the thick mascara-layered lashes, were the same startling blue. When she smiled, her front teeth still angled slightly inward.

"I remember you," I said, resisting the urge to tell her she looked nothing like the girl she had been.

My eyes wandered back to the stairwell, prompted by another chorus of laughter. Was it in poor taste to laugh so hard at a funeral? A girl with white-blonde hair was propped up on the stair beside the boy from the front row.

"That's Harry Clark," Charlotte said with a smirk. When I didn't say anything, she kept going. "He's the preacher's son. Lyla Rae Harrison Jr.—I'm not kidding—is on his left. And Marie McClain and Shane Green on the steps below." Charlotte studied her nails like they were suddenly the most interesting thing in the room. She had them painted a cherry red to match her lips. "I'd introduce you, but that would require us to run in the same circles and, well, we don't."

I nodded because I wasn't always one to fill silence. When I'd visit in the summer, Gran called me a one-word wonder.

"If you stick around until school starts, you'll have the pleasure of seeing Lyla Rae Jr. parade down the halls in her cheer uniform like it's her job. As if we all don't know she's cheering for the worst football team in the state." She smiled at her own jab. "You think you'll stick around till then? Everyone in this town loves to talk, and from what I've gathered, you and your mom don't stay places too long."

We'd been here less than twenty-four hours, but our reputation had preceded us.

"I give us a week, tops," I said with a shrug.

"Well, if you need a tour guide, I'd be happy to show you around. They leave this town off most maps. It'll take me all of one day to get you acquainted. Plus, I kind of promised my mom."

I'd been the new girl at enough schools to know no one actually wants to show you around, especially not when adults are the ones making them do it. Toting me around the school hallways was bad enough, but forced acquaintances during summer?

"You don't have to. Seriously."

Charlotte rolled her eyes. "Don't be dramatic. I'm not giving you an organ."

Charlotte left with her mom and a promise to call me tomorrow. I resisted the urge to tell her again she really didn't need to. She didn't seem like she'd listen. Plus, it wouldn't be the worst thing in the world—having someone show me around. It might be nice to spend time with someone my own age, even if it was only for a week.

One by one, families began to make their exit, each group making sure to stop and squeeze Gran's arm on their way out. Some offered hugs, and I just knew Gran hated all the attention. Wrapped up in the arms of a particularly stout woman, Gran caught my eye and mouthed "Help me!" I slipped away to the kitchen, leaving her to fend for herself.

Karl found me hiding out by the egg salad, which truly was good enough for me to question the motives and condolences of everyone who had joined us for the reception.

"I'm about to walk home if you want to join," he said, reaching down to ruffle my hair. The gesture reminded me of Jay, and for the first time since hearing the news, I felt a pang of sadness thinking of him. So far, my tears had been for Gran, but in that moment his absence felt like my own loss.

"I'll stick it out, but I appreciate the offer."

Karl placed his weathered hand on my shoulder. "Come find me in the evening if you want to meet this year's roses, okay?"

"Okay."

He slipped out the back door in the kitchen, avoiding the leftover crowd in the living room. I worried that of the people I'd met thus far, the person I felt most similar to was a seventy-year-old widower.

Mom found me a few minutes later. "Gran's ready to go if you are."

This made me laugh. "I've been ready since we walked through the front door."

"Like mother, like daughter," she said before offering me her hand. "I've been ready since we started on Highway 24."

In the living room, I spotted Gran at the front door, smiling up at a man with brunette hair and a thick beard. He towered over her, in a black T-shirt and blue jeans, making him stand out in a room full of people in their Sunday best. When Gran looked our direction, so did he.

"Whoa," Mom whispered under her breath.

One of the girls from the stairwell, Lyla Rae Jr., ran up to him. He put an arm around her shoulder, his wedding band catching the light.

I stuck an elbow in her side and let out a long exhale. "Mom. He's married. The ring."

"Oh, Aurora," she said, swatting my arm away. "A girl can look, can't she?"

4

I woke up to Gran at the foot of my bed, tapping my leg.

"Yoo-hoo," she sang, reaching for the arm I had draped over my face. "Aurora."

I rolled over so my back was to her, pressing my face into the pillow. "It's *summer*."

Gran was persistent, tugging the pillow out from under my head. I covered my eyes and peeked out between my fingers.

"Come on," she urged, her face close to mine. The smell of whiskey was unmistakable. "Get up and hang out with your old gran. I could use a friend."

She was surprisingly—and perhaps concerningly—upbeat for the Monday after burying her husband. Willie Nelson swore whiskey was the cure to a broken heart—maybe there was some truth to it.

Resistance was obviously futile, but I figured I'd give it one more shot, burying myself beneath the comforter.

She rose from my bedside and made her way to the foot of it. I could feel her gathering the bedding, pulling from the bottom until it was entirely on the carpeted floor.

I opened my eyes with the sole intent of glaring at her. Gran winked. "Come on—breakfast is ready. You know your mom won't last a week here. I got to take what time I can get."

My cutoffs were in a heap on the floor—I paired them with my favorite striped T-shirt.

Mom was already at the kitchen table with a cup of coffee. Gran's bottle of whiskey—notably empty—served as the table's centerpiece.

"Did she wake you up too?" I asked, using the back of my hand to cover my yawn.

Mom, with her chin cupped in the palm of her hand, looked particularly beautiful in the morning light. When she got ready for a night on the town, she wanted her beauty to be an in-your-face kind—thick lashes, ruby lips, bombshell curls. I preferred her like this—soft features and kind, tired eyes.

"No—unfortunately my mind does that for me."

Her forced, close-lipped smile kept me from prying.

Gran rounded the corner. "See? I made breakfast," she said, gesturing to the cereal box on the table.

"Before you get your hopes up, there's no milk," Mom said, pressing her fingers to her temples.

I could tell Gran was getting on her nerves already. I wondered if we'd even last a week.

Gran looked me up and down. "Nice shorts. You ever think about switching up your look, Miss Aurora?"

Gran wore a printed shift dress that showed off her trim figure, complemented by a kitten heel. She wasn't old. She could have been my mom, even. The years of drinking had aged her some, but she worked with what she had, and her honey-blonde hair made up for the frown lines. That and the workout routine she did after her soaps made her pass for late forties at least.

"Not really," I said, crossing my arms across my chest.

Mom smiled. "Aurora keeps a simple wardrobe."

"Might have something to do with the cardboard box she has to shove it into every couple months," Gran snipped back.

She was picking a fight. Her biting remark and the empty bottle confirmed any lingering suspicions. I wondered how long she'd waited—was it the morning she found him? The next day?

I waited to see if Mom would take the bait—she was always good for a quick-tempered response. Maybe it was because we'd buried Jay less than forty-eight hours ago, or maybe it had something to do with the thoughts that woke her up before the rest of the house, but whatever the reason, Mom stayed silent.

Charlotte, the girl from the funeral, strolled down the stone path like she didn't have a care in the world. She was wearing jean cutoffs and a red tank top cropped well above her belly button. Her hair fell in waves down her back. She must sleep in curlers to get it to look that good.

I watched her from the big picture window while she stopped to chat with Mom, who'd been tanning on the lawn. The two looked like old friends. Charlotte pushed her feathered bangs back from her eyes and laughed at something Mom said.

She left Mom behind, strolling up the steps. I moved to the door, opening it before she could knock.

"Oh, hi," she said, stepping past me before I could invite her in. "I'm here to fulfill my tour-guide duties. Also, your mom is kind of a babe and, like, *really* cool." She looked back in her direction before I shut the door. "Like, not a mom. At all."

"I get that a lot."

Charlotte smirked. "I bet. So do you drive?"

I shook my head. It's not like I couldn't. I'd been driving without a license for a few years now. When I was thirteen, Paul, the guy Mom had been seeing, gave me lessons. He liked having someone to drive on the nights they couldn't see straight. After they broke up, Mom kept my driving in her back pocket, using it on an as-needed basis.

"I'll be sixteen in August," I said, giving the simpler answer.

"Lame. Everything's better with a car. So, what are you doing now?"

I looked at Gran. She was in Jay's recliner with the footrest propped out.

"Don't look at me," she said. "I'm not your keeper."

"Um . . . nothing really."

What remained of my afternoon would consist of hours in front of the TV, with Gran's endless commentary. A good time, but I suppose that amounted to "nothing really."

"Well, since you don't have a license, you got a bike?"

I shook my head to answer no while Gran chimed in.

"We do," she said. "Jay's got it somewhere in the garage." Her eyes betrayed the pain saying his name caused. "You girls gonna head to town?"

"Promised my mom I'd show her around." Charlotte shrugged. "Figured town's the only place to start."

"Start and end," Mom chimed in, joining us inside. "That'll take you all of five minutes."

She'd taken the time to do her hair and makeup, so I knew she wouldn't be spending the afternoon at home. We'd been in town for three days, and she already had plans—typical Mom. I wondered if it was Phil the Cop or if I'd missed the signs of another suitor. We had been separated for most of the reception, and she wasn't one to waste time.

Gran looked her up and down, seeing what I was seeing. "Where the hell you going?"

Mom rolled her eyes. "Dinner with Phil, but don't you get any ideas."

"I liked that Phil." Gran's grin bordered on obnoxious. "Probably had something to do with why you *didn't* like him. Girls, garage opens with a good tug on the lever."

Mom collapsed on the couch. "I might be gone by the time you get back, Aurora. Phil's coming around six, but I shouldn't be too late."

Mom's famous last words. I'd heard them plenty of times, and they were rarely true.

Charlotte led the way outside, the garage creaking while she tugged the lever. I used both hands to force it above our heads.

I didn't know how to break the news, but the truth was I'd never learned how to ride a bike. When I thought about it, I wasn't sure I'd ever asked for one. Bikes don't fit in cardboard boxes, and Santa would never have managed to secure the funds.

When I was seven, Mark from just outside of Muncie promised he would teach me come spring. He had a bike in the garage, left behind from previous tenants—all it needed was a shot of air in both tires. It wasn't a fair promise to hold him to, but I didn't tell him that. By the time the snow had thawed and the weather warmed up, we were long gone.

"Is it this hot where you moved from?" Charlotte asked. "Feels like this kind of heat should be illegal."

"Unfortunately, everywhere in Indiana is this hot."

I stepped into the open garage. It was like Jay's own personal museum—tools none of us would know how to use, an old grandfather clock in mid-repair, a collection of WWII photos. He looked particularly handsome in one, like a soldier you'd see on TV. I spotted the bike I had no clue how to ride, resting up against a wall in the back corner.

"Wait—where'd you move here from?" Charlotte asked.

"Technically, we came from Sherwood, but we were there less than a year."

"Where were you before that?"

"Logansport."

"How long?"

"Four months? Maybe five?"

"Whoa. How many places have you lived?"

This answer came easy. I'd been keeping count since move five, tiny lines marked on the inside of my box.

"Eighteen."

It wasn't a number I shared all that often, mostly to avoid the shocked look on people's faces. Charlotte did her best to recover.

"And I thought *my* life was messed up."

I didn't know how to respond to that. I'd never thought of my life as "messed up." I'd just thought of it as my life. One dictated by the whims of a mother who preferred to leave when things got hard. It could be worse—plenty of kids get left behind. I counted myself lucky to have a mom who took me with her.

I shrugged. "You get used to it."

I dragged the bike out into the driveway, one hand on each handlebar. "This might be a good time to tell you I have no clue how to ride this thing."

I waited for Charlotte to laugh, to point out just how strange it was that I'd been on the earth for fifteen years and never learned how to ride a bike. Instead, she put her hand on my arm, and the way she tilted her head reminded me of the girl I'd met all those summers back.

"You know what? It's hotter than hell, but I think today might be a perfect day to learn."

Charlotte, despite her initial enthusiasm, wasn't the best instructor. She told me to push my feet down while staying upright, which only resulted in me tipping over onto the asphalt.

"Exactly like that, but try not to fall," she said, which earned a laugh track from our audience. Mom and Gran, noticing the commotion, had come out to sit on the lawn and watch.

"How wonderful," Gran said, taking a long pull from her sweating glass. "This is a rite of passage."

Mom had a glass of her own. I suppose she figured if she couldn't beat Gran, she might as well join her.

"I had no clue you couldn't ride a bike," she said. She smiled when she said it, but I detected a hint of guilt.

I wasn't surprised this fun fact was news to her—Gran called it a rite of passage, and there were plenty of those I'd missed out on over the years. Mom kept busy—work, men, moves—and I was just along for the ride.

After my third tumble in the middle of our street, I decided it was time to call it quits. I had legs capable of getting me where I needed to go, and pretty soon I'd have a license.

"You've got to push your pedals faster," an unfamiliar voice said. "Get some momentum going to keep you balanced."

I turned to discover the mailman had been watching the show—his truck parked a few houses down from ours.

"And stay upright," Charlotte chimed in, as if the same advice she'd been offering for the last fifteen minutes might suddenly become helpful.

"Just press that right foot down hard and fast." He kept his voice low as he approached. "And then the left, and then get that rhythm going. One, two. One, two."

Upon second glance, I realized I knew him after all. His voice was unfamiliar, but the tanned skin and warm brown eyes were not. This was the married man from the funeral, the one Mom had been ogling. One glance at her on the lawn confirmed that she too had recognized the unexpected guest.

He set his satchel on the curb and placed both hands on the rusted handlebars. "I'll hold the bike up until you get going."

I listened, mostly because his instructions were the most useful I'd heard all day. I pressed down hard and fast with my right foot, and then my left. *One, two. One, two.* The mailman kept his promise, keeping up with me as I picked up speed, holding tight onto the handlebar. About fifteen feet down the road, he let me go, and I *finally* managed to stay upright, pushing one pedal after the other.

Charlotte, Mom, and Gran erupted into a chorus of cheers. I flew down the road, unsure of how to turn around or how I'd manage to stop. The breeze that rarely graced us with its presence pushed my hair back.

"Turn the handlebars!" the mailman yelled. "But slowly!"

I navigated a half circle and pedaled my way back to them.

"A natural!" he called out.

Gran let out a cackle. "*Natural*'s a stretch, but she did manage to get there."

I slammed my shoes down into the asphalt, causing the bike to skid to a stop.

The mailman hoisted his satchel over his shoulder and made his way up the driveway. I watched Mom adjust her hair so it fell over one shoulder, using her hands to shield her eyes as she tilted her head up to look at him.

"Some help you two were." He sifted through the satchel and grabbed a stack of mail, passing it to Gran before turning to meet Mom's eyes. "I'm Tim, by the way."

"Oh, I know who you are." Mom's voice was teasing. I watched her put on her best smile. "There's not a girl from Monroe High who wouldn't remember Tim 'take-his-team-to-state' Harrison."

Tim's laugh was low, loud, and contagious. "Just when I was starting to feel like people had forgotten me," he said. "I'm obliged to remind you we did lose at state, though."

Mom laughed. "And he's humble too."

Tim was, admittedly, quite handsome for an older man. His eyes, when they landed on you, had a way of making you feel seen, so much so that you felt the need to look away. Or at least *I* felt the need to look away. Mom, with her bright smile, was like a moth to a flame.

Tim looked toward Gran. "How you holding up, Katherine?"

I knew she hated questions like this, but she gave it her best. "Doing all right. He would have loved seeing Aurora learn to ride a bike at the ripe age of fifteen."

This made Tim smile. "Well, I know Jay hated you reading that trash," he said, pointing to her stack of mail, "so in his honor I'm going to remind you what you got in your hand there is absolute garbage."

Gran waved the *National Enquirer* in front of her face. "I caught that man reading it at night, over my shoulder, when I left it open on the kitchen table. He loved pretending like those headlines didn't catch his attention too."

Tim laughed, pushing his hat back so it sat on the top of his head. His free hand scratched his beard, and there was a beat of awkward silence, almost like he was trying to think of something to say. "Well, you ladies have a good afternoon." His eyes landed on Mom, staying there for a moment too long. I'd seen the look plenty of times throughout the years—everyone thought she was pretty. "I'll see you tomorrow."

Once Tim's truck rumbled to the end of the cul-de-sac, hooking a left, Mom and Gran returned to the comfort of the indoors.

Charlotte, my original instructor, stood at the edge of lawn, straddling her bike. I hadn't noticed before, but it had pink and purple streamers hanging down the handlebars and a wicker basket attached to the front. The bike was an unlikely pairing with the girl in dark makeup and notice-me clothes.

"So, you up for a ride to town or what?"

I wasn't confident in my ability to navigate an open road or being able to brake without ten feet of room to skid to a stop, but it was worth a shot.

"Only one way to find out."

5

Lucky for me, Monroe's roads were practically deserted. We were passed by three cars total in a span of fifteen minutes, all of them giving us a wide berth. We passed the highway exit Mom and I had used less than a week before. Just after, King's Bar and the bowling alley were on opposite sides of the street.

"Here's the alley," Charlotte said, fulfilling her obligation as tour guide. "It's one of, like, two fun things we have in this town."

"What's the second?"

She swerved between paint lines with the confidence of someone whose dad had taught her how to ride a bike. "Drive-in movies about a half mile out."

"And that's King's?" I asked, as if its name wasn't spelled out on a neon sign.

"Yeah—my mom's the bartender there. That's why she knows your grandma so well, from back when she was a regular."

I'd heard plenty about King's—the backdrop of most of their stories. The way the jukebox got updated and everyone complained until they brought back the old selection. How Gran was banned from song selections after wearing out Elvis's "Hound Dog." And perhaps most notably, how my mom met my dad and brought me into existence.

Charlotte, unaware of King's significance, pedaled a bit faster.

"They got a new bartender—*Stevie*." She said his name like she wanted to savor it. "He's cute—that's as much as I know."

While I was sure this was a normal conversation between two girls our age, I struggled to formulate a response. I'd spent most of our time in Sherwood in the back row of classrooms, eating lunch alone in the library, choosing the empty bench seat on the bus. I was, admittedly, out of practice in the art of small talk.

I settled on "Cool," which certainly gave away my inexperience. Downtown came into view, and I mentally prepared to stop the bike, hoping I'd manage to do so without falling over.

"Have you ever had a boyfriend?"

"No," I answered honestly. There was no point in lying—she clearly knew the answer. "You?"

"A handful." She hit the hand brake, sliding her bike to a graceful stop just inches before the curb. "But I haven't had one who felt like the real deal."

I pressed my heels into the asphalt, and my old sneakers took their second beating of the day. Charlotte maneuvered her bike up the curb and propped it on the Tommy's Hardware brick wall. I followed her lead—placing my bike beside hers.

"Today, you learned to ride. Tomorrow, you learn to brake."

"Deal."

Charlotte laughed and linked her arm in mine, like girls at school did walking down the hall. We fell into step, crossing the street toward Rexall Drugs.

"So, this is downtown," she said, waving her free hand halfheartedly.

Downtown Monroe took up one block in total. There were businesses on both sides, some that had seen better days: a hardware store with cardboard covering a shattered window, a pharmacy, Norma's diner, the law offices of one J. R. Priestly, a women's dress shop Gran said wasn't worth a second look.

The courthouse was at the center of it all, a looming brick building with a county jail right beside it. All in all, it didn't look much different from the smaller towns we'd lived in throughout the years.

Charlotte pushed open the door to Rexall, a bell announcing our arrival. The boy at the counter was about our age—maybe a few years older. He didn't look up from his notepad.

"Hi, Robby." Charlotte singsonged his name.

Robby perked up at the sound of her voice, wearing a lazy smile. "Hi, Charlotte," he sang back, his voice matching her cadence.

His eyes landed on me, and I remembered how strange it was to be an outsider in a town small enough that everyone knows everyone. "Who's your friend?"

"Robby, this is Aurora. She's new to Monroe."

"Lucky her," he mumbled.

"And Aurora, this here is Robby."

Robby's eyes had found their way back to Charlotte, but he offered a halfhearted "Nice to meet you."

"You too," I said, letting Charlotte guide me away from the checkout.

"Gotta pick up a few things," she explained.

Charlotte walked with a destination in mind. I stood at the end of the aisle, examining the mismatched shelf. There were cans of bug spray next to hairbrushes, and a jar of peanut butter with no matching friends in sight. I was starting to think Robbie might be bad at his job. Charlotte was at the other end, opening Revlon lipstick tubes to test them on the back of her hand.

"Aurora," she whispered, calling me over. "What do you think?"

She placed her hand over her mouth so I could examine the colors. There was a red, a pink, and some shade of purple.

"The red," I answered. "It's classic."

I wasn't confident in boy talk but I'd spent plenty of years helping Mom get ready for nights on the town. Charlotte flashed a pageant smile and dropped the lipstick into her purse. My stomach dropped, and I hoped my face wouldn't betray me.

Spotlighted by the fluorescent lights of Rexall Drugs, she reached over and placed her hand over my mouth, staring intently.

"You take the pink," she said, attempting to place the tube in my hand.

"No." I shook my head, keeping my hand balled shut. My heartbeat sped up at the thought, my palms pooling with sweat. "I don't need it."

"Aurora, come on." She tilted her head, her eyes peering into mine. The whole thing felt like a test I was destined to fail. "Robby's cool. No one will know."

"Really, I'm okay." My voice quivered, betraying my nerves. *"Seriously,"* I said, hoping my voice seemed nonchalant, tossing in an eye roll for good measure. "I really don't need it."

Charlotte tossed both in her purse. "You can borrow it sometime." I must have looked upset, because she dropped her voice to a sympathetic whisper. "Calm down. I knew you wouldn't. I just had to try."

She walked down the aisle, expecting me to follow. I did. If I was good at anything, it was following someone else's lead. Charlotte let out a long, exhausted sigh and waved at Robby. He gave a slow, delayed wave back.

The sun was beating down on us, the air thick. The sidewalk radiated heat back to the sun. It was almost painful. Charlotte turned to me and offered her arm like the scene in the drugstore had never happened. I wanted to forget it too, so I hooked my arm in hers.

"You up for more adventure?" she asked.

"What did you have in mind?"

"The only thing in Monroe that makes summer bearable: Norma's milkshakes." She tugged me toward the diner. "And don't worry, we'll pay for these."

⊙～⊙

Diners always felt like home to me. The checkered floors. The vinyl booths. The jukebox lullaby. The tall stools that spin. The silver chrome lining on a red Formica tabletop. Norma's looked, sounded, and smelled like the one thing that had been consistent in all the places we called home.

Before Mom had felt comfortable leaving me home alone, she'd sign up for the bus to drive me to whatever diner she was working in at the time. My home address had been listed as Dale's Burger House, Dino's Diner, and Sweet as Pie. The bus drivers didn't question it, tugging down on the lever so I could take the steps two a time toward an afternoon milkshake and Mom's warm smile.

Charlotte slid into a booth, and I slid in opposite her. I always sat at the counter with the other solo diners—truck drivers making a pit stop; downtown workers stopping in for an afternoon cup of coffee; or in my case, girls with schoolwork and a mom serving up afternoon specials.

Charlotte scooted the menu across the table toward me. "You can't go wrong with the chocolate milkshake and fries."

I scanned the menu and read through items that sounded just like the fare in other diners throughout Indiana. Of course, Norma's had added their own personal touch—Norma's Sweet Peach Cobbler had a gold star by it, making sure we knew it was special. I had a suspicion it tasted pretty similar to Patty's You're a Peach Cobbler in Sherwood, and Miss May's Peach Slice in Logansport, but I'd have to order it to be sure.

"So, do you have a dad?" Charlotte asked.

Her question caught me off guard, but so far everything about having a friend caught me off guard. Maybe this was what friendship was—riding bikes, shoplifting, exchanging your most personal life details over milkshakes.

"Well, she's not Mother Mary," I quipped.

This earned a smile. "You know what I mean."

I wondered how to explain it, but I supposed simply put it was a story as old as time. "I don't know him," I said. "I mean, I know things about him, but he doesn't come around if that's what you mean."

"Who was he?"

"His name was Gene. They met at King's Bar, but he wasn't around after I was born or anything."

Norma herself approached our booth with a pad in hand. "Hi there, ladies," she said. "Charlotte, nice of you to take the time to show Miss Aurora around. Miss Aurora, Katherine holding up all right?"

"Yes, ma'am," I said, manners I didn't know I had kicking in on instinct. When you're new to a town, all you have are first impressions. I always felt desperate to make a good one.

"Well, that's good to hear. And your mama?" I nodded my answer while Norma continued. "I'll tell you, I don't know how long Laine plans on sticking around, but if she's looking to work, I've got plenty of aprons and plenty of customers. You'll pass that along for me, won't you?"

"Yes, ma'am," I said, like those were the only two words I knew.

"Good. So, what can I get you girls?"

Charlotte ordered a chocolate milkshake and fries, so I said to make it a double. She seemed confident in her order like she seemed confident in most things.

"Do *you* have a dad?" I asked once Norma walked away.

Her mouth turned up at the corners like she knew this question was coming.

"Yeah, I do, but he's not around anymore." My face must have betrayed my sympathy because she quickly shook her head. "No, it's a good thing. We don't want him around. Actually, he left right around the time we went to Indiana Beach."

"Yeah?"

"Yep. Gran and Jay offered to take me for the weekend while my mom packed up his things. Changed all the locks and everything. I was riding the Ferris wheel with you while she told him to get the hell out of Dodge."

I thought back to the timid girl I'd met all those summers ago—the quiver in her voice, the silence she never tried to fill, the strained smile when the World's Tallest Tower brought us up, then down, up, then down.

"He had a temper that went from zero to one hundred in no time at all," she continued, answering questions I wasn't asking. "The good days were good, but that summer there were more bad days than good. Mom spent years putting up with his fists, but once they turned on me . . . well, that was her final straw."

"Oh," I managed. "I'm sorry."

Whatever sadness Charlotte felt about her dad she kept tucked away, preferring a forced nonchalance. She shrugged, and Norma delivered our fries and milkshakes. She took a fry from the top of the pile and dipped it in the chocolate.

"I'm not," she said. "But I'll tell you this: count your blessings. Having a bad dad is a whole lot worse than no dad at all."

I dipped fries in my milkshake too and struggled to keep up while Charlotte gossiped about all the kids in town. She was impatient when I'd forget a name, so I did my best to remember. There were girls we hated and boys we loved, and all sorts of people in between. She promised she'd introduce me if I stuck around long enough.

At some point, the afternoon crowd switched to the dinnertime rush, and a gaggle of teens came walking through the front door, the dinging bell announcing their entrance. I recognized some from the funeral—the blonde-haired girl with her hair pulled back into a ponytail so tight it had to give her a headache.

"Lyla Rae Jr.," Charlotte whispered. "That's the mailman's daughter."

A girl with short, cropped brown hair linked her arm with Lyla's, and they made their way to the corner booth. "And Marie," Charlotte added, "the one who spread that rumor about Lisa Ann last winter."

One by one the characters from her stories walked past us. Shane—cute but awful. Took a few girls behind the bleachers but ignored them in the school halls. Jillian—quiet and kind when she was away from the dynamic duo. Marie and Lyla Rae Jr.—the dynamic, avoid-at-all-costs duo. And finally, trailing them, the boy from the funeral with the curly brown hair and too-short pants. He was the last to enter, the bell above him letting out a final ding.

"And I'm sure you remember *Harry*," she said, kicking my leg beneath the table.

I kicked her leg right back, turning around to face her so he wouldn't catch me staring over the red and white vinyl seat. I held my breath, waiting for him to pass, not sure why his walking by made me all that nervous.

The footsteps stopped by our booth, and when I looked up, his blue eyes were staring down at me.

"You're Jay's granddaughter, yeah?" he said, his voice smooth and kind.

Charlotte kicked me beneath the table again, and I did my best not to react.

"Yeah—Aurora," I said, the name I'd had my whole life sounding strange coming out of my mouth.

He stuck his hand out to shake mine, which felt like an oddly formal gesture for a teenage boy, but I reached my hand out to grasp his.

"Harry," he said, shaking my hand once before letting it go.

My arm lingered in the air for a beat too long before I quickly returned it to my side.

"Hi there, Harry," Charlotte chimed in, in the same singsong voice she'd used for Robby.

"Hey there, Charlotte," he mimicked back, while she tossed her hair behind her shoulders.

Harry looked over at me and opened his mouth like he was going to speak, but before the words came out, a girl's voice called out his name. "Harold Clarrrrk!" Lyla Rae Jr. squealed. "Come here right now and tell Shane he has absolutely no shot at varsity."

The group erupted in a chorus of laughter, Harry smiling with them. His teeth were white and perfectly straight, and I felt a sudden, surprising desperation to be the one on the receiving end of that smile.

Charlotte locked eyes with me and mouthed, "Blah blah blah," rolling her eyes. I bit my lip to stop my laugh from escaping. I was used to watching from the outside, but it felt good to be on the outside with someone else.

Harry held his index finger up to Lyla Rae Jr., asking for a moment, before turning back to us.

"Nice to meet you, Aurora," he said, already taking steps toward the crowded corner booth. "I'll see you guys around."

"'Harold Clarrrrk!'" Charlotte imitated, dropping her voice so only I could hear.

She let out a sharp laugh and I joined in, the two of us earning a glare from Marie, which only made us laugh harder.

I didn't have enough experience in friendship to know if she was taking the time to be nice to me because she felt bad for me, because her mom was forcing her to, or because she really wanted to be my friend. My time in Monroe wouldn't be all that long—a silent countdown started as soon as we'd pulled into Gran's driveway. With the boldness of a looming goodbye, I put a voice to my racing thoughts.

"Can I ask you a question, and you promise to answer honestly?"

Charlotte seemed like the kind of girl who held her secrets close. Sure, she told plenty of stories, but I was left with the feeling that she gave the world what she wanted it to have, keeping back the parts she didn't want anyone to see for herself. I watched her mull over her answer—blind honesty was a big ask.

"Okay, sure—shoot," she said.

"Are we friends? Or are we still here cause your mom asked you to?"

Charlotte smiled a big, broad smile, the stolen red lipstick highlighting the smallest gap between her two front teeth. "Honestly?"

"Honestly."

"Honestly, Aurora, if *you* could use a friend . . ." I could tell it took effort, removing the practiced irreverence she wore like armor. "If *you* could use a friend, *I* could use a friend."

I smiled back, startled by my relief, by how much I wanted this day to be real.

"I could use a friend too," I said, matching her honesty.

"Then it's settled," she said, scooting out of the booth with a squeak and offering me her arm for the third time that afternoon.

Walking arm in arm past the booths in Norma's diner, I felt like the girls I'd see in the school halls, heads bent together, laughing at secrets no one else could know. I'd spent so long watching them, telling myself it wasn't all that great, that I was lucky to enjoy my own company (Mom's words, not my own). But walking with Charlotte, I couldn't help but think I'd spent all those years being wrong.

It was nice to have a friend.

6

I loved the freedom Jay's bike gave me. Even when I had nowhere in particular to go, I'd spend the moments before dusk biking up and down unfamiliar streets, learning Monroe like I'd never learned any of the places that had come before. Gran also loved the freedom the bike gave me, particularly when that freedom could get me to the liquor store and back in less than ten minutes.

Jerry didn't mind that I bought the alcohol underage, so long as I had a handwritten note from Katherine and swore up and down I wouldn't touch the stuff myself.

"Once you start, you can't stop," he said.

Gran had stopped for years, but I suppose none of that counts if you start back up again. I was uneasy bringing back bottles of whiskey for Gran, but it didn't seem like a request I could refuse. Plus, she was nothing like the Gran in Mom's stories. There was never any yelling, no fights. Really, the whiskey just brought out an extra dose of sass and a cackle that carried to the neighboring houses.

It was Thursday, and we'd been in town just shy of a week. Mom and Gran had managed to avoid any knock-down, drag-out fights, but that didn't keep me from feeling like our boxes might be packed any minute. It was a feeling I was used to, the fear that everything could change at the drop of the hat. But the more time I spent in Monroe, the more worried I became. I wanted to learn the rest of the streets by heart. I wanted to hear Gran's thoughts on our soap's many love triangles. I wanted to spend more time with Charlotte.

I lived most days painfully aware they could be my last here.

Halfway home from the liquor store, I hit a rock with my front tire and toppled into Mr. and Mrs. Shephard's yard, Gran's bottle of whiskey crashing with me. The glass hit the cement before I did, shattering into the Shepherds' azalea bushes. I'd met the Shepherds on my Tuesday trip to the liquor store. They'd called me up to the front porch to ask how Gran had been getting along since Jay's passing. If they'd noticed the fifth, wrapped in a brown paper bag, they didn't say anything.

The front tire had a slit two inches long. I felt tears spring to my eyes. I wondered what sort of tools Jay kept in his garage, not that I'd have any clue how to use them. A good piece of tape might keep the tire from giving out completely.

The glass bottle had shattered onto the sidewalk, a few stray shards landing in the street. I tried to pick up some of the bigger pieces before giving up. I walked in the direction of home, warmer than before, dragging the bike behind me. Maybe Gran would drive me back with a broom this afternoon. It seemed rude to leave such a mess.

I made it about three houses past the Shepherds' before the mail truck pulled up beside me, Tim "take-his-team-to-state" Harrison at the wheel.

"You all right?" he asked. "I thought you figured out how to ride this thing."

"Sliced tire," I said continuing to drag the bike along.

Tim stopped the truck completely, getting out and squatting down to examine the flat tire. "It's a doozy," he said, taking the bike's handlebars out of my hands. "Here—I'll put it up in my truck and give you a ride home."

He was lifting the bike into the back before I had a chance to object.

Our mailbox was at the end of the driveway, but in the few days since the afternoon he taught me to ride, he'd stopped putting the mail in our mailbox, delivering it directly to our door instead. Mom liked to answer, always beating Gran and me to the door. They stuck to small talk, but she laughed at his jokes, even when they weren't all that funny. She knew he was married, but that didn't stop her from pulling out all the stops.

I rolled my eyes when she tossed her hair behind her shoulder, feeling a little sick at how blatant it felt. I knew Mom enough to know when she was flirting—the hair toss was a dead giveaway. Gran, with her narrowed eyes, knew too.

"You sure?" I asked. With a little over a mile to go, I'd have accepted a ride from just about anyone to escape the heat, but I didn't want to take advantage. "Won't it ruin your route?"

"Nah." He patted the empty seat next to him. "We're close. I'll give the Harvey Street girls their mail a little early."

He drove past the houses who'd go without mail a little longer, throwing the town's routine out of sync. The closer we got to our little blue house, the smaller the houses got. In the development side of town, white picket fences marked property lines.

Tim pulled directly into our driveway. Karl, tending to his roses out front, offered a polite wave.

Tim unloaded the bike from the back. "I don't have my tools on me, but I'd be happy to look at that tire if you'd like."

"Oh, you don't have to do that." I dragged the toe of my sneaker on the sidewalk. The ride was enough of a favor.

"I want to," he said. "I'll stop by tomorrow at the end of my route. Around five or so."

"Okay," I said, keeping my bike steady with one hand and holding our mail in the other. "Thanks for the ride."

"Don't even worry about it." He flashed a swoon-worthy smile. I looked away, embarrassed. "Say hi to your mom for me, yeah?"

༺ ༻

"What was that about?" Gran asked before I had even shut the front door.

"I popped a tire. He said he'd help fix it."

"I'll bet," Gran said, pouring what was left of her bottle into an almost-empty glass.

Mom, usually posted up on the couch, was nowhere in sight.

"Where's Mom?"

"Norma's."

General Hospital started back up on the TV, switching over from a commercial break.

"Will you turn it up?"

I walked to the television set and adjusted the dial. I knew better than to talk through her soaps, so I waited until the next commercial break to ask my follow-up question.

"What for?" I asked.

Gran looked at me like I had a third eye. "What do you mean 'what for'?"

"What did Mom go to Norma's for?"

Gran gave me a wink. "A job."

A warmth spread from my chest down into my stomach. "We're staying?"

Gran shrugged, but her smile gave away her excitement. "She says for the summer while she figures out what's next. Said she worries about me—I guess she thinks I might need some sort of babysitter."

"Am I the babysitter?"

Gran smiled. "Looks like it. Speaking of—where's my whiskey?"

When I thought of the shattered fifth in the Shepherds' driveway, I couldn't help but laugh. "It's kind of a funny story, but before I tell it, do we own a broom?"

<hr />

Tim kept his promise. The next day, just after five, he ended his route at our house. Mom went to the store before he came, and made lemonade, swearing it was just proper hospitality, a thank-you for him giving me a ride home. The recipe was a box mix, of course, but she'd bought a lemon to slice up for show. Gran bit back her commentary, but I could tell she was irritated by the whole production.

The three of us—Gran included—sat out on the front lawn, watching while Tim stripped down to his undershirt and sat in our front yard with a toolbox and a new tire. Mom's eyes seemed to watch his every move.

"This really is too kind of you," she said.

Tim looked up from his project and winked. "It's no problem at all. It's nice to feel useful."

"Well, consider yourself useful. If you didn't come by, this bike would've returned to a life of gathering dust in Jay's garage."

"So Tim," Gran chimed in, "how's Lyla doing? She still over at D&D Dental?"

Tim furrowed his brow before straightening out his expression. He pulled a cloth out of his pocket, using it to wipe the sweat from his forehead.

"Nah," he said, not offering many details. "She's been home for a while now."

"Sad to hear it." Gran angled her body toward Mom. "Laine, you remember Lyla Rae, don't you?"

Tim stopped cranking the wrench, looking up at Mom while she answered.

"Not really," she said, with a passive shrug. "Different circles, I guess."

Gran, satisfied with her sudden spotlight on Tim's marital status, leaned back on her elbows to soak up the sun. "Aurora, you ought to start going to the pool and working on your summer tan."

I rolled my eyes. "First my clothes, now my tan."

"Your lack thereof," Gran said, letting out a cackle. "I'm just saying, the sun is good for you. I saw it on the six o clock news."

Tim continued to silently tinker with the bike, but one corner of his mouth was turned up in a grin.

Mom chimed in. "Aurora doesn't get tan. She keeps her fair complexion all summer long. Our very own Snow White."

"Can we find a new subject?" I asked. "Preferably one that has nothing to do with me."

The three of them joined in a chorus of laughter but honored my request. We had a guest much more interesting than me. Mom began peppering him with questions about the people in the town, who stuck around, where the others ended up. He was a Monroe encyclopedia, filled with facts and anecdotes.

"And what about you, Miss Laine?"

"What about me?"

Tim used his free hand to block the sun, looking over at her like he was trying to study her face. In that moment, with Gran and me bearing witness to his bold gaze, it was obvious the spare tire wasn't out of the goodness of his heart.

"Where have you been all these years?" he asked.

I looked over at Mom, whose eyes were fixed on Tim's.

"It's a long story," she said.

Tim smiled. "I'd like to hear it."

Gran let out a sigh that only I could hear.

"Well, there's a Miller in the fridge with your name on it, if you aren't busy."

"A cold beer sounds great right about now." Tim began gathering his tools, returning them to the toolbox. "Let me just get these back in the truck."

"All right," Mom said, wiping grass off the back of her tan thighs as she stood up.

She led the way back into the house, Gran trailing her at a close distance.

"Laine," Gran hissed as soon as the door shut. "He's *married*."

Mom narrowed her eyes, the stubbornness she'd carried with her for the last thirty-one years rising to the surface. "It's just a beer," she said, walking toward the kitchen.

Gran followed, and I hurried to keep up. The fight I'd been dreading was finally here. "You and I both know this isn't just a beer," she countered.

Mom opened the fridge, pulling the bottle out and setting it on the counter, a single act of defiance.

Gran crossed her arms over her chest. "You might have carried on this way for the last fifteen years, but this is still my house."

Mom grabbed a second beer, setting it beside the first. "Fine. Tim and I can take these to go." She turned to face me. "Aurora, pack your things while I'm out."

My stomach dropped. I guessed today really was my last.

Mom turned back to Gran, wearing a cruel smile. "Her and I will be gone by morning."

I waited for Gran to shout "Fine!" or to throw up her hands in exasperation. Instead, she dropped her arms to her sides.

"Laine," she said, her voice softer this time, "you don't have to do that. I'm just telling you to think before you act, that's all."

"I *do*," Mom said. "I've been living my life without you for the last fifteen years. I'm grown, even if you don't see me that way."

Tim, right on cue, knocked twice on the front door.

"Come on in!" Mom yelled, her voice chipper.

Gran turned to face me. "Aurora, you hungry? You haven't lived until you've had a burger from Norma's."

I wasn't all that hungry, and I wasn't too keen on leaving Mom behind with the mailman, but the way Gran asked it made me feel like it wasn't a question.

"I could eat," I said.

Gran smiled, the empty glass of whiskey still in her hand. She set it in the kitchen sink. "Good. But you gotta drive. You fly, and I'll buy."

"Fine," I said.

By the time Gran gathered her things, Mom and Tim were at the kitchen table, both of them holding a cold beer. He wanted to know about the last fifteen years, and I knew there was quite the story to tell. I wondered if she'd share the highlight reel—the years on the road with me in the passenger seat, all of Indiana laid out before us. Or maybe she'd be honest, letting Tim in on the secrets she kept from everyone, even from me. Maybe she'd tell him about how she'd spent fifteen years running.

Part of me wanted to stay behind and hear her tell it, what she'd been up to for all these years and all those miles, but Gran was dead set on a burger and dead set on getting me out of the house. I think she knew what was going to unfold, and although she was powerless to stop it, she didn't want us to stand by and watch either.

7

Mom settled in the chair facing the window, halfheartedly flipping through last week's *National Enquirer*, delivered by none other than the former high school quarterback. Elvis Presley had been dead two years, but he was alive on the cover, sporting his signature collar and lopsided grin.

Gran's glass and whiskey bottle were fixed to the nearest TV tray, which still held the remains of last night's TV dinner pot roast. She kept still in her recliner while I stayed sprawled on the living-room floor, waiting for my freshly painted toes to dry. Minimal movement was essential to surviving summer. Minimal movement and wall fans.

We coped with *One Life to Live* on the television.

"Turn it up, Aurora," Gran said. "Can't hear a word over that damn fan."

I shot her a look.

"Don't sass me. You're the closest."

I crab-walked to the TV from my spot on the floor to turn the dial, careful not to smudge my toes.

Mom dogeared her spot before flipping the magazine shut. She'd taken Norma up on her job offer, falling into her familiar rhythm of early mornings behind the counter. Her apron was draped over the couch.

We all watched the familiar soap opera format fall into place, our newly adopted ritual. Gran made a dent in the bottle I procured for her, while Mom watched the window more than the show. For once I didn't care. I'd begun to cherish the rhythm of our summer afternoons.

The wall clock was broken, keeping us stuck forever at nine in the morning or nine at night, our sense of time dependent on one thing.

Really, one person. Mom's dreamy haze shifted to a nervous energy Gran and I suffered through. Gran's sass took on an edge. The change in TV programming was our only real indication of time—that and the arrival of our mailman.

Ten minutes before *General Hospital*, we heard the familiar knock on the door. Mom was already up, straightening the stack of magazines and checking her hair in the hallway mirror.

Gran poured herself another glass, the second past her unspoken limit, and rolled her eyes. "Mail's here," she said.

Mom opened the door and Tim stepped inside. She took the stack of mail from his hands, which found their way to her waist. She tossed the bills and ads on the side table, on top of the ashtray with its cooling cigarette. He grabbed her chin, tilting her face toward his. His other hand moved to the small of her back, pulling her closer. I looked away just in time.

⁂

Two weeks had passed since she'd invited him in for a drink, which led to two, which led to this. Just like that, something that wasn't suddenly was. When she asked him in, and he said yes, I guess I should have known what was coming. Mom said it was just drinks, and I wanted to believe her.

But by the next afternoon, he was barefoot in Gran's house, flipping through Jay's records, playing us his favorites. He grabbed beer from the fridge like it was his own, reaching down to tousle my hair like he'd raised me. Mom never lingered long in the in-between.

I tried not to wonder how long it took them to get up from the table after we left, or where his wife thought he was, if she noticed the smell of Virginia Slims heavy on his skin. I tried not to think of the lies he told his daughters on the nights he came home late. Seven of the last twelve. I tried not to dwell on the ache deep in my gut while my mind told me stories about the other life he lived. I was sure he left our house in time to make it home to a real family dinner, a table with warm casseroles where his daughters told him about their day while he lied to them about his.

Once Mom got a job and a boyfriend (albeit a married one), I figured we'd be here for more than a few weeks. The end was still guaranteed, that much I knew, but until then, I figured I'd find ways to occupy my time, preferably in ways that got me out of the house between the hours of three and five PM.

Being Katherine's granddaughter and Laine's daughter wasn't particularly helpful in the job hunt. Like in any small town, Gran and Mom filled their roles: the relapsed drunk and her wayward daughter. The town didn't know me at all, and for all they knew I might be Laine reincarnate. They didn't necessarily want their establishments stuck with the comings and goings of the Taylor girls.

I biked up and down main street, getting a polite but firm "No" three times.

I was too young to be a bartender, but King's might be the only establishment willing to accept me. I stood on the sidewalk, holding my bike's handlebars, ready to call it quits. Across the street, Paradise Bowl's neon sign loomed large. I remembered Al the owner from the funeral, specifically the scowl on his face. His hate for Mom and Gran was plain as day, but rejections start to sting less when you get three of them in a row.

I walked into the bowling alley, the familiar sounds of crashing pins washing over me. The floor stuck to my shoes like there was a layer of spilled soda coating the floor. Maybe they needed a janitor? I wasn't above mopping the floors. I'd be sure to mention that.

The buttery smell of popcorn was thick, and I was grateful for the familiarity. We'd had a bowling alley in every town we'd lived in, and Mom loved a Friday night at the alley. She would put me up at a lane before heading to the bar.

I approached the shoe rental, where a tall, lanky man with a wiry mustache was staring off into space.

"Excuse me," I said, trying to get his attention.

The man blinked his way back to earth, offering me a delayed smile. "Yeah?"

"Um, is the owner in today?"

His smile drooped at the corner. "Office on the right," he said, pointing past me to the glass door.

"Thanks."

I wiped my nervous hands on my shorts, not sure what had inspired me to pick Al of all people. Gran and Mom had plenty to say about him, particularly how he was a drunk and a cheat. Gran had no room to comment on the drinking, but she had been a faithful wife to Jay. Al's second wife had burned his clothes on the lawn, taking out the front room of the house in the process. She was gone with the kids before the smoke cleared.

The third wife was a disappearing act with much less showmanship. One day she was here, the next she was gone. There were no kids to take, but Gran swore up and down to Mom over dinner a night ago that there was a bit of money. Gran said Al drank a little more than he did before, which seemed like the pot calling the kettle black. Apparently, he had a few strikes against him, but the town needed a bowling alley, and Al needed a town.

In spite of their stories, I was desperate enough to stand outside his office. I knocked twice before I could change my mind.

"Jim, I swear if you broke that popcorn machine—" The door swung open, and Al cut his speech short.

"Can I help you?" he asked, taking a step back.

All day I'd felt like the ghost of my mother, come back to haunt Monroe with their past.

"I was hoping you might be hiring," I managed, delivering the same line I'd recited all day. This time my voice sounded defeated.

Al walked back to his desk, plopping down in a red leather chair that looked out of place in an otherwise simple room. I followed him in, feeling a flutter of hope when his "no" wasn't immediate.

I waited in front of his desk with my hands in my pockets, trying hard not to fidget. The office had one chair, and he was in it, his belly out almost as far as his legs.

"Your mom doing okay?" he asked.

I nodded. "Yep."

"Heard she's over at Norma's diner. That mean you girls are sticking around?"

I shrugged. "Seems like it."

I watched his eyes wander. "And Katherine? How's she doing with everything?"

"She's all right."

His office was covered in papers. There were frames on the wall—his diploma, his ex-family, and a shot of last year's bowling league champions.

His eyes landed on my exposed legs and stayed there. "Good to hear." There was a pause. "But I'll be upfront, and I don't want you to take no offense to it. I know we don't know each other all that well, but—"

I knew what was coming, but I just smiled. "Go ahead," I said, giving him permission to turn me down.

He furrowed his brow and frowned.

"Did you meet Jim out there?" he asked.

Al's question caught me off guard. "Not really," I said. There had been no formal introductions made between me and the space cadet running his rentals.

"Well, if you had, you'd know I'm a little short-staffed on competent people. It's Aurora, isn't it?"

I nodded.

"You competent, Aurora?"

"I got all A's this last year, sir," I said. A flutter of hope settled in my gut. "And I pick things up really fast."

He ran a hand over his face, like this decision was painful. "I believe it. Say what you want about your mom and Gran, but they aren't short on brains." He let out a long sigh, and I resisted the urge to fill the silence with more of my accomplishments. "Listen, if I give you this job, Katherine and Laine don't need to be coming around here." He shuffled around some papers on his desk. "I don't want any of that trouble—I've been there, done that, and it's probably best they keep their distance." Al paused, like he might be changing his mind. "I'm giving *you* a clean slate, Aurora, not them. It's up to you what you do with it."

"It'll be good," I promised, letting out an exhale like I'd been holding my breath all afternoon. "No problems."

I could hardly believe it. I wanted to say more, to thank him, to tell him how much this meant to me, but I didn't want him to change his mind. I'd prove him wrong—show him I was worth the clean slate. There'd be no problems.

He whistled through his teeth. "We'll see about that. You can start Monday."

When I walked in the living room, Mom was draped across the couch, leaving little space for anyone else. Her apron was a heap on the floor. Gran was where I'd left her, asleep in her recliner. I stood behind them, unnoticed. One person was missing from our new normal.

"No Tim?" I asked, walking around the couch and taking my spot on the floor.

Mom kept her eyes on the TV. "Not today."

"I got a job," I said.

Gran stirred. She'd been listening. "Where?"

"Don't laugh, okay? Paradise Bowl."

Mom's eyes moved from the figures on the screen to meet mine. Gran spun her recliner.

"What'd you do that for?" Mom asked. "Al hates us."

"You two," I corrected. "He hates you two. He doesn't know me yet."

I explained Al's rules and Mom laughed. "He's ridiculous. I love that we're the one causing trouble. That man's rap sheet is a mile long."

"Damn that Al," Gran said, piping up from her TV room throne. "As if I'd want foot fungus from that God-awful alley."

Mom's eyes crinkled with her smile. They were back on the TV. "How are you getting to and from the alley, Miss Aurora? I watch enough of the evening news to know you can't be riding your bike that late on dark roads. You get that far in your sneaky plan to get a job?"

I had anticipated this question. I crawled toward the couch and stood, picking up her long, tanned legs and taking the cushion next to her. She kept limp, dead weight. I batted my eyelashes, but she didn't look impressed.

She set her almost-empty glass on the coffee table and raised her eyebrows. "What do I get out of it?"

"A very happy daughter. And one who can pay for her own movie tickets."

Last summer, I'd gone to see *Grease* once a week. Mom said I'd bankrupted our family.

"I'll drop you off and pick you up, but just three nights a week. This can't turn into a second job for me." She paused to light her cigarette. The ashtray was full. "You'll call when your shift ends, and Gran or I will pick you up. Are we allowed in his parking lot, or is that sacred too?"

"Thank you, Mom." Ignoring her questions, I leaned over to hug her, shocked she'd said yes. She extended her lit cigarette away from our embrace, squeezing my shoulder with one arm, careful not to burn me.

8

I'd been at Al's for a little under two weeks. Of the five shifts I'd worked, they'd only forgotten me twice, tonight being the second. I sat on the curb, waiting, and stared down the road, desperate for headlights. The neon sign above me read "Paradise Bow," the *l* in *bowl* no longer lit. My vest smelled like burnt popcorn and Al's spilled beer. The parking lot was close to empty, just the cars of the few bowlers still finishing their games. After fifty-five minutes staring down an empty road, I went back inside.

The bowling alley felt good, which said more about Indiana than the alley amenities. Al ran two wall fans at either end, and they mostly just pushed hot air around. Lane 9 and lane 11 were the last to finish their games.

Lane 9 was taking his time wrapping up the third game of the night. His wife had called twice to check in. He had four kids at home and came twice a week—Fridays for practice, Tuesdays for league. Al kept a tally whenever she called. We all placed bets—if the wife called two more times, I'd get free soda for the week. If she showed up, kids in tow, I'd cover Jim's Saturdays for the month. Jim was a go-big-or-go-home kind of guy, and I wasn't one to shy away from a bet.

Two lanes over, it looked like the last group of the night was halfway through frame 9. Harry, the pastor's son, was with Shane from the diner, plus a few characters I didn't know yet. All five of them sported freshly cut hair and tanned summer skin. They were the kind of boys you noticed in the hallway—handsome and comfortable taking up space on this earth. Each took turns walking down the divider like it was a balance beam, the only discernable finish line a ball stuck halfway down the gutter. Three beers ago, Al might've noticed.

A few hours before, I'd watched them enter the alley with boyish chaos, commanding everyone's attention, including my own, and ordering four bags of popcorn to share and two bottles of Coca-Cola each.

"Keep the change," one of them said, winking. Unlike the others, with five-dollar barber-shop cuts, his mom cut his hair, and it showed.

"Shut up, Jerry," Shane said, shoving him from behind.

I'd rolled my eyes, because I'd watched Mom enough to know that's what you do. The boys laughed, play fighting as they walked toward their lane, spilling popcorn onto the patterned carpet. Harry was the last to grab his sodas. He smiled a perfect, straight smile—Charlotte had told me over peanut butter and jelly sandwiches on the town green that he was one of three kids in town to get braces, getting out of school early for trips to the orthodontist two towns over.

When I told Gran about it, she said that's why she didn't go to church. She said that seemed like a silly use of the town's tithes, but when his smiled landed on me, I didn't feel so sure she was right.

"Sorry about my friends." He added another smile for good measure.

I shrugged, ignoring the flutter in my belly, and passed him his second Coca-Cola. "No big deal."

Of the boys walking up and down the gutter, Harry got the farthest. He almost tipped over, then found his balance, extending his arms out like a seasoned gymnast. His friends cheered. When he turned to face them, he caught me staring, and when he bent over to take his bow, I looked away.

"Aurora, still no sign of them?" Al called.

He was at an empty lane with his friends. They had finished more than a few beers, and the bottles were littered across the table. I'd noticed games on the house weren't helping business. Neither was drinking on the job, but as the snack bar attendant, I didn't have much of a say in these things.

"Nope," I said. "Mind if I try the phone again?"

"Go ahead."

I opened the office door. Lane 11 laughed at something I couldn't see.

"That's Katherine and Laine's girl," Al said, a drunk excuse for a whisper. "My latest hire."

There was a collective grumble in the crowd.

Al's desk was littered with bills and the remains of a spilled ashtray. The framed picture of his ex-wife and two kids wasn't balanced, tilting to the left. I flopped down in his desk chair and spun before picking up the phone and dialing the number again, willing someone to answer. The busy signal mocked me for the third time that night.

"Shit," I said, slamming the phone on its receiver.

I spun twice in the chair before standing, steadying myself on the desk. The office was quiet, but I could hear faint sounds of the alley, the crashing of the pins and the hum of laughter. I closed my eyes and tried to focus on this rather than worry about where my mom was or who she was with, even though I could guess. The pang in my gut was familiar, and so was my panic. It was better with Tim—married or not. There were no more strangers, no more nights out. My body didn't know what my mind did, though. I took a deep breath and opened the door.

"No answer?" Al bellowed, his volume turned up a notch with each beer.

I shook my head.

"Need a ride?"

I nearly laughed. "I'm okay. She might be on her way."

He didn't even pretend to believe me.

"Check the bar!" one of them yelled, followed by a chorus of men's laughter.

Al shushed him, and I waved before exiting the alley. I could feel my cheeks turning red. My spot on the curb was vacant, and the parking lot was clearing out. Across the street, the King's Bar parking lot was washed in a neon glow. With the small-town traffic, you could walk straight across the two-lane highway. Heck, you could crab-walk without any real danger. Even before they'd suggested it, I'd checked. No one had seen them tonight.

Lane 11 came out of the double doors like they'd been trailing me. I avoided their collective gaze and focused on the scuffed toes of my sneakers, dragging them along the asphalt's edge. When I heard their cars pull out of the lot, I let myself look up.

"Need a ride?"

Five feet to my right stood Harry.

I looked back down the empty road. "Someone's coming."

He took a seat on the curb, maintaining the five feet of space. "I don't mind waiting."

"You don't have to. Al's still here. I'm safe."

Right on cue, Al emerged from the alley with friends on either side. They half dragged, half carried him across the street to King's.

"See you tomorrow!" Al yelled. And then, loud enough to make an echo, "George wants your mom to give him a call!"

Music flooded the silent street as the men entered the bar. As quickly as it came, it was gone again. Harry looked at the bar and back at me.

"I'll just stay," he said. "It's Aurora, right?"

I nodded but kept my eyes on the road, painfully aware of my vest and name tag.

"So you working at Paradise now? Does that mean you guys are sticking around?"

I wondered how much he knew about me, what stories were told at his dinner table about Laine Taylor and her return to town.

"For now," I said, which was the truth. I wasn't guaranteed tomorrow, let alone next week.

"That's cool," he said, matching my two-word answer with one of his own.

I knew I could say more. He was clearly nice enough to wait with a girl he barely knew while she sat in an empty parking lot. I had so little practice in talking with a boy my age, so instead I settled into a painful silence.

We stayed like that for fifteen minutes, me looking down the road, him watching the bustling parking lot across the way. I wondered if he'd be the one to break the silence, but he never did. I thought he'd leave, but he stuck around. When I saw the one-headlight car down the stretch of road, I stood up and brushed the dirt off my jeans. He followed my lead and stood too.

"This is them," I said.

He squinted down the road. "You can tell from here?"

Gran had hit a pole the week before, so we were down to one headlight. I nodded toward the car as it came closer. "The headlight."

One corner of Harry's mouth turned up in a smile.

I squinted to see who was driving and hoped it wasn't Gran. It was. She was hunched over the wheel, probably trying to figure out who I was with.

She stopped close to the curb, and I was grateful she didn't hit it. I walked to the car, and when I pulled at the passenger door, it stuck. Gran's accident had altered the car just slightly, making the process of getting in and out a difficult one. Gran knew the drill. She stretched her leg over the center console, using her bare foot to push while I pulled. The door dislodged and I stumbled back.

I looked over to explain, but Harry was already walking toward his car.

The TV was on, but Mom slept through the sound. A glass with melting ice was in its usual spot on the coffee table. The watered ring stains were permanent. I turned the TV off and tossed a blanket over her, picking up her half-filled glass on my way to the kitchen. Gran was at the kitchen table, grinning and flipping through a magazine. She had her bottle of whiskey in front of her and a fresh glass.

"So, who's the boy?" she asked, not even looking up.

It had been a silent drive home. I'd stared out the window and ignored her excuses about the phone being off the hook and how Tim hadn't shown up when he said he would. I didn't care.

"The preacher's son." I dumped Mom's drink in the sink and set the glass in with the others. Nobody did dishes until it was absolutely necessary. "You know I called *five* times." It was really three, but I was angry, and five sounded better.

"I told you: the phone was off the hook." She started to laugh, but I couldn't laugh with her. "I'm sorry, hon, really. You saw your mom in there. She threw a fit, drank a little whiskey, and fell asleep. Probably took the phone off the hook so he couldn't call. I was the one who was supposed to get you. I should've checked the phone, but by the time I did, it was so late."

"He didn't show?" I asked.

Gran shook her head. "No, he did. Sometimes that's worse."

"Well, if things don't work out with Tim, Al's friend George told me to have her call."

Gran threw her head back and laughed too loud. When I pulled out a chair and joined her at the table, she scooted her glass toward me with the back of her hand. Her eyes were glassy. I wondered how much she'd had to drink and how much of it had to do with Jay. Sometimes her eyes would stay fixed on something I couldn't see, and I knew she was plagued by grief she'd never show.

"Want some?"

I slid the glass back toward her. "Whiskey's not my poison."

"It's definitely mine," she said, her voice tired.

I was tired too. "Is Tim Mom's poison?" I asked.

Gran took a sip before answering.

"For now."

9

As simple as the popcorn machine was, Al made a big deal of showing me how to use it. Even after three days of unnecessary training, complete with a graduation certificate, he was always nearby, ready to step in if I was being too stingy on the salt—or too generous. I never gave the right amount of butter to a customer. Sometimes the bag spilled over, and if it didn't spill over, he'd think we looked cheap. It was Friday night, which meant we were actually busy. Half of the town was at the drive-in. We got the other half, the ones who had seen the movie on the two-week cycle last week. Al was working the shoe rental and assigning lanes because Jim flaked. Despite the crowd, Al managed to keep an eye on my popcorn.

"Aurora, get over here!" he bellowed.

I walked over to the shoe rental.

"I saw the bag you gave lane seven." He paused and waited for my response. I didn't have one. "Lane seven, the couple. You know, with the guy in the leather jacket."

I nodded, still not sure what was wrong with their popcorn.

"It was just," he continued, "a little sloppy. I'm running a business."

It took all of my energy not to roll my eyes. "Sorry about that." This was the fourth correction of the night. "I'll do better next time."

He smiled and pointed at the snack bar's growing line. "Now's your chance."

I gave him a thumbs-up and walked the ten feet, adjusting my crooked name tag. The line was three people deep. My stomach did a twist. The first person in line had a white-blonde ponytail. I prayed it wasn't her.

Tim had two daughters. I peppered Charlotte with questions about them, doing my best not to reveal Mom's secret. One was my age, and the other a few grades below. Lyla Rae Jr., Tim's daughter and his wife's namesake, was my living nightmare. Charlotte swore she was the absolute worst, and I felt relieved. Imagine if Mom had struck up an affair with a nice person's father.

In a town this small, I knew it was bound to happen, us running into each other. I'd been living in constant dread. If Tommy's Hardware had hired me, I wouldn't have had this problem. I entered through the snack bar's swinging door, steadying myself on the counter.

I was supposed to ask what she wanted, but I was mute.

"Two popcorns," she said, looking at me, then back at her friends. They were renting shoes from Al. "Size eight!" she yelled.

I stood still, staring, willing myself to disappear. A spontaneous evaporation. Maybe I'd melt like the witch in Oz—I'd have poured water on myself if that were even a remote possibility.

"Two popcorns," she repeated, much more slowly than her first request. She looked down at her nails. They were painted pink to match her top.

The man in line behind her cleared his throat.

I turned to the machine, willing my concrete-heavy legs to work, and filled the bags, avoiding the burnt bits in the bottom. It was the least I could do. "One dollar, twenty-five cents," I said, the words thick on my tongue.

She handed me two crisp dollar bills. When I looked at her, I couldn't help it—I saw Tim twirling my mom in circles, the carpet soft under their feet, my mom's cloud of smoke filling the room.

I passed her the change, and she grabbed the popcorn, running to catch up with her friends. The bag was too full, and a couple pieces dropped to the floor.

I glanced over at the shoe rental. The bits of popcorn were now crushed into the carpet. I'd have to vacuum at the end of the night. Al crossed his arms over his chest and shook his head.

The man next in line stepped up to the counter. When he ordered, he made sure to enunciate each and every syllable. "Two popcorns and a pitcher of orange soda."

I could feel Al's eyes on me as I scooped the popcorn. I was careful to fill the bag just enough, and I drizzled the butter in an X formation. My ratio of soda to ice was perfect. The man balanced the bags in one arm and held the pitcher with the other, nodding thanks before he left. When I looked over, Al was smiling.

༶

To my left, yards away, Lyla Jr. sat on the curb. Mom had actually answered on the first ring, and I thought about mentioning her. If I'd known we'd end up on the same curb, staring down the same road, I might've told her. I probably should have.

"I hate when they're late," she said, a peace offering.

I moved my eyes from the road to meet hers. "Who?"

"Parents. I need my own car."

I nodded, unsure of what to say. The familiar sinking in my gut returned.

"So you work here?" she asked.

I nodded. "For a couple weeks now."

"That's awesome." She tightened her ponytail. "I should look for a job."

I'd known plenty of girls like Lyla Jr. throughout the years. It felt like high school was built with them in mind. They made sure everyone in the hallways noticed them, while I did my best to fly under the radar. I couldn't imagine she'd take the time to talk to me if her friends were around, but maybe this parking lot was the great equalizer.

"It's nice to get out of the house," I said, remembering to speak. *The house with your dad in it,* I thought.

"God, I can imagine." A pair of headlights appeared down the road, and as they came closer, pulled into the parking lot. Both were working. "Speaking of."

Lyla stood and I couldn't help but notice her cherry-print shorts, suddenly self-conscious about my own worn-out denim pair. Tim pulled up beside the curb, and I fixed my eyes on the approaching headlight. Our winking car wasn't far behind, and Lyla, blissfully unaware, didn't move fast enough for any of us. Mom pulled up beside Tim right as Lyla climbed into the passenger seat. I stared at Mom, who stared at Tim, who was pressing the gas pedal before Lyla could even shut her door.

I went to open the car door, and it stuck. Mom absentmindedly extended her leg and pushed while I pulled. The door came unstuck.

"What the hell?" she asked. "What was he doing here?"

"That was Lyla Jr., Tim's daughter. The older one." I gave her the facts and fastened my seat belt, hoping she'd share in the guilt I always seemed to carry. "He was picking her up. She was bowling with friends."

She nodded and stared ahead, pulling out of the parking lot and driving with more focus than the sleepy road required. When we pulled into the driveway, she turned off the car but didn't move. I sat still too, staring at our front window, trying to see what she saw. The blinds were a little crooked. Once Jay died, Karl had taken over keeping our flowers in the front alive.

"He didn't even look at me." She unbuckled her seat belt. "Not even a glance."

Mom came out of her room at ten till three. I hadn't seen her all morning, not since she'd locked herself in the night before. She was dressed for the diner, her hair up in a knot and the checkered apron around her waist. I knew she wasn't scheduled. It was Saturday afternoon, and the mail would be here any minute.

"It's Saturday," I said.

"I picked up a dinner shift. Maureen called. Ate something that's not sitting right—not like I've got anything better to do."

Gran had one phone with a ringer shrill and loud enough to hear two houses over. It hadn't rung once all morning, but I didn't call her on her bluff. She leaned down to tie her shoes and adjust her socks. "If Tim shows up, tell him I had to work."

Gran tried to give Mom the half-eaten peanut butter and jelly sandwich left on her plate. She shook her head and reached for the watered-down glass of whiskey instead, downing what was left of it. She leaned over to kiss my forehead before moving to the door.

"Good luck!" Gran called.

"Make lots of tips," I added.

She offered us her sad smile, the forced one, before heading into the sun she'd avoided all day.

Gran waited until the car was out of the driveway to twirl her recliner to face me. "What the hell happened last night?"

I told her about Paradise, about Tim picking up Lyla Jr., about Mom's silent drive home. I left out the part about Lyla and me talking on the curb, because for some reason it felt like a betrayal. In the month we'd been in Monroe, I'd realized there wasn't much I kept from Gran. She let me say everything that came to mind, and it felt good to have a captive audience. Still, we were a loyal bunch, and the conversation with Lyla Jr. had left me uneasy.

"Well," she said, the word like a sigh, "I guess it was bound to happen. He has a wife and kids, and this town isn't all that big. It's good for her to get a dose of reality, no matter how painful." She shook her head and refilled her empty glass. "I hope you know being with a married man isn't right, Aurora."

I nodded.

Satisfied, she turned her chair back to the TV.

My lessons on right and wrong followed a similar pattern. Mom usually did the wrong, and then told me to do the right. Gran was following in her footsteps. It was the opposite of lead by example, and for most of my life it had worked.

A knock at the door interrupted the Sunkist commercial. Gran and I exchanged looks. In all of our talk about the married man, we'd forgotten he was coming.

She fixed her eyes straight ahead to let me know it was my job to get rid of him. I stood up and moved toward the door, dragging my feet. He knocked again. I don't think he'd ever waited more than ten seconds.

When I opened it, his dopey smile sank a little at the corners. I knew I was a disappointment. His blue postal shirt was covered with small spots of sweat. His satchel was empty except for our small pile of mail. His hat sat a little crooked on his head.

"Your mom home?" he asked, peering around me.

"She picked up a shift." I shuffled my weight from one foot to the other.

Tim looked more awkward than I'd ever seen him. In spite of the circumstances, he usually existed in our house like it was his own, exuding an inexplicable ease. I stuck my hand out for the mail, hoping to end the moment for the both of us.

"You liking the new job?" he asked, the pleasantries surprising me.

It felt a little weird for Tim to be talking just to me, but it was nice to have his attention.

"It's okay," I said.

I felt a little guilty, like I should elaborate, fill the empty spaces with my words. Sometimes I just couldn't.

"Shows real initiative," he said, "you getting out there and working. Lots of kids your age stay lazy for the summer."

"Thanks, Tim."

He smiled before looking over at Gran. The TV continued to make noise, and Gran stayed put in her recliner. If she was feeling hospitable, she might've invited him in. But I think her hospitality for Tim was waning.

I wondered how often he told Lyla Jr. he was proud of her, and if she felt this same lightness in her chest. His opinion shouldn't have meant all that much to me, but it felt good to be noticed.

"How was the mail today?" I asked, unsure what other topics would be appropriate.

"Hotter than hell. Pure misery."

I nodded my agreement, embarrassed at how silent I'd become.

Tim shuffled from one foot to the other, adjusting the strap on his satchel. "Well, I should go. I offered Karl a trip to the store, and he takes his sweet time on the produce aisle, like he's buying a car instead of a head of lettuce."

Gran chuckled, proving even she could be charmed by Tim. Even still, she kept her eyes fixed on the TV.

"Will you tell Laine I say hello? Tell her I'll try and call later?"

"Sure thing," I said.

When the front door clicked shut, Gran looked over and raised her eyebrows high enough to wrinkle the skin by her hairline.

I crawled toward the TV to turn up the volume, and took a spot by Gran's feet. She reached down to run her hands through my hair, which had grown past the middle of my back. I'd get a back-to-school haircut come August. Maybe I'd be at Monroe High this fall. It wasn't probable, but it was possible.

I pictured Tim walking up and down the food aisles of IGA, choosing between nearly identical heads of lettuce. I'm sure Tim was kind enough to humor Karl, debating the merits of varying cucumbers and eggplants. I could picture him loading up Karl's groceries in the back of his mail truck, securing the bags, making sure they wouldn't tip.

"You know what I hate?" I said, feeling brave enough to fill the room with my words.

"What's that?" Gran ask, her hands trailing my back.

"I hate that I like him."

Of course I didn't hate Tim—that would be too easy.

I felt Gran's warm breath on the back of my neck as she let out a long sigh.

10

The fridge was empty, and so were the cupboards. We'd used the last of the Wonder Bread for PB&Js—the last-resort meal. I reached for the lone brown banana in the almost always empty fruit bowl and poured myself a cup of coffee. We were in the middle of a standoff, which of us would buy groceries first. Both Mom and Gran hated the store. The first time we walked the aisles of IGA, three different men asked Mom to dinner. For Gran, it was the condolences. "I don't know why people bringing up my dead husband think they're doing me any good," she said.

Mom prolonged trips as long as possible, offering to bring home our Norma's favorites instead. Gran said she'd gained ten pounds since we'd shown up.

I sat opposite Gran at the kitchen table, peeling the speckled banana. When I offered her half, she took it.

"It's hotter than hell," she said. "Checked the almanac, and we are way ahead of schedule with this heat."

It wasn't even nine AM, and I could already feel the beads of sweat forming on the back of my neck and thighs. Gran was a few steps ahead of me, with sweat drips moving from her hairline down the sides of her cheeks. She swept an old kerchief across her forehead.

I nodded in agreement but drank the hot coffee anyway. It'd hold me over until lunch. Gran's glass with ice had orange juice and hopefully nothing else. She flipped through her magazine and took a small sip.

"You work today?" she asked.

"I wish." I could tell the day would only get hotter, the thick kind of heat that made me long for the wall fans in Paradise Bowl.

She tapped her nails on the table. "We could go to the pool."

"The pool could be nice."

There were pros and cons to a day at a community pool. Pros? Man-made holes of water were invented with days like today in mind. Cons? With limited options—pool, alley, drive-in, repeat—chances are a trip to the pool could result in another Lyla Rae Jr. run-in.

I stood up to toss the peel in the trash. "Let's just stay home," I said, listening to the single con. I usually favored cons. "I don't want to miss the shows."

Gran used her kerchief to wipe down the back of her neck. "Shows will be here tomorrow, recaps included. The pool might be our only chance of survival." She downed what was left of her juice and set the empty glass on the table. "But I have a headache, and that means you have to drive."

⁂

I drove our one-headlight car without a license, and we hoped Phil wasn't out on patrol. A week ago, he'd caught me in the parking lot of IGA. His partner had driven our car home with me in the passenger seat, Phil trailing us down the cul-de-sac with his lights on.

Gran said the siren in our driveway was too much. Karl Saunders was out in his driveway, babying the roses. He couldn't stop himself from smirking. Phil said I could be in jail, but everyone assured me that wasn't true.

"They've got special jails for the youth," Gran had said, doing a poor job of reassuring me. "It's more of a correctional facility than anything. A boot camp, if you will."

Karl assured me she was yanking my chain, but since then we'd been cautious. Or, more accurately, I'd been cautious, hence the lack of groceries. It was hard to stock the fridge without a car, and hard to drive the car without a license. I liked rules. There weren't many to follow in our house, but the law of the land seemed like a good place to start.

I drove the two blocks to Charlotte's house, hunched over the wheel, car crawling. Gran reached over and pressed down on my right leg to speed us along.

"Gran!" I squealed.

"You driving at the speed of a snail is going to draw more attention."

"It's called caution," I said, swatting her hand away.

I missed the mailbox by a yardstick and flew up the curb. Charlotte was on the porch, waiting for us. She seemed relieved when I called, and I was glad her offer of friendship extended past the week I'd promised her.

Gran pushed the door with both hands while Charlotte tugged on the handle. It came unjammed, and Gran collapsed her seat forward so Charlotte could climb in back. Her blonde hair fell well past the middle of her back. Her boobs were bigger than mine, and she kept them up and out on display. Gran looked over at me with a knowing smile. It took me two tries to back out of the driveway before Charlotte's mom Beatrice came outside to guide me.

The community pool smelled like chlorine and sunblock with a dash of coconut. There were old, white-turned-yellow chairs scattered across the weathered cement. Distracted moms occupied most of them, leaving floatie-bound kids splashing in the shallow end. Gran looked out of place at the community pool, but I think she knew that.

She stole Mom's ancient black one-piece and had wrapped some sort of scarf around her to look like a dress. Her sunglasses were too big for her face, and her hair was pinned on her head. When she emerged from her room, I told her she looked dramatic. She looked me up and down in my faded denim shorts and tank top.

"You could use a bit of dramatic."

I laid my towel on a chair, and Gran laid hers beside me, Charlotte taking the chair on the other side. Charlotte undressed like people were watching, and they were. The boys treading water in the deep end smiled and nudged one another. Gran cackled. She appreciated Charlotte's sass. I shimmied out of my shorts, careful not to take my stretched-out bottoms with them. Charlotte was Marilyn Monroe, and I was just limbs.

"Too hot to linger," Charlotte announced, tossing her clothes in a heap by my feet.

Everyone watched her launch into the deep end.

Gran passed me last week's *National Enquirer*. We both lay on our stomachs and flipped through our magazines. After fifteen minutes she flipped over to tan her front, and I did too.

"I like the lifeguard," she said.

I propped myself up on my elbows and shielded my eyes from the sun, squinting to see the guy she was talking about. Harold Clark was up in his tower, shielded by a striped umbrella. Charlotte told me he worked as the lifeguard. Seeing him, it felt like my heart skipped a beat.

I lowered myself back onto the chair. "He's the boy from the bowling alley."

"Is he?" She acted surprised, but I knew she recognized him. Gran couldn't lie. She sounded like a bad actress delivering her lines.

I nodded. "Harry Clark."

Charlotte climbed up the ladder and out of the pool, and made her way toward us. The boys watched her go. She took the magazine I hadn't finished and adjusted her pool chair so she was sitting up.

"Charlotte, what do we know about that Harry boy?" Gran asked.

Charlotte nodded toward the boys in the deep end. "We know he's got a car and a job, and that's more than any of those dweebs can say."

Gran reached back to adjust her chair, sitting up too. Both of them were focused on the lifeguard tower.

"He's got great teeth," I said.

"Oh yes," Gran said, suddenly remembering. "Is he the one who got the braces?"

Charlotte and I exchanged looks. I laughed.

"I can look past that." Gran continued to stare at the tower, and I worried he would notice.

"Stop staring," I said.

She swatted my leg with the back of her hand and shushed me. "I think he's cute."

Charlotte stretched out so her legs weren't shadowed from the sun. "Might be a little young for you, Katherine."

Gran reached in her bag. She pulled out a flask I hadn't seen her pack and took a long drink. I looked around to see if anyone had noticed. Harry looked over at me, not Gran. He smiled and waved, and I waved back before looking down, all too aware of Gran and Charlotte's growing smiles.

"He's not too young for you," Gran whispered, wiggling her penciled-in eyebrows.

<hr>

I had packs of peas on my lower back and frozen carrots on my bare legs. I'd forced Gran to stop at the store. She cackled while I waddled through five aisles so we wouldn't starve, filling our cart with TV dinners and anything instant, plus the carrots and peas for my own survival. Gran was sober enough to drive, and I was incapacitated.

When I'd fallen asleep in the chair face down, Gran hadn't had the good sense to wake me, and Charlotte had been otherwise occupied. The parts of me that my hair didn't cover had baked in the sun, turning a patch of my lower back and all of my legs lobster red. Gran had laughed so hard she cried. When Mom got home, she tried to stop herself, feigning maternal concern because that was her role, but eventually she laughed too. I picked a spot on the floor by the fan and stayed there, barely dressed, in just a tank and underwear. Mom switched out my peas and carrots for fresh ones every half hour.

"I just don't get it," Mom said, speaking blasphemy of Johnny Carson. "He's not funny."

Gran ignored her, laughing at something I'd missed in the monologue.

Mom leaned over and grabbed my thawed veggies, standing up to head to the kitchen.

"Thanks," I said, attempting to bend my fiery legs.

Gran's empty glass was on the side table by the lamp, and Mom reached to grab that too. With eyes still on the TV, Gran placed her hand over the top of the cup. Mom sighed but moved past her, surrendering before the battle could begin. I watched as Gran poured another, the leftover ice cubes dancing in the bottom.

Mom was still in the kitchen when we heard a knock at the door. Gran looked over at me. It was just before midnight.

"Laine!" Gran called. "Get the door!"

Before Mom was back in the room, the front door swung open. Tim walked in and smiled. I sat up, panicked, forgetting my burn and remembering my underwear.

"Oh shit," he said, turning to face the wall. He placed his hands over his eyes.

"I didn't know you were—" Mom walked in and smiled at Tim before noticing me. "Oh God, Aurora. Go put some pants on."

I sped up my waddle toward the hall to my room, ignoring the sting on my legs. When I looked back, Gran's eyes were locked on Johnny, but the corners of her mouth were turned up in a smile.

"What're we watching?" I heard Tim ask.

Safe in my room, I flopped on my bed, mortified. Mom had taken over Gran's room around the time Tim and her started up. Gran didn't seem to mind—I think the room held too many memories for her. She swore she was fine in her recliner, and Mom didn't fight her on it. I was grateful for plenty of reasons, but most of all because I loved having a place of my own.

I thought about hiding in my room all night, but the peas and carrots were out there, and my room was the hottest in the house. The backs of my legs were on fire. Plus, unlike Mom, I liked Johnny. My pajama pants were in a crumpled ball on the carpet. I sniffed them before slipping them on. Today, groceries. Tomorrow, laundry.

Tim never came over at night. His visits were strictly late afternoons. I wondered how he had escaped. I had this vision of him crawling out his bedroom window like a teenage boy, but with a wife asleep in the room. Maybe she wore a long-sleeve, floor-length nightgown, her hair prepped in curlers, tied up in a scarf. Nothing like my mom in her oversized T-shirt, unkempt, dark hair down past her shoulders. In reality, he probably used the front door. Mom said they kept separate rooms.

I rounded the corner, and everyone kept their eyes on the TV, doing a terrible job at hiding their smirks.

"Ha ha," I said. "Aurora was in her underwear—*very* funny."

Tim tossed me my bag of peas. "You should wear sunscreen."

Mom and Tim were on the couch, his arm draped around her shoulder. Gran was glued to her recliner, per usual. I took my spot on the floor. Maybe this is what it felt like to have a real family. A mom, a dad, a gran, and a kid watching late-night TV. If anyone could see past our always-shut blinds, they wouldn't know any different.

I didn't let my mind wander too far, though, because the truth was we weren't a family. An outsider might not know any different, but I did. I wouldn't let myself get caught up in the fantasy. I'd been there before—expectations beyond reality lead to heartache.

Tim got up for a beer and fluffed my hair as he passed. I suppose he was caught up in the moment too—the inexplicable *normalcy* of it all. I reminded myself it wasn't real, a reminder I found myself needing more and more. *I'm not his daughter.* He had one of those. *He isn't my dad.* He belonged to someone else.

Mom didn't mind living in delusion, but I wouldn't let myself go there.

○○○

When I went to bed, Tim was still there, but when I woke up, he was gone. I guess he had somewhere to be. Gran was where I'd left her, asleep in her recliner. Mom was missing from her spot on the couch, and the kitchen table was empty. Nobody had made coffee yet, so I started a fresh pot.

I walked down the hall to Mom's room. Her door was open a crack, and I pushed it further with my foot. The light from the hall spilled across the floor, a spotlight on the bed. She was on her back, arms by her side, eyes open, staring at the ceiling. It looked like the scene in "Snow White," after the bad apple. We just needed the prince to kiss her back to earth.

"Hey," she said, eyes still fixed above.

I took a step into the dark room. "Hi."

She broke her staring contest with the speckled white ceiling and turned on her side to face me. Her smile was forced. She lifted the covers and scooted back, an invitation. I crossed the room, bare feet sinking into the carpet, and slipped into bed beside her. It was a familiar scent I knew from the years we'd shared a single bed—cigarettes and vanilla.

"You're sad," I said, her sadness as familiar as the smells.

I felt her chin against my back when she nodded. "A little." She ran her fingers through my hair. "I'll be okay, though."

I turned so I was facing her. "I put on some coffee."

"He'll never pick me," she said, sitting up and scooting so her back was against the headboard. I did the same.

"Did you ask?"

"He's got his kids, Aurora. And Lyla's not great, but they've been together since high school—even I remember that. That's his family."

I looked over. Her eyelids were swollen, dried streaks of mascara beneath them.

"We're not his family, even if I want us to be. I'm just the secret at the end of the cul-de-sac."

Everything she said sounded like she was convincing herself of its truth. I nodded, unsure of what to say.

She reached over and held a hand to my cheek. "Am I screwing you up?"

"I don't think so."

She took my hand in hers and brought it to her lips before dropping it. "Good." She pulled her knotted hair into a ponytail. "So, what's on the agenda today, Boss?"

"Practically speaking, laundry."

She scrunched up her nose. "And impractically speaking?"

"Still laundry."

I climbed out of the bed and offered her my hand. She sighed loudly, but she took it.

The laundromat was empty when we showed up. Gran bought us each a soda while Mom sorted the darks from the lights. I took a seat in the corner chair. The plastic was hot on my burn, so I pulled my legs up to my chest, resting my head on my knees. I was pink almost everywhere.

At some point Gran had possessed her own washer and a line strung up for drying in the backyard. But according to her, the washer had broken down two summers ago, and Gran decided to convert it into a flowerpot, much to Jay's dismay. Karl helped her drag it out of the garage, and he helped her plant the lilacs that spilled over the sides. It was unrecognizable to anyone who didn't know what was beneath. Jay was a handyman, through and through, but I think back then Gran secretly liked the visits to town and the hours spent in air-conditioning at the laundromat. I bet this summer she regretted her choices.

"Aurora, is this your bathing suit?" Mom called out.

She was holding the tattered bottoms in one hand and the tattered top in the other.

"Yes," I answered.

"This is shameful." She shook her head. "Please tell me this isn't what you wore to the public swimming pool."

It was old and pilled, the elastic stretched beyond repair. I couldn't even remember when we'd bought it. It might have been a hand-me-down from Mom, come to think of it.

"It is," Gran said, ratting me out. She was starting to laugh. "It's a wonder it didn't fall right off."

"We're *not* poor enough for you to wear something like that." Mom tossed it in the trash and continued sorting. "We'll get you a new one. Preferably one with elastic in the waistband. God, I can only imagine what people thought."

Gran walked over to grab a load of darks. She scooped it up using both arms and headed to the wall of washing machines. Her upper arms had loose skin that shook when she moved. Even her devotion to Richard Simmons couldn't stop the passage of time.

"You know what will make this go faster, Aurora?" Gran called out.

"What's that?" I asked, playing into her bit.

"You and that sunburned behind getting up to help."

I stuck out my tongue and rose from my chair. My thighs peeled off the plastic, and it was so painful I had to check if part of my skin had been left behind. Mom handed me the pile of whites, and I chose a washer by Gran's, tossing in the pile of our underthings. Gran loaded her pile in but paused, bending over and leaning in to grab something out. Her hand emerged holding a pair of boxers.

"Laine," she yelled, "Are you ser—"

I looked over to see what could get Gran to stop a good scolding. I hadn't heard the front doorbell ring, and I was just as shocked as Gran. Mom was talking to Phil. He wasn't on duty, and I almost didn't recognize him without his uniform. He was dressed like he was on a tropical vacation on our country's East or West Coast, instead of the middle. I admired his confidence. It was a brave man who wore a floral-print button-down and khakis in Central Indiana.

He noticed the boxers before Mom did. "What have we here?" he said, his smile fading.

Mom's eyes moved from Phil to the boxers.

"You seeing someone, Laine?" He sounded disappointed, which wasn't surprising.

Her face and neck turned red, with splotches spilling down her chest. I faced the open machine, adding in the detergent and starting the load. My stomach knotted, and I couldn't bear to look. Gran looked at me and back at them.

"If you must know, I've taken a lover," Gran said loud and clear, like a line from her soaps.

Mom tried not to laugh while Phil looked to her to explain.

"What she means is she's seeing someone." Mom scooped up a final load and walked toward the machine by mine. "God, Phil, don't look so shocked. It's rude."

I laughed. "Gran's a hot commodity these days. You might be surprised."

Phil looked from Mom to Gran, to me. The three of us could barely hold it together. I'm sure we looked suspicious, and Phil looked like he was putting together puzzle pieces that didn't quite fit. "Do I know him?"

Gran shrugged. "Maybe you do, maybe you don't. That's what makes it fun."

Phil reached for his laundry bag on the floor. "You three are crazy."

There were two spare machines, and our clothes filled the others. I took my corner chair by the wall. Gran took the seat beside me. Someone had left behind their *Women's Daily*. She flipped through two pages before tossing it aside. Recipes would do her no good.

Mom leaned against the washer next to Phil's and let out a laugh. Her eyes looked less swollen than they had that morning. When Phil turned to start his load, Mom looked at Gran and mouthed, "Thank you."

11

When Mom left home, it took her a few years to establish a routine. She was good at charming people into tips, so she'd figured out the job part right away. It was the rest of it—the house, the food, the kid—that made her feel like she was in a boat without a paddle. She was sixteen, with a baby in tow and no clue how to make a life of her own.

I think that's where the men came in. It never took long for someone to step in and show her the way. They weren't always boyfriends, although all of them wanted to be. They were bosses or landlords or night clerks. She rented small furnished apartments or motel rooms by the month, keeping me in the same bed with her for all of my life.

The first man I remembered had a bird. This one was a boyfriend. His name didn't stick, but I remembered the way he called me "kiddo" and the plush red carpet in his living room. They'd met at the diner, and he'd mentioned the two-bedroom apartment, said he wanted to help her out while she got her bearings in town.

Rosie's cage had gold wire, and she repeated back curse words and things like "Shut up!" and the theme song from *The Flintstones*. She splashed in her water and only ate the green bits from her multicolor food, tossing the others in a pile at the bottom of her newspaper-lined cage. I could spend all day watching her. Some days I did.

It was a Tuesday, and Mom had picked up a shift, leaving me behind with the man. She had always been careful with me, making sure I had places to be while she worked. But it was summer, and the shift was last minute. We needed the money for car repairs, and he was a good guy. Every man was a good guy until he wasn't.

The man slept on the couch with the TV on. I stared at Rosie in her cage and wondered if she missed flying. When I opened the door of the cage, she looked confused, like the open door didn't exist. I stood on my tiptoes and reached in, offering two fingers like I'd seen him do. She placed each claw on my finger and I lifted her out. She paused on my fingers and stretched out her wings, showing off. Or maybe she was making sure they were still there.

There was a moment's hesitation before she took flight, the wind from her wings blowing back my hair. He must not have trimmed her wings in a while, because she could fly. She hadn't forgotten how. I sat on the floor and watched her fly all around the room in desperate circles.

There was a window by the sink, with almost-dead plants littered across the windowsill. I pulled out the silverware drawer to use as a step and climbed up to the counter, positioning myself on my knees to open the latch. The man had noticed me, but I hadn't noticed him. When I reached for the latch, he grabbed my hand. Not hard enough to leave a bruise, but hard enough to stop me. He picked me up off the counter and carried me to the couch, taking the seat next to me.

We waited in silence for Rosie to tire herself out. It had to have been a full hour-long episode before she did. She landed on one of the plants Mom was struggling to keep alive. I watched Rosie look out at the view, which was just a parking lot. I told myself that the world outside the window wasn't much to miss out on. Her back was to the man when he grabbed her. He trimmed her wings before dropping her back in the cage with the newspaper bottom. I hadn't noticed the tears staining my cheeks, and I plugged my ears at the sounds of her cries.

<hr />

I wasn't sure if Charlotte had friends before me. If she had, she'd never mentioned them. We'd established a routine of morning calls where we'd list out potential plans for the day. If I was working, she'd let out an impatient sigh before telling me she'd call tomorrow. Of course, there wasn't all that much to do in town, which meant we spent most of the call going around and around before settling on a bike ride to town.

Charlotte loved a trip to Rexall. She'd escalated from lipsticks to nail polishes, and on the most recent trip she'd tucked a magazine into her waistband, pulling her shirt longer to keep it hidden. After the first trip, she never asked me to steal, but she did ask me to stand at the end of the aisle to keep watch.

I watched her browse the aisle for something worth pocketing, wondering what she'd take next. She stopped by the sunglasses, trying on one pair after the other, looking over at me for a thumbs-up or a thumbs-down.

"You look like Jackie Kennedy," I said.

She returned that pair to the shelf.

"You want to come over after this?"

She pulled the white-framed glasses to the tip of her nose. "I can't. Kevin is taking me out."

"That's the pair," I said, offering a thumbs-up. In part, because I was over being an accomplice, but also because they looked amazing on her. "Who's Kevin?"

"From the pool. The one I was swimming with."

I tried to picture just one boy, but many surfaced. She may not have had friends before me, but she'd definitely had boyfriends.

A beat passed before she continued, tucking the sunglasses down her shirt. "Turns out they weren't all dweebs. This one has a car."

The door chimed when we left Rexall, and the sun hit us with light and heat. Charlotte pulled the sunglasses from her bra and put them on. Being friends with her felt like being friends with Miss America.

I pulled my bike out from the bike rack, and she climbed on the pegs, placing one hand on each of my shoulders. A few weeks ago, when she'd noticed mine had pegs, she'd decided her bike was unfit for the public, leaving hers with its streamer-covered handlebars in the garage.

I pedaled unsteadily at first before gaining speed. We headed toward home, and I dropped her off at the end of her driveway. She promised to call me tomorrow and spare no details. For the life of me, I couldn't picture Kevin.

End of August

The mail truck was at the end of the street, and Tim was four houses into the cul-de-sac. When I passed on my bike, he'd waved and mouthed, "See you soon!" If Mom was dropping hints by picking up a shift, Tim wasn't recognizing them. I propped my bike against the garage door and smiled at the cracked blinds, just in case Mom was watching.

When I opened the door, she was back in her favorite spot. Gran looked like she'd just worked out, with sweat stains under each armpit. She had a fresh glass of whiskey for her cool-off.

"Great timing," Gran said. "*General Hospital* is just about to start, and you're the perfect person to turn up the volume."

I walked to the TV, turning up the sound before taking my place on the floor. Mom's eyes were on the cracked blinds.

"He's three houses down."

She turned her chair to face the TV. Her hair looked freshly curled, and I could smell her perfume, even at a distance.

"How's Charlotte?" Mom asked.

"Good. She's got a date tonight. Some boy named Kevin."

"Yep." Gran nodded like this wasn't news. "That's the one from the pool."

"You remember him? Why do you know more than I do?"

"Sure I remember him—don't you? Oh wait, of course you don't. You were asleep for most of the day." She started to laugh at her own comedy routine and then stopped. The show was starting. "To be continued. We can talk at the commercial."

Mom and I giggled before Gran shushed us. We all watched the TV and Tim slipped in unnoticed, setting the mail in its spot on the side table. He knew better than to knock during *General Hospital*. I kept my eyes on the television, but in my peripheral vision I could see him lean down to kiss her cheek. She took his hand and brought it to her lips before leading him down the hall. Gran's eyes moved from her show to theirs, and I pretended not to notice any of it.

When the commercials began, I crawled toward the space by Gran's feet and leaned back into her legs. She massaged my scalp and brushed her fingers through my hair. The man in the TV said this deal was once in a lifetime and that if we called now, he'd throw in an extra set of hair curlers for free.

"What a liar," Gran said. "Just look at him. How could he know anything about hair curlers?"

⁂

Tim left just before dinnertime, offering an awkward wave to Gran and me. We'd maintained our positions on the floor, with the TV at high volume, just in case. When Mom emerged from her room, she seemed more upset than usual. Her day's highs and lows were easily charted, the peak time around three PM, a knock on the door responsible for the sudden spike. The chart always angled down just after six. A few of his visits ended with yelling, and other times tears. Mom always alternated between two extremes—elation and devastation.

She joined us in her usual pajamas, an oversized T-shirt and underwear. When I was little, this had been her pajama of choice for me too. She'd bathe me before bed and then put me in a fresh-from-the-laundry T-shirt. Band tees, sports tees—you name it. When I got older, I realized these T-shirts didn't belong to her, at least not at the start of their lives. The graveyard of stolen T-shirts. Gran was the one who bought me my first real pair of pajamas—a matching set with a ditsy floral print.

"I guess we'll be dining at home," Gran said, standing up to go start the TV dinners.

Mom flopped on the couch and stared at the screen. It was just local news. Her mascara was smeared under her eyes, but there'd been no yelling, so I knew she was more sad than mad.

"Did I miss anything good?" she asked, her eyes still fixed ahead.

It took me a minute to realize what she was talking about. "On *General Hospital*?"

She nodded. "What's Laura up to? Nothing good, I'm sure."

I tried to play along. "Nothing good happens in Port Charles. Couldn't be a TV show if it did."

Mom let out a bitter laugh. "Nothing good happens in Monroe."

"Do you really mean that?" I asked. "Don't you like it here?"

She gave a noncommittal shrug. "The world is bigger than Indiana, Aurora. Even if we've never seen it."

"But isn't everyone supposed to pick a place they call home?" I asked.

Every day that summer I'd felt it more and more, this desire to settle in a place of my own. I suppose I'd never known what I was missing out on. I'd kept my distance, making sure not to want anything that couldn't be mine. But since our arrival in May I kept finding things that felt like mine—a room of my own, a friend of my own, a gran of my own. For the first time in my life, there were things to lose.

There was a look she had that I'd learned to notice over the years—one like Rosie's in her cage. Mom had escaped her own "cage" once before, and she could do it again. She might even find the door this time, taking me with her.

"I never did," she said, offering little reassurance.

We watched the news in silence until Gran walked in with two TV dinners, and Mom stood to set up the trays in front of the couch.

"It's a good one," Gran said, setting a TV dinner on each of our trays, "if I do say so myself."

Mom sat back down and used the edge of her fork to cut into her meat loaf while I stirred around my mashed potatoes. I didn't have to eat a bite to know what they would taste like.

Gran looked back and forth between the two of us. "Any big plans tonight?"

We shook our heads in unison. Gran set up a TV tray in front of her recliner and went back to the kitchen to grab her dinner. She'd taken the last pot roast, everyone's favorite. Mom and I exchanged knowing smiles. Gran paused in front of the TV and returned it to its normal volume. Jimmy Carter was smiling on the screen, shaking some man's hand.

I thought about Tim's dinner and whether Lyla Sr. was a good cook. Maybe it was real meat loaf, prepared from scratch. I couldn't picture the inside of their house, and I wanted to. The walls might have framed pictures or paintings, more things than could fit in a single cardboard box. Maybe Lyla Jr. took Tim's spot in the bed with the floral quilt, so her mom wouldn't be alone at night. Or maybe Lyla Jr. went on in life like nothing had changed. Maybe she didn't suspect a thing.

12

Charlotte's feet were propped up on the wall by her John Travolta poster, her hair fanned out around her and cascading down the side of the bed. It was Friday night, and since I wasn't working, she'd called earlier in the afternoon and invited me over for a sleepover. I had never been to a sleepover, another rite of passage I'd finally experience this summer.

I hadn't been at Charlotte's for more than an hour, and she was already desperate to leave. She scooted back so her head was hanging off the bed, upside down. The bored expression on her face was familiar to me by now. I could tell she'd slept in curlers the night before. Her naturally straight hair was waved like a movie star's, or a pageant queen's. I recognized her red lipstick from that first day at Rexall.

"We should go somewhere," she said, for the third time.

I'd biked the two blocks to Charlotte's in plaid pajama bottoms and a white spaghetti-strap tank top, assuming this was how girls dressed for a sleepover. I mean, the word *sleep* was in the name. My hair was pulled back in a sloppy ponytail. Karl had been in his yard, talking to his roses, and I'm pretty sure I heard him mention my outfit. The others on the route smiled and waved, tending to their geraniums. The sun relented in the evenings, making that the prime time for gardening.

"I came for a *sleepover*," I said, for the third time. "You know . . . TV? Snacks? Maybe a prank call or two? Sleep?"

I did my best not to betray my naivete. All of my facts about sleepovers came from magazines and television and the questions Gran answered while I packed my overnight bag.

"We'll sleep, eventually." She sat up and her smile looked mischievous. "When we're dead. But at this present moment, we're young and I'm not at all tired. Are you?"

I wasn't because it wasn't even past seven. "Obviously not, but just look at me."

She looked me up and down. "Aurora, this is such an easy fix. And if we're fast, we can make the eight o' clock."

She stood and moved toward the closet. Charlotte always moved like there was an audience and a soundtrack. She threw open the closet door with flair and waved her arms like she was one of Bob Barker's girls showing off a prize. I rolled my eyes, but her energy was contagious. When she offered her hand to pull me up from my spot on the floor, I took it.

I searched the closet for something that wouldn't remind me of our difference in chest size. When I reached for her Eagles T-shirt, Charlotte let out an audible sigh.

I walked back to the bed and flopped down. "Fine, you go ahead and pick."

Charlotte smiled and winked at the invisible camera. "Why, I thought you'd never ask."

She flipped through each item with a concentrated stare, as if this humid summer night in Indiana could be anything but that. I waited on the bed, afraid to see what she'd choose.

"Aha!" She pulled a dress off a hanger and held it up. On her it was too short. On me it would be a shirt. "This one."

"That's a . . . ?"

"It's a dress." She looked down at the dress in her hands and back at me. "This is totally a dress."

"On who? Definitely not on me." I flopped back onto the bed, and the dress landed on my face.

"Just try it. It's longer than it looks."

Unsure of how that could be possible, I gave in to her demands, slipping out of my pajamas and into the gingham print dress. The fabric in the chest hung loose. I reached back to feel for the length, but the fabric covered my butt. It was too short by anyone's standards, but Charlotte was smiling and nodding, up from the bed to take down my hair.

"What's playing?" I asked.

She shrugged. "Does it matter?"

"Well, some of us watch the movie," I said.

Charlotte had told me stories about the town drive-in, specifically about the back row of cars and the people who parked there. They weren't worried about what was playing on the screen.

She rolled her eyes and ran her fingers through my hair, reaching for the makeup on her dresser. "I'm sure it's that scary one."

I made a face.

"C'mon," she said. "It'll be fun."

I let her coat my eyelashes black and puckered my lips while she applied lipstick, an unnatural shade of pink. When she turned around to grab the bottle of cheap perfume, I wiped the lipstick off with the back of my hand. She sprayed me and I coughed, tugging at the sides of my dress.

"Wait," I said, grabbing a pair of shorts off the laundry pile. I slipped them beneath the dress and smiled. "There. Much better."

Charlotte rolled her eyes. With a hand on each shoulder she guided me to the mirror beside her bed, the one above her vanity. Side by side we gazed into the same mirror. She smiled at her work. I took two steps forward and smiled back despite myself.

"Don't take this the wrong way, because it's totally a compliment, but you look just like her."

"Who?" I asked, even though I knew. I squinted at the figure squinting back at me, with dark hair falling past her shoulders and blackened eyes.

"Your mom," Charlotte said. "You're a babe."

<hr />

Kevin from the pool picked us up from Charlotte's. Her mom worked nights, which made sneaking out simple. Charlotte took shotgun, and I crawled into the back seat between two boys. A cloud of cigarette smoke had settled in the car, and the smell made me think of home. Kevin kept one hand on the wheel and the other on Charlotte's bare thigh. I spent the whole car ride fidgeting with the hem of my dress, adjusting myself between the two almost strangers—Mike and Dan.

Just before the entrance, Kevin pulled off the road toward the trees.

"I have the money," I said, proud of the dollars I had saved up since working at the alley.

"Are you seventeen?" he asked.

I shook my head, and Charlotte undid her seat belt. I waited for Mike to let me out, and when he didn't, I climbed over, glad I'd slipped on the shorts. Dan snickered.

Kevin opened the trunk for us and pushed aside a bag of tools and his spare tire. "Your chariot."

Charlotte playfully punched his arm and climbed in first. Her underwear was bright, and I watched Kevin pretend not to notice. He turned away when I climbed in. We were squished in like spoons in a drawer.

Charlotte giggled as the car roared to life.

Kevin had a lead foot, and each time he braked, we flew forward and backward.

"God, he's a terrible driver," she said.

I laughed and she shushed me. We could hear voices. The car dipped and I could feel it slow when it rolled onto the grass. The sounds grew louder, and eventually the car stopped. The trunk flew open, and a group of boys stood over us, grinning. The movie hadn't even started, and I was terrified. Kevin parted the sea of strangers while I scrambled to get out of the trunk.

"Underage girls make cheap dates, huh, Kevin?" a toothy boy asked.

Kevin shoved him, and the others laughed.

"Don't speak so soon," Charlotte said, adjusting her cutoffs once her feet hit solid ground. "This girl needs some popcorn."

She put out a hand and waited for his. He hesitated but took it, and she led him away to a chorus of whipping sounds and cackles. The boys were like a pack of hyenas.

Charlotte and I were outnumbered five to one, and without her I felt a little panicked. Fortunately, once the crowd dispersed, Mike and Dan took little interest in me. They scanned the lawn for someone better, and I looked for a friendly face. After a month working at the alley, most of the faces were vaguely familiar. I tried to orient myself and hoped my smile looked pleasant.

Three cars made up the back row of the drive-in. The screen was just a small box, far away. I doubted the back row cars even turned their dial to connect to the sound. I began to walk toward the snack bar, weaving my way between the parked cars and avoiding the fogged-up windows. At least my well-earned money could get me a snack.

The grass in front of the screen was littered with blankets and girls who looked like Charlotte and me all those years ago, small and freckled and shy. I wished I could sit there with them, ditching the boys who'd snuck us in. I wondered who had snuck those little girls in.

I joined the back of the line and scanned it for familiar faces. There was no blonde ponytail in the line, and I felt instant relief. *Alien* didn't seem like her kind of movie.

"Aurora?"

I turned around, and Harry was standing in line behind me with Shane from the bowling alley. Shane looked past me and surveyed the line, probably trying to find his opportunity to cut.

"Oh, hi," I said, taking a step forward as the line moved.

Harry scanned the line too. "You here with anyone?"

"Just some friends," I lied, not sure how to explain my situation.

"That's cool."

I couldn't think of how to respond to that. This boy–girl thing was uncharted territory. Other than the advice I'd read in *Seventeen* magazine articles, or my observations of my mom and Charlotte, I had no idea how it all worked. Harry nodded toward the gap between the person next in line and me, and I hurried to close it.

"They've got the best nachos," I lied again. I'd never even had their nachos.

"Really?" He flashed his brilliant smile, and I couldn't help but smile back. "And how about the popcorn?"

I shrugged and tugged on the ends of my hair. "Not the best in town, but it's all right."

One of the articles said to make a joke. Harry let out a laugh, and I took it as a victory for *Seventeen* and myself.

"I heard they're switching movies next week," Harry said.

"Don't hold your breath. Rumor is they're playing *The Muppets* again. Charlotte knows the marquee guy."

Harry let out a long sigh. "It'd be nice to live in a town with new movies every week."

"Not for people who like the Muppets."

Harry laughed again, and I could feel my skin flush. This feeling was addicting, and I was disappointed when we reached the front of the line.

I reached down the top of my dress for my money and hoped Harry didn't notice. "I'll have an order of the nachos."

"You sure?" the attendant asked.

I nodded my answer, thinking that was pretty poor salesmanship on her part. She passed me the nachos, soaked in unnaturally yellow cheese, and I turned to leave the snack bar.

"Aurora," Harry called out, and I turned around to face him. "Maybe I'll see you around."

I smiled, and he moved forward to order. He ordered the small popcorn, and I felt mildly betrayed. I doubted it was as good as Paradise popcorn. I kept walking, even though part of me wanted to see her butter-drizzling technique. More than that, I wanted to know if he was watching me go.

I thought about going back to the cars and the boys, but Charlotte and Kevin were probably fogging up the windows by now. The classier girls in town wait for the movie to start. Instead, I walked toward the grassy area in front of the screen and settled in, the cool grass on my bare legs a relief from the warm night. The popcorn and soda on the screen danced with each other. I pulled a nacho out of my basket and took a bite. It tasted terrible.

When Kevin dropped us off it was just after one, and the driveway was still empty.

"Is your mom working?" I asked.

"She should be off by now. Probably met some guy. Even worse, the same guy." Charlotte pretended to gag and opened the front door with the key she'd pulled out from under the ceramic ladybug. "Ever since things ended with my dad, she's been on the hunt for Prince Charming. Just frogs so far, but that hasn't stopped her from working through the town roster. The family rule is his place, not ours. Is your mom still screwing the mailman?"

"Shh," I said, even though no one was around to hear her.

Charlotte was loud but decent at keeping secrets. Even still, I never would have told her. But Mom let it slip to Charlotte's mom after a fourth glass at King's, and she'd let it slip to Charlotte. As the bartender, she carried the secrets of most of the town. Lucky for us, she wasn't the judgmental type.

"She is, and it's actually kind of serious."

Charlotte turned on the hall light, and I followed her to her room. We both crawled into bed with our clothes on, too tired to care about pajamas.

"You can't think it's serious, Aurora. He's married."

I shrugged. "They don't really get along, though."

"Mom had a married man once too, maybe two years back. He was from two towns over, and he had kids. In the end, they pick their family."

I knew she was right, but for some reason I'd never imagined Tim having to choose. Sure, he had his family, but couldn't he have us both? I didn't say that, though, because Charlotte read *Cosmopolitan* and was well versed in the ways of the world. I hated to feel naive.

We both pulled the covers up to our chins. She had missed most of the movie. What knowledge she lacked about *Alien* she made up for in knowledge of all things Kevin. What he said and where he touched, that he might give her his class ring just like Danny gave Sandy his. He had plans to take over for his dad at the auto shop, learning the family trade—it was a familiar trajectory. In the end, we become our parents.

And what did that mean for Charlotte and me? Dead-end jobs? A revolving door of men only willing to throw us crumbs?

I shook away the thought and nodded, forcing my eyes to stay open. Eventually she reached over and turned off the light by her bed, exhausted from her monologue. I turned so I was facing the wall. Once she was asleep, I let my mind wander to Harry and the "See you around." It didn't mean much, but it was something. I drifted off to sleep full of this new feeling, a weird, fluttering hope. It didn't hurt to hope. And then again, it did.

༻✦༺

I biked the two blocks home while the sun warmed up Indiana. Every morning we started new, with the hope for a breezy day, but God popped us back into the toaster. Karl wasn't in his front yard, and I was grateful, but I knew the roses would fill him in later.

The front door was unlocked and the TV was on. Even though Gran hated Saturday morning cartoons, she hated silence more. Her recliner was empty, but I heard her and Mom talking in the kitchen. I went to join them. Mom was pouring herself coffee, and Gran was at the table.

Gran looked up and smiled when she saw me. "Your makeup looks beautiful, hon."

I reached up to rub under my eyes and found bits of mascara. I'd biked home without looking in a mirror.

Mom turned around to get a good look and laughed.

"Bite me," I said, pulling out my chair to join them.

Mom propped herself up on the counter. She seemed happy, and I wondered if Tim had made an appearance last night. I was happy too. And Gran was just Gran.

"How was the sleepover?" Mom asked.

I shrugged. "Okay. Mellow."

would look at me, it was like she wasn't really looking, and the voice she used didn't sound like her own. But she always came back to me, and I knew she'd come back to us. Life didn't always give her what she wanted, but I think she'd gotten used to it by now.

"Can't," I said, and Gran scrunched her nose in response. "Mom threw away my suit."

"So, we stop at the store. Or you borrow one from Charlotte."

She winked. Charlotte's bathing suits were much tinier than her dresses.

"The store it is," I said.

⁂

The fluorescent lights in L. S. Ayres weren't unlike the ones in Rexall, and they did nothing for my skin tone. Mom and Gran were golden, but the sun didn't stick on me. This was a Gene thing. When I walked out of the dressing room in the black one-piece, Gran put on her sunglasses and cackled.

"I'm blind!" she yelled.

"You're fabulous!" a woman working the cosmetics counter yelled back.

I flipped Gran the bird, and she brought her hand to her chest, feigning shock. The sales associate lingered by the dressing room, folding and refolding tops on a nearby table. She was charmed by Gran's over-the-top behavior. When we'd walked through the double doors, greeted by the cold air, Gran had yelled out that this place was heaven, and too many heads turned to stare. My skin shifted from pale to pink.

The nearest mall was twenty miles away, but Gran had insisted. She'd said it was an emergency. She told the sales associates it was an emergency too. A fashion emergency. They smiled at her and paid too much attention to us. We didn't have much money, but Gran acted like she owned all of Indiana.

"This won't do," Gran said. "Sheila, you agree, right?"

Sheila, always close by, emerged from behind a rack. "Of course, Miss Katherine, it's much too plain."

"Plain and boring. You're sixteen. Live a little!" Gran threw a red bikini at me, and I caught it.

"This doesn't cover anything," I whined, holding it up against me.

"It covers the important bits."

"It's true," Sheila chimed in. "And you've got the body for it."

I had a body, but not *the* body. My boobs were taking their time showing up to the party, and the rest of me was long like uncooked string beans. Gran called me skin and bones.

"Just try it," Gran said. "It's my dying wish."

"You're not dying."

"Well, knock on wood," she said, and Sheila laughed. "Not yet."

I exhaled a dramatic sigh full of the teenage angst I reserved for moments like this and went back into the dressing room. Three versions of me stared back, and none of them looked like a girl who should wear a red bikini. I slipped out of the one-piece. My underwear and purposeless bra were in a pile on the carpeted floor. The three versions of me were stark naked. I looked at my pale skin and dark hair. Her eyes were staring back.

The bikini bottoms hung a little loose in the back, but the top fit my boobs. There was still too much skin in the mirror, but I didn't hate what I saw. I opened the door a crack and stuck my head out. If I couldn't expose myself to Gran and Sheila, I had no idea how I'd walk through the metal gates at the pool.

"Come out!" Gran yelled.

I pushed the door open a little further and took a step out. Her mouth spread into a smile, and Sheila clapped her hands.

Gran let out a whistle. "Now this—this is a bathing suit."

My hands flew up to cover my face. I peeked out between the cracks in my fingers. "It's not too much?"

"Not at all," Sheila answered, and Gran shook her head.

"Can we get it?" Gran asked.

I hesitated. "Okay," I said. I rushed back into the dressing room before the two of them began their applause.

The twenty-mile drive back to town felt too short, and I began to tug at my shorts. The red bathing suit peeked out of my tank top, and I was overwhelmed with buyer's remorse. It was smaller than the one Mom had tossed in the trash, and brighter. Gran must have sensed my panic.

"You look great in it," she said, reaching over to squeeze my hand.

The pool played the Beach Boys on loop, an attempt to transport us from central Indiana to somewhere coastal. When we walked in, "Barbara Ann" greeted us, and Gran exhaled through her nose. Charlotte was on the other side of the pool already. I recognized Kevin, but there were other boys too, different boys from the ones at the movies. She waved us over, but I just waved back.

Gran laid her towel down on a chair and took her magazine from her bag. "You can sit with them."

I laid my towel on the chair next to hers. "I'm okay."

Gran raised her hand to shield her eyes and squinted up at the lifeguard tower before she smiled and opened to a bookmarked article about face transplants performed on monkeys. I knew why she was smiling, but I didn't look up. My stomach had the increasingly familiar flutter.

I took off my clothes quickly and shoved them under my chair. I don't know what I was so worried about. Even in a bright two-piece, no one looked my way.

Before I could even adjust my chair, Charlotte screamed, and the whole pool took notice. Kevin had her cradled like a baby while she squealed and flailed. Another boy grabbed her arms while Kevin held her legs. They swung her three times before releasing her. She crashed into the water, and we all waited for her to surface. When she did, she was laughing. She pushed her hair back from her face and flipped over to float on her back, smiling into the sun. Harry blew his whistle and climbed down from his tower. Gran raised her eyebrows at me.

"Showdown," she whispered.

Harry talked to Kevin, but it looked like it was just for show, because Kevin was smiling afterward. Harry looked over then, from across the pool, and I looked down. Gran looked down too, pretending to read the same article she'd been reading before.

"He's coming," she whispered through clenched teeth.

I quickly adjusted my hair, so it was falling over one shoulder, grateful I'd taken the time to wash it. His shadow blocked the sun, and when I looked up, he was standing above me, smiling with those perfect teeth his parents had paid good money for.

"Hey," he said.

I could see Gran fighting a smile, in my peripheral.

"Hi." I adjusted my legs. "This is my gran," I said, not sure what to say next. Introductions seemed polite and appropriate. Gran looked up at the mention of her name, as if she hadn't been tracking Harry since we'd walked through the rusted metal gate. "Gran, this is Harry."

"Oh, hi," she said, reaching to meet his hand. "You can call me Katherine."

"It's nice to formally meet you," he said. "I knew your husband."

"Nice to formally meet you too, hon."

She smiled and returned her eyes to that same article, pretending to offer us privacy.

We were silent for a beat too long before we both started to speak at the same time. Gran winced for us.

"You go," I said.

He was pink, either from embarrassment or the sun. I watched his eyes shoot over at Gran before returning to meet mine.

"Do you work Friday?" he asked. "At the alley?"

"I do," I said.

"Oh."

I wasn't sure why he was asking or why my response made him so awkward. He looked down, and I looked across the way.

"Aren't you off Saturday night?" Gran asked, moving us along.

I moved my hair from one side to the other, something I'd seen Mom do. His eyes followed its movement. "I'm off on Saturday."

"So I've heard." He smiled at Gran, who was still pretending to read. "Would you maybe want to do something?"

I nodded, shocked this was the question he'd chosen to ask, and then I remembered to use my words. "Sure."

He smiled and I smiled back. "Little Surfer Girl" started up on the speakers. Gran let out an audible sigh.

"Hey." Gran leaned toward Harry with a conspiratorial look in her eye. "How much pull do you have with the music man?"

Harry pressed his lips together and tried not to laugh. He returned her gaze with one equally as serious. "Katherine, I am the music man."

She threw her hands up in mock surrender and flopped back onto her lounge chair. When I laughed, the sound almost startled me, and I realized it had been a few days since I'd really laughed. Even when I wasn't in the house, the cloud followed me, but in that moment it was just clear skies.

"I'll call you about Saturday," Harry said before walking back to his tower.

Gran gave up on her magazine and tossed it back in her bag. "He's handsome, but he has terrible taste in music."

We decided to visit Mom at work in case the happiness was contagious. Norma's was a two-minute drive from the pool, but we took the long way. "Tequila Sunrise" was on, and that was Gran's favorite song. She took it as a sign that the good mojo was back, swerving the car between the two empty lanes, singing along. I grabbed the wheel when she started to sway too close to the cornfields, making sure we stayed on the road. Part of me felt guilty for being so happy, but Gran said that wasn't how happiness should be.

The sun was high in the sky, and my skin was still warm from the pool. I laughed, my hands still on the wheel. The song was ending, and Gran looked over and winked. For Mom, Gran had been unpredictable and wild. But for me, Gran was my steadiness. She was like the perfect day in spring, when the sun has finally thawed through the last of the winter snow and the world turns green again.

"Just because your mom's sad doesn't mean you have to be." She took the wheel back and reached to turn down the radio. "That's her own stuff she's got going on. It has nothing to do with you." I knew Gran was sad too, but she was better at hiding it.

I looked out the window. Gran made a right turn back onto the main road, toward the downtown strip.

"You've got too big of a heart, Aurora. Just let yourself be happy. She'll catch up. You're going on your first date on Saturday. You didn't get sunburned. The bikini looks great on you." She pulled into a spot in front of the diner and turned to face me. "Days like this, you count all your blessings, big and small."

I nodded and undid my seat belt, not willing to offer any promises. It's hard to shake sadness that's not your own. Mom's moods always stayed with me.

Norma's Diner looked empty from the outside, and I could see Mom behind the counter. Gran was putting on lipstick in the rearview mirror, and Tommy was watching her from inside his hardware store. She exited the car, fresh-faced, and he waved from behind the window. She waved back before turning to me with wide eyes. We linked arms and headed toward Norma's.

The bell on the door dinged above us, and Mom looked up from her spot behind the counter. It was just us and a man in the corner booth. We'd made it in time to beat the dinner rush. Mom smiled for a heartbeat, like she'd forgotten she was supposed to be sad.

"Hey," she said. Wisps of hair clung to the sweat on her neck. "You two coming from the pool?"

Gran took a seat at one of the stools by the counter, and I took the seat next to her. Mom pushed herself up on the counter and leaned over to kiss my cheek. I thought of the after-school days in diners, before Gran and before Monroe. I'd walk to the diners Mom worked at, or the bus would drop me off. She'd set me up at the counter with my schoolwork and a snack—on Fridays, a milkshake. She always leaned over to kiss my cheek. Even when I grew big enough to be embarrassed by that sort of thing, I never told her to stop.

"We are," Gran said, reaching for a menu. Usually, she'd have to talk about every special they had before settling on a cheeseburger with a side of ranch. "I had to get out of the house."

"How was it?" Mom's eyes were on the food ticket, with her pen poised to write. "Cheeseburger, Aurora?"

I nodded. "Yes, please."

Gran shut her menu. "Make it two."

Mom half smiled. "Well, that was fast, Mom."

"Why waste time with the inevitable?" Gran was grinning. "Well, Aurora, your mom asked you a question. How was the pool?"

Both of them were giving me their full attention, which was rare. It felt like even the man in the corner booth was staring. Mom looked like she knew what was coming, and I thought of what Gran said about her sixth sense.

Both my palms were pressed against the cool metal on the counter, and I began to swivel the spinning stool, the squeak competing with the juke box. "It was fine."

"Just fine?" Mom asked, turning around to slip the order ticket through the kitchen window.

I tucked my feet under and spun the chair in three complete circles. "It was fine," I said, when my back was to the both of them.

"She has a date!" Gran practically yelled, startling the man in the corner booth. She grabbed the bottom of my seat to stop my spinning.

"*What?*" Mom spun around, hands on her hips. "Is she serious, Aurora?" I nodded and Mom grinned. "Aurora, the pool was so much more than 'fine'!"

P.J., the chef in the back, poked his head through the window. "Aurora has a *date?*"

He was the kind of person who went from stranger to family as soon as you were introduced. By the third time I'd eaten at Norma's, he'd figured out how to prepare my cheeseburger "Aurora style"—double the cheese and extra pickles.

"It would seem so!" the man from the corner booth called out. He let out a sigh before turning back to his newspaper crossword.

Mom turned around to shush P.J., but not soon enough. He gave me a thumbs-up and a warm smile. He was another one of Mom's accumulating admirers, even though she insisted that wasn't true. She'd been coming home with food on the house. He wrote notes on the bag, signing his name with oversized smiley faces.

"I'm so excited for you," she said, and I hoped she meant it. "I needed good news today."

When Mom walked away to grab me a soda, Gran looked at me and winked. "I told you so," she mouthed.

○──○

P.J. served me a celebration sundae, and I made a mental note never to bring Harry to Norma's. Too much opportunity for humiliation. Gran, full of cheeseburger and hot fudge, declared the bad mojo officially gone. But then we turned into our tract and noticed the mail truck parked on the corner of the street before ours. At the end of our cul-de-sac, the little blue house was still dark. I wondered if Gran felt a little less lonely having us around. I hoped we were helping and not hurting, but with Mom's current state, I couldn't be sure.

Karl Saunders was out front, wearing a straw hat, a dress shirt, and pajama bottoms. He cupped a rose between his hands, and I could see his lips moving. When Gran pulled into the driveway, he turned to wave.

Our mailbox was full of four days' worth of mail. Gran flipped through what was mostly garbage, stopping on an envelope with no address. *LAINE* was written on the outside.

She flipped it over and tugged gently on the flap. "It's sealed."

"Lots of mail today," Karl called out. "Timothy said something went wrong at the Post Office. Our mail was sent one town over."

"It's crazy how something like that can affect one street," she whispered. "Crazy!" she called back to Karl.

When we got inside, she held the envelope up to the light. She passed it to me. "I can't make out a thing. You try."

All I could tell was that it was a letter, and that seemed pretty obvious. The envelope felt like it was on fire. I set it down gently on the side table, with the bills and a coupon sheet from Pete's Pizza. It'd be the first thing Mom would notice.

I walked around the couch and stretched across it. "I wonder if it's good or bad."

Gran flipped on the TV for background noise and sat in her recliner. "We'll know soon enough."

Soon enough was really an hour, and the hour dragged on. Eventually we heard P.J.'s squeaky brakes and Mom's footsteps up the walkway. She opened the door and stopped with it open, so I knew she saw the mail. I twisted around to face her. Gran spun her recliner, but Mom was focused on the pile. She didn't see us.

"The mail came," she said, her voice just above a whisper.

"It did," Gran said. "A neighbor probably called to complain."

We watched her grab the letter and leave the rest of the pile. Her feet were silent on the carpet down the hall, but the slam of her door shook the house. She left the front door open, and I stood to shut it.

"I'm thinking it'll be bad," Gran said.

She walked into the kitchen and returned with a full glass of whiskey. The man on the TV droned on and on about temperatures and forecasts when, really, he could've just said, "It's going to be hot!" The house was still. Gran had the volume down low, and we listened for any indication of the letter's contents. Shattered glass, cries, yells. Instead, Mom gave us silence, not a single clue.

I smelled her perfume before she reentered the living room. Fifteen minutes had passed. She was in a black dress, and her hair was curled. Concealer had removed all signs of the sleepless nights, and her lips were painted a sharp red. She looked good.

"I'm going out," she said, walking through the front door before Gran or I could ask questions.

"I'm guessing it was good," Gran said, taking a long drink from her glass. "Although sometimes good is just bad dressed up in Sunday clothes."

I woke up to Mom in my doorway, the light from the hallway spilling around her shadowy shape. "Are you up?" she whispered.

I shut my eyes. "I am now."

I listened to her quiet footsteps. She slipped into my bed, under the covers.

"Where'd you go?" I asked.

She brushed my hair back from my face. "To meet Tim."

I opened my eyes. "So it was a good letter?"

"It was a great letter."

She smelled like her cigarettes and men's cologne. I couldn't smell her perfume. I only smelled Tim.

"Did you ask him why he disappeared?" I asked.

"He disappeared because he loves me too much, and that's scary. It's a big deal. It means big changes for him. Big changes for all of us."

I rolled over so I was on my back. Her eyes were so full of hope, it hurt to look at them. "So that means he's leaving her?"

There was an unfamiliar bitterness in my voice, and it startled both her and me.

"Eventually." She was defensive. "Nothing can happen right away. It's too complicated for you to understand, but I want you to be a part of it. This is a good thing for us."

I forced a smile because I wanted to believe her. She smiled back, and she looked relieved.

"You think it's good?" she asked.

I opened my mouth to speak but yawned instead, nodding.

"Oh no, you're so tired." She climbed out of my bed and leaned down to kiss my forehead. "I'm sorry I woke you up."

She moved to leave but hesitated in the doorway. I had so many things to say but I didn't say them. I closed my eyes and listened for the door.

She exhaled like she'd been holding her breath. "I love you," she said before shutting my door behind her.

When I opened my eyes, the room was dark again. I looked around at the things I had, the things that made the blue house home. I had clothes hanging in the closet. My work vest crumpled on top of the dresser. My popcorn graduation certificate taped to the mirror. Charlotte's pink lipstick she'd "accidentally" left behind. It had only been six weeks since we'd pulled into Gran's driveway, but Monroe felt like more of a home than anywhere we'd been before.

Maybe Mom didn't need *things* to make Monroe home. Maybe she just needed a person, one person. Gran wasn't enough, all those years ago. Maybe I couldn't be enough either. Maybe Tim was what she'd been needing all along. Maybe Tim could make her stay.

My body felt weighed down, paralyzed with something like desperation. I didn't know what I was hoping for. If it worked out, she'd have a reason to stay. Part of me knew it wouldn't, though. It couldn't.

14

Tim ordered his eggs fried and covered his plate with more salt than I'd ever seen anyone use. I don't know how he even tasted the food. Since the letter there'd been an arrangement, one of many changes he'd promised. On Fridays, I'd meet him for lunch at Norma's diner, during the rush. We were supposed to arrive separately and take seats at the counter, side by side, where Mom would serve us. She said it was important for me to get to know him outside of the TV room and drawn blinds. We were "forming our own relationship," a phrase she had to have picked up in a magazine. But of course, our own relationship included her hovering five feet away, distractedly pouring coffee, straining to hear our every word.

"Can you even taste the eggs?" I asked. Five minutes in, and I was struggling for banter.

He grabbed the salt and poured a second helping. I laughed.

"So you're seeing Harold Clark?" He stacked two pieces of salty bacon and took a bite.

"Did Gran tell you that? She's exaggerating."

Mom stopped by to refill Tim's still full coffee. "They have a date," she said.

I narrowed my eyes at her. She mouthed an insincere "Sorry" before continuing her route down the counter, stopping to refill coffee cups along the way.

"He really is a good kid, sometimes hangs out with—" He caught himself and left her name out in the air somewhere. I could fill in the blanks. "And I know him from church too . . ."

His voice trailed off again. Without the distraction of the strangers on the TV, we were forced to talk about the characters in our real lives.

It was much more painful. I couldn't help but think of Lyla Jr. the whole time, and the meals they shared. It couldn't be the same with me, and Mom shouldn't expect it. But Tim and I both loved her. She was our common interest, so I ignored the pang in my gut and put on a good show. I think he did too.

I took a drink of my black coffee, and the steam warmed my nose. "He hasn't even called yet."

"They've got some creamer here. It's good."

I looked at him over the edge of my cup. "I hear their salt's pretty good too."

Tim grinned. "You know he'd be an idiot not to. To call, I mean."

I blushed and then I hated myself for blushing. I hated myself for caring what he thought, like his opinion mattered or changed things. I alternated between hating Tim for pretending to care and loving him for caring. Because sometimes I thought, in the part of my thoughts I refused to say aloud, that maybe he wasn't pretending. Maybe we could be his family, and the little blue house could be his home. Maybe that wasn't so much of a stretch. But there were the things I wanted and the things that were. I'd gotten used to the two rarely lining up.

I wouldn't admit it, not even to myself in the quiet moments, but it scared me how much I wanted to believe him, how much I wanted him to love her, how much I wanted him to love us. I guess I wondered what it'd be like to be chosen for more than a season.

I followed his eyes across the diner, down the counter, past the scattered coffee cups and half-eaten burgers. She was at the register beneath the kitchen window, chin resting in her cupped hands. Her hair was in a loose ponytail, tied back in the midst of the lunch rush. The long, dark curls fell down her back. I watched her look over and notice him staring, meeting his blatant gaze. No one else seemed to notice, and they didn't notice anyone else.

I couldn't think of what to say to Tim when he turned to face me, so I just smiled, hoping that was enough. Tim wiggled his eyebrows and reached for the salt shaker, shaking a third helping across the last few bites of eggs. I forced a laugh.

That afternoon Tim dropped off the mail early, before she got home. I tried not to blame myself. I wondered if Mom did. Even with the mail on the side table, she stared out the window, waiting. Then the phone rang. He said one of the girls had a sleepover, and he had to drive her there. Lyla Sr. was "under the weather." Mom had the phone cradled between her neck and ear. She was using her hands to braid my hair.

"Uh-huh," she said, nodding even though he couldn't see her. "No, I know. That's what we talked about." She was silent for a bit. Her fingers hooked strands of my long hair and tugged on the tangled spots, a little aggressively. "I'm not mad. Do I sound mad?"

"Ow," I said, my head tugged to the left.

Gran came around the corner to the spot by the wall phone, the old laundry room. Mom shooed her away.

"Well, I can't help it if I sound disappointed. I wanted to see you, and now I can't see you. Disappointed seems fair, doesn't it?" She motioned for me to hand her the hair tie on my wrist. I passed it to her, and she secured the second braid. "God, nobody here is saying anything about you."

Mom covered the receiver with her hand. "Have fun," she whispered. "Tell Charlotte hello."

I kissed her cheek, and she clenched the phone cord between her fingers.

She sighed. "I already said I'm fine."

I rounded the corner and bumped into Gran, listening on the other side of the wall, out of sight.

"I'm going to stay home and watch TV." Mom's voice had an edge. "I'm not going out, but if you say one more thing about it, I swear—" Mom took a deep breath, and Gran pressed her lips together. "Okay, fine. Have a nice night. Hope Lyla feels better soon. Be sure to tell her hello for me."

Mom slammed the phone on the receiver. Gran and I moved fast and took seats at the kitchen table, where Gran opened up her magazine.

When Mom rounded the corner, she held her earlobes between her thumbs and forefingers, a nervous tick.

"Nice try, guys," she said. "Mom, you learning to read upside down?"

"Yeah, Gran. Is it any good?"

"Aurora, didn't you say you were headed to Charlotte's?" Gran tossed the magazine at me, and I ducked. Her aim was bad. It flew past me and slid to a stop on the checkered linoleum floor. "And what about you, Laine? Got any big plans tonight?"

Mom reached her fingers up into her hair and shook out the curls she'd pinned up for Tim. "As a matter of fact, I do. I'm headed to King's."

⁓

Charlotte's clothes were short and small. The pile of rejects was growing into a mountain, and even Charlotte looked discouraged.

"I've never been out with a preacher's son," she said with a shrug. She tossed the denim miniskirt onto the pile before I even had a chance to try it on. "I just don't think anything I've got is going to cut it. I can't believe I'm saying this"—her hand was over her heart—"but you might just have to wear something of your own."

"We're forgetting the most important detail." I flopped on top of the pile of tiny, tight tops and cutoff shorts, some made even shorter as a result of Charlotte's handiwork. "He hasn't even called yet."

She waved her hand in front of her face as if this wasn't a problem at all. "Kevin calls me from the pay phone downtown. That gives me three minutes' notice. Four if there's a red light. I'm not concerned."

She was fighting with Kevin, which is why she was okay staying in on a Friday night. Supposedly he'd been seen with Carrie at the movie theater in the town with the Dairy Queen. And just being in the same town as Carrie was enough, because, in Charlotte's words, "Well, you've seen Carrie." She mimed a pair of boobs much bigger than hers and raised her eyebrows.

In true Charlotte fashion, she insisted she'd already known he was out with Carrie before anyone had told her, but I don't think she did, and I'm sure she hated hearing about it from girls in town.

When I came over, her hair was in a single braid and her face was bare. She looked just like the Charlotte I'd met all those summers back. But then she put her hand on her hip, narrowed her eyes, looked me up and down, and I remembered how much had changed.

She began lining up her growing lipstick collection. "So where's Laine tonight?"

I told Charlotte about Mom's fight with Tim and the sudden change in plans. A sick wife at home had ruined her Friday night plans, but Mom wasn't one to waste her curls.

Charlotte's mouth spread into a smile. "Laine's an icon."

After the fight, Gran had decided to join Mom at King's. She told me it was to keep an eye on things, and I pretended to believe her. I stuck around a little longer than I'd planned and watched as Mom remade her face. She added more coats of mascara than I'd seen in a while. Her denim shorts looked like Charlotte had had a hand in their creation, and if that wasn't enough, she'd tied up an old plaid shirt, showing off her belly button. Nothing about her was preacher-son appropriate.

"Wait." Charlotte's smile seemed suspicious. "We should go."

"To King's? *Why?*"

"Because it could be fun." Charlotte was already applying a coat of lipstick, the idea taking root. She shook her hair free from the braid.

"Stevie will be there."

"So will *our moms*," I countered. "And what about Kevin?"

She looked at me like I was crazy. "Kevin can spend his Friday night with Carrie. It's time I set my sights on someone new."

When she offered me her hand, I let out a sigh, but I took it. She pulled me up off the pile of rejects and moved around me to grab the denim miniskirt and red tube top. She tossed a blue floral-print romper in my direction and began adjusting her boobs in the mirror. I slipped out of my shorts and tank top and shimmied into the tiny one-piece. I was too long for it—all legs—but Charlotte insisted.

"This isn't a date with Harry," she said, wiggling her eyebrows. "This is King's."

At ten at night, the parking lot of King's was quiet enough to disguise what went on inside. So much life could be contained within four walls and a roof. There was a whole other world through the double doors. Al's bowling sign was blinking across the street, and I worried he might lose another letter. I'd mention it tomorrow.

I propped the bike up against the brick before adjusting my jumper. "Shall we?" Charlotte offered me her arm.

We were greeted with the steady hum of conversation and the heat of bodies packed tightly together. The thick smell of smoke was familiar, and the jukebox was playing "Hound Dog," so I knew Gran was around, with her usual drink, drowning the sorrows I saw peeking out when she thought no one was looking. A couple of men on bar stools turned to look at us, probably fathers of girls our age. One of them was the man Charlotte's mom was seeing. I recognized him from their kitchen table. His eyes lingered a little too long, booze and the smoky haze his only excuse.

I tried to shake off the unsettled feeling while Charlotte stuck her finger in her mouth, pretending to gag.

Her mom hadn't noticed us, and that was probably a good thing. Charlotte and her mom fought constantly. Neither of them held their tongue, and I'd been witness to plenty of jabs back and forth.

We walked toward the tall, wooden table by the jukebox. Everything at King's was wood, and everything felt damp. Even the air felt damp and smelled damp, as if the collected spilled drinks had found a permanent home. Gran was perched on a stool with her usual glass of whiskey. At home in her recliner or on a stool at King's, she looked the same. Mom wasn't with her.

"Tsk, tsk," Gran said, waving her finger in our direction.

Charlotte sauntered over to the table, hands on her hips, the world her catwalk. Gran leaned her head back and let out a cackle, so I knew it wasn't her first glass.

"Is Stevie working?" Charlotte asked.

Gran smiled. "Sure is, but so is your mom, missy."

Charlotte rolled her eyes. "Aurora, you want anything?"

I shook my head. "Gran, where's Mom?"

She pointed to the bar. Mom was perched on a stool, and Phil was beside her. That was the thing about King's: it was the only bar in town. Cops off duty got driven home by cops on duty. I'd heard they sometimes slept the night off in empty cells, waking up in time to work their morning shifts. I couldn't get used to Phil in plainclothes. His taste for Hawaiian vacation wear made him stand out. Mom's hand was on his arm, and her bare legs were crossed. She was laughing at something he said.

Gran pursed her lips like she tasted something sour. "Interesting, huh?"

Charlotte came back with the drink I didn't ask for. "Don't be a dud," she said, handing me the glass. "It's so fruity you won't even taste the alcohol."

"I doubt that."

Gran put her hands over her eyes, and I took a small sip before letting out a dry cough. "What's in this?" I asked. "It's disgusting."

Neither of them answered. Gran looked like she was seeing a ghost.

"Aurora, that better not be a drink in your hand."

I didn't have to look to know who was talking. When I turned around, I collided with Tim, my head hitting his chest. My drink spilled on his shirt and the floor. He was smiling, but his eyes were glassy, and his cheeks were red. He reached over and ruffled the top of my hair. I'd never seen him drunk before. Two glasses of whiskey, sure. But this was more than two glasses.

"Hey there, Katherine," he said, each word slow and enunciated.

Gran lifted her glass in greeting, but her eyes kept switching focus between him and Mom. Mom had a lit cigarette dangling from her lips, which meant she was really flirting. Phil had inched closer.

"So, where's Laine?" Tim sort of swayed from one foot to the other, and he reminded me of the trees just before the lumberjack yells, "Timber."

"One . . . two . . ." He was counting, moving a finger from me to Gran. "Where's your third musketeer?"

I reached out and grabbed his arm, hoping to steady him. Gran rose from her stool, instantly sobered.

"Hey, Tim, maybe we ought to get you home." She latched onto his other arm and directed him toward the door. "Aurora and I will drive you."

He leaned back against our pull causing both of us to stumble.

"I think I'm going to stay," he said, his voice a little too loud, even for King's.

Charlotte had run over to Mom, and I could see her whispering in her ear. People were starting to stare. Phil looked over at us. His eyes narrowed, and I was afraid he'd guess our secret. Or her secret, really. Mom started to walk our way, with Phil trailing behind her.

"Hey, guys." Mom's voice seemed steady, but I could hear the panic underneath the forced pleasantries. "Are we heading home?"

"I think so." Gran had regained her grip on Tim's arm, and I held the other. "We were just telling our good old mailman here that we could give him a ride."

It was probably the cop in him, but Phil watched interactions like a tennis match. I could see him tracking the ball between players.

"Not if Aurora's driving." Phil winked, and I smiled back at him. He put a hand on Mom's arm. "I'll take you ladies home and find an officer for Tim."

All of us—Mom, Charlotte, Gran, and me—winced in unison. Tim broke our hold and grabbed Mom's other arm. His grip was tight, and she gasped like it hurt. He'd never done anything like that before.

"Can we talk?" he asked.

I could feel the room shrinking in on us, and heads turning in our direction, one after the other. I watched the color drain from her face.

"That's fine," she said, her voice finally faltering. "You three want to meet me outside?"

Phil looked concerned. "Laine? You okay? Hey, Tim, you might want—"

Mom looked at him with panicked eyes and shook her head. He fell silent, and his eyes stopped moving between the five of us. Game over.

Mom and Tim went through the front doors, and the three of us followed. Charlotte intertwined her fingers with mine, and I noticed her hands were shaking. She squeezed my hand, and I squeezed back.

Outside, under the yellowed parking-lot lights, Tim looked kind of pathetic—and much less intimidating. His shirt was untucked in places, and I noticed a spot of sweat on the center of his back. When he turned to face us, he looked like the Tim who had fixed my bike. His eyes were a little glazed over, but they were still kind. I didn't want to feel bad for him, but I did.

"I think we ought to get out of the parking lot," Gran said, looking back at the doors to King's.

Mom was holding her arm with her hand. "Aurora, are you okay to drive us?"

She and Gran and Tim looked like children who'd broken a vase. They were glassy-eyed and staring at the ground, counting on a fifteen-year-old to get them home.

"Sure," I said. I turned to Charlotte. She knew what I was going to ask.

"I'll call Kevin from the phone inside. He can give me a ride home."

"Are you sure?"

She looked at the four of us and smiled. "I mean, as fun as this has been, I'll pass."

⁂

I woke up to ringing. My head was cloudy, and I felt hung over, which was impossible because I'd had only one sip of my drink. I waited for the phone to shut up, but then it began to ring again, and my brain started to fill in the details. Saturday. Harry. The date. Harry was supposed to call.

I jumped out of bed and ran down the hall, through the living room, tripping over the coffee table. Gran was asleep in the recliner, with the TV on. Not even my flailing body crashing into the table could wake her.

The magazine was still on the floor. Nobody had started the coffee. The whole house was asleep. I rounded the corner and picked up the phone.

"Hello?" I answered, horrified by my raspy voice.

"Hi, um . . . is Aurora there?" It was Harry.

I deepened my voice. "Um, let me get her."

I dropped the phone so the chord was dangling, the phone bobbing up and down. When I rounded the corner, Gran was at the kitchen table with her magazine right side up. I never could figure out how she moved so fast. Her hair, teased from the night before, was flattened on one side.

"Who's the phone for?" she asked.

I raised my finger to my lips. "Shh."

I cleared my throat.

"Aurora!" Gran yelled, shaking her head. "Phone for you!"

I made sure to emphasize my steps around the corner, not that he could've made out the sounds. "Hello?" I answered, this time sounding much more like myself.

"Hey."

"Hi."

Gran coughed in the kitchen.

"It's me, Harry."

I laughed. "I know."

"Oh good . . . well."

There was noise in the kitchen. Mom was up, and Tim was with her. The night before came back to me all at once. Tim had fallen asleep on the drive home. Nobody knew how to drop him off, or how to explain to Lyla her passed-out husband in our back seat. Every now and then he'd mutter, "Sorry, Laine," which wouldn't have helped our case. So we took him here and helped him stumble into her room. Our street was dark, but Karl Saunders had a light on in his front room.

"So tonight?" Harry asked. "You still free?"

"Tonight is perfect." I curled the phone cord around my finger, an unsteady flutter settling deep in my gut. "I've got a day shift, so I should be home from work around five."

Tim began to laugh, and I covered the receiver with my palm to mute the sound.

"I'll pick you up at six," Harry said.

Gran and Mom joined in on the laugh, and I hated the feeling that things were moving on without me. And I hated that nobody seemed concerned by Tim's presence. Nobody thought about the house on the other side of town, the girls waking up to no father, and the wife walking out to an empty couch. I hung up the phone and walked into the kitchen. Mom was wiping a tear from her eye, and Gran was holding her side.

"How's Tim getting home?" I asked.

He looked over and smiled. "Hon, your guess is as good as mine."

The three began again to laugh together, and suddenly I couldn't stand the sight of them. I couldn't stand that I was the only one who woke up with a pit in my stomach. I walked past them, through the living room, and out the front door. Then I walked back inside, quietly opening and shutting the door I'd just slammed. I didn't want to ruin my exit, but Al wouldn't appreciate me showing up for work in my pajamas. I slipped into the tank top and jean shorts I'd decided on as a uniform. My vest still smelled like popcorn.

It would take me just over an hour to walk to the bowling alley, and the heat would do me no favors. I thought of my bike propped on the side of King's and hoped it would still be there to get me home. My desperation to get out of the house outweighed the inconvenience. I made sure my second exit was quieter than the first.

꧁ ꧂

The bowling alley Saturday day crowd wasn't much of a crowd at all. It was a few of the older men from the league and the occasional kid birthday party. Marty, the league chair, always bought a round of Coca-Cola's and tipped me a quarter.

When I walked in with my knotted hair, Al scribbled a note on his clipboard, but he didn't ask questions. My cheeks were pink, and I could feel the sweat dripping between my shoulder blades. I wondered if he'd been at King's the night before. I couldn't say for sure how many people had been paying attention, but Mom and Tim's first public appearance was sure to raise suspicion. I thought of Harry. I thought of his parents. I could only hope that the people who went to King's weren't the kind of people who spent Sundays in church pews, but Tim's existence proved otherwise.

I kept looking at the clock, keeping track of the time, which only made the day go by slower. Every now and then I'd catch Al staring, but he'd quickly look away, never meeting my gaze. I straightened the snack bar with as much attention as I could muster, cleaning crushed popcorn bits out of crevices that hadn't been touched in years.

Nobody new had walked in for the last hour, and I had another three left in my shift. Not that I wanted to go home, because I didn't. I was sure Tim was home by now, armed with reasons why he'd never made it home the night before. And I was sure Lyla Rae Sr. ignored the discomfort she felt in her bones, dismissed it, because I'd seen it happen before. Mom let men lie to her too. And Charlotte's dad, before he'd left for good, had been gone for weeks at a time. The women I knew swallowed men's lies whole.

I hated having so much time to think. I was beginning to understand why Gran had the TV on all day. Al was busy scribbling away on his clipboard, stuck at the shoe rental station because Jim had finally quit. When he looked up, I waved, and he gave a quick nod before looking back down at his clipboard. I tried not to feel too paranoid.

The double doors swung open, and sunlight spilled onto the stained red carpet. Tim, Lyla Rae Sr., Lyla Rae Jr., and the youngest blonde walked in, smiling and laughing. They looked like a family in a movie. Lyla Rae Jr. was talking with her hands, telling a story that had the whole group paying attention. She was in a pair of red gingham pants and a matching cropped halter. I recognized the set from the Sears catalogue. Her blonde ponytail, topped off with a red silk ribbon, swung from side to side.

Tim caught my eye for just a second, but he didn't break his stride or his grin. I was, quite literally, invisible. The youngest of the group tugged on the bottom of his T-shirt. The four of them looked over in my direction, and I couldn't even force myself to look away. He nodded, reaching in his pocket for a wallet, handing his younger daughter a five-dollar bill.

The little blonde ran over, and I thought she looked ten, maybe eleven. She was a miniature of her older sister, with the same blonde ponytail and a different-colored ribbon. I smoothed my own knotted hair.

She looked proud to order on her own. "Can we get two popcorns and a pitcher of Pepsi?"

"We just have Coke." My voice was unfriendly. She was too young to resent, but that didn't stop me. "Is that fine?"

She glanced back at her dad, who was renting shoes. "Coke's fine," she said.

I scooped the popcorn into bags and was careful not to fill them too much, not with Al carrying his clipboard around. I set the bags on the counter next to the pitcher of Coke and stacked four cups beside it.

"Dad!" she yelled, and Tim looked over.

He had no shoes, just socks. She pointed at their snacks. He slipped on his bowling shoes and walked over with untied laces, careful not to look at me when he tucked the bags of popcorn under one arm. The little blonde handed him his change, and he stuck a dollar in the tip jar, still avoiding my searching eyes. I don't know what I was looking for, what he could give me with one look. I could feel a pang in my gut, and my eyes watered before I blinked the tears back.

Al was watching me again, from the shoe rentals, but this time when I looked up, he waved me over. I had filled their bags just right, so there was nothing to bust me for. The snack bar was immaculate.

Caroline, I remembered. The little blonde's name was Caroline.

"Aurora, it's too slow for me to be paying a snack bar employee. I doubt many people are coming in in the next couple hours, and Frank's coming in for the night shift." He looked over at the family of four picking out bowling balls by lane seven with a pained smile. "You're okay to go, I'll see you . . ." He looked down at his clipboard. "Tuesday."

I looked over at Tim and his girls, bowling on a Saturday, painfully aware of our role in his storyline. In the light of day, in the real world, it all felt so obvious. We were just a distraction from *this*—bowling on a Saturday, family dinners, a life so full we paled in comparison. Al reached over and squeezed my shoulder, and I knew he knew. And if he knew, it was only a matter of time before all of Monroe knew too.

15

My bike was still on the side of King's, and I counted my blessings that a drunk hadn't used it as his ride home. I started to bike home the same way I'd come, but the sun was higher and brighter, and I could feel the sweat dripping down my back before I'd even made it out of the parking lot. King's had three cars in the lot. I tugged on the heavy door I'd opened just twelve hours before, greeted by the same smells. The sounds were different. Afternoon drinkers were silent drinkers, and no one bothered with the jukebox. Beatrice was wiping down the counter, and she waved me over.

"Your Gran's not here," she said.

I climbed up on a stool and rested my head in my hands. Harry would be at my house in three hours.

"I know." There was a gouge from a knife fight in the wood, and I traced it with my finger. "Mind if I use the phone?"

"Of course not." She pulled her hair back into a ponytail. Charlotte and her mom looked nothing alike, but their movements were the same. "You know where it is?"

I shook my head no.

"Down past your Gran's table." She gave me a knowing look. I guess she had seen us last night after all. "Down the hall just before the bathroom."

The men who saw the inside of King's more than their own living rooms nodded as I walked past them toward the hallway. Phil was at the end of the bar, on the same stool he'd sat in last night. His red button-down with the white plumerias was rumpled. He had an empty glass with melting ice cubes.

"Hey, Phil," I said.

He looked up. "Oh, hey, Aurora." The circles under his eyes gave him away—he hadn't slept. "What are you doing here?"

I pointed toward the hall. "Calling for a ride."

He stood up and smoothed his wrinkled shirt. "I can give you a ride."

"Can you?" I nodded toward the glass on the counter.

"Ask Beatrice—I just had the one." When he smiled, he looked more sober. "I'm a man of the law, Aurora. You know that."

"Okay," I said. "Sure."

I didn't know him all that well, but Phil seemed like someone you could trust.

We left King's and its dampness behind, hopefully leaving the dark of the night behind us too. The sunlight hit us both at the same time.

"This is mine," he said, using his key to unlock the passenger door. His green Grand Torino was covered in a thick layer of dust. "Is that yours?" He nodded toward my bike.

"Yeah. It's too hot to ride home."

He walked over and grabbed it, angling it on its side so it'd fit in the back seat.

"I don't mind," he said, shutting the door.

I slipped into the passenger seat, grateful I didn't have to swallow my pride and call home for a ride. I wanted them to worry a bit longer. I wanted them to know I was angry.

Phil turned the key, and the car roared to life.

"So," he said, pulling out onto the road, "someone told me you have a date tonight."

"That someone have long, dark hair? And a big mouth?"

"That's the one." He looked over and smiled. "You excited?"

I could feel the heat rising to my cheeks. "Sure."

"Sure?" He shook his head. "No, no. This is a *date*. You've gotta be excited."

"Okay, okay. I'm excited." I slouched in the seat. The cracks in the leather dug into my bare shoulders. "Can this conversation end?"

"Sure," he said, laughing at my discomfort.

"What about you?" I asked.

When he squinted, the lines by his eyes grew deeper, but his mouth was still turned up at the corners. "What about me?"

"Well, it's Saturday. You have any dates?"

I knew I was walking a fine line, but still I forged ahead.

"Doesn't look like it." I watched his pointer fingers drum on the steering wheel to the beat of the missing music. "Although . . ."

He stopped himself. I looked over expectantly. "Although what?"

We made a right into the housing tract. He knew the route by heart. I watched him navigate through the streets, each one bringing us closer to the little blue house.

"Nothing." He made a right onto our street. Karl Saunders was on his front lawn, wearing his pajamas. "Karl still doing okay?"

I nodded. "Screws are a little looser, but Gran thinks he'll outlive us all."

Phil smiled and I unbuckled my seat belt. I knew they were watching. When I looked over at the cracked blinds, they fell shut.

Phil put the car in park and stepped out. He set my bike on the driveway, his hands on the handlebars keeping it upright.

"When you gonna get some real wheels?" he asked.

"I'll be sixteen in August. Maybe I'll get my license then."

"If you need lessons from a capable driver—no offense to Laine and Katherine—I'd be happy to help." He smiled. "Not that a lack of license has stopped you before."

"I'll keep that in mind." I reached for the handlebars, dragging the bike to the lawn and letting it fall on the grass. "Thanks for the ride, Phil."

"Sure thing, Aurora."

***

Mom and Gran were smiling when I opened the door, and a yellow dress was draped over the couch's edge. Tim and his girls were probably finishing their second game by now, the pitcher of Coke due for a refill.

"Is this for me?" I asked, pressing the dress against my body.

"Do you like it?" Mom asked. "It won't be much shorter than your knees."

"Preacher-son appropriate," Gran chimed in. "No chance of you getting smited or any of that."

I wasn't sure I wanted to let go of the night before, to let go of my anger, but standing there with the yellow dress in my hands, it didn't feel like I had much of a choice.

"I love it so much," I said. They looked relieved. "It's perfect."

And it was. The straps were thin, and they tied at the top. Tiny flowers were stitched all along the bottom. I remembered seeing it at L. S. Ayres when we bought my bikini. I'd run my hand along it, but it was too much money, and I'd never have asked for a dress like that. Gran was always such a sneak.

"If you shower, I'll do your hair," Mom offered.

"That'd be great," I said, still clutching the dress to my chest.

Gran was back in her recliner. "I'd offer to do your makeup, but God knows what I have to offer wouldn't be preacher-son appropriate. We could always call Charlotte." She let out a cackle.

The three of us were in our spots: Mom on the couch, Gran in her recliner, and me lounging on the floor, with my dress fanning out around me. The fan did its best to keep me from sweating. Mom had curled my hair to look like hers, and it fell down my back. I tucked it behind my ears.

"Do you think he'll be on time?" Mom asked. "Men are rarely on time."

I'd kept her from the spot by the window. Her watching made me anxious.

"I'm sure he'll be on time," I said.

The TV volume was all the way down, and the figures in the little box walked all around it. Our eyes were on them, but our ears listened for any coming cars. At the start of the evening news, we heard his truck pull into our driveway. Right on time. The three of us stood in a panic, and then Gran sat back down.

"I don't know what I'm standing for," she said.

Mom hurried over to me and licked her palm, brushing down my flyaway hairs.

I stepped back. "Ew, Mom."

She pulled on the front of my dress and worked to smooth the crease I'd gotten from sitting on the floor. Harry knocked.

"I don't know why I'm nervous," she said. "I'm not the one going on a date."

I grabbed her hands to stop her fussing, and leaned in to kiss her cheek. Gran waved goodbye. When I opened the door, Harry was wiping the palms of his hands on his shorts.

"Should I come in?" he asked, peering around me.

"No need." I shut the door behind me before he could get a good look inside. "No one's home."

He sped up down the walkway to beat me to the car door. When he opened it, I turned and gave a small wave to the slit in the blinds. I knew two hands on the other side waved back.

16

Harry kept his hands on the steering wheel and his eyes on the road, and the speedometer never went past fifty, but every now and then I'd catch him looking at me from the corner of his eye. "I already said you look pretty, right?" he asked.

I looked out the passenger window to hide my smile. The trees floated by in a sea of green. "You did."

"Okay, just checking."

Harry's truck didn't smell like cigarette smoke, and I didn't have to compete with anyone for shotgun. There were no boys in the back seat, and he didn't put his hand on my leg, even though part of me wanted him to.

We drove in silence, and I thought of things to say, and then I didn't say them. I had never been with a boy who was mine. Not that Harry was mine, but he wasn't Mom's. And he wasn't Charlotte's. I watched as the road went on without much change in scenery. We drove down the road by the river with trees on either side, and then past the neon signs small businesses in a small town felt they needed. As if, without a flashing pink sign, we'd forget to go to the only market in town. Harry was all mine, and I was blowing it, stuck in silence.

"Are you hungry?" he asked.

I was starving. "A little."

Despite the silence, Harry wore a grin while he stared at the road. The trees began to disappear and reappear in patches. I noticed the change. The untrained eye might not notice, but in a road that stretched on too long, you had to focus on the details. We were almost a town away from Monroe, and soon we'd see the familiar glow of neon signs, different but the same.

And then, like a mirage in the desert, different parts of the different town greeted us. They had no bowling alley, but they did have an indoor movie theater that kept up with box office hits. On the nights too hot for cheap cars without air, Monroe kids played town swap, taking over their theater while they bowled in our alley. Al said the kids from Riverside were better tippers, and so far, they'd proven him right.

Harry used his blinker with no one behind him and turned into the Dairy Queen lot.

"This is my favorite place," I said. "How did you know?"

Harry glanced over and smiled before readjusting his parking job five spaces away from the only other car in the lot. He shut off the engine while I unbuckled my seat belt and reached for the door.

"Oh no, let me get that." Harry opened his door and ran around to open mine.

He walked ahead of me and reached for the Dairy Queen door before I could.

I laughed. "You always this polite?"

His neck turned pink around the collar. I walked into the Dairy Queen and was met with cold air, a relief from the warm night. There was no line at the counter.

He fixed his eyes on the menu. "Do you know what you want?"

I moved to order first. "I'll just have a dipped cone." I reached for my back pocket and realized I didn't have one. There was no space for money in this dress.

Harry moved past me and handed two crumpled bills to the boy behind the counter. "I'll have the same. Two cones."

The cashier, whose name tag said "Allan," looked like he'd rather be anywhere else on a Saturday night. He sighed and unfolded both bills, placing them in the register. "I'll call your number when your order's up."

We were the only two people in the shop.

"What number are we?" I asked, trying not to smile.

Reaching up and adjusting his paper hat, Allan looked right at me. "One. Order number one."

I took a seat by the counter, on a stool that spun.

Harry was smiling with his teeth in a way that made me smile back. "You're kind of a smartass," he said.

I raised my hand to my heart and feigned shock. "Me? Never."

"I think Allan might hate you."

I looked over at Allan, who was holding our two cones in his hands. "Order one," he called out to the empty room, avoiding eye contact with both of us.

I hopped off the stool before Harry could, and grabbed our cones. "Thanks, Allan."

He walked through a door into the back area. Harry took his cone, and I sat back down on the stool.

"Thank you for the ice cream."

"Thanks for coming." He moved to tap his cone with mine, saying, "Cheers!"

I ate my ice cream and worried the silence might return.

"So you come here often?" Harry asked.

I couldn't help but laugh.

"What?" he asked.

"It's just the way you asked. It sounds like a line from one of Gran's soaps. But no, I don't come here too often. I just like knowing it's here. Mom and I always ask around about the nearest Dairy Queen. Whenever we move to a new town it's the first thing we ask, and it sort of became our joke. As long as there is a Dairy Queen in driving distance, we know we'll be okay.

"We haven't been to one since we got here, but I've been wanting to find—" I stopped and smiled. Ice cream was dripping down my hand, and I licked it before it could land on my dress. "Sorry, that was a ramble. But no, I don't come here often."

There was a piece of melted chocolate stuck to Harry's bottom lip, but I didn't point it out.

"Well, we could always come back here." He smiled, and with the chocolate on his lip, it was almost cuter, if that was possible. "And it wasn't *that* long of a ramble. I'm just glad I got you talking."

I moved to punch his arm like I'd seen Charlotte do to Kevin.

He leaned back and grinned.

"You said *towns* as in towns *plural*? How many places have you lived?"

I wondered how much to tell him, and I wondered how much he already knew. I didn't want him to pity me, so I kept my answer pretty vague.

"I've lived lots of places." I took a bite of my cone, melted ice cream spilling down the back of my hand. The air-conditioning unit was working overtime, but it couldn't keep up. "What about you? Have you lived anywhere other than Monroe?"

"Nah—Monroe born and raised. Us Clarks live here until we die. And then we get buried in the cemetery by the church." Harry shook his head. "Sorry. That was kind of bleak."

I shook my head. "Don't be sorry. It's kind of nice—knowing where you'll end up."

Harry shrugged. "It's kind of nice seeing other places too."

"Well, if it makes you feel better, I've only ever seen everywhere in Indiana. We're cursed. We never make it past state lines."

Harry laughed, and I told myself not to keep count. There was something addicting to making him laugh.

"That puts to rest some of the rumors."

I put my hand to my chest. "Rumors? About me?"

Harry let out a long sigh. "It's a boring town, Aurora." His saying my name filled my stomach with an inexplicable flutter. "You have to know people are talking."

"I've been the new girl plenty of places. People don't always talk."

He shot me a look like he didn't believe me, but I wasn't lying. There were plenty of towns where I came and went with little fanfare. I was good at staying unnoticed, taking the corner seat in the classroom, the furthest lunchroom table.

"Well, Monroe doesn't even keep a town paper. We had so little news, they went out of business. Yes, people are talking."

"What have you heard?" I raised my eyebrows, hoping my face didn't betray my panic.

I couldn't imagine the rumor mill was kind to Mom. And while I wasn't sure where this was headed, or if he'd even call me after tonight, I knew I didn't want Harry to think any less of me.

Harry wore a mischievous smile. "Some people said your mom left to be a model."

"A *waitress*," I corrected.

"Most said she left because of a bad breakup."

"Not true."

He finished off his cone, reaching for a napkin to clean the ice cream off his hands. "But mostly people said you guys have been gone for a while and that your mom isn't known to stay one place for long."

"That's fair," I said, relief flooding my body.

I didn't want him to think less of me—or to think less of *us*, really. Harry's opinion suddenly seemed very important to me, and I was desperate to stay in his good graces.

"So," he said, looking up at the clock on the wall. "I've got two hours until curfew. What's next on the agenda?"

I smiled at the thought of his curfew, glad to have had him figured out. I liked the image I had of his dad sitting in a chair by the door, one eye on the clock. He'd have a Bible in his lap, of course, open to something New Testament—and no TV in sight. The house would be silent. Maybe the faint sounds of the gospel station on the radio, but still quiet enough for his wife to sleep in the next room.

"I have to choose?" I asked.

"I guess not." I liked how his face showed he was thinking. There was a dent between his eyebrows, and I waited. He stood. "Okay, let's go."

I walked through the Dairy Queen door he held open and sped up my walk so I'd beat him to the car, opening my door before he could.

Charlotte had given me the rundown on how dates in Monroe worked. According to her, boys usually took girls to the drive-in or to the river, where they got lost in the trees for a while. But Harry didn't seem like the boys from her stories, or at least I didn't think he was. He was a cautious driver, never speeding up to pass slowed cars on the two-lane highway. He was the slowed car.

But then I noticed the little red cup on a stick, just by the road. I was surprised when he turned off into the small space between the two trees. I'd never been to the river with Charlotte, but I'd heard plenty of stories. She'd promised to take me one day, and up until now I'd managed to avoid her keeping that promise.

Other towns I'd lived in had their equivalent of the river—places where the teens from town created their own lawless land. I'd hear about it in the school halls or in stories overheard at lunch tables. In Logansport, it was Wayne's Field. Wayne had been dead for ten years. His widow was fighting his kids, which left his property uninhabited. The teens in town claimed it as their own, and the cops left it alone.

Nobody was swimming. When Charlotte told her stories, I pictured everyone in bathing suits, but I couldn't have been more wrong. The shore was littered with red-cupped proof that this was *the* spot. Other than the red cups and broken glass, it might've looked like any other patch of land beside the river, but the way Charlotte talked about it, the river seemed almost magical.

The headlights from senior boys' cars, set up in a half circle, illuminated the clearing, letting us all see one another. The mating ritual was one of keg drinks in the light of the circle followed by darkness in the trees, or so I'd gathered. Harry pulled off behind the circle of cars and shut off the engine.

The river smelled vaguely dangerous, like there was a spill of something radioactive. Charlotte was in line for the keg. Stepping onto the dirt, I could feel her eyes on me. The yellow dress was too much for the river.

"You want a drink?" Harry asked.

It seemed so unnatural. His hands were in his pockets. His striped polo looked freshly washed, and his shorts seemed ironed.

"I'm okay," I said, looking around.

The sun was still working on its descent, filling the sky with streaks of red fire. Every sunset this summer looked like the end of the world. Charlotte had two drinks in her hand when she headed in our direction.

"Fancy meeting you here," she said, pushing a drink into my hand before jabbing my chest with her finger. She took a long drink from her cup and smiled at Harry. "Hi, Harry."

"Hi, Charlotte."

Kevin came over to our group. "Lifeguard Harry!" he called out, his voice mocking.

Charlotte leaned over. "Nice dress," she whispered with a smirk.

I rolled my eyes. Her skirt exposed all of her tanned legs, and she'd cut down the neckline of her mom's old T-shirt, tying up the bottom so we could see her belly button.

"You should drink," she said. "It'll help."

"With what?"

She nodded toward the trees. The sun was already leaving us. "With the nerves."

I brought the cup up to my mouth but kept my lips pressed shut, denying the cold liquid its entrance. She nodded, satisfied, before taking Kevin's hand and dragging him off mid-sentence. He looked back at us and waved.

I watched her disappear into the land untouched by car headlights. The crowd of kids drinking and laughing was overwhelming, and I wanted nothing more than to be at home, listening to Gran hurl insults at the people on TV.

Harry's voice broke my trance. "We could sit." He nodded toward the rock outside the circle, but still in the light.

"Okay," I said, unsure what to add.

His hands hovered by my waist as I climbed the rock. When I turned around, Harry climbed up with more ease than me. He sat down, maintaining enough distance so our legs weren't touching.

"Do you come here often?" I asked.

He smiled and shook his head. "No, it's not really my scene."

I looked out at the group of boys standing around the keg. They were disheveled and rowdy. Harry just seemed so clean, and his teeth were so straight. He looked like he had a mom who made casseroles. He looked like someone worried about where he went at night.

I fiddled with the hem of my dress, suddenly self-conscious. "I could understand that."

Another boy approached us. When he got closer, I realized it was Mike from the drive-in.

"Reverend!" he yelled, startling Harry, who hadn't seen him coming.

"Oh, hey, Mike," Harry said. The crease between his eyebrows was returning. "What's up, man?"

"Not much, not much," Mike slurred. He shifted weight from foot to foot, swaying like Tim in the bar. When he noticed me, he raised his eyebrows. "Fancy seeing you here," he said, and I hated him for the smile he gave me. "When you're done up, you don't look so bad. You could do better than a preacher boy."

Harry's body tensed, and Mike took notice. "Lighten up. I'm kidding, I'm kidding."

"Hey, Mike," I said, "I think Charlotte was looking for you."

"Shit." Mike took a swig from his cup and wiped his mouth with the back of his hand. "You serious?"

I nodded emphatically. "Dead serious."

"And Kevin?" he asked, eyeing me with drunken suspicion.

I shrugged. "Trouble in paradise, I guess. Didn't you hear about Carrie?"

He turned and ambled away like Frankenstein's monster. He'd be disappointed when he found out the truth, but I knew I could count on him not remembering.

Harry was red with embarrassment.

"He's an idiot," I said, pouring my full cup out in the dirt beside the rocks. "And can I be honest? This isn't really my scene either."

"No?" he asked.

I shook my head. "And I kind of hate that you thought it was. I've been here all of five minutes, but I'm calling it: this place sucks." His face looked so relieved I had to laugh. "If you hate it too, which I'm assuming you do based on the look on your face, why are we here?"

"It's not you," he said, avoiding eye contact while he answered. "I guess I just wanted to seem cooler. I mean, cooler than I really am, you know?" He laughed a nervous laugh and ran a hand through his hair while the nerves in my body slowly eased their grip. "Embarrassing, huh?"

I shook my head. "Not embarrassing. But you don't have to do that. *Really.*"

Harry looked over at me and smiled.

"Okay, let's make a promise," I said, sticking out my pinky, suddenly bold, waiting for him to hook his in mine. He did, and even though it was just our pinkies touching, it sent the smallest thrill from my head down to my toes.

"What am I promising?" he asked, leaning closer to keep eye contact.

"Let's promise to be ourselves, even if that means we look uncool. *Especially* when it means we look uncool."

Harry kept eye contact, and I resisted the urge to look away. "Okay, Aurora. I promise."

He let go of my pinkie and hopped off the rock before offering me his hand. "Let's get out of here."

I wiped the pool of nervous sweat off my hand before grabbing his, and hoped I was quick enough he didn't notice. Far from graceful, I half crawled, half walked down the rock, and even in a dress as long as mine, I'm sure he saw my underwear.

We walked, and I waited for him to let go of my hand. He held it for a few seconds more than necessary, and when it dropped to my side, I felt a sudden pang of disappointment.

"I don't think you're like I expected," he said, talking to me over the roof of the car before sliding into his seat.

"What do you mean?" I asked.

He looked at me like he was going to be quizzed on my facial features. "I don't know," he said, like he was really thinking about it. "But I'll let you know when I figure it out."

He was exactly like I'd expected, cautious and polite with a perfect smile. But I liked that I was surprising him. Gran, Mom, and even Charlotte now—everyone knew me too well. I lived life feeling like a book that everyone had read. Even Al wore a knowing smile. It felt nice to be a mystery.

I smiled at him and blinked my coated lashes like I'd seen Mom do when she was teasing with Tim. "I can't tell if that's good or bad."

"It's not good or bad." He reached over and grabbed my hand. "But this—I mean tonight—it's good. Okay," he said, returning his hand to its rightful place on the steering wheel. "It's your turn."

"My turn?"

He started up the car. "To pick. Clearly, I'm not good at it."

"Don't count yourself out. You're one for two—Dairy Queen was perfect."

He turned out onto the road, and his headlights took over the job of the missing sunlight. "Batting five hundred."

The trees on either side of the car flew by in a blur. "Okay," I said. "I have a place."

―⁂―

Paradise Bow was now "Paradise ow." The *B* had disappeared overnight, and I wished I could have been there when Al found out. I wondered who drew the short straw and had to tell him. Through a series of turn rights and turn lefts, we'd ended up in Al's parking lot, per my instruction.

"Really?" Harry shut off the car and shook his head. "But you work here. You were here hours ago."

"Exactly." I unbuckled my seat belt and opened my car door before he could. "I work here. Therefore, I really never come here. Believe it or not, I can't bowl on the job."

He trailed behind me, and I didn't dare look back. King's parking lot was a lingering omen from the night before. When I walked through the double doors, there was no relief from the warm night, but the chorus of scattering pins eased my nerves.

"I feel like I should ask if you want popcorn," he said, "but that seems so silly."

I could feel his warm breath on my neck. I turned around to find his face just inches from mine, causing my voice to catch in my throat. "A small bag with extra butter," I managed. "And a Coke too."

He shook his head like I was crazy and headed toward the snack bar. "Size eleven!" he yelled.

"You're not scheduled tonight, Miss Aurora." Al was working the shoe counter. "You look nice—I don't know if I've ever seen you in a dress."

"Tonight I'm a patron."

Al raised his eyebrows. "Two shoes?"

"A size eight and a men's eleven."

He leaned down beneath the counter. "Did you notice the *B*?" he asked.

"I did." I pressed my lips together so I wouldn't smile because that would just set him off. "It's terrible," I said, offering my condolences for the missing letter. "When did you notice?"

"About twenty minutes ago. Jim was the bearer of bad news." I opened my mouth to speak, but he raised his hand to silence me. "Yes. He's back. *For now.* I know I'm an idiot. I scared the pants off of him, though." Al chuckled. "Hell, probably scared the pants off a few customers."

Harry came up behind me with popcorn and drinks. He set them on the counter and reached in his pocket for his wallet. Jim underfilled the popcorn bags, and I hoped Al would notice and take note. The man was a disaster.

Al shook his head when Harry tried to offer him money. "Shoes and game on me. After putting up with me all summer, this girl has earned it."

"Thanks, Al," I said, grabbing the shoes by their laces and dragging Harry away before Al had a chance embarrass me.

"For being the new girl in town, you're pretty well connected."

"Are you impressed?"

"A little."

"Well, Harry," I teased, bumping my shoulder into his, "maybe there's a lot you don't know."

I silently thanked Al for giving us lane 12, the closest to the wall fan.

"You think you guys will stay?" Harry asked, with no context at all.

I looked up from tying my shoes. "What?"

"I'm just wondering how long you'll be in Monroe."

I walked toward the wall of bowling balls, each color a different size and weight. I grabbed the third heaviest, and he raised his eyebrows. "Honestly? I'm not all that sure. Mom doesn't like a plan."

He grabbed the second heaviest. "What about you? Do you like a plan?"

I smiled. "I love a plan. But you get used to it after a while. Like, at some point the unpredictable becomes the predictable, you know?"

I watched him take a drink of his Coca-Cola, the crease between his brows deepening. "But do you like it here? I mean, would you want to stay if you were the one making the plans?"

Nobody had asked me that before, but I didn't have to think long to answer. "I love it here," I said with enough enthusiasm to make him laugh. "Don't you?"

He shrugged. "I mean, it's all right."

Charlotte felt the same. I thought most kids here did. Like the world outside of Monroe was bigger and better and filled with things that could make you happier. But I knew the world outside Monroe was just the same, except the world outside Monroe didn't have Charlottes and Harrys and Grans.

I pointed at the lane. "You first."

He stood and stretched, giving his best serious face, and I let out a giggle. It felt good to laugh, and I tried not to feel any guilt in my gut. He bowled a seven and then a gutter ball.

I stood up, cradling my ball and stepping toward the lane. I did a little shimmy before launching the ball down the lane. The pins scattered. A single one remained, swaying from side to side before falling to the left. It was a strike.

"Whoo-hoo!" I yelled, lifting my hands above my head and swaying side to side.

I was much more competitive than I'd let on. Harry laughed at my victory dance. "Now I know why you wanted to come here. Trying to embarrass me." The machine returned his ball, and he reached for it. "Does your mom like it?"

"Bowling?" I asked, even though I knew what he meant.

"No, Monroe."

She likes Tim, I thought, but of course I couldn't say that. We'd promised to be honest, but there were some things I had to keep to myself. "She likes *parts* of Monroe," I said, which was the truth.

"But she left," he said, and I wondered if he knew more than he let on.

"She was young," I countered, tossing a piece of popcorn in my mouth.

Harry bowled a spare and flopped down in the orange plastic chairs. I watched as a piece of hair usually swept back from his forehead fell forward. I resisted the urge to push it back. "My parents have never left, not even on a vacation. They honeymooned at Indiana Beach."

I smiled, thinking of the tourist attraction by the fake lake, the Ferris wheel lights. The pins remained scattered across the wood, and I pressed down on the button to reset them. "There's nothing wrong with Indiana Beach."

Half of his mouth turned up in a smile. "There's got to be more than Monroe."

"So you want to leave?" I asked.

"Someday," he said, and I found myself hoping that someday wouldn't be anytime soon.

⁂

The TV light flickered behind the blinds. They were fifteen minutes into *The Love Boat*, but I wasn't sad to miss it. The clock on the dashboard said nine fifteen, and his curfew was nine thirty on Saturdays.

"I should go," I said, reaching for the handle. "Thank you. I had fun."

He reached across the divider to stop me from opening the door. "Wait, I'll get it."

"Someday I'm going to prove to you I'm capable—"

He was already out of the driver's side. I watched him jog around the front of the car and open mine. "I'll walk you," he said, tipping his chin toward the front door.

"You going to open my front door too? After a night with you, I'm not sure I remember how."

He laughed and reached for my hand, intertwining my fingers with his. I hoped he wouldn't notice the pool of nerves on my palms. Our stone walkway was short, no more than a few yards, but each step we took was slow and small.

"You coming to the pool Monday?" he asked.

I nodded, feeling defeated when we finally reached the door. I wondered if anybody had watched us on the other side of the blinds. Harry let go of my hand, and we stood facing each other. He dragged his toe on the ground before looking up. When his hand reached for the side of my face, I'd seen enough movies and soap operas to know what was supposed to happen next.

"It's a beautiful night!" Karl Saunders called out, causing Harry to take a quick step back.

Harry's head collided with the porch light, and I gasped. I hadn't noticed Karl in his yard, and apparently neither had Harry. Karl was on his knees in a bed of dirt, shaking packets of seeds into the ground.

"Are you okay?" I asked, instinctively reaching a hand to Harry's head. His curls were as soft as I'd imagined. Not that I'd spent too much time imagining touching his hair, but the thought had crossed my mind.

He forced out an embarrassed laugh, moving his hand up to scratch the back of his head. "I'll try and survive."

"You should go," I said, thinking of his curfew—and his pride. Karl was still watching across the way. "I'll see you Monday."

"Okay," he said, looking back and forth between Karl and me. He reached out a hesitant hand and patted my shoulder. "I'll see you."

The dim porch light spotlighted his brisk walk to the car. I bit my lip and tried not to laugh. Karl and I watched Harry's car pull out of the driveway. He drove down the street, away from the little blue house, and turned left at the corner.

"Hi, Karl," I called out. "How are the roses?"

He turned toward them as if they could answer for themselves. "The heat's been hard, but they're persevering!"

"Well, I wish them the best of luck!"

"If you look up, you can see the Buck Moon!" he yelled after me.

I walked toward the end of our driveway. The sky was littered with stars. I crossed the street to his garden.

The moon was a perfect circle and a vibrant orange. It looked close enough to touch. "Doesn't happen too often, but when she's there, she's beautiful."

From his vantage point, I could see the little blue house perfectly. The blinds were shut, and the lilacs were washed in moonlight. Tabby, the stray Karl had decided to feed and name, walked across our roof. Gran had told Karl if the cat took a shit up there, he was the one who was going to clean it.

The more I studied the little blue house, the more I didn't want to return to it. "Can I sit for a while?"

"Be my guest." Karl gestured at the two lawn chairs in his garden: one for him, one for visitors. "The roses love your new dress."

"Do they?" I looked over and curtsied at the rose bush. "Thank you for noticing."

We looked up at the night sky, mostly in silence except for when Karl wanted to point out a constellation. At some point I yawned, and Karl smiled.

"You should go in," he said. "They're probably waiting for you."

"Maybe." I wasn't sure if that was true.

"Goodnight, Aurora."

"Goodnight, Karl." I turned to the roses. "Goodnight, roses."

The little blue house always smelled the same to me, smoke mixed with must and leftover meat loaf. It was a strange, familiar combination, and when I left the cool night air, the house surrounded me. The light from the TV washed the room in shades of blue, lighting up Gran's face. It was like the tank in the Chubby Lobster, the restaurant Gran had begged us to go to for her "fortieth" birthday, the age she'd decided on as her last. We didn't make it to dessert. Mom blew up at dinner, driving through the night so we'd be home by sunrise.

Mom and Tim were on the couch, and he held her feet in his lap. No one noticed I was home. I watched him press his thumb into the arch of her foot, tracing small circles. The moment felt intimate, like I wasn't supposed to witness it. The affection between them seemed easy. Sometimes it felt like they'd been together for years instead of weeks. There was a wife somewhere out there who had earned this easy intimacy, and thinking of her made me feel sick.

"Hello," I said, knowing I was interrupting them.

The three of them turned around to face me.

"Aurora!" Gran looked excited.

Tim smiled at me, and I couldn't help but think of this morning and the smiles reserved for Lyla Jr. Ours were secondhand. Mom took turns looking between the two of us. I wondered if he'd mentioned Paradise or if it was another secret I was expected to keep.

Gran patted the spot on the floor by her feet, and she stood up to turn down the TV. "Come, tell us about the date."

I stayed behind the couch, and the room felt split in two. I shook my head, willing myself not to cry. I don't know why I wanted to cry. I'd had a perfect night with a perfect boy. But the feelings, like the stagnant air, suffocated me.

"I can't," I said, the quiver in my voice betraying me. I took a second to sort myself out, and I tried to make my voice sound bright. "I'm just beat. Can I tell you about it tomorrow?"

Before Gran could stand back up, I hurried down the hall to my room, careful not to slam the door behind me. There was an ache in my throat I couldn't swallow. I couldn't stand to be there. Harry would be home by now. I wondered what he had walked in on. His dad prepping for Sunday's sermon? His mom on the couch with her needlepoint? Did they ask about me? I'm sure the air in his home was fresh, carried in through the open window. The married mailman hadn't taken up residence on their couch.

I walked to my bedroom window, unhooked the latch, and pushed it open. The night air smelled better than meat loaf. I sat on the sill and took a deep breath before swinging my legs to the other side. The green grass was cool on my feet, and I realized I'd slipped off my shoes by the front door. It was too late now.

I headed toward Charlotte's. I wasn't sure of the time, but if it was as late as it felt, she might be home already. Not that I wanted to see her after the way she'd treated me. Treated *us*. Still, she was my only friend.

Barefoot in my yellow sundress, I walked the blocks I'd begun to know by heart. Norma of Norma's Diner lived on the street before Charlotte's. Her curtains were a red floral, and she'd tied them back. I don't know what made me want to get a closer look, but I did. I had an itch to see what was inside.

The window opened to a living room like ours, and a light beside the yellow couch lit up the space. She didn't keep her curtains drawn because she had nothing to hide. Norma's husband's picture was on the mantle. His reading glasses were still on a side table, folded on top of a stack of

Auto Trader magazines. She kept shrines to him like Gran kept shrines to Jay. I wondered if putting the little things away—the remnants of them—would be the worst kind of loss.

Most of the houses were dark. Some had porch lights left on. I liked the windows that opened to living rooms, framing their lives. There weren't all that many of us in Monroe, Indiana, but in that moment, my world felt full of people.

When I reached Charlotte's, her mom was on the front steps, looking up at the night sky. She noticed me before I could slip away, offering a tired smile. Her hair was knotted on the top of her head. She rarely missed a Saturday night. Saturday nights paid the bills. I couldn't figure out why she was home, but it didn't seem like I should ask.

"Charlotte's not home," she said.

"That's all right."

"It's a little late for a walk." Her voice seemed weighed down by whatever she was carrying.

"Clearing my head," I said, knowing she would see through a dishonest excuse.

She nodded like she understood.

"Charlotte is glad to have you. She keeps her feelings close to her chest, but I know she's happier this summer than she's been in a while."

"I'm glad to have her too," I said, meaning it.

"Want to sit a moment?"

I walked up the pathway, taking a seat on the porch step below her. I wondered if she was lonely, and that's why she was always looking for someone to spend time with. Charlotte made it sound like the men came in a never-ending rotation. She said she'd stopped trying to learn their names.

"You getting along okay here?" she asked.

"So far."

"This town isn't always easy on people." She said it like a warning. "Charlotte's dad wasn't a good man, but there were plenty of people who took his side. Still, your gran and Jay were the first to stand up for me." She placed a hand on my shoulder. "I hope you know you'll always have us in your corner."

Gran had told me about him and what he'd done, and I couldn't imagine anyone taking his side. But Gran had also said life wasn't fair, and there was no point waiting for the rights and wrongs to balance themselves out.

"Thank you," I said, hoping there'd be no need to cash in on her loyalty.

We stayed like that for a while before she sent me on my way.

"Don't make your gran worry," she said.

I walked home under a blanket of stars, exhausted. The bottoms of my feet were black. My dress had a tiny tear from Karl's rose bushes. The curls in my hair had begun to fall out. Our date had ended just hours before, but it felt like I'd lived another life since then.

I tried to think about Harry because that's what normal girls do after dates with boys they like, but I was stuck on thoughts of Tim's front window. I wondered what room it opened up to and if the TV was on. I'd never seen his house. It was on the other side of town. I'd looked it up in the phone book, but I'd never gathered the courage to ride by. Tim entered our world and left his behind, never mentioning it.

Was his house blue? Yellow? Green? Did Lyla Rae Jr. set the table for dinner with china from her parents' wedding? Was there an empty place kept for Tim on the nights he came home late? My body ached like a summer flu, which is the worst kind, and I felt the urge to run. I wanted to run across town, and I wanted to see the house. The front porch light holding vigil, waiting for him to come home. Lyla Rae Sr. waiting by the window facing the street. His daughters asleep in their beds. They had to be in bed by now. Church had one service—the early one—and I doubt they ever missed it.

Or maybe his wife slept through his absence. Maybe she knew where he was, and maybe she didn't care. The inside of Tim's house—the girls' school pictures on the wall, and the quilt made from their baby clothes—was really just a world I'd made up in my mind.

When I turned onto our street, Karl was still out front. I liked to think he was waiting for me, making sure I got home okay. He had a glass in his hand and raised it in salute. I wondered how much he'd seen that night. Who had come and gone. I could only hope his roses would keep our secrets too.

◦◦◦

The TV volume was low, just a steady hum, so I knew Mom must have turned in for the night. I assumed Tim was gone, driving across town and quietly entering his house, armed with excuses, though more and more I had the feeling his girls never asked.

I sat by Gran's feet, and her hand stretched out to smooth my hair. "I thought you were tired," she said, her voice thick with sleep. I turned to face her. "You had fun?" she asked.

I rested my chin on her knee. "He was perfect."

"Nobody's perfect, but I'm sure he was close." She leaned down to kiss the top of my head. "Speaking of imperfections . . ." I could tell right away where this was going, my thoughts going straight to her. I wondered what Tim had said or done, what she had said or done. "Your mom does her best. It's not always enough, but she's trying."

This was true. Mom did do her best. But sometimes, her best wasn't good enough. Before this summer, I'd never had so much to lose. We'd leave jobs and towns and schools, and it didn't matter because we had each other. And I made sure to have nothing else. But now I had a world of my own. I had a gran. I had a room. I had a friend. My world might seem small to some, but it was mine. For the first time, I had everything.

"I know," I said, giving Gran peace before her night's rest.

She smiled and took my hands between hers. "You're good, Aurora. Always have been."

Tears blurred my vision, and I blinked them back. I stood and leaned down to kiss Gran's cheek before hurrying down the hall toward my room. Mom's door was open a crack, and the light spilled in the hallway. She was awake. I wanted to go in and let her be a mom. But if I didn't go in, she wouldn't have the chance to hurt me, I wouldn't have the chance to hurt her, and I could pretend. I could pretend she asked the right questions, pretend she cared about where I was, who I was with, what we did. If I didn't go in, she could stay perfect.

When I shut my door, I pressed my back against it, sliding down to the carpeted floor. Before that day I couldn't remember the last time I'd cried so hard, and then it was twice in one day. They were hot, panicked tears, and the tightness in my chest spread. I was too full of everything.

17

Gran always said things looked better in the morning. My eyelids were still a little swollen, and my new dress, now draped atop my dresser, was still torn. But my chest didn't feel so tight. The house smelled like diner food, so I knew she'd made breakfast. The TV was off, and Mom and Gran were at the kitchen table with pancakes and bacon and eggs. Mom hadn't mastered any cooking skills beyond breakfast, but sometimes breakfast was enough.

When I walked in the kitchen, Mom stood to pour me a cup of coffee, and I pulled out a chair to join them. She'd even put the syrup in a fancy glass pitcher Jay kept in the cupboard.

"So how was it?" Mom asked.

I began to fill my plate, suddenly starving. "It was good."

"Where'd he take you?"

I could tell it was just pleasantries because her eyes were far away. Still, I told her the details of my night, and she nodded along and smiled when she was supposed to. My whole life I'd seen her disappear for a while, even when we were in the same room. That summer it happened more and more. She'd do what she was supposed to when she was supposed to do it, but her eyes never seemed to focus.

Her hair was in a knot on the top of her head and she had old makeup under her eyes. Tim never came over on Sundays, so there was no one to get dolled up for.

"He seems really great," she said, her voice falling flat. "Maybe bring him by sometime and I can meet him."

"Yeah, or maybe the four of us could go on a double date."

My voice was harsher than I'd intended. She came back to the world we were all living in, her eyes clear for the first time that morning. She looked like I'd hit her, and I half expected her cheek to turn red from a slap I didn't remember giving.

"Aurora," Gran said, and it was almost a scolding. Almost.

That's all it took, and I was flooded with guilt. It wasn't a very nice thing to say. It wasn't a very Aurora thing to say. Gran had said I was good, but I didn't feel good.

"I'm sorry," I said, not sure that I was, not sure that I wasn't.

Mom stood and I watched her unsteady hand set her mostly full plate in the sink. "It's okay," she said, when her back was to us. I knew it wasn't okay.

She ran her fork under the faucet and set it in the sink. "I might go out for a little bit. I was thinking of taking a walk."

"Just stay," I said, my voice sounding desperate. "It was a terrible thing to say. I'm already sorry I said it."

"I know. It's okay," she lied. "It's not that, I promise. I just need some sunshine."

She walked down the hall and I moved to follow her, but Gran grabbed my hand.

"Let her go," she mouthed, squeezing my fingers.

When I heard the door shut, I sat back down. I still had two pancakes on my plate and three slices of bacon, but I wasn't so hungry anymore.

"I don't know why I said that."

Gran smiled. "God, if you knew how she talked to me at your age. Hon, you ever heard of karma?"

"I'm not mad at her," I said, not sure whether it was her or me I was trying to convince.

Gran reached over and stole a piece of bacon. "It's okay if you are."

"I'm not," I said, defensive.

"Okey dokey." Gran rose from her chair like she was twenty years older than she was. "Well, get up. You better get ready. The preacher on the TV's going to tell us the story of the guy with the boat and all the animals, and I've just read about a new step routine to give us better behinds."

18

The pool gates opened at ten, and Gran was ready by nine. When I walked out of my room, she was in the recliner, wearing just her bathing suit, while a man in a suit and too white teeth told us the weather would be the same as the days before.

"It's a good day for a swim," she said.

"Apparently."

I had on my red bikini under an oversized T-shirt I'd stolen from Mom's pajama pile. I hoped Gran wouldn't notice the mascara and lipstick I'd put on. I'd never hear the end of it.

"You're wearing that?" she asked, looking me up and down.

"What do you mean?"

She grimaced. "I mean, honey, you've got a body. We aren't doing step aerobics for shirts like that."

"We're going to the pool, not the prom. I take it off once I get there, and at that point everyone sees every last bit of my body."

She shrugged. "To each their own."

I sat on the floor by her feet. She took my hair up in her hands.

"Let's at least curl it," she said.

"Gran! Can Harry not like me for my personality?"

"A seventeen-year-old boy? That's unlikely. But even if he's as perfect and pure as you say, a little effort never does any harm."

She was persistent and I was tired, so I let her curl my hair and tie the shirt up in a knot. When she was finished, she smiled.

"You look like her," she said. "It always sneaks up on me."

I knew it was a compliment. She was beautiful by anyone's standards. But for some reason it made me feel nervous.

We picked up Charlotte on our way to the pool. She didn't say anything about my hair or outfit, but I could tell she wanted to.

"Sorry about Saturday," she said before I had a chance to say anything. "We had been fighting for most of the night, and then you came in with the glow of new love. I shouldn't have been a brat, but I was. And if it makes you feel better, I threw up in my hair by the end of the night, so I got what I deserved."

I had left that part of the night out of my recap, but Gran didn't say anything.

"All's forgiven," I said, and I meant it.

Charlotte looked genuinely relieved. As much as I needed her, she needed me. We needed each other.

"Speaking of . . . how are things with Kevin?" Gran asked.

Charlotte released an exaggerated sigh. "Love is the worst."

"Love?" I asked.

She nodded. "Love."

Gran did her best not to laugh. "I can imagine," she said, looking over to wink at me.

"He's the best and the worst thing to ever happen to me." Everything with Charlotte was pure drama, like a soap opera come to life. Maybe that's why I liked her so much. "And when I don't want to kill him, things are really great."

Gran pulled over and put the car in park. The chain-link fence surrounding the pool made my stomach do a flip. I didn't want to get out of the car, but Charlotte was pushing my seat forward, forcing me out onto the sidewalk.

"Who's on duty?" she asked, her voice teasing. I watched her extract herself from the back seat, climbing over the front, flashing all sorts of parts in the process. Her sunglasses fell to the tip of her nose.

"You know who's working," I said, crossing the vacant street with Gran close behind.

The gate creaked when it swung open, announcing our presence to the empty plastic chairs scattered across weathered cement. It was still early. Gran insisted we leave, saying she wanted to have her pick of seats. Thank goodness we weren't the first ones, or I might have died of embarrassment. There was a group of moms putting sunscreen on toddlers, attaching floaties to arms. Harry was up in his tower. He shielded his eyes from the sun and looked down, smiling.

I remembered to inhale and exhale, and to put one foot in front of the other, but my stomach turned over on itself again and again. Gran not so subtly picked a spot closest to the tower, tossing down her towel while Charlotte laughed.

Playing it cool was difficult, and when I pulled the T-shirt over my head, it got stuck. I tugged it off and pushed my hair back from my face. His eyes were on me, and I was instantly warm. Each movement felt slow and strained, me doing my best not to embarrass myself.

I pretended not to notice him climbing down from his tower and Gran pretended to read *To Tame a Vixen*, the book she'd picked up at Rexall Drugs. She found it on a shelf with the sunblock and said it was like a soap opera to-go, except it took a lot more work.

"Oh hey, Harry," Charlotte said, just before I looked up.

He nodded a greeting and walked to the edge of my lounge chair. I scooted my legs to make room, watching his eyes track their movement. It felt good to be noticed.

"Hey," he said, sitting down. "How are you?"

"Hotter than hell," Gran said, her eyes still on her book. "Thanks for asking."

Harry smiled. "And you, Aurora?"

"Same," I said.

"And you, Harry?" Charlotte asked, her eyes hidden behind dark lenses.

His eyes stayed on me. "Probably more of the same."

There was an inch of space between us, and I was watching it closely.

"So, do you work tonight?" he asked.

I shook my head.

"Well, I have to teach the swim lessons this afternoon, but I'm off around four." I missed the moment when he scooted closer, but our legs were touching, just barely. "Would you maybe want to do something?"

"Sure," I said, too aware that Gran was probably tracking my word use. *"She used two whole words,"* I could hear her saying. *"Two words in an entire conversation."*

"I mean, I'd like that."

"And no river," he said, laughing.

I laughed. "No river."

"Okay." He looked back at his tower. "I should probably go. Keep an eye on the pool. Save some lives."

"I was planning on drowning in the next couple minutes," Charlotte said, flipping her hair to one side.

"I was kind of hoping it would be Aurora." He grinned out of the side of his mouth.

I watched Gran's eyes narrow and her lips pucker. She kept focused on her book, but I knew her well enough to know she was biting her tongue about Charlotte. I was too smitten to feel annoyed.

Harry waved goodbye to us, and I leaned back into my chair, letting the sun soak into my skin as a delighted feeling coursed through me. When "Barbara Ann" started up on the speakers, Gran muttered curse words under her breath.

"She was a little flirty, huh?"

I looked over at Gran in the passenger seat. She'd lost her sunglasses in the handful of yards between our car and the pool, and was now refusing to drive, as if without sunglasses she was legally blind.

"Charlotte?" I asked. We'd dropped her off a few blocks before.

She nodded. "With Harry."

"I didn't notice," I lied.

I'd noticed, but I was too happy to care, and I didn't want to let my mind go there. For all that Charlotte was, she was the best friend I'd ever had. The *only* friend I'd ever had.

"Well, let's just hope I'm paranoid." Gran pretended to study her nail beds. "But I'll warn you now because you're young, and at your best you're naive: girls like Charlotte don't always have loyalty. Hell, most girls don't have loyalty. I'd be careful."

I missed a stop sign and began to scan the street for Phil and his friends. "Did Mom know Lyla Sr.?"

"Turn right here," Gran said, pointing in the opposite direction of home. "I need to stop at the store."

I turned right and waited, wondering if she hadn't heard me.

"I don't think she did," she said, a few minutes later. "At least not well. Tim and Senior were a few years older than your mom, and she was—well, you know, otherwise occupied." She mimed a growing belly. Right. I'd happened. "Different sides of the track, if you will."

"So, she's not disloyal?" I asked. "Because they weren't friends?"

"Now, I didn't say that." Gran pointed at the liquor store beside the gas station. "Pull in here."

I obeyed and pulled into the spot by the door.

Gran undid her seat belt and turned to face me. "Here's what I'll say on the subject, and then we'll table this discussion for another day. Life's not all black and white, it's just one gray blob. Of course we shouldn't go around stabbing one another, but there's always a story that gets a person to that point. Pointing fingers isn't going to get us anywhere good."

She took a breath and looked like she wanted to say more. "Your mom and Tim? Maybe it's a darker shade of gray, more black than white, but it's still gray. No bad guys, just people. I'm not saying I like it. It just is what it is." She reached over to tuck my hair behind my ear. "Now I'm going to go in and grab myself a drink, and you a Cola, and then we're going home, and you're going out with Harry. Let's just be grateful for another day of sunlight, okay?"

I nodded. "Thanks, Gran."

"What for?" she asked, opening her door and planting one sandaled foot on the asphalt.

"I don't know—just for being you." I took in a deep breath, and the thoughts that had been plaguing me tumbled out. "I like being here. And I like being here with you."

I waited for her to make a joke or a snide remark, but she didn't. She just reached over and cupped my cheek with her hand. Her hand was warm and weathered and smelled like the sunblock she'd bought from Rexall and forced me to use. It smelled like home.

―――

The mail truck was down at the corner, and I realized I hadn't factored Tim into my plans with Harry. On our date I'd managed to avoid him crossing over into the little blue house without Tim in it, but with Tim actually there, the risk was just too great. I had to cancel. I'm sure the pool had a phone I could call. There was no reasonable way to explain the mailman on our couch and my mom draped across him.

"He might be gone before then," Gran said, like she was reading my mind.

I pulled the car into the driveway and braked so hard Gran's seat jolted forward. "And if he's not?"

"Then we—or, more accurately, *I*—will politely kick him out."

Mom turned around to smile at us when the door swung open. The sunlight flooded the darkened room with the drawn blinds, and then the light was gone.

"Hi ya," Tim said, his standard dad-like greeting.

"Hey, Tim," I said.

Satisfied by the pleasantries, Mom turned back to face the TV. "You guys almost missed your soaps."

Gran opened a new bottle, topping off her glass. "When your life is a soap, you find you need television less and less."

Tim smiled with just one corner of his mouth. "Your life is a soap opera?" he asked without any irony.

Gran didn't say anything. She just sat in her recliner and pulled on the lever that lifted her feet. I turned up the volume before taking my spot on the floor. Tim was stretched out across the couch with his head on Mom's lap.

"I meant to ask about your date," he said.

Mom's hands massaged his head, and my stomach turned a little. "It was fine."

"It was more than fine," Mom said, shaking her head at me. Sometimes I think she was a more conventional mother with Tim around. Or at least she pretended to be. "The kids had a great time."

Tim closed his eyes, and the show began its opening credits. "He's a good boy, so he's got my approval."

"I'm not sure how much your approval matters," Gran said, clearly irritated. I could tell by her face she immediately regretted saying it. She'd done her best to avoid Mom's minefields ever since we'd arrived.

I watched as red blotches splattered across Mom's chest and neck, and I tried to figure out if she was embarrassed or angry. After fifteen years I could usually read her moods like the weatherman. I should have started a daily forecast.

"*Of course* his approval matters, Mom," she said, and even with her blotchy skin she managed to keep her voice even. Gran opened her mouth to say something and then closed it. "Tim's a part of this family too."

Tim sat up so fast he knocked his beer off the couch arm rest, brown liquid pooling on the carpet. "Shit," he said. This was clearly news to him. His hat hair stuck out in both directions, and Mom offered him her best smile, reaching down to squeeze his knee.

"Does he know that?" Gran asked.

And then, with one look, I didn't have to wonder if Mom was embarrassed or angry. She stood up and her face was pure fury. Tim stood up too, and he looked a little terrified. It was always a wonder how someone so beautiful could look so ugly, like all of the ugly bits came out at once.

"Laine," he said softly, with a hand on her arm. "Maybe I should just go."

"No!" she yelled, and he stepped back from her like she'd slapped him. "You don't have to go," she said, softer this time, but her face was still pinched.

Gran was fiddling with the lever, trying to get the footrest to fold down. It took too many tries, but when it did, she stood. She wore a mocking smile.

"Tim"—she said his name like it was a curse word—"I think that might be for the best."

"No," Mom said, but this time she didn't yell. Sometimes her quiet voice was even scarier. "Tim can stay. You can't tell him to leave."

Tim stared at her hand on his arm like it was burning him. He looked like an actor who'd forgotten his lines, and for a second I almost laughed, because to an outsider the scene would have been comical. But I had a part to play too, and there was no way the daughter was supposed to laugh. That wasn't in the script.

"God, look at him, Laine," Gran said, taking a step toward the two of them. "The boy wants to leave, let him leave."

"Do you want to leave?" Mom asked, and suddenly Tim had three sets of eyes on him.

"I just think it might be best," he said, and Mom let out a long, shaky breath. She bent down to grab a cigarette out of her pack on the coffee table, and he reached in his pocket for a lighter. Her hand shook as he helped her light it. "I'll call you tonight. Or swing by another day."

The soap went on without us, and Laura was crying on the TV. Mom exhaled a cloud of smoke, and I wondered if she'd crack. Sometimes she let him get out the door before things fell apart.

"Did things change?" she asked.

He shook his head and leaned over to kiss her cheek, but he offered no parting words. We all watched him leave through the front door. Gran lowered herself back down into her recliner, and I stayed still in my spot on the floor. Mom's eyes remained on the space where he'd stood seconds before. She had two choices: walk to her room, or turn around and give us the whole of her wrath. I held my breath.

She took one step forward, toward the hall, before spinning around on her heel. Her blue eyes could have been red as fire for all the rage they held.

"I hope you're happy," she said, each word thick with her anger. The minute he left, she returned to the Mom I knew. "Thirty-three years old, and you still treat me like a damn child."

"Thirty-three years old, and you still act like one," Gran shot back. She began to fiddle with the recliner's lever again, so I knew she was gearing up for a fight. "He's not leaving her," she said, and her voice was just a little softer but still stern. "He's got a family he goes home to. I know he visits at the end of his shift, but there's no future in that, Laine. I see it. Tim sees it. Aurora sees it. You're the only one falling behind, the only one missing the memo."

Mom was the queen of turning her pain into anger. I watched the pain splash across her face, and I watched her fight it. I don't think she liked her sadness. She always shook herself free from it. The whole room shifted with her mood, and I could feel her anger leaving her body, filling the room, suffocating us all.

"You don't know that," she said. "You don't know his marriage. You don't know his life. His feelings for me. You're lonely and bitter and sad and mean."

Mom's comment hit too close to home—Gran was sad and she was lonely, but she had every reason to be. For a moment, Gran's face cracked wide open, betraying the sadness she'd kept hidden this summer. I could tell she was fighting against it, though, and as quickly as the sorrow came, it was gone.

Gran shook her head. "I never knew if you were optimistic or just plain stupid, but now I'm leaning toward the latter. And you can't be stupid when you've got a kid, Laine. You can't be selfish, not when—"

"Ha!" Mom practically screamed. I remember that laugh like an earthquake, shaking the walls, breaking down the foundation. "You want to talk about selfish? How about a twelve-year-old spending weekends alone while Mom's on a bender? Or a sixteen-year-old getting fucked in the back of the bar while Mom sleeps off the night? You know what? You're toxic. This town is toxic. Don't you *dare* call me selfish."

"Mom," I said, speaking up for the first time that afternoon, my voice quiet. Barely above a whisper. "You don't mean that. Don't say that."

She looked down at me in my spot on the floor. "Stay out of this, Aurora," she said, a stern warning.

"No," I said, forcing myself to stand. "You shouldn't say those things. People change."

Mom looked back and forth between Gran and me. "You're so toxic you turned her against me too."

I stepped toward her and she took a step back, bumping into the coffee table. "I'm not against you," I said. "No one is against you."

She turned so her back was to both of us and bent down to flick the cigarette's ashes into the ashtray. "You're all against me. This town is against me."

Gran sat back down in her recliner. "God, you're melodramatic."

Mom reached for Tim's half-empty Miller bottle. She spun around and held it over her head before throwing it past me. It shattered against the wall. Glass shards and beer rained down while Gran shielded her head.

Before anyone could yell or say anything, Mom was out the front door, slamming it behind her. Tears sprung to my eyes, but I brushed them away. I took a step toward Gran, and my bare foot landed on a sharp edge.

"Shit," I said, lifting my foot. The tears I'd been fighting forced their way out. A drop of blood landed on the carpet. Why was she like this?

"Don't move," Gran ordered.

Frozen, surrounded by broken glass, I watched her maneuver through the obstacle course of debris. Mom didn't have aim, but she had power, and the remains were everywhere.

Gran came back in the room with a broom, dustpan, and a Band-Aid for my toe, which was staining the carpet with drips of blood.

"Don't move," she said, lowering herself onto her knees.

She grabbed the big pieces first, careful not to cut herself on the shards. One by one she piled them into the dustpan. She worked in silence, and the world of the TV went on without her, figures continuing their storylines while we sorted out our own. The pieces collided with one another, the sounds of glass meeting glass. I focused on Gran's hands and their precision. Her watered-down whiskey was on the TV tray.

She looked up at me. "She wasn't aiming at you."

"I know." I nodded, biting my lip in an attempt not to cry.

She turned back to the task at hand. "Shit, this is a lot of glass."

When the pieces were too small for her fingers, she reached for the broom, which was ineffective on the carpet. She began sweeping around me, the broom tickling my toes. The pan was full of the remnants, and the tiniest pieces were embedded into our floor.

"I didn't even know we had a broom," I said.

Gran smiled. "Believe it or not, Jay did the housekeeping. I had to look pretty hard."

She set the pan aside, and I stared into it, piecing together the bottle like puzzle pieces with a bad fit. Gran waved her hand for me to sit, and I lowered myself back to the couch. She raised my foot to her eye level, examining my toe.

"No glass in there." She reached for the Band-Aid. "Had to search for this too. He had a kit under the sink. I swear that man thought of everything."

I could see just how much she missed him.

She wrapped it around my toe and held it tight. My chipped purple nail polish peeked out of the top.

"Really." Gran kept my foot between her warm hands. "It wasn't aimed at you."

There was a knock at the door, and Gran smiled.

"I'll tell him to leave," I said.

Gran stood and walked back to her recliner. "Why the hell would you do that?"

"Don't you want me to stay?" I asked.

"No. I want you to go out with that boy and have fun. I want you to forget about this place for a while."

"What if that's not possible?" I asked.

She smiled. "Then try. For me."

The glass-filled pan became the room's centerpiece, a reminder not meant for me.

"Should I move this?" I asked.

"No," she said. "Just leave it there. But turn up the TV before you go."

It felt wrong to leave her, but I knew that was what she wanted. Gran carried the weight of Jay's loss on her own, missing him in the moments no one was around. Sometimes I wished she'd share it with me, let me help, but that wasn't Gran. She wanted my happiness, and today, this afternoon, the person who could provide that happiness was busy knocking on my door.

I honored her request, twisting the dial so the sound filled the room. Before I left, I bent down to kiss her cheek, hoping it would communicate the things we'd never say aloud.

19

I studied Harry while he drove with both hands on the wheel. He'd reached over to manually roll down my window, and with each breath of warm summer air, I tried to forget. I tried to forget about my throbbing toe and my blood soaking the Band-Aid. I tried to forget about the things Mom said and would probably regret. I tried to forget about how quickly Tim left.

Harry's brown eyes narrowed while he watched the road with too much seriousness for a boy of seventeen.

"You're a careful driver," I said.

He laughed and glanced over at me briefly. "Shane always makes fun of me. Says I drive like my dad."

"So you drive like a preacher?"

"A preacher *and* an old man—which is worse." His body relaxed with his laugh. "I guess it's 'cause he taught me. It's his first driving rule: better safe than sorry."

I thought of Mom and Gran and the lives they'd chosen to live. That rule never made our family list, driving or otherwise. I reached my arm out the window. The trees were too far away to touch, but that didn't stop me from trying.

Looking at Harry, I couldn't help but smile. Just being near him filled me with an inexplicable warmth. There was something comforting about his driving, even if his style was kind of funny. It wasn't just knowing we'd arrive safe. It was the in-between, the "getting there" part with Harry that put me at ease.

"So where are we going?" I finally asked.

Any time Harry smiled at you, you just had to smile back. "The best spot in all of Monroe."

I rested my arm on the window and felt the rushing air escape between my fingers. I was shaken up from the fight, hoping my unsteadiness wasn't showing. "That's certainly something to look forward to."

He turned left, in the opposite direction of downtown. I was relieved the best spot in Monroe wouldn't be populated with half the town.

"I bet Gran—I mean Katherine—is bored when you're not around."

"I think it's the opposite."

He pursed his lips, and I thought of the scene on our porch. I couldn't help but smile. Saturday seemed like forever ago, but really only two days had passed. Summer days were always long, but this summer the days felt like lifetimes.

"What do you mean by that?" he asked.

"Well, I mean, you've seen her. I'm not the one who brings the fun to the party. She's got her own supply."

He took one hand off the wheel to playfully shove my shoulder. "I bet you bring some fun."

I rolled my eyes and reached over to shove him back. "Maybe more fun than a preacher's son, but I don't think that's saying much."

His mouth fell open in mock surprise before he laughed. "Well, you inherited her sass, that's for sure."

"I'll be sure to tell her you said that. Right after I tell her you keep calling her *Gran*."

Harry put the car in park. I'd missed him turning off the road into a clearing.

"You won't do that," he said, "because you want her to like me."

Without his hands on the wheel, he looked much more relaxed. He turned in his seat to face me.

"You're feeling pretty sure of yourself." I gestured to our surroundings. "But I will say this looks an awful lot like the river, so you might be overestimating your appeal."

"Stay put," he said before quickly opening his door and getting out of the car. I laughed while he ran around the front to open mine. I liked that things about him were becoming familiar. He offered me his hand with more confidence than he had Saturday night.

"This is the best spot in Monroe?" I asked, gesturing my free hand at the surrounding trees.

He shook his head. "No, the best spot takes a bit more work. You'll have to follow me."

And I did. I trailed a few feet behind, following him, step for step, for what seemed like forever. Twenty minutes in, I realized the path to wherever Harry was taking me wasn't an easy one. I don't know if you could even call it a path. We walked across logs and climbed over fallen trees. I scaled a rock with his hands around my waist. It didn't help that the sun was relentless, finding ways to beat down on us between the shaded patches from the trees.

"You're trying to kill me," I said, out of breath.

Harry was up on a rock he'd just climbed, looking down at me.

"You're cute when you frown," he said, and then he blushed.

Whenever Harry complimented me, his face turned the best shade of pink.

"I don't know how cute I'll be when I'm angry."

He offered me a hand, and after a dramatic huff I took it.

"I'm sure you'll still be cute, but don't worry—we're almost there."

I watched him hop off the rock with ease, and he turned to face me.

I crawled down its side, too scared to jump. "Do you know what I'm normally doing at this time?"

"What?"

"Watching *General Hospital*, maybe *Edge of Night*." Tim always made a case for *M*A*S*H* reruns, but Gran never gave in. I looked up at the sky to track the sun. "Well, maybe local news if it's after five."

He raised his face to the sky, radiant in the sun's glow, extending his arms out from his side, like he was one with nature. "Isn't this so much better?"

"I don't know. *Edge of Night* is pretty good."

He took my hand to guide me over a rotted log. "We don't have a television."

I stopped atop the log, stunned. "What?"

He tugged on my hand and I jumped down.

"What I said." He studied my face and then laughed, startling the birds in the surrounding trees. "My family never had a television."

Of all the things that made us different, it was this I couldn't fathom. "Are you serious?"

He nodded emphatically, still laughing. "Is that so shocking?"

"I don't know. I mean, I guess not. Is that why you spend your time climbing up rocks and jumping over logs?"

He continued walking and I trailed behind him, matching each of his steps. "I guess. It's not like I've never watched television. I have friends, you know."

I smiled. "I know."

"And it's nice to be outside." His fingers brushed against mine. "Especially outside with you." There was that perfect pink again. "Don't you think?"

"I think Monroe is too hot for this kind of physical activity," I teased.

"Well," he said, finally taking my hand in his and dragging me along even farther down the invisible path toward the invisible destination, "one of these days you can invite me over, and I'll experience your idea of a perfect summer afternoon. But today it's my turn."

"Fair enough," I said, letting myself get pulled along. "Am I your perfect travel companion?" I gave him my cheesiest smile.

"My perfect travel companion is less of a complainer."

"Hey!"

"Don't worry." He wrapped his arm around my shoulder. "What you lack in positivity you make up for in good looks."

"Gran always says positive people are overcompensating for something."

"I'm probably her worst nightmare," he said before stopping suddenly. "Okay, we're almost there. Close your eyes."

"What?"

"Will you just humor me and close your eyes?"

"I think this is the part where I die. If you dump my body in the lake, it'll wash up on the shore. You're better off with a bonfire." Gran liked shows with a dash of murder. "Some sort of cremation."

He pressed his pointer finger to my lips, silencing me. Not that I could have founds words to speak, with him standing this close. "Can you just close your eyes?"

I closed them. "Okay, okay. They're closed."

With both my hands in his, I let myself be pulled forward. Branches brushed against my arm, and then they didn't. I could tell the dirt and mud had switched to sand, and I could smell the water, hear the way it swished around, while waves from boats pushed against the shore.

"Keep your eyes closed," he said, like he knew me well enough to know I was desperate to peek. He grabbed my shoulders and turned me a little to the left. "Okay, now open them."

The sun wavered on the water's surface, the lake sparkling the world's reflection back at itself. I could see the Ferris wheel in the lake before I looked up at it, looming across the water. It was spinning in endless circles. The lake itself was littered with tourist spots across the water, the places I'd gone when Indiana Beach was just a place to visit. Our patch of land was clean, the trees ending by the sand bank that led to the water.

When we'd first visited Monroe, I couldn't believe Gran lived somewhere with an actual lake. But then Mom told me the lake was artificially created, just a poor man's attempt at an ocean. She said there were bigger and better lakes all throughout this country. Everything outside of Indiana was bigger and better.

Harry was staring straight ahead, beaming with those teeth of his. "Pretty great, huh?"

"The lake does look pretty from here," I said.

"It *is* pretty. Or at least parts of it are."

He was grinning so big I had to laugh. "You're feeling really proud of yourself, huh?"

He sat down first, leaving plenty of room for me. I ignored my instinct to sit with feet of space between us and sat close to him, my bare legs pressed against his. I hadn't changed out of my shorts and tank top, and I hadn't had time to do much to my hair.

"How did you ever end up here?" I asked.

"Well, I didn't have a TV, so I had to find my own entertainment. My dad used to come out here with me, but he's got bad knees now."

"Your dad is kind of . . ." I searched for the right word, picturing the preacher in his ill-fitting suit at the funeral.

"Old," Harry filled in. He laughed. "You can say it."

I smiled. "I just always had a young mom, I guess."

"He is really old. Truth is, he and my mom had a hard time having kids. A really hard time. She was thirty-eight when the doctor told her it was a lost cause." He squinted out at the lake, and I tried to match his gaze. "The week before she turned forty-three, she threw up six days in a row, and then she took a test. My dad thought I must be a miracle, God ordained, but that didn't mean he wasn't terrified. The whole church fasted and prayed for months, taking turns. Each Sunday they celebrated her."

"And here you are," I said, swinging my knees so they bumped his. "I'm on a date with a miracle."

The corners of his mouth turned up, but just for a second.

"It's quite a bit of pressure, though?" I reached for his hand, and he let me take it. "To be this great gift from God?"

He let out a sigh, and it sounded like he'd been holding it in for all his seventeen years on the earth. "I don't really want to be a preacher." He said it like a confession.

"Are you supposed to be a preacher?"

"Well, I don't know. It's just sort of implied. My grandpa was the preacher, his grandpa too. We've all been stuck in this same town for too many years now. No one's ever told me I have to be the preacher, but no one's told me I don't have to either."

"What do you want to be?"

He shrugged. "I don't even know. I mean, what's the point of thinking about something that'll never happen?"

I knew what he meant, more than I could even explain to him. I knew what it was like to tell yourself there was no point in hoping for what could never be. No point in wanting something you'd never have. And yet here I was, on the shore of the lake with Harold Clark, hoping and wanting for more than I'd ever allowed myself. I didn't want to stop hoping. I didn't want to stop wanting. I didn't want him to stop either.

He'd offered so much about himself, and I wanted to do the same. I could tell him the things I was afraid of, the things that weighed me down. But I knew that telling him those things would send him running, and I wasn't ready to let him go. I couldn't be honest with him, and in that moment it felt unfair.

That conversation was the longest I'd gone without seeing his toothy smile, and I was desperate for it.

"Well, Harold Clark, I think you've spent seventeen years on this earth, and it's about time you start letting yourself dream. You're not your dad, and I'm not my mom." It was the smallest confession, admitting that I didn't want to become her. But saying it aloud released some of the weight on my chest. Harry's fingers intertwined with mine, and my stomach did the increasingly familiar flip. "We're just Aurora and Harry. Maybe we can be anything we darn well please."

He squeezed my hand. "You always this sure of yourself?"

I shook my head. "Almost never."

"What happened?" he asked.

He was looking at my toe.

"I stepped on some glass," I said, tucking my feet under my legs.

"Ouch. Didn't Gran teach you not to walk around barefoot?"

I didn't tell him it was in my own house. "She's not big on life lessons."

"Well, I'll invite you over, and my parents can give you a rundown of the basics. Do unto others as you'd have them do unto you. Be kind and honest. If you're too lazy to plow, don't expect a harvest."

"The Ten Commandments?"

He laughed. "If you think those are the Ten Commandments, I've got to get you to church."

I actually knew a handful of the commandments from the TV preacher, but I didn't know if I should tell him that or not. I think Mom and Gran had broken most of them, some more than once. I was still doing okay except for the smaller ones. Even I lied every now and then.

"So, if I break a commandment, I go to hell?" I asked, curious where I stood with the man upstairs.

"Well, no, not if you ask for forgiveness."

"But what if I break a commandment because if I don't, something bad will happen? Like what if it seems right at the time? Are there situational passes or anything?"

He looked stunned, but then his face broke into that glorious smile. "I really should have you over for dinner. I think my dad would love it."

I laughed. "I don't know about that. I'm worried he'll see my bad parts before you do."

He reached over and took my hand. "You always do that."

"Do what?"

"You know, pretend you aren't as great as you are."

I rolled my eyes. "I'm definitely not as great as you think I am."

He turned away from me but kept my hand in his. I watched him look both ways. He looked back at me and leaned over to the right, checking behind me for who knows what. I turned around to see what he was seeing, but there was nothing. Just trees.

"Hello?" he called out, cupping his hands around his mouth so his voice carried across the lake.

"Harry, what in the heck are you looking for?"

He smiled before he leaned in closer, taking my chin in his hand. "I'm just checking for Karl, making sure he's not hiding anywhere."

I threw my head back and laughed. He was funnier than I'd ever expected. And I loved that he knew nothing about the world I'd left, filled with broken glass and yelling. His world was filled with life lessons and Ten Commandments and cautious driving. To me, Harry was like the best parts of summer, the moments just before the world swallowed the sun, the sudden relief from the too hot days.

There was no Karl to stop us, and no Tim on the other side of the door. It was just the two of us on the muddied patch of land that was so much better than the river. I smiled just before his lips met mine, and I tried to remember everything about that moment. Not because I wanted to tell Charlotte or Gran or Mom, but because I couldn't think of a time I'd ever felt so infinitely happy.

"I think you might be right," I said, breaking apart so I could look at him.

His teeth were even nicer up close. "About what?"

"This might be the best place in all of Monroe."

And then I kissed him again.

∽

The house was exactly as I'd left it. The TV was still on. The dustpan was in the center of the room. Gran was in her recliner. The only difference was the cold pot roast on the side table.

"You're home early," Gran said.

I took Mom's spot on the couch. "Preacher's son curfew."

Gran smiled. "Do you want a curfew? I could give you one."

"Sure."

"Home before sunrise, not a minute later."

I rolled my eyes. "Maybe we should start with midnight and work my way up."

"Okay midnight it is. How's the Prince Charming?"

"He's fine," I said. President Carter was on TV, and he looked like he was going to tell us the world was ending. "Is Mom home?"

Gran shook her head. "She needs time to cool off. I made sure the phone's on the hook in case someone from King's calls."

"I'm going to be sad to leave," I said.

"Leave?"

"Leave here." I pulled my hair back into a ponytail. "Monroe."

Gran stood up and walked to the TV. She turned the dial, and the screen went black.

"Who said anything about you leaving?"

"Well, no one. I'm just looking at the signs."

She sat back down in the recliner and turned so she was facing me.

"What signs? Enlighten me."

"I mean, the Tim thing's bound to explode. You saw him this afternoon. He's been blowing smoke—there's no way he's leaving them." In that moment, I felt wise. I felt like a realist. "I just know her well enough to know she can't survive this one. She won't even try to."

All this time I thought Gran knew what was coming. Even this afternoon, she'd been the one saying it couldn't work out. I'd assumed she knew the end was in sight, but the look on her face told me she hadn't considered this part of the aftermath.

"Gran," I continued, explaining the way things worked, "I've been enrolled in thirteen schools, and I'm only a junior. The fact we didn't leave days after the funeral is a miracle from above."

"But you like it here?" she asked.

I nodded my head. "Of course I do. I love it here." And then I said four words I'd never said in my fifteen years on earth. "It feels like home."

"Then let's not count the eggs before they hatch. Nothing's happened yet."

I thought of the Band-Aid on my toe and Mom's sharp laugh and the tiniest bits of glass still embedded in the carpet. So much had happened.

Still, I smiled at Gran because I thought she needed to see me smile. "Maybe you can come with us."

She didn't laugh like she was supposed to. I watched her rise from her recliner and grab her pot roast off the TV tray before heading into the kitchen. When she came back, she had a glass with ice and a clear liquid, which was far from her usual.

"You out of whiskey?" I asked. "I can go get you some."

She shook her head, taking a sip and making a face. "I'm all right."

20

Whenever I got upset when I was young, Mom would tell me to close my eyes and fall asleep. "The world might look different when you wake up," she'd say. And even though I'd wake up in the same bed in the same room, with the same caged bird by the window, my world always felt turned around. The bad was made right just by eight hours of shutting my eyes. It was my favorite magic trick.

Close your eyes, and the world might look different. Maybe that was the first rule she taught me: avoid the problem, and hope it fixes itself.

That next morning, I woke up to the sunlight spilling onto my bed sheets. My shelves were lined with the same layers of dust. I was wearing the same pajamas. And when I walked down the hall barefoot and opened the door to her room, Mom's bed was still empty. The world felt the exact same as it had the day before, and that terrified me. She might've stayed up all night for all I knew, never giving herself a chance to work her magic.

Gran was still in her recliner, and the TV screen was still black.

"No Mom?" I asked, and she just shook her head. "Should we call someone?"

"No, she'll turn up. I'm never too worried about her."

I didn't believe her, and I could tell she didn't believe herself. In the weeks turned into months of Tim, we'd gotten used to Mom coming home every night. Nights like the one at King's were a thing of the past. The panic was familiar, but it had been so long neither one of us knew what to do.

Gran rose from her recliner and moved toward the kitchen. "What's on your agenda?"

I followed close behind. "I told Harry I'd go to the pool, and I told Charlotte I'd pick her up. But I can always cancel."

She reached in the cupboard and pulled out a glass. I knew the routine, what she'd reach for next, which is why I was surprised when she moved toward the fridge. She twisted off the cap of the orange juice and brought it up to her nose, inhaling.

"Is this still good?" she asked.

I shrugged. "Beats me."

"Go to the pool." She poured a little bit in her glass, pausing to taste it before filling it to the top. "You can take the car if you want. I'm going to sit this one out, in case she calls. And don't you dare offer to stay home again. You know I won't let you."

I left her in the kitchen, drinking her orange juice and pretending like she wasn't worried about where her daughter was. And even though I felt bad leaving her in the house filled with stale air, I was relieved when the sunshine hit my face.

I decided against the car because of the Phil factor—I was one month away from my license, and there was no point in pushing my limits. The two of them—Mom and Gran—could talk their way out of anything, but I'd missed out on that trait.

My bike carried me down the street, and I took a left at the corner, past Norma's hand-sewn curtains. Charlotte was on her front porch.

"Oh God," she said when she saw me, "Where's Gran? Where's the car?"

She walked down the driveway like each step was taking all of her energy.

"You're not even the one pedaling. You just get to ride on the pegs and look pretty."

"There's nothing to stop the sun from beating down on me," she whined. Resigned, she placed a perfectly manicured hand on each of my shoulders. "You didn't answer my question. Where's Gran?"

"Sitting by the fan," I said, starting to pedal. "Watching her shows."

"And Laine?" Charlotte was terrible at keeping secrets, always ruining punch lines before the end of the joke. Her voice betrayed her.

I placed both feet on the asphalt, bringing the bike to a sudden stop in the middle of her street. Her body slammed into my back.

"Ow," she said.

I twisted around so I could face her. "What do you know?"

She pursed her lips when she smiled. "Well, I know she went to King's last night and was seen leaving with a certain someone."

"Tim?" I asked. If Charlotte knew they'd left together, who knows who else had seen them. They were careless with their secret—I could hear the countdown from the invisible clock.

Charlotte shook her head. "A certain cop," she said, stopping my spiraling thoughts in their tracks. "Dressed in his tropical best."

"Says who?" I asked.

"Says everyone." She pretended to study her nails. "Or at least my mom."

I guess I should have spent less time worrying over where she'd gone and more time worrying about who she was with. I wondered who else had noticed her leave with Phil and what had transpired. In a town like Monroe, no one was more than two degrees of separation from any other person. Tim would find out. That much I knew.

I began to pedal, the starting up the hardest part. My legs shook as I pushed each pedal down before I found my rhythm.

"Wait," she said when I turned left at the corner. "Where are we going?"

"The pool."

The sun was relentless.

"Don't you want to tell Gran?" she asked.

I shook my head, and for a brief moment a breeze blew through my hair. I relished it.

Of course I wanted to tell Gran. Almost more than anything in the world. Almost. Because more than wanting to turn the bike around and pedal straight down the cul-de-sac, past the rose bushes, and into our driveway, I wanted to see Harry. I wanted him to smile at me from the top of the lifeguard tower. I wanted Charlotte to throw her head back and laugh at things that weren't that funny. I wanted to soak up sunshine.

I didn't turn around. I continued to press each pedal down, forcing myself forward, away from the little blue house and the secrets it held. They would be there waiting for me when I got home. That much I knew.

My time at the pool, my time with Charlotte, my time with Harry—all of it would disappear any day now. There was no way we'd stick around until my birthday. I'd celebrate with Mom, like I'd always done, propped up on a stool while she worked the counter. I wasn't ready to say goodbye to Monroe. Not yet.

The pool was more crowded than usual. I think the heat was starting to get to everyone, and the whole town was searching for relief. Harry's tower was empty, and I began to scan the crowd for him.

"Oh shit," Charlotte said, us noticing the same thing at once.

Lyla Rae Jr. was holding court with her friends. Harry stood beside them in his red lifeguard shorts, and Shane was stretched across a lounge chair.

"Aurora!" Harry called, noticing us as we noticed him.

He waved me over, and Charlotte reached for my hand.

"This should be interesting," she whispered, dragging me behind her, ensuring I wouldn't make a run for it.

We walked around the edge of the pool to the lounge chairs populated by people we'd never talk to otherwise. Lucky for me, Charlotte was confident enough for the both of us, managing to lead the way with her signature charm. Only I could tell the smile she wore was menacing.

When we reached the group, I remembered to smile.

"Hi," Harry said, just to me.

"Good to see you, Harold," Charlotte said.

"Charlotte." He gestured to the group of familiar faces. "I'm sure Charlotte knows everyone, but Aurora, this is Lyla, Ronnie, Marie, and of course Shane." He reached for my hand. "Guys, this is Aurora."

The girls wore strained smiles, and Shane looked like he might fall asleep.

"Hey—I know *you*." Lyla smiled, and I felt my stomach drop. "You work at the bowling alley, right?"

"Yes, she does." Charlotte began speaking for me when the silence went on a beat too long. "She practically runs the place."

We stood before them like defendants awaiting a verdict. Would they ask us to sit? Or would they make us stand there for all of eternity? Harry's hand was warm in mine, and then he let go.

"I've got to get back," he said, nodding toward the tower. "I'll come say hi on my break."

"Okay," I said, too full of nerves to find more words.

Lyla stood and squished herself beside Marie, the two of them sharing a lounge chair. "Sit, sit," she said. "You guys can share my seat."

Charlotte laid out her towel, seemingly unnerved by the whole situation. "Thanks."

She shimmied out of shorts, and peeled off her tank top, waking Shane up in the process. I watched Lyla pretend not to care and Charlotte pretend not to notice the audience observing her. She took the side of the chair closest to Lyla, winking at me.

I undressed much faster, sitting beside Charlotte, in the spot closest to Shane.

Marie angled herself toward us, cutting Ronnie out of the group. Her one-piece was modest, but it looked expensive. I remembered that her parents owned the Italian restaurant in town, Norma's sole competition. On Fridays, you could eat dinner by candlelight. The boys on the rich side of town took their dates there. Charlotte assured me it wasn't as nice as it sounded.

"So you and Harry are . . . ?" Marie's voice trailed off.

"Dating," Charlotte answered. "Aurora and Harry are dating."

"He really likes her," Shane said.

I looked over to offer a smile, but his eyes were shut.

"For how long?" Marie asked. "I know you've been in town for, like, a minute."

"Not long," I said.

"And you like him, yeah?" Lyla propped herself up on her elbows to look at me, her sunglasses slipping to the tip of her nose.

"I do," I answered.

"And you're a good person?" she asked.

I wasn't sure how to answer that—I tried to be good, but how many of Mom's decisions reflected back on me? Was I responsible for her? For Gran? The town treated Mom, Gran, and me like we were cut from the same cloth. And sometimes, when Tim left earlier than expected, turning down our offer for a frozen TV dinner, I felt a pang of sadness. But it's not like I would have wanted this—not really.

"The best person," Charlotte answered when I didn't. I wasn't sure how much her opinion mattered to this particular group, but I was grateful for her confidence in me.

"Good." Lyla lowered herself back onto the chair. "Harry is the nicest guy I know, so he deserves someone nice."

My body felt frozen despite the heat, a cold sweat covering my skin.

"Well, Aurora is the best person I know," Charlotte said, each word drenched with her attitude. She adjusted her sunglasses. "So it looks like they're perfect for each other."

She threw in a pageant smile for good measure. Charlotte and I had exchanged minimal words on the subject of Harry, but it felt good to have someone on my side, in my corner. Charlotte grabbed my hand and squeezed it.

The problem was I didn't feel like a good person. I felt like I might throw up. I closed my eyes, but when I did, I saw Tim with his head in Mom's lap. I saw the smoky haze of the living room, her leading him down the hall. I saw Lyla Rae Jr. in the bowling alley with her dad. I forced my eyes open and looked up at the sun, hoping to burn the images from my mind.

Charlotte stood up with her hand still in mine, dragging me up with her. "It's too hot to sunbathe—let's swim."

Lyla Jr. rose from her chair, and I realized her hair wasn't in her signature ponytail. It cascaded down her back in long blonde spirals. Her one-piece was coral to match her nails and lip gloss, and her body looked more like Charlotte's than mine. All curves and breasts. Shane seemed to notice too.

"I'll join you two," she said.

Marie's eyes fluttered open, a shock of blue. "Me too," she said, rising from her chair.

"Great," Charlotte managed.

As each girl moved, Shane observed the two of them with a lazy smile, their long blonde hair attracting the attention of the boys at the pool. Marie and I trailed behind them, and when I looked up at the tower, Harry was smiling at me. It felt good to be watched by someone.

"Are you seeing anyone?" Charlotte asked Lyla Jr., taking a seat on the shallow end step.

Lyla Jr. shook her head. "This town doesn't have much to offer. You?"

"I'm not sure if you know Kevin Martin—he's older." Charlotte flipped her hair with the back of her hand. "He graduated this year."

In the world of the soap opera, this was the start of a catfight. Throwing down the gauntlet with subtle brags, each girl's attempt to show off. I was interested in who would come out on top, and grateful mine was just the supporting role.

"College plans?" Lyla asked, probably knowing that wasn't the case.

Charlotte faltered, but only for a second. "Actually, he works at the auto shop. His dad owns it, so it's only a matter of time before he takes over."

Lyla's smile wasn't sweet. "That's so great." She turned to face me and smiled, and I could have died right then. "You really did luck out with Harry."

I just nodded, too terrified to try and find words.

"We only dated a few months, but he was the best boyfriend," she said, tossing her final trump card on the table, unaware that I had the ultimate trump card in my hand.

Really, we were all just supporting roles, the small bits between the love story spilling over into multiple seasons. Luke and Laura. Chuck and Donna. Tim and Laine.

Charlotte's green eyes narrowed into slits. "I had no idea you two had dated."

"Oh really?" Lyla kicked her feet in the water. "It was the end of our sophomore year. Don't worry," she said, making sure to make eye contact with only me, "we're both totally over it."

"Well, I'd hope so," Charlotte said, and for a moment I wondered if I could sink beneath the water, if anyone would notice. Maybe their conversation could go on without me. Charlotte's voice was flat when she said, "It's great you two can still be friends."

Marie spoke up. "Best friends," she clarified.

"Aurora!" Harry yelled, and I flinched at the sound of my name. He was waving me over, but I felt little relief.

"Excuse me," I said, rising from the water. I hated myself for sounding so mousy.

He climbed down the ladder, and his smile was so big I had to smile back. "What are you doing two hours from now?" he asked.

I gestured at the pool and the people in it. "Well, this."

He shook his head. "Wrong. You're coming with me."

He reached for my hand and intertwined my fingers with his. I wondered if this is what Mom felt with Tim or with the other men who'd come and gone. Maybe she just wanted to feel a tingling down to her toes, like her heart might float outside of her body, up, up, and away to the sky.

"Harry, I'm starting to think you don't like to share me." It was so much easier to use words with him, and the panic I'd felt just moments before was slowly subsiding. "You just want me all to yourself."

He grinned and tugged me closer. "Is that so bad?"

Before I could overthink it, I leaned forward and kissed him, blocking out the rest of the world when I closed my eyes. It was short and sweet, just enough to anchor me.

He ran a hand through his hair and smiled, like I'd shocked him into silence.

"Come get me when you're off."

Charlotte, Lyla, and Marie were in the shallow end, watching, and Charlotte's stunned expression morphed into a smile. She wiggled her eyebrows, reminding me of Gran.

Lyla Jr. stood up before I could reach them, walking past me to her chair and her towel. Marie trailed close behind.

"Well done, Aurora. I think that shut them up." Charlotte grinned. "I didn't know you had it in you."

I rolled my eyes, embarrassed.

"And Aurora?" she said, tilting her head to the side, reminding me of young Charlotte on the Ferris wheel.

"Yeah?"

"I hope you know you're not your mom."

༺ ༻

If Charlotte didn't hate Lyla before, that afternoon sealed her fate as enemy number one. Still, despite her indignation, Charlotte remained with me in the pool for the next two hours while our fingers and toes turned to prunes. And when Harry came over at the end of his shift, she offered to ride my bike home.

"Are you sure?" I asked. She wasn't the type to do favors.

"I mean I might die of heatstroke, but yeah, I'm sure."

So once again I was following Harry to an unknown destination. I couldn't help but wonder if Mom had come home yet. I hoped there were no nearby breakables, and I hoped Gran hadn't poured herself too many drinks.

Much to my dismay, Harry turned right toward downtown.

"Are you hungry?" he asked. "I'm always starved after my shift."

I watched the businesses as they came into view, shop after shop, stacked side by side. They were different colors with different window displays. I liked how in a town every shop had its purpose.

"I'm hungry," I said, resigning myself to the inevitable.

He pulled into a spot in front of Norma's. Through the glass I could see her, her signature work ponytail cascading down her back. Of all the places I'd thought Mom could be, work was not one of them. She never thought twice about missing a shift.

I pointed toward the diner. "My mom's working."

"Oh." Harry put the truck in park and unclipped his seat belt. "Will that be weird?"

I shook my head and offered a closed-mouth smile. "No. It'll be nice for you to meet her."

He reached over to tuck a stray hair behind my ear. "I love the way your hair looks after you swim."

I sucked in a breath, feeling dizzy.

"And if your mom didn't have a clear view out Norma's window, I'd kiss you right now."

"Maybe you can owe me one," I said, my voice coming out like a whisper.

"Deal."

Harry jumped out of his seat, running around the front of the car to get to my door. I waited because this was something I'd gotten used to.

He took my hand when the door dinged above us, Mom's busy eyes flicking over our way. She looked startled, but she forced a smile, and I waved.

I took a stool at the counter. "We can sit here."

Harry followed my lead and took the stool beside me.

"Aurora," Mom said, "what are you doing here?"

"What are *you* doing here?" I reached past Harry for a menu, setting one in front of him. "I didn't think you had a shift."

She shifted her weight from one leg to the other, her hip jutting out. "Picked it up this morning."

Harry wiped his palm on his shorts before reaching his hand across the counter. "I don't think we've officially met. I'm Harold Clark, but everyone calls me Harry."

"Oh, sorry," I said. "Of course. Mom, Harry. Harry, this is Mom."

"Nice to meet you, Mrs.—" He caught himself.

"You can just call me Laine." She smiled her best smile. "It's nice to meet you, Harry. I've heard only good things."

"Same here," he said.

Mom reached for her notepad. "That's a relief. So you two hungry or what?"

He studied the menu. Beads of nervous sweat had formed on his neck. "Starving."

"I'll just get my usual," I said, reaching under the counter for his hand.

He looked over at me and smiled. "I'll take Aurora's usual."

Mom stacked our menus and slid them between two napkin holders. The place was busy, the lunch rush still going strong. I watched her move down the counter and refill drink after drink, brushing her hair back from her eyes. I wonder if she'd stopped at home for her uniform or if she wore a spare. Maybe Phil drove her after their sleepover. Tim obviously wasn't spending the afternoon at our house.

"So what have I gotten myself into?" Harry asked.

"What do you mean?"

"Well, I'm a little scared of 'your usual.'"

"Oysters, the season special," I said, laughing when his eyes got big. "It's a cheeseburger with extra pickles. We're at a diner in Central Indiana. I think you're safe."

Mom set two Coca-Colas in front of us before continuing her endless route.

"Is your mom dating anyone?" Harry asked.

"No," I said, with enough emphasis to make Harry take notice.

"That big of a *no*, huh?"

I laughed. "I just mean, no, she's not."

"It's weird to talk about parents' dating lives, huh?"

"A little."

Just then the door swung open, the ding announcing someone's presence. I saw Mom's eyes flicker to the door, and then they stayed there. I turned in my stool to see what she was looking at—who she was looking at. I didn't really have to look to know. Her face gave her away.

"Tim," I said before I could catch myself.

Harry followed my lead, spinning his stool to get a better look. He hopped down and walked to the door, wearing his friendliest smile and stretching a hand out in greeting. "Mr. Harrison!" he said.

Tim pulled Harry in for a hug. "Harry! How are you?"

Mom exchanged looks with me, but then a man asked for more coffee, and she moved to get the pot. Tim was in his mailman uniform.

"Lunch break?" Harry asked.

"I guess not." Tim shook his head. "This place is too crowded for me. A coffee to go!" he yelled.

"You sure? There's a spot by us." Harry waved me over. "Aurora, this is Lyla's dad, Mr. Harrison. We were just at the pool with Lyla."

"We've met," I said.

"She's on my mail route," Tim explained.

Harry smiled like this was the most natural interaction in the world, and I watched Mom watch us. She came around the counter with a to-go cup. Tim said a polite thank-you. She walked to the nearest table to see if they needed anything. To Tim's credit, his eyes never lingered.

The whole diner felt too small, and I was relieved when Tim clapped Harry on the back before offering me a polite wave. He made brief eye contact with Mom just before the door swung shut behind him.

I sat back down on my stool. "You never told me you dated Lyla."

Harry grinned and swiveled the stool so he was facing me, our knees touching.

"You jealous?"

"I didn't say that. I just said you never told me."

"It's okay if you are." He looked cocky when he took a swig of his Coca-Cola.

"Ew," I said, reaching over to push his shoulder.

He choked on his drink when he laughed. "I'm kidding, I'm kidding. It was so short-lived. I dated her, like, a week sophomore year. We're friends. It was nothing like—" He stopped himself, his voice trailing off.

"Nothing like what?" I asked, nudging his knee with mine. "Nothing like me?"

Pink washed over his skin, starting in his cheeks and making its way down his neck.

"Harold Clark, are you trying to say I'm someone special?"

"Dang it, Aurora," he said, laughing. "Haven't you figured that out already?"

Now it was my turn to blush. I couldn't imagine why he'd chosen me—what in the world would make him ask *me* out. I told Gran that once, how it made no sense to me at all.

"It makes sense to me," she said.

Just then Mom set our plates in front of us. He looked relieved, but she didn't.

"Thank you," he said.

Her voice was strained when she said, "Of course."

I watched him pick off all eight pickles, setting them on my plate. "I actually hate pickles," he explained.

And even though Mom looked upset, I couldn't help but laugh.

❧

Less than an hour after Harry dropped me off, Mom walked through the front door. She looked exhausted. Her eyes were swollen like she'd been crying.

"Hi, hon," Gran said, her voice soft.

Before Mom could speak, she burst into tears, a silent, open-mouthed sob as tiny droplets rolled down each cheek. Gran rose from her recliner and moved to hold her, but Mom stepped back and shook her head. She walked down the hall, leaving us both behind.

"What the hell?" Gran said.

I shrugged. "Your guess is as good as mine."

"Are you going to check on her?"

"Are *you*?"

Sassing Gran was a losing battle, and the moment the words left my mouth, I regretted them.

"That's your mom in there," she said, scolding. "Get off of your ass and go check on her."

"Okay," I said. *"Gosh."*

I rose from my spot on the floor and emphasized each step down the hall toward her room. The door was shut, so I knocked.

"No," she said.

"Mom, it's Aurora." I turned the door handle and pushed against it. "I'm coming in."

She was in her bra and underwear on top of the covers. Her uniform and apron were in a crumpled ball on the floor. Thick curtains covered the room's single window, but they didn't stop the heat from making its way in.

I searched the closet for an empty hanger and bent down to pick up her uniform, hanging it in the closet before taking a seat on the edge of her bed. She'd thank me later.

"Do you want to talk about it?"

She shook her head, and the silent tears started up again. I watched them fall down the sides of her cheek, landing in her hair and soaking parts of her pillow.

"I bet you'll feel better," I said.

She sat up and scooted back against the headboard, patting the spot beside her. I crawled across the bed and stretched my legs out.

"Remember Lafayette?" she asked.

I nodded. "Barely. Was that the one with The American Diner?"

"Yes." She wiped her tear-stained cheeks with the back of her hand. "That manager had the mole between his eyes, and you asked him why he had three eyes."

I laughed. "How old was I?"

"I think you were six. Maybe seven. After that we went to Fort Wayne."

"With Sean," I said, his name suddenly coming to me. "He was the one with the bird. Rosie."

"Yes! I totally forgot about Rosie." Her gaze was fixed on a spot by the dresser Gran and she shared. "She always freaked me out."

"I freed her once," I said. "Opened her cage and let her out."

"You did? Where was I?"

I brought my knees up to my chest. "Working."

"Harry seems nice." She reached over to brush my hair back from my eyes. "I'm sorry Tim showed up. I didn't know he was coming by. Promise."

"Were you really at Phil's last night?"

She nodded. "Poor Phil. He's too nice for his own good."

"I think he loves you," I said.

"I think so too."

"But you love Tim?"

The tears were back, like a faucet turning on and off. "I love Tim."

"Is he going to do it? Is he leaving them?"

She reached over on her nightstand for a cigarette and lighter. Her hand shook, so I took the lighter, helping her light it.

"You want to try one?" she asked, slipping one out of the pack and handing it to me.

I held the cigarette between by teeth like I'd seen her do, closing my lips around it and inhaling as I lit the end. The flame from the lighter danced before me. I don't know why in a world as hot as ours we'd bring in more heat. I coughed out the smoke, and she smiled.

"We talked," she said before taking another drag. I waited for her to elaborate. "Tim and I have plans to go away for a little. Not long—just a weekend. He's taking a 'fishing trip' with the boys. I think we need the time just for us. It'll be good."

I thought back to the look on Tim's face when she called us a family, the pure shock. How fast he left us behind. But Mom seemed hopeful, like she really believed in him—in *them*. Or maybe she was just trying to.

"Okay," I said, taking another long drag from my cigarette. This time I didn't cough.

21

With the big trip on the horizon and the hope for some sort of resolution, the house seemed to breathe a little easier. Gran and Mom maintained a polite silence, me the go-between. Nobody yelled. Mom dumped the shattered beer bottle remains in the trash. Things were looking up.

On the Thursday before her trip, she decided she needed a new bathing suit, hers older than mine had been. Shifts at the diner and afternoons with Tim left little time for the pool and little need for a bathing suit. But she thought they might go somewhere with a pool or a lake, and she wanted to be prepared.

"Want to shop?" she asked.

I was on my stomach by the fan, watching the same weatherman tell us the same weather, waiting to see if Harry would call. Our phone, usually silent for days at a time, was now in use almost nightly. Gran worried we'd run out of things to talk about.

I propped my head up on my hands. "Where?" I asked.

"L. S. Ayres?" She looked hopeful. She looked like she needed company.

"Fine," I said, and she offered me her hand to help me up. "You coming, Gran?" I asked, knowing she wouldn't.

Gran shook her head, her eyes never leaving the screen. "You two have fun."

The same Sheila who sold me my bathing suit was working the women's section. When she noticed me, she looked around, most likely in search of Gran.

"Back for another suit?"

"No," I said, gesturing to Mom. "She's on the hunt."

Sheila asked what she had in mind, and Mom shrugged.

"Something sexy?" Sheila asked.

Mom smiled. "I guess a little bit of sexy wouldn't hurt."

My stomach turned at the thought of what—or who—that sexy was for. I trailed behind the two of them as they perused the racks, Sheila stopping every few bathing suits to add to her pile. Eventually we reached the end of what an Indiana department store had to offer, and Mom went into the dressing room. I sat on the same leather sofa Gran had sat on weeks ago.

"Anything working?" I asked.

Mom opened the door a crack.

"Just come out," I said.

The door swung open, and she was standing in a two-piece just as tiny as mine was, except she had the body for it. Breasts I wondered if I'd ever get and olive skin. She'd freed her hair from her work ponytail, and it fell down her back in dark waves.

"Is it too young?" she asked.

I thought about answering honestly, but I didn't know how much honesty she could handle. "Not at all," I lied. "You look amazing," I added, and that part wasn't a lie.

"You think?" She turned around and looked at the three Laines that stared back in the mirrors.

"Oh, hon," Sheila spoke up. "You've got the body, the face. You're the real deal."

Mom laughed and tucked her hair behind her ears. "Okay," she said, exhaling. "I guess we'll take it."

<hr />

Ten miles into our twenty-mile drive I spoke up. "Have you and Phil ever . . . ? Well, you know."

Mom looked shocked. "Are you asking if Phil and I have ever had sex?"

"Oh gosh, Mom, no." I covered my face with my hands. "I'm asking if you've ever dated."

"Aurora!" She laughed. "For future reference, that's not what 'well, you know' refers to. And it's a no to both."

"Good to know."

"Why do you ask?"

I cracked my window to let in some air. "Just curious. Has he always liked you?"

"I guess so. He had a pretty big crush on me in high school, and I suppose I strung him along." She let out a sigh. "That was such a long time ago, though."

"Do you think he knows about Tim? Because of what happened at King's?"

"He might. He'd never say."

I fixed my eyes on the trees flying past, watching us edge closer to Monroe. For a moment, I worried she'd keep driving, leaving all of it behind. She'd made a pretty big mess this time. Leaving would be easier. But I knew she wouldn't. Tim had a pull on her like no man had ever had—I knew she'd see things through. The power was all his.

"I don't mean to hurt him, but I know I do," she added after a long minute. "I guess in the same way Tim doesn't mean to hurt me."

But they did hurt each other. All of them. In the soap operas, people split up and remarry their secretaries, and the aftermath is usually an episode of tears. Some yelling. But then two episodes later, the world reorients itself around the new way of doing things. New couples become old couples, and the audience forgets. I hoped Monroe could be like that, but it didn't seem likely.

Our life wasn't one of our soaps—it was real. We were real.

On the eve of her trip, I sat cross-legged on a pile of laundry, an awkward pretzel of too long limbs. Mom stared blankly at the empty, open suitcase on her bed. Her hair was pinned up in a new set of curlers. She was in a T-shirt, but no pants, and I worried about the possibility of her being ready to leave by morning.

"Shit," she said.

"Just pack something." I picked up a lacy red thong on her dresser I'd never seen before and grimaced. "Start with underwear," I said, throwing it in. "Then go from there."

She pointed her finger in the air like that was an idea she couldn't have thought of herself. I watched her yank the drawer out of its slot in the chipped orange dresser. She dumped the contents into the now partially filled suitcase.

"It's only two nights," I said, counting the ten pairs.

She nodded like she'd heard me, but moved on, removing nothing from the suitcase.

"And pajamas?" she asked, turning to me for approval.

"Pajamas are important," I said.

She cautiously moved about the room, grabbing items and holding them up for my approval. My whole life she'd seemed so glamorous, so in control. But now she was just a girl like me, nervous about a date with a boy.

I nodded yes to the too small shorts and the too small tank top. I rolled my eyes at the striped sweater.

"It's the end of July," I said. "Almost August."

I dug through the pile of clothes for the red dress she said she absolutely needed to bring. And because nothing in the little blue house was normal, it all felt strangely natural, helping my mom pack for her weekend away with the married mailman.

I watched Mom survey the suitcase. She had three pairs of shorts, jeans for nighttime, three tops—a compromise from the five she'd tried to pack—two dresses, and one tiny new bathing suit. She started to laugh. I laughed too.

"It's two nights," she said, repeating my words back to me.

Gran hovered in the doorway unnoticed before joining us. She sat on the edge of mom's bed. At this point Mom was laughing so hard she was crying. Gran started to laugh too. Eventually we all fell silent. I looked at the two of them.

"In the end," Gran said, the mood suddenly serious, "in the end, I'll bet he chooses you."

Gran picked at her hangnail, but Mom didn't notice that. She looked relieved, grateful for Gran's peace offering, the closest either of them could get to an apology. I was relieved too. But even in my relief I was nervous. Mom gave men the power to break her, and they usually did just that.

And when they had the power to break her, they had the power to break me. To break us. Our lives had been one for so long now. She was so willing to place our world in his hands, trusting that he wouldn't shatter it. But I wasn't so sure. Whatever he decided, nothing would be the same.

⁂

Sometime before the sun rose, Mom woke me up to drive her.

"Gran won't budge," she said. "Thought she'd left us to join Jay."

I rubbed my eyes. "Are you serious?"

"Phil isn't on patrol. The roads are empty. You'll be fine."

Her hair was curled, and her eyelashes were coated in thick layers of mascara. I wondered if she'd slept at all or if she'd spent all night preparing. Our street was silent when she lugged Jay's old suitcase out into the driveway, opening the car door to toss it into the back seat. It felt like we were going out to dump a dead body. Why else would someone be out this early?

She pointed out where to turn when she needed to, and spent the rest of the drive staring out the window. I thought she seemed nervous, even more so than usual.

"Where are you going?" I asked.

She shrugged. "I'm not sure. Probably not far. I should be back late Sunday."

"Are you scared?"

"Not scared. Just a little anxious, I guess." She pointed right. "Turn here. Three full days with me, and he might change his mind."

"I doubt it," I said.

"This is his," she said, when we approached a car stopped on the roadside. It was a pickup, and I realized I'd never seen him drive anything other than the mail truck. There was fishing equipment in the back, and I remembered the lie, and I remembered the girls he kissed goodbye while they slept. The wife. My heart wilted a little, and I wondered if Mom ever thought about them—the family. Did she just ignore the worry? Bury the thoughts? Or maybe—and this option scared me most—she didn't think of them at all.

She leaned over to kiss my cheek. "You know how to get home, yeah?" I nodded.

"Well." She smiled, and there was lipstick on her front tooth. "Wish me luck."

I motioned for her to wipe her tooth, and she did.

"Better?" she asked, smiling.

"Perfect."

I got home right as the sun chose to join our side of the world. Gran was in her recliner with the morning news on low volume.

"How was she?" she asked.

"She managed to stuff all of her clothes into that one suitcase, so she seemed okay. Hair curled, makeup done, prettiest smile."

Gran nodded. "That's Laine for you."

"If you had to guess, what's the end of all this?"

Gran seemed to really consider her answer. "What do I *think* happens? Or what do I *want* to happen?"

"Both."

"I don't know what will happen. Really, no clue." She paused to drink the clear liquid in her glass. "And what I want to happen? Well, I want her to be okay. I could give a shit about Tim. She's my only stake in all this."

"Mine too," I said.

"So, no mom in the house. What're your plans? Charlotte? Boys? A huge party?"

I rolled my eyes. "Hardly. I asked Harry to come over for our soaps. The house will be safely Tim-free. And then I work Saturday night."

She raised her eyebrows. "You're inviting the preacher's son into our house to watch *General Hospital*?"

"He wants to," I said.

"Oh, hon," she said, standing up from her recliner. "Boys don't want to sit on a couch with you and your gran and watch daytime television. I hate to tell you, but we might be dealing with some ulterior motives."

I followed her into the kitchen. "What kind of ulterior motives?"

She turned on the faucet, filling her cup with more water. "Oh Aurora, you're not that naive." She wiggled her eyebrows and winked.

"Oh gosh, Gran. Harry's not the kind of guy to have ulterior motives."

"All guys are the kind of guys to have ulterior motives."

"What's with the water?" I asked.

She shrugged. "It's hot and I'm keeping hydrated."

I didn't ask any more questions because her tone wasn't exactly inviting.

Harry was early because I'd warned him that interrupting a soap was a federal offense. He had Norma's to-go boxes, and when he gave Gran a side of ranch with her burger, she said she wanted to kiss him, and I had to ask her not to. His cheeks went red, but he laughed. I'd told him to get the ranch because Harry was pretty determined to remain on Gran's good side.

"What's first?" he asked, settling into Mom's usual spot.

"*Days of Our Lives*." I took the cushion next to him. Tim's spot.

"Sounds dramatic." He took a bite of his French fry and faced the television as the opening credits began. "Who's that?" he asked, nodding toward Tom.

"That's Dr. Tom Horton," Gran answered. "And that's his wife, Alice."

Harry zoned in on the television in the way only a kid without TV could. He only broke his focus to take bites of food and ask Gran questions, all of which she knew the answer to. There was little Gran knew more about in this world than her daytime soaps.

"How come he can ask questions, but when I speak, you bite my head off?"

Gran shushed me. "Don't make me miss something."

We went on like that for the next three hours, Harry asking questions and Gran answering them. At some point he placed his hand on my knee, and Gran pretended not to notice. When the local news started up, he looked over at me with watery, bloodshot eyes.

"I think you might have overdosed," I said, and he laughed.

"What time is it?" His eyes landed on the clock, and he sat straight up, clearly panicked. "Is it nine already?"

Gran laughed. "Clock's broken," she explained, "and I promise you the sun is still out behind those closed blinds. But the news is on, so it's a little after five."

Harry checked his watch and released an unsteady breath, his heart rate no doubt returning to normal. He wasn't the kind of kid to miss curfew.

"So what's your favorite?" Gran asked him.

He ran a hand over his face. "*General Hospital*."

"Good answer." She stood up to turn down the voice of the news anchor. "You two have any Friday night plans?"

Harry looked over at me and smiled. "I'd say we could catch the eight o'clock, but I don't know if I could look at a screen for another two hours."

"Well," Gran said, "I'm about ready to doze for an hour or so. I think it's best you two skedaddle." She not so subtly winked at me. "I'll see you before dawn, Aurora?"

I rolled my eyes and stood up, dragging Harry up alongside me. "Okay, old lady. I'll see you later."

"Bye, Katherine!" Harry called, and she offered him her best Queen of England wave.

When we reached his car, he looked up at the sun in the sky, closing his eyes. "That's a lot of TV."

"The other day? That was a lot of hiking."

He smiled. "I guess both just take practice. So where are we going?"

"I'm out of ideas."

He stood with his hand on my door, thinking. "Gosh, our town is boring."

I loved the way he said *our town*, like it belonged to the both of us.

I started to sit, but then he said, "Wait." His hand moved to the small of my back, and he pulled me toward him. When his lips met mine, I felt the kiss all over.

"I wanted to do that all day, but I didn't think Gran would appreciate it."

I laughed. "Well, you better hope she's not peeking through those blinds."

After narrowing down the options to the main three: the river, Paradise, and the drive-in, we decided to give the river another chance. Shane was supposed to be there, and so was Charlotte. I didn't want to go to Paradise, and Harry didn't want to go to the movies. In Monroe, these were our options.

He kissed me again before we got out of the car, and this kiss was much longer than the one in our driveway. My hand reached for the back of his neck, and I didn't want it to end.

When he pulled back, I took in an unsteady breath. "You sure about this?"

"If it's lame, we can leave," he said.

"Deal."

I opened my door before he could. He grabbed my hand while we walked, and I thought of what Gran said about ulterior motives. The river was crowded. By the time school started in the fall, these faces would be familiar to me. I'd spent the summer paying attention, gathering facts from Charlotte, sorting out who was who.

I spotted Charlotte right away. Her hair was in big curls, and her makeup was dark, each lash thick with the extra layer of mascara. I thought I recognized the dress, black with a self-made slit up the left thigh. She smiled when she saw us.

"*Harry!*" she yelled.

"Hello, Charlotte," he said.

She swayed with each step, and I watched Harry catch hold of her elbow.

"Are you okay?" I asked.

She let out a loud cackle. "So serious." She waved her finger close to my face. "I'm fine. Harry's fine. You're fine. Everyone's fine, *Aurora*." Her voice was loud, and her words felt mean. Kevin came up and snaked his arm around her waist. He pressed his mouth to her ear and said something we couldn't hear. Harry let go of her elbow.

"Okay," I said, taking a step back. "Have fun. We're going to go find Shane."

Before we even turned away, they were kissing in a way that made me feel nauseous.

"This might have been a mistake," I said, tugging Harry away from them.

Harry scanned the crowd. "Fool me once, shame on you. Fool me twice, shame on me."

"What?" I asked.

"That's another one of my dad's rules. I'm feeling like a fool."

"Let's just find Shane," I said, searching the collection of faces. "Look"—I pointed over at the keg by water's edge—"there he is."

Harry didn't look at all relieved, but Shane smiled when he saw us.

"Hey!" Shane called. He offered Harry a drink when we got closer, but Harry shook his head.

"I'm good."

"You?" Shane asked, shoving the drink in my direction.

I took the cup from his hand, with little intention to drink it.

"Harry doesn't drink," Shane explained. "Doesn't stop me from trying."

"That's okay," I said, and Harry smiled. "I'm not a big drinker myself."

"C'mon." Harry pulled me away from the circle of cars, leaving Shane behind. We were back at the boulder where we'd sat on our first date, that first night at the river. Harry's hands were much less hesitant when he helped me climb up. Our legs weren't miles apart. I draped mine over his and leaned back so I could stare at the cloudless blue sky. It'd be washed orange soon, my favorite color. Harry stayed sitting up, watching me. I liked how it felt to have him study my face.

"I like you," he said.

"I like you too, Harold Clark."

I didn't have to look at him to know he was smiling.

"I like you more than any of these people," he said.

I laughed. "That's not saying much. I like you more than any of the people in this town. Besides Gran and Mom, of course."

"And Charlotte?" he asked.

"Eh," I said. "Ask me in a couple of days. She's a terrible drunk."

"Well, I like you more than any of the people in Indiana," he said.

I sat up. "Now that's saying something."

He grinned, and I scooted closer. I leaned forward so our foreheads were touching, wiggling my eyebrows suggestively. "You want to go kiss in your car?"

Harry laughed, his eyes crinkling at the corners.

"More than anything in the world."

༺ ༻

Harry dropped me off at quarter till ten. Gran snored in her recliner, and even me slamming the front door didn't wake her. I grabbed the blanket from the sofa and tucked it around her lean frame. Since Jay died, she'd spent every night in her recliner, letting Mom claim the room as her own. She'd go in to change, to brush her teeth, to apply her makeup—but she refused to sleep in the bed. Mom used to insist, telling her she didn't mind sharing, but once Tim starting hanging around, they both dropped the subject. Gran looked most at home in the living room.

A glass was on the side table, and when I sniffed it, there was no smell. I took a sip. It was lemonade. I took it to the kitchen, along with her half-eaten meat loaf, setting one in the sink and the other in the trash.

I was too wound up to go to sleep, but I didn't want to disturb her. When I opened the door to my room, I hesitated. I headed down the hall to her door. Mom's room was a disaster. The rejected clothes were strewn across the floor. I walked across the discarded dresses and climbed into her bed, inhaling her scent. She always kept cigarettes on the nightstand. I slipped one out of the pack. The room felt like it missed her usual smoke. I searched for her lighter and couldn't find one. The side table drawer was open a crack, and I opened it further.

Her lighter was sitting on top of an envelope, the scrawl with her name familiar to me. I lit my cigarette and reached for the letter, unfolding it carefully. His handwritten words were barely legible.

> *Dear Laine,*
>
> *I'm sorry I got scared. I know you're scared too.*
>
> *Some things are complicated, but some things are simple, like the fact that I love you and you love me. I'm sorting it all out. Give me time.*
>
> *Meet me at our spot at 6:30.*
>
> *Yours,*
>
> *Tim*

I tapped the ash out in her ashtray. I wondered if they'd gotten to wherever they were going. I wondered if it was somewhere she could wear that bathing suit. I wondered what would happen when he finished all that sorting out.

And then, because I didn't want to think of Mom and Tim, I forced myself to think of Harry. I thought of the things about him I liked and the way I felt when his lips made their way to mine. Somewhere across town, I hoped he was thinking of me too.

When I put out the cigarette in the ashtray, the room seemed darker than when I'd entered, washed in moonlight from the open curtains. I brought an unsteady hand up to my cheek and wiped away my tears, not sure when I'd started to cry.

22

Gran was at the kitchen table, flipping through a brand-new *National Enquirer*. Yesterday, a mailman Mom hadn't slept with had slipped mail into our rusted mailbox. No front door delivery.

I sat down across from her. "When did you know you loved Jay?" I asked.

She looked up from her magazine and smiled. "Where's this coming from?"

"You guys met at Rexall Drugs, right?" The trick was to get her talking, and then she'd never stop.

"Nice try," she said. "I'm no fool. I know you know this story."

"I don't remember it," I lied.

"Sure you do."

"Just give me the brief version." I wasn't above begging. "Please."

The truth was I knew the story by heart. The summers before Jay died, I made him tell it, and that always got Gran to tell her version because the two were vastly different.

All those years ago, Gran walked through Rexall Drugs with three bottles of whiskey in her hand. I don't know how much she drank a day, but it was enough to give Mom reasons to hate her for years to come. I was sheltered from that version of Gran—this summer, she cut herself off after half a bottle.

According to Jay, she stumbled around the corner on aisle four and slammed into him, dropping all three bottles on the floor. She says he bumped into her, knocking the bottles from her hands.

He said something like, "That stuff'll kill you anyways."

And in the story he told, she told him to go screw himself, but I always had the feeling that was the censored version. He didn't get mad, though. He just laughed and offered to pay for the broken bottles. She couldn't afford the broken bottles in addition to the ones she needed to actually drink, so she let him, and then he asked her if she wanted a cup of coffee. She said no.

"What if I buy you a bottle?" he asked, and that she couldn't refuse.

They sat in the car outside of the liquor store for five hours that night, neither of them even opening the bottle. It turned out Jay didn't touch the stuff, not once in his entire life. His dad beat his mom, and he said he'd seen the worst of men because of it. That was the other stuff he left out of his version, but she told me later how his eyes filled with tears when he talked about his childhood. Gran's life wasn't peaches either, and even though I didn't ever hear much about Great-Gran Ruth, I knew enough not to ask about her.

Gran's eyes began to water.

"Dammit," she said, wiping under her eyes. "Now you've got me crying. I guess I knew I loved him that day. Day one. Five hours was the longest I'd gone without drinking in God knows how long. And then at the end of it all, I left the bottles in his car. I didn't even remember to take it with me." She winked. "Of course I stopped off at the liquor store and fixed myself a drink as soon as I got home, but that's not the point. The point is he was enough for me."

"I like that story," I said.

"I know you do. You're a little shit for making me tell it." She laughed and cried all at once. "I like the woman in that story."

"The woman who stopped drinking?"

Gran nodded. "It was easier then. Everything was easier with him around."

"You think Grandpa Jay saved you?" I asked.

She drummed her fingers on the table. "I wouldn't say he saved me. I think he was just the first person who told me I could save myself."

I liked that idea of love. It was different from the one on the soaps we watched or the Friday night movies. It was different from the love Mom knew.

"I miss him," I said, and I meant it.

Gran patted my hand before she pushed her chair back, rising like the woman who was sixteen years older than the one in the story. She opened the fridge and stared at its contents, sniffing the orange juice before pouring herself a glass.

"I miss him too."

⁂

Saturday night at Paradise was the busiest of all. My spot at the snack bar afforded me a front row to the town's weekly parade. I worried about the day when Monroe would search for more entertainment than Al's rundown bowling alley. I think Al worried about it too.

Even though I didn't want to, I kept thinking of Mom and Tim. In so many ways Tim was unlike the men she'd dated before, but in so many ways he wasn't. We thought all men were different in the beginning, and even though the summer had moved slowly, the truth was they'd been together all of two months. A little less. And what even counts as *together*? Hours in her room after he cut his shift early. Stolen late nights while his family slept.

But then there was the way he looked at her. He always wore this expression of amazement, like he couldn't figure her out but he wanted to. There was the way he laughed louder at the things she said, the way he ruffled my hair when he walked in the living room. I liked that he liked all of us, or at least he seemed to. Our ragtag group wasn't conventional, but he didn't seem to mind it.

I was relieved when a man walked up to order a soda refill, the spell I'd been under suddenly broken. He gave me a dollar, and I passed him the change, half of which he added to my tip jar. A line had formed behind him. The snack bar was only busy in short bursts.

I distractedly filled bags of popcorn and pitchers of soda. I was careful, though. Al was always watching. I was so focused on the popcorn and my own spiraling thoughts, I didn't even notice when Harry walked up to the counter.

"What can I get you?" I asked.

His laugh surprised me, the familiarity of it bringing me back down to earth. "A large popcorn and a kiss from my girlfriend."

"I'm so distracted," I said, pressing my fingers to my temples, "I didn't even see you." I turned to fill up a bag with popcorn. "I didn't know you were coming to bowl tonight."

Harry was almost always smiling. "Last-minute decision. Shane called because a group was going, and I knew you were working, which might've swayed my decision a little."

He rested his elbows on the counter. I took my time dealing with his popcorn.

"Do you get a break?" he asked.

"I already took it." I set the popcorn on the counter between us. "Fifteen minutes ago."

"Shoot." He ran a hand through his hair. A man behind him cleared his throat. "Well, I should probably get back. It might be my turn."

"No tip?" I asked, nodding toward the jar.

He pushed himself up on the counter, leaning over to kiss my cheek. I swatted him away.

"Al's watching," I said, shooing him off.

He laughed and grabbed his popcorn. "I'll come by for a refill."

I strained to watch him go, wondering who exactly constituted a *group*. Lane 11, the designated lane for teens thought unruly by Al, was populated with familiar faces. Shane held two balls up in the air. Marie was tying her shoelaces. Lyla's hair caught the light, and I reminded myself to take a breath. She threw her head back, laughing when Harry approached, a move I recognized from years observing Mom.

From my side of the counter, I watched them play two games, but by the end of the second, I could tell they were getting bored. Al says bored bowlers ignore the art of the game. They start rolling it between one another's legs, using two hands instead of one, or two balls at one time. Poor etiquette, he called it. It looked fun to me. I watched Shane toss the ball high in the air. It landed with a thud on the lane before making its way, slowly, to the gutter. Zero pins.

"You two steady?" Al asked, startling me.

My hand flew up to my heart. "What?"

"Harold Clark." He nodded toward lane eleven. "Pastor Clark's kid."

"Oh yeah," I said. "We're seeing each other."

Al came around the counter and fixed himself a cup of soda, light on the ice. "Hmm."

"What's the 'hmm' supposed to mean?" I narrowed my eyes at him, and he threw his shoulders up in an animated shrug. "C'mon, Al. Just give it to me straight."

"Where's Laine this weekend?" he asked, and my stomach sank in response.

"What do you mean?"

"Heard she was taking a girls' weekend with her old friend from high school—what's her face, starts with an *S*."

"Sophie," I filled in, knowing the story she'd told people. Sophie lived in Arkansas, and she'd agreed to keep up the lie to anyone who asked. "What are you getting at?"

"I'm just asking questions," he said, and then his voice dropped really low. "I know about her and Tim. I'd say everyone knows, but that'd be a lie. Enough people know. And if he ditches those girls, the whole town's going to know, including the Clarks. You might not think I do, but I care for you, and I care for Laine and Katherine too, even if they drive me crazy. I just want to prepare you for the worst."

"Who told you?" I asked, too tired to keep up the lie.

"Tommy from the hardware store. He's Tim's cover for the weekend."

Just then I saw the group approaching—Harry, Shane and the rest of them, including the one person most affected by our whispered words.

Al squeezed my shoulder. "Tell your gran."

Stunned, I tried to force a smile when the group approached.

"Hey," Harry said, "I think we might head out. What time do you get off?"

"Hi, Aurora!" Lyla's wave seemed insincere, but I waved back.

"I get off at closing," I said to Harry. "Past curfew."

"Gran coming to get you?"

"If she remembers."

He didn't laugh. "Maybe my parents will let me come."

I shook my head. "Saturday curfew is hardly flexible. Don't worry about it. She'll come."

He leaned over to kiss me, and I let him, even though there were people watching. I didn't know how much longer these kisses would be possible. Especially not after what Al had shared.

"Call me if she doesn't," he said.

"Okay."

Harry walked toward the door, and the rest of them followed. Marie and Lyla flanked him on either side. They linked their arms in his, and I watched them go. Maybe their parents were doing things they didn't know about too, things that would affect their lives for better or worse. Or maybe their parents sat at home, waiting for their arrival, cross-stitching pillows and humming along to songs on the radio.

⁂

I called Gran at ten till eleven, and she answered on the third ring.

"Hello?" Her voice was much friendlier for strangers.

"It's me," I said, "Aurora."

"What do you want?"

"I want a ride home."

"Prince Charming called and said he'd take care of it."

"What? He has curfew."

"Well, as far as I know, he asked for a little bit of an extension to pick you up and drive you home. I'm starting to think he might not trust me so much."

I laughed. "No, I have a feeling he just wants to spend time with me."

"Ulterior motives?" Gran asked.

"Goodbye, Gran." I hung up Al's phone and looked up at the clock.

In an empty parking lot, I spotted Harry's car right away. It was hard to miss, with him sitting perched on the hood.

"How'd you manage this?" I asked.

He smiled. "Got an extension on curfew."

"So Gran said. Now truth. Where do your parents think you are?"

He lowered his voice, even though we were the only people around. "Truth? They think I'm in bed."

"Harold!" I reached over to smack his arm. "I can't believe you lied to your parents!"

"It's not a lie." He bit his bottom lip to stop himself from smiling. I refused to smile back. "C'mon, Aurora. They were asleep when I got home. They go to bed at eight. No one checks on me. They'll never know."

"But why?" I asked.

He hopped off the hood of his car and wrapped his arms around me. I relaxed into him, breathing in the familiar scent. No amount of soap could remove the aroma of sunblock. I wondered what he'd smell like in the fall, hoping I'd have a chance to find out.

He tucked his chin against my neck. "I just wanted to make sure you got home safely."

The community pool at night looked much different than during the day. It was the same white-turned-yellow lounge chairs, the same unnatural blue water, and the same burning smell of chlorine and sunblock. But the people were missing. The distracted moms and their kids with oversized floaties were gone. Lyla Jr. was asleep in her bed. Or maybe she was keeping her mom company, filling in her dad's space in the bed made for two.

On a hot summer night in early August, I stood and watched as Harry, the preacher's boy, trespassed onto property, stripped down to his briefs and launched himself into the community pool.

"Are you coming?" he asked, treading water in the deep end.

"I've got no swimsuit."

He put his hands over his eyes and peeked through the cracks in his fingers. Before I could stop to think, I shimmied out of my shorts. I turned around and pulled my tank top over my head, setting it on the closest chair. I looked down and noticed a string of elastic on my underwear that trailed down the front, shocked Mom hadn't thrown them away. I pulled it off and jumped in.

I shot up to the surface and wiped under my eyes to check for mascara before swimming toward the edge.

"A pit stop?" I asked.

Harry flashed his perfect smile. "It *is* a pit stop."

"You know Gran could have driven me home," I said, gripping the ladder by the pool's edge. I could swim well enough, but I'd never had lessons. I always felt better holding the side.

Harry treaded water with the ease of a merman. "I know."

"Do you?"

"Remember the night I sat with you at Paradise? Where was Gran then?"

"The phone was off the hook," I said, suddenly defensive.

"But why was the phone off the hook?"

"What are you getting at?" I submerged my nose and mouth beneath the water's surface, and the bubbles started up when I exhaled.

He tilted his head so his eyes met mine. "I just think there's things you don't tell me."

"Like what?" I asked, terrified of his answer.

"About home."

"What about it?" I could hear Mom's edge in my voice. The defensiveness.

He swam toward me. His voice was gentle. "I just want you to know you *can* tell me things. We don't have to have secrets."

He couldn't have been more wrong. Our survival was contingent on secrets.

"I know, Aurora." Those three words could have sunk me. Everything keeping me afloat was slipping away. But then he added, "About the drinking."

I could have laughed I felt so relieved. Gran's drinking was hardly a town secret.

"Oh," I said, hoping to sound somber. "I just don't talk about it much."

"Well, I hope you know you can talk to me about it. You can tell me anything."

His voice was sincere enough to make me cry, but I forced myself not to.

"I know," I said. "I'm sorry. And I'm not sure what you heard or who you heard it from, but it's not so bad anymore. The drinking, I mean. She's still crazy, but sobriety won't fix that."

Harry rolled over so he was floating on his back, and I thought about telling him everything. I had this vision of me starting from the beginning, the men Mom had seen before, the towns before, the life before Tim. And then I'd tell him about Tim, how he was nice to us, good to her, and sure, he had a family, but maybe *we* could be his family. Or I could say that I hated my mom for what she did, which wasn't totally untrue. There were versions of the story playing out in my mind, but at the end of every make-believe scenario, Harry's response was the same.

I couldn't risk it. I couldn't risk losing this—the flutter that expanded in my abdomen with every kiss, the certainty that someone cared, the way I felt when his eyes searched mine. I knew then—looking at Harry in his briefs, floating in the deep end—I knew then, I'd never tell.

I pushed off of the ladder and swam toward him.

"So, Harry," I said, desperate to change the subject, to keep him here, "is this where you take all the girls? Some grand gesture? Breaking the law for love?"

I ignored my fears, willing away the weight of their secrets. I wanted to float too, and I would not let Tim and my mother have this moment.

He looked at me from the corner of his eye. "You got any particular girls in mind? Maybe a blonde?"

"Stop," I said, splashing him. "I was only joking around."

He smiled and shook his head, flipping right side up, bobbing up and down in the water. "Aurora," he said, swimming toward me, closing the gap, "never in my life have I climbed out of my bedroom window and broken into the pool. Not for anyone on this green earth."

His hands reached for me beneath the water's surface, and for a second I was terrified at what he might find, like the secrets I carried were visible on my bare skin. But it was just flesh. This wasn't our end. Not yet.

"Do you believe me?" he asked, grabbing my waist and pulling me closer.

"I believe you," I said, tilting my head to meet his kiss.

23

I woke up to Gran at the foot of my bed, shaking my foot.

"Why?" I said, throwing a dramatic arm over my eyes.

When I'd come in the night before with soaking wet hair, she'd smiled and said, "No ulterior motives, huh?"

She continued to shake me awake. "Your mom's here."

I shot up. "Already?"

Gran laughed. "I'm kidding, hon—she's not here. But God, did that wake you up fast."

I hid my face beneath my pillow. "Gran, what are you doing?"

"I'm bored and I want company." She pulled the pillow away from me. When I opened one eye to look at her, she was smiling. "Just get up out of bed and spend time with your gran before chaos returns. We've got one day left of peace—no sense in wasting it."

"Okay, okay," I said, swinging my legs over the side of the bed. My feet met the carpet. "But no step aerobics. That doesn't sound fun."

"What about a Sunday morning drive?"

I was beginning to realize there was nothing I loved more than a drive with Gran. "I'm in."

༺❀༻

We decided not to talk about Mom and Tim because we'd be talking about them soon enough. It was a new rule. This felt like our last day of freedom, and we agreed not to waste it. Still, they were on our minds, the silent pauses in our conversations full of sound. I couldn't shake them.

"You want to tell me about last night?" Gran asked.

I couldn't stop myself from smiling. "Well, it's safe to say his parents didn't know he was sneaking out and breaking into the pool."

"No way," she said, turning left toward the open road, leaving downtown behind us. "He surprises me sometimes. I bet he's feeling tired this morning."

I thought of him in the pew closest to the front, mumbling the words to the hymn he'd probably known since birth. A few rows back the Lyla Raes joined in with Sunday morning worship in well-ironed dresses and ribbons in their hair, washed in the Technicolor of the stained glass. I hadn't been inside the church since the funeral, but I remembered the stained glass above the pulpit, the way it caught the morning light.

"You nervous about him finding out?" she asked.

"Isn't this breaking our rule?"

"Not if we don't mention them by name."

"Well, then, yes. I'm nervous. I just, when it comes down to it, I don't want to lose this."

Talking about it made my insides feel topsy-turvy.

"Lose Harry?" she asked. Gran was good at getting me to elaborate.

"Not just Harry. All of it," I said, gesturing at the road, hoping I made sense. "I worry about the big things—you. Harry. Charlotte. But then I worry about the small things too. The bowling alley and Al. I worry about missing Miss Norma's apple crisp in the fall. What about when Karl's roses bloom next May?"

"Well, take me off that list. I'm not going anywhere." Gran reached across the car to hold my hand. "So what do you want to happen? In a perfect world, I mean."

"I guess I'm hoping they just—" I paused. "Well, that it all just disappears." I'm sure Gran knew what I was getting at. I'm not sure when I'd switched sides. Maybe last night. Up until then I think I'd been rooting for him to pick her, but I wasn't so sure anymore, not after the way I felt in the pool with the preacher's son. "I know that's naive."

"A little." She took in a long breath followed by an even longer exhale. "I want you to be naive though. You're fifteen years old, almost sixteen, and it's not right for you to be so practical. I like that you think boys don't have ulterior motives and that bad things might disappear. Don't let her change that."

"Al knows," I said, suddenly remembering last night's conversation. It had been lost beneath the pool's chlorinated water and soft hands and long, breathless kisses. "He told me last night."

Gran's hands squeezed the wheel so hard I saw the whites of her knuckles. Then she relaxed, only skipping the slightest beat in conversation. But I didn't miss much these days.

"Oh God, well, that's never good. But Harry can't blame you for your mom's choices. You didn't take up with a married man."

"I don't think it works that way, and I know you don't think so either."

I might have cried, but we'd made a promise to keep Mom and Tim out of this car ride. We were choosing happiness, which meant no tears, no worries, no panic.

Gran reached over to turn up the radio. She always could read my mind. "Okay, enough of all that. Let's be happy while we still can."

"Agreed," I said, reaching out the car window to feel the warm breeze. "Our world might look different tomorrow."

⁓⁓

When we pulled into the driveway, the house looked dark in spite of the sunlight. I swear there was a cloud sent to intercept the rays supposed to light up the little blue house. I wondered where Mom and Tim were and if they'd had a good time, quietly hoping against it.

"Aurora!" Charlotte yelled just before I could open our front door.

She was across the street in the lawn chair beside Karl's. I watched them say their goodbyes. She made her way from his side of the street to ours with the same runway walk she used in the bar, but when she got closer, I could tell she'd been crying.

"Can I come in?" she asked.

I stepped into the hallway, and she followed. Gran was ahead of us, already in her recliner after flipping on the TV.

"Can we go to your room?" Charlotte asked.

Whatever she had to say she couldn't say in front of Gran, which was rare. We didn't have the same lines between child and adult in either of our homes. There was rarely a need to hide things from parents.

"What is it?" I asked, easing my door shut behind me.

She threw herself on my bed and pressed her face into my pillow.

"Charlotte," I said, sitting on the bed beside her, running my hand through her tangled blonde hair. "What is it?"

When she flipped over to face me, I could tell just how much she'd been crying. Her eyelids were swollen and free from their usual dark rims.

"He's staying with us," she said, and by the way she fixed a mean glare on the ceiling, I knew she was trying not to cry. "She broke the rule. She said *she* makes the rules."

"Which one is it?" I asked, because this summer, with her mom, we had trouble keeping track.

"Austin," she said, and I couldn't help but remember the way he'd looked at Charlotte in the bar. "The worst of the lot. He came out in his boxers this morning. No shirt. My mom was at the stove making eggs—mind you, she hasn't cooked me a meal in years, I didn't know she still knew how—and he grabbed her ass. And then, as if that wasn't enough, he smiled at me. *Smiled*."

"That's gross," I said. It was a familiar story, a world I'd lived in for too long. "Did she say how long?"

Charlotte shrugged. "Indefinitely. I mean, there's no end date. They'll end, of course, because Austin is no Mr. Forever, but no one has *ever* made it to the moving-in stage."

"If you decide to murder him, I'll help bury the body," I said, hoping to lighten the mood.

Her features began to soften. "He's kind of big, Aurora." She was doing her best not to smile. "You know he's got a gut like Al's. I don't know if we could manage."

I smiled and nudged her with my elbow. "I'll bet Gran has beef with him. She can help, and if we get her drunk enough, she'll think it was just a strange dream."

Charlotte, unable to help herself, began to laugh. "Karl has a sympathetic ear," she said, the potential murder plot taking shape. "Who knows? He might be willing to get in on the scheme."

The four of us in the old Vega spewing smog with Austin in the trunk was a good thought, and it was nice to have something to laugh about. We laughed until we couldn't laugh any more.

"When's Laine coming home?" Charlotte asked when the silence began to fill the room.

"Tonight," I said, lying down beside her on my twin bed.

"Are we still placing bets on how it all ends?" she asked.

I shrugged.

She sat up and scooted so her back was against my headboard. "I hope you stay."

We'd avoided the topic all summer, pretending I'd be at school come fall, never mentioning a looming goodbye. She told me about the teachers—who to avoid, who was an easy grader—and what table we'd sit at during lunch. I never corrected her, never warned her of what might be coming.

"I hope I stay too," I said.

I didn't want to be a realist, and Gran said I didn't have to be. I could let myself daydream about homecoming with Harry and afternoon milkshakes with Charlotte. There was no reason to dread tomorrow—today had enough trouble of its own.

We dropped the subject and spent the afternoon painting our nails. While Charlotte told me the latest on her saga with Kevin, I didn't let myself worry about when these afternoons would come to a sudden end. Instead, I told myself we had forever, that it'd always be like this. And then, because I was letting myself be optimistic, it started to feel true.

❧

After Charlotte left, I got on my bike and rode across town. Harry's house, which up until then I'd never been to, was on the other side of Main Street, across from the church. It was Sunday afternoon, and I knew they'd be sitting down to dinner soon. But it was also my last night without the weight of my mother's life crashing down on me, and I wanted to see him smile.

When I knocked on the door, his mother answered. I'd planned for this, swapping my tank and shorts for the yellow dress I'd worn on our first date. Maybe she'd think she'd missed me in the pews during the service. Like his dad, she was older. Frail and grandmotherly, even more so than my own.

"Hello," I said, extending my hand. "I'm Aurora. Is Harry home?"

"Ah," she said, and I was relieved my name elicited some sort of recognition. She took my hand in both of hers and smiled. "So, you're Aurora."

"I'm Aurora."

"Come in, come in." She guided me inside, keeping my hand in hers. Her hands were cold and weathered. They seemed like the hands of someone who'd uprooted and re-rooted too many gardens to count. *Hands like Karl's,* I thought. "Harold is setting the table. I'll let him know he has a visitor. Please, sit."

She gestured at a chair in their front room before heading down the hall. On the table beside the chair was a needlepoint pillow in progress, and I loved that I had been right about her choice in hobby. The house smelled like Sunday dinner, or what I imagined Sunday dinner to smell like. Cooking—real cooking—fills the house with enough smells to confuse the senses. Our dinners smelled like hot plastic, burnt meat loaf, and nothing else.

I saw Harry before he saw me, watching as he tugged on the bottom of his button-down and smoothed his dress slacks.

"What are you doing here?" He sounded surprised, but he was smiling, so I knew it was a good kind of surprise.

"I missed you," I said.

His smile grew wider. "Since yesterday?"

I shrugged and smoothed my dress. "Your mom's nice."

"She is," he said, and then he crouched by my chair. "So why are you really here?"

"I was in the neighborhood?" Lie.

He shook his head. "Try again."

"I wanted to get out of the house." Not a total lie. "And of all the people in this little town, you're at the top of my list of faces I'd like to see." Truth.

This answer seemed to appease him. "One day you'll have to give me reasons for you wanting to get out of that house."

"But not tonight," I said.

He shook his head. "No, not tonight. Because tonight you have made my mother the happiest woman in Indiana, and she's pretty insistent you stay for dinner."

"Okay," I said, a small smile creeping onto my lips. I couldn't help myself.

"She's staying!" he yelled, and it seemed like his voice shook the delicate house run by the delicate woman.

"Don't yell!" she yelled back.

He pushed his hair back from his forehead and rolled his eyes before sneaking a sudden kiss.

"Good surprise?" I asked.

"Best surprise."

༺ ༻

Harry, or Harold as he was known in this house, was sent to fetch his father. Harold Sr. spent Sunday morning in the pulpit and Sunday afternoon in his office, meeting with members of the congregation who needed prayer. Maybe Lyla Rae Sr. was there, waiting in the chair outside his office. Whether she knew it or not, she was in need of some serious prayer.

Despite my offering, Claire-Anne, as she insisted I call her, would not let me help her in the kitchen. She did let me pull up a stool to watch, but she was very particular that guests have no part in making the meal they would soon consume.

I loved seeing her smash actual potatoes and grab things from a stocked cupboard to add to already complicated dishes.

"What's that, Mrs. Clark?" I asked.

"Claire-Ann," she corrected. "Just garlic salt. It adds a bit of zest."

Our meat-loaf tray dinners were zestless. Our pot roast, just one step above.

"It's almost more fun to cook than to eat," I said.

She laughed. "One night, when you're not a special guest, I'll teach you. Harold Sr. and Jr. have very little interest in the kitchen beyond the ice cream they sneak into my freezer."

"I would love to learn," I said, hoping these were plans I'd have a chance to keep.

Harold Sr. was nothing like the preachers on TV. His suit was ill fitting and cheap looking, and his hair wasn't dyed. He was grayed and weathered and sincere. The three of them had so much warmth I felt like I might cry, but I didn't, thank goodness.

"So Aurora," Harold Sr. began, "it's so nice to meet the girl Harry's been talking about all summer."

"We asked to meet you weeks ago," Claire-Ann chimed in, smiling as she scooped me another helping of mashed potatoes. I didn't know they could taste this good.

"I was keeping her all to myself," Harry joked.

"I suppose so," Harold Sr. said. "He tells us you and your gran both have quite a wit. Always keeping him laughing."

"Oh goodness, did he say that?" I looked over, and Harry wore a guilty smile. "Gran has passed on the sassy gene to both my mom and me."

"And it's just the three of you?" Claire-Ann asked.

I searched her voice for any hint of judgment, but there was none to be found.

"Yes," I said. "My mom grew up here but left around the time she had me, but we came back in May."

"For the funeral," Claire-Ann added, nodding sympathetically. "We knew Jay pretty well. Although I suppose everyone knows everyone in this little town. But he was a great, great man."

Harold Sr. raised his glass of iced tea. "I'll second that."

"I wish I could've spent more time with him," I said, the weight of his absence hitting me all at once. "We came back to Monroe every now and then. But it doesn't feel like enough."

"He spoke fondly of you," Harold Sr. said. "Called you Rory?"

I nodded. Jay was the only one who'd ever called me that.

"He said you two were a lot alike. Said you preferred to watch the world around you—didn't always feel the need to chime in unless you really meant it."

I was surprised Jay had been paying that much attention, but I guess that's where he and I were alike. I felt guilty that I hadn't paid as much attention to him. Sometimes it felt like Mom and Gran took up all the space in the room, but even then, Jay took the time to see me.

"These potatoes are so good," I said, taking another bite from my plate. If they noticed my abrupt subject change, they were polite enough to ignore it.

"You don't eat a lot of mashed potatoes?" Harold Sr. asked, amused.

"We prefer our food to be of the instant variety. That or prepared by Norma's Diner. But Norma's has nothing on Claire-Ann's mashed potatoes."

Claire-Ann winked at me. "I'm going to teach her a few tricks."

"Oh are you?" Harry asked, laughing. "Remind me to skip dinner that night."

"Harold," she said, "don't sass us. She's got more of an interest in the kitchen than you do, and she's probably got more of a knack for it."

"That I'd like to see," Harry said.

Harold Sr. laughed, loud and heartily, before taking a long drink of his sweet tea.

⁂

Pastor Clark and Claire-Ann insisted Harry drive me home. I said my goodbyes to the two of them, and Claire-Ann made me promise to return sometime this week. We were going to make a real meat loaf—one that would put our frozen meals to shame.

"How about Wednesday?" she asked as Harry loaded my bike into the bed of his truck.

"I'll be here," I promised.

Pastor Clark covered his yawn with his hand before laughing. "Sun's not quite gone, and I'm already ready for bed. We're early risers."

They waved from the driveway while Harry reversed out onto the street.

"What'd you think?" he asked.

I fiddled with my seat belt. "Why'd you want to keep me all to yourself?"

He ran a hand down his face, a gesture I'd noticed his father do. "I knew you'd ask that."

I leaned over the center console to rest my head on his shoulder. "I'm not mad. Just curious."

"If I'm being honest," he started, "I just thought they'd bore you. That sounds terrible. I love them so much. But your gran is like a box of fireworks. Your house is loud and fun." He paused. "We eat dinner at five thirty every night on the same china. Not a minute early, not a minute late. Right now, they're brushing their teeth, and by the time I get home, they'll be fast asleep."

"Harold," I said, tilting my head so I could see his face. He smiled at the sound of his full name. "I could have sat at that table all night, and not just because you were sitting across from me. Your parents love you as much as I love you, and that makes me love them. Not to mention the food. I filled and cleaned my plate three times, in case you weren't counting."

He laughed and turned onto my street, pulling over a few houses before mine, putting his truck in park.

"I have something for you," he said, turning his body so he was facing me.

I watched him reach in his pocket.

"A gift? For me?"

"Something like that," he said. "Here. Give me your hand."

He took my hand and slipped a watch on my wrist. It was one of those LED ones from the magazines, with the numbers in a futuristic red. I turned my wrist to admire it.

"It's a little loose," he explained, "but we can get some of the links removed. It's my old one. I just want you to be able to know when I'm coming to pick you up."

I leaned over to kiss his cheek, which felt like a proper way to say thank you. "I love it."

Harry looked pleased with himself. "Aurora, I gotta ask you, did you mean what you said just now?"

I looked up from my watch. He was wearing a lopsided grin. "Mean what?"

"You said you love me?"

Heat rushed to my cheeks. "Did I say that?"

"Before you answer, I'd like to say something." He reached over and ran an unsteady hand down my cheek. In the movies, boys didn't look nervous when they touched you, but I liked the real thing so much more. "I love you too, if you meant it. Shoot, even if you didn't mean it."

I unclipped my seat belt and climbed over so I was on his lap, pressing my face into his neck. I breathed in the smell of sunshine and chlorine, desperate to memorize everything about him. "I love you too," I whispered.

When I leaned back so our faces were just inches apart, he pressed his lips against mine, running his unsteady hands down my back. We kissed and kissed and then kissed some more. And then I stayed there with my head against his chest, an ache starting in the back of my throat. This hollowed feeling haunted me in my happiest moments, a constant reminder of all I stood to lose. I willed it away, willed myself to be present. We stayed like that, in a silent state of bliss, until his parents were sure to be fast asleep.

When I walked down the block toward my house, Karl waved from across the street. I was wearing the stupidest grin and laughing at nothing in particular.

"He loves me!" I yelled, too happy to feel embarrassed.

"Well, that I knew!" Karl yelled back.

24

I fell asleep in Mom's bed. It was just before midnight, 11:57 to be exact, and she wasn't home yet. She'd phoned, and Gran had answered. We could expect her sometime after one AM. Gran had offered me the phone, and I just shook my head. I wasn't sure what I'd say, and I was tired of lying to the people I loved.

With each passing day, my anger toward her grew. It was a surprising feeling—I'm not sure I'd ever let myself be mad at her before. Sure, I'd been disappointed by her. Or hurt. Or embarrassed. But this anger was settling deep into my bones, unfamiliar and jarring.

I woke up to the sound of her creaking door. I knew her routine and could imagine her setting her purse down on the floor. I could feel her eyes on me, and her body standing over me. I kept my eyes shut and slowed my breathing, listening to her opening and closing drawers. She dropped her earrings on the glass tray that held her perfume.

When she slid under the comforter, snuggling up beside me, I could smell the cigarettes and suntan lotion. Her feet left a trail of sand in the bottom of the bed. I continued to fake sleep, even when her hand tugged on a strand of my hair.

"I'm so sorry," she whispered.

I don't think Mom slept that night, and when I woke up, she was gone, the sheets on her side barely rumpled. By the time I reached the end of the hall, closest to the kitchen, I could hear them. Their whispers were hardly quiet.

"Good morning," I said, announcing myself.

Mom stood up to hug me. "You were out last night. Didn't even wake up with all my moving around."

I took a seat at the table. "I was pretty beat."

"So am I," she said, covering a yawn. She clasped her hands on the table like we were in a business meeting, a smile plastered on her face. "Aurora, there's something I have to tell you."

My newfound anger settled into my gut, a hot, unsteady feeling taking over. I knew what she was going to say. I knew what she was apologizing for last night.

"He's actually leaving her? Leaving them?"

The mention of her and them caused her smile to falter, but just for a moment. "How'd you know?"

Gran spoke up. "Probably figured it out when you weren't a puddle of tears."

Mom released a strained laugh. "Well, yes, he is coming. Tim's going to join this family. Soon. And really, I think it's best we just keep up our normal appearances. I don't see how this should affect either of you at all."

"You've got to be kidding me," I whispered when my back was to her. I poured myself a cup of coffee.

Mom turned around in her chair. "What's that?"

I took a step back. The Aurora I'd been for the last fifteen years told me to say nothing, to let the moment pass. But a voice I didn't recognize told me, *Just say it*. And I listened.

"I said, 'You've got to be kidding me.'"

"I'm missing the joke," Mom said, and her voice was sharp. "Forgive me, but I thought you'd be happy. This means we're staying. We're staying in Monroe."

I wanted to scream. But instead, I said, each word full of venom, "Are you stupid?"

It would have been better if I'd screamed.

"Whoa, whoa." Gran, suddenly a peacekeeper, rose from her chair. She didn't know this version of me, but neither did I.

"I just don't get it," I said, my voice catching on a sob. I wanted to stay angry, but my tears betrayed me. I turned to face her. "I could lose everything. And for what? He's leaving them. Who's to say he won't leave us? How long do we even have with him?"

Mom shook her head, her anger diffused by my tears. "Honey," she said, her voice soft. "It's not like that. I promise."

She reached out to touch my arm, but I took a step back.

"I don't think you understand." I tried to keep my voice steady, but my tears made my voice shake. "What about me?"

She remained silent. I tried again, my chin trembling. "What about what I want? Have you thought about me at all?"

"Oh, Aurora." She took my hands in hers and squeezed them, hard. "Honey, I think about you always. I want what's best for you—for *us*. You gotta trust me. What Tim and I have is real and it's *good*, honey. I know that's hard to see right now, but we're going to be a family. He's going to be—*he wants to be*—your dad."

Gran remained silent. I wanted her to speak up, to take my side, tell her this was crazy, but I knew better. She wouldn't fight her on this.

"How long until he comes?" I asked. There was no use in putting up a fight. I knew how it'd end.

"He said one week, just to prepare everything."

Everything. I guess everything was all-encompassing—and better than the truth. He had a week to say goodbye to the tiny blondes he'd raised since birth, goodbye to the wife he'd taken to prom, goodbye to the town who'd soon chew him up and spit him out. How long until he figured out we weren't worth it? That she wasn't worth it? I stormed out of the kitchen with both Mom and Gran trailing close behind.

"What are you doing?" Gran asked when I flung open the front door.

"Enjoying my last days of happiness."

It was a melodramatic thing to say, and I'll never forget Mom's face when I said it. Her painted red lips parted, the wideness of her blue eyes stark against her freshly tanned skin. My words might hurt, but in the end, they wouldn't matter. She would always choose herself.

I'd sassed her so few times in my life there was no other look for her to wear than one of pure shock. I glanced at Gran, and even with her hands planted on her hips, I swear she was trying not to smile.

Six days.

With Tim's arrival in mind, I began to live each day like my last. There was no time to be mad at Charlotte, no time to worry about spilled popcorn, no time to not kiss Harry.

I sat on Charlotte's floor and watched her paint her eyelids black.

"I still can't believe he's doing it," she said. "He's actually doing it."

"Well, let's wait and see what happens on Sunday."

"God, your mom must be good in bed."

"Ew, Charlotte. That's disgusting."

"I'm just sayin'." She turned to face me. "No man is going to destroy his entire life for mediocre sex. It's just not going to happen."

"Oh my gosh, *stop!* I'm going to throw up."

She threw her head back and laughed. Charlotte had made her transition from girl to woman of the world seamlessly. She'd drawn a line between herself and the virgins in town thanks to Kevin, and was now proudly smiling at me from the other side.

"I wonder what his exit plan is. Like does he just tell the girls and split? Is it bad that I wish I could see Lyla's face when he does it?"

"A little," I said.

"Maybe I should be more sympathetic. Losing a bad dad sucked, but losing a good dad probably sucks a lot more."

My stomach turned at the thought of it, and I wondered what Tim's final days looked like. Was he sitting down for nightly dinners? Was he kissing the girls' foreheads before bed? I wondered if his exit would be jarring, a sudden absence they'd never planned for. Or had it been a slow disappearing act—coming home late, leaving in the middle of the night, an inexplicable distance in his eyes. Maybe it wouldn't be a shock at all.

"What about you?" she asked.

"What about me?"

"Well, how are you going to tell Harry?"

I had run through a million different scenarios. In one I pretended that this was complete news to me, this torrid affair. But that'd be a lie, and I knew enough right and wrong to know lying didn't put me on the side of the good guys.

"Just be honest with him," Charlotte said. "If he splits, that's on him. He doesn't deserve you anyway."

"Maybe," I said, unconvinced.

He'd told me he wanted to know my secrets, the things that I held back from him. I'd had plenty of chances to be honest, but I let each and every one pass me by.

The final scenario, the one I'd decided on, was waiting as long as possible. I'd waited this long—would a few days really matter? They might be all I had left.

As far as any of us knew, Tim was scheduled to arrive on Sunday morning. That gave me six days to ignore the inevitable. Six days to sit with Charlotte poolside. Six days to drive with Harry in his truck. Six days to pretend the little blue house wasn't covered in gasoline, with my mom poised to drop her cigarette.

Charlotte flipped onto her side to face me, risking an uneven tan in the process. "I just thought of something," she said.

"What?"

She lowered her voice. "Isn't this what you wanted? I thought you said things were serious, that he might actually do it. What changed?"

For the first half of the summer, it had been my favorite daydream, Tim, Mom, Gran, and I—the happy family. I let myself think of it in the quiet moments of summer, what it'd be like to have a dad. But daydreams don't make good reality. It was stupid not to see the world outside our four walls. Not that I hadn't thought of his family every day. Weeks before I was sure it was worth it, that Tim was worth it.

But even though I saw how happy he made Mom, I also saw how unhappy he made her, how sad she was when he left, how often he left.

What would happen when her charms wore off? What would happen when things turned sour? All summer she'd been the best version of herself when he was around—warm, maternal, doting, flirty, dependable. Sure, there were fights. But then they'd make up, and all would be well again. Every moment with them felt stolen, but now there'd be nothing but time.

"I guess I just changed my mind." I shrugged. "I mean, it's not exactly realistic."

Charlotte smiled before flipping onto her stomach. "My little Aurora, all grown up."

"Shut up," I said, looking up at the tower and the boy with perfect teeth smiling down at me.

"What does Gran think?" she asked.

"She says things that burn that bright don't last all that long."

"Someone oughta tell that to this damned sun." She shielded her eyes, casting a shadow on her face before looking over at me. "Can I tell you something?"

"Of course."

"Remember when I was telling you about my dad bailing?"

"Yeah," I said.

"Well, before he left, I'd never really had friends. My mom was pretty strict about people coming over for, like, their own safety and stuff. And then when he was gone, she planned this whole sleepover, letting me invite the girls from my class."

I knew where this story was going, but she looked like she needed to tell it.

"So I passed out invitations and everything, and Mom bought me a new pajama set now that he wasn't there to police her spending. She cleaned the house and baked cookies. It was a whole thing. And, well, no one came."

Charlotte, despite her breasts, red lips, and blackened eyes, would always be the girl in two braids to me. "I'm so sorry," I said, reaching over to grab her hand.

She squeezed mine before letting go. "I've recovered, Aurora—don't worry. But what I'm saying is that my whole world was in pieces, and no one showed up. And next week if you throw a sleepover, I guarantee no one would come. But I will. Hell, I'll show up with bells on.

"I know what it's like to have the town look at you sideways. But you won't have to walk the Monroe High hallways alone—promise."

My eyes filled up with tears, and I blinked them back.

"Oh God," she said, "pull yourself together."

I wiped under my eyes.

She stood. "Your prince is on his way, and I'm going to take a dip." And just like that she was gone, submerged beneath the water before rising, her long hair sticking to her bare back. She smiled at the pool, her audience, commanding their attention. It felt good to have someone like that on my side.

"Hey," Harry said, taking a seat on her vacant chair.

"Pool looks a little different during the day," I said.

"Not quite as magical." He looked up at the increasingly overcast sky. "It looks like we might have a summer storm after all. Weatherman said possibly all week."

"I wish we wouldn't."

"Why?"

I hated summer storms. The way things changed all at once. The sunshine covered by clouds and the air thickening with moisture. And then, suddenly, lightning and thunder and more lightning and thunder. There was nothing predictable about a summer storm. Mom and I had pulled off the road for plenty, and there was no way of knowing how long you'd be stuck. Minutes or hours. I told Harry this, and he smiled.

"I think they're beautiful," he said. "Awe inspiring and terrifying at the same time. My dad used to let me stay up late to watch out the window."

He watched from the window of a home. I watched from the window of our Vega.

"My mom keeps talking about your cooking plans," he said. "I can tell she's really excited."

"You brave enough to try my cooking?"

"I might swing by," he said, reaching his hand over to tug on the end of my braid. "Just to see if you look good in an apron."

"Harry!" I swatted his hand away, laughing.

Wednesday would be day three of my seven. I hated the way the thought kept jumping out at me, even in my happiest moments.

25

Harry had volunteered to paint the front steps of the church, and I'd volunteered to watch him. I was messing with my hair, trying to style it, which had become a new habit of mine. I finally understood why Mom slept in curlers. It was nice to have someone to dress up for.

There was a knock on my door. I never used to shut it.

"It's me," Gran said. "Can I come in?"

I faced the mirror. "Sure."

"You look nice."

I reached up to smooth my hair. "Thanks."

Gran appeared beside me in the mirror. She looked pale, like she hadn't seen the sun too many days in a row. "Where you headed?"

"Harry's painting the church steps and I'm keeping him company."

"Can I tag along?" she asked, smiling at me in the mirror.

I turned to face her, not sure when she'd ended up in my line of fire. "Is this a peace offering?"

She shrugged. "There's no war between us, Aurora."

"We're allies?" I asked.

Gran wasn't always affectionate, but when she was, you knew she meant it. She reached over to tuck my hair behind my ear and smiled.

"We'll always be allies."

Harry didn't look surprised when I walked up to the church gate with Gran. He had already started the chore, and half of the steps were a fresh white. Harry was a good dresser, always in colored polo T-shirts and pressed shorts. That or his lifeguard getup. But his painting clothes were more casual than that. He wore a white T-shirt with rolled sleeves, like Danny in *Grease*. His bare feet stuck out of old highwater jeans, now covered in splatters of paint. Even his hair seemed a little messier.

"You two here for the show?" he asked, flashing his perfect teeth.

I opened the gate and climbed up the faded side of the stairs, reaching down to ruffle his hair when I walked past. Gran plopped down on the grass in front, in the shade beneath the single tree.

"This is as close as they usually let me," she said, nodding toward the church.

"Gran's pretty nervous she'll catch on fire," I said. "Been up to no good lately."

Harry laughed. "I'll have to ask my dad, but I'm pretty sure that's not how it works."

I watched Gran tuck her feet under her legs. "How'd you get stuck with this job?"

He pointed across the street at his house with the white picket fence, the same shade as the wood steps leading up the church. "Perks of being the son of the preacher man. Better than when I have to clean off the headstones."

Gran's eyes wandered over to the cemetery beside the church. Jay's headstone was somewhere in the back. We hadn't visited once—she'd told me there was nothing left of Jay in that plot of land.

"You know what would make it go faster?" Harry said, grinning.

"What?" I asked, giving in to his bit.

"Six hands instead of two."

Gran and I looked at each other and laughed, shaking our heads. "No thanks," we said in unison, before falling into another fit of laughter.

"It's so much more fun to watch," I said, still laughing.

Harry shook his head and kept painting.

"So Harry," Gran said, "I've got a question for you."

He wiped the sweat above his brow, leaving a thick streak of white paint across his forehead. Neither of us said anything.

"We'll see if I have the answer," he said.

"So, sin," she started, and I let out a long sigh. She held up a hand to shush me. "As far as sin goes, are some sins worse than others? Like, is there a ranking system?"

"I'm pretty sure that's not how it works. I think my dad would say all sin is the same in God's eyes, and I have a feeling that's a direct quote from the Bible." He pointed up at the sky. "Which is a direct quote from, you know, God."

Gran's eyes narrowed, and I could tell she wasn't buying what he was selling. "But do you really believe that?" she asked. "Like a man killing his wife and kids is committing the same sin as Aurora telling a little white lie?"

Harry looked like he'd painted himself into a corner.

"Gran, what in the world are you getting at?" I asked.

She shook her head. "I don't know, I'm just curious. It just seems strange God would look at us all the same."

"Well, I don't know about that," Harry said. "I mean is this murdering man praying for forgiveness? Does he believe in God? Does he feel remorse? Same for Aurora. Does she feel bad about the lie?"

My stomach somersaulted on itself, but I forced a laugh. "I don't know how I got dragged into this."

Gran smiled like she knew what she was doing.

"I have a lot to ask my dad," Harry said. "But it's not like we can really know for sure. Really, I'll have to ask God when, you know, my time comes."

"Do you think the big man will let you telephone your answer down to me?" she asked, pointing down to the ground beneath her.

My mouth fell open, but Harry just laughed, shaking his head.

"Never a dull moment," Harry said, reaching for his paintbrush. "Never a dull moment."

When Harry finished painting, he went over to his house to change. Gran asked him to join us for ice cream, and he'd answered with an enthusiastic yes. The two of us decided to walk the neighborhood while we waited.

"Can we?" I asked, pointing to the cemetery.

She stared off toward the back. "Sure," she said. "I don't mind."

The white gate creaked when I pushed it open. I thought I might remind Harry to grease it some afternoon. He'd get a kick out of that.

"This way," Gran said dutifully, turning right after the first row of graves.

Plenty of bodies were buried in this tiny cemetery. The bodies of people who'd spent their whole lives in Monroe, and the bodies of the people who'd managed to escape only to be dragged back for eternity.

"Here," she said.

JAY EASTMAN

1924–1979

Beloved husband, father, and grandfather

She knelt on the grass, and I knelt beside her. The cemetery was shaded, so the grass was cool on my bare knees, sending a chill down my arms.

"Pastor Clark said he was a good man."

Gran nodded. "He was a good man. Loved his church on Sunday morning."

"Did you ever go with?" I asked.

"Handful of times." She smiled. "When his birthday fell on a Sunday, he convinced me, and sometimes on Christmas. They had your boy Harry dressed up as Baby Jesus one year in the reenactment. I think Mary said Joseph's line, or something like that. I got the giggles, and Jay covered up my laughing with a cough."

I could picture it exactly as she told it.

"And then the funeral, of course. But you were there for that." She let out a long sigh, using the bottom of her dress to clean the dust off his headstone. "I was awful to him about it. Church, I mean. All the time. Told him if I'd wanted to marry a pastor, I would've married a pastor."

"He loved you," I said. "I'm sure you weren't that bad."

"I hope not."

"What was up with all the sin talk?" I asked.

"Just making sure you aren't too guilty by association."

"I'm not worried," I said, which was a lie. Guilt always spread throughout my body like a spider weaving its web. "Don't you worry either."

Gran frowned.

She used her pointer finger to trace Jay's name. "I don't know what he'd think of all this," she said, the words tumbling out like a sigh. "None of this would even be happening if Jay were alive. I never can keep things in control."

"If by *things* you mean Mom, no one can. She's never been one to be controlled. Especially not by Jay."

"I drank a lot," Gran said, "too much. I wasn't a good mom. Hell, I wasn't a good person. Jay wasn't there for all of that, just the aftermath. Your mom—she has a right to be mad at me."

"Everyone forgives you," I said.

"She doesn't."

"Have you asked her?"

Gran shook her head. "I know the answer."

"The thing about Mom is she'll always surprise you, and I don't mean in the bad ways. She's not as predictable as she seems. Give her a chance—see what she says."

A breeze ran through the cemetery, a rarity this summer. Gran closed her eyes. Maybe it was Jay's way of saying hello.

"I have lots to be sorry for," she said.

I reached for her hand. "Then maybe saying sorry is a good place to start."

I heard the door across the street slam and looked over in time to see Harry crossing the street toward us. He'd returned to his colored polo, a light blue to match his eyes, and pressed shorts. The weight on my chest I'd been trying to ignore pressed down.

Gran wiped the wet spots from under her eyes. "How'd you get so wise about things?"

I smiled. "You may not have been a good mom, but you're an amazing gran."

⁂

His mole on his neck, just below his ear.

The teeth. All of them.

His nervous hands. His hands on the steering wheel, stuck at ten and two.

The way he looked at me when he thought I wasn't looking.

How he could take me and Gran on a date and not ever complain about it.

The things I loved about Harry had begun to stack one on top of another, one by one, sitting on my chest like an elephant. I was overwhelmed in the best way. He liked long drives down Indiana roads. And I liked long drives in his passenger seat. Although that night, I let Gran have shotgun. I sat in the back seat, watching the two of them.

"You drive like you're eighty-five," Gran said. She reached over to press down on his leg like she always did to mine, speeding the car along. "Let's just try and get somewhere before sunrise tomorrow."

"Hey," he said, nervously glancing at her out of the corner of his eye.

"I'm just trying to get you to the darned speed limit." She put a hold on the cursing in front of Harry. "Heck, I want ice cream and you know I turn into a pumpkin at midnight."

Harry looked back at me in the rearview mirror, widening his eyes.

I smiled. "I'd help you out, but you know I've got no say in this."

"The motto in this car is: better safe than sorry." Harry shook his leg free of her hand, adjusting his grip on the wheel. "You oughta try it some time."

Gran looked impressed. "Sass looks good on you Harold Clark."

I leaned over the front seat so my head was between them. "Gran, if you could please refrain from flirting with my boyfriend, that'd be great."

She clucked her tongue. "And jealousy does not look good on you, Aurora."

The three of us laughed, and the lights from the town over became visible down the road.

"We might've gone bowling," I said, "but Gran's banned from Paradise."

Harry turned on his blinker for the left he'd make in a quarter mile. "What in the world for?"

"Don't tell him that." She spun around to glare at me.

"I'll fill you in later," I promised.

Harry smiled. "Well it's a shame you'll never see Aurora in action. She's a star at scooping that popcorn."

"Hey!" I reached over to slap his arm. "Don't mock me. There's a whole process. I took Al's class, and I passed on the first try. Not everyone does."

The Dairy Queen lot was empty. Harry parked in the same spot he'd parked in on our first date. Allan was behind the counter with that same paper hat and sour expression on his face.

"Don't sass Allan," I warned Gran. "He doesn't take well to it."

"Besides, it's Aurora's job to sass the Dairy Queen worker," Harry explained.

Warmth spread through my chest, replacing the anger that had been poisoning me for days. It felt weird, having to explain a part of my world to Gran. It felt weird, but good. Like I was inviting her into something that was just mine. I'd never been the host before, just a guest.

She walked through the door Harry held open for us, raising her eyebrows at me.

"He's just so polite," she whispered.

Allan looked up at us and exhaled loud enough for us to hear.

"You okay, son?" Gran asked him.

Allan nodded and his paper hat tilted a little to the left. "What can I get for you?"

"I'll have a dipped cone."

"Make it two," Harry said.

"Make it three." Gran leaned over the counter and lowered her voice. "But, Allan, can you do me a little favor?"

"What?" His voice was lifeless.

She smiled and tucked her hair behind her ear, batting her lashes like a schoolgirl flirting with the star football player. "Can you cover mine in those little peanuts?"

"A dipped cone with peanuts?"

Harry reached past her to pay for the ice cream, fighting a smile. He whispered an apology to Allan and dropped his change in the tip bucket.

"What's our order number?" I asked.

"One. You're still order number one."

Gran was already in a swiveling chair, moving it back and forth like an antsy child. I joined her. Harry waited by the counter for our cones.

Allan called out our order number, which made me think he was keen on the joke. Harry turned to face us, balancing the three cones in his two hands.

"I feel like your babysitter," he said, "and neither of you have earned your ice cream. Poor Allan."

Gran picked the peanuts off of the chocolate coating and popped them in her mouth.

She looked around at the inside of the Dairy Queen and tilted her head back, staring at the blue and white ceiling tiles. "I needed this."

"Ice cream?" I asked.

"No, just a day out. Sunshine. You two. Ice cream."

Harry took a bite out of his, quickly wiping for any stray chocolate flakes. "Guys, how long did I have that stripe of paint on my forehead?"

Gran bit down on her bottom lip so she wouldn't laugh. "Just most of the afternoon."

―・―

Harry said goodnight to the both of us in the driveway, already cutting it close for curfew. Gran was insistent he'd be fine, and told him he could always tell his parents he had been with a responsible adult. He looked around the car and in the back seat before asking, "Where's that responsible adult hiding?"

Before joining Gran in the driveway, I leaned over the center to kiss his cheek.

"I'll see you tomorrow," I whispered.

"I love you," he whispered back.

"I heard that!" Gran yelled.

By the time the two of us reached the front door, Harry's car had reached the end of our street. Both of us walked like our feet were full of lead.

"I don't want to go in," Gran said.

I reached around her for the doorknob. "That's my line. You sound like a child."

I went in first, and Gran followed. The record player had come to life. Mom was singing along to "Hotel California," missing most of the notes. A bottle of whiskey was half empty on the coffee table. Gran took in a sharp breath.

"You two home?" Mom hollered from the kitchen.

"Yep!" I yelled back.

She came around the corner with a smile. She was still in her work outfit, but her apron was on the table by the front door.

"Where were you two?" she asked, like the house hadn't been suffocated by her silence for the last two days.

"With Harry," I said.

"The both of you?" Mom asked, stepping into Gran's line of sight.

Gran didn't say anything.

"Yes," I answered for her.

Mom's smiled drooped at the corners, but I watched as she forced it back into place. "Well, that sounds fun." She walked to the coffee table and bent down to grab the bottle. "Mom, you want a drink?"

Gran just shook her head. It was so unlike her to turn down a drink, but at this point, I think she'd have said no to anything Mom offered.

"Suit yourself." Mom plopped herself down on the couch. "Anything good on tonight?"

I willed Gran to speak up, to meet Mom halfway, but I knew she wouldn't. I don't know if she could. When she walked down the hall, without a word, toward the bedroom she hadn't used all summer, I wasn't surprised.

Mom's head fell into her hand. "I'm trying," she said. "I'm really fucking trying."

I took the spot by her feet, even though the one beside her was empty. "I know."

"It's not easy for me either," she said. "I know it's hard for the two of you, but it's hard for me too. I've got people in this town I care about. People who won't look at me the same. Phil. Norma. P.J."

"But maybe you're the only one who has something to gain. Something to balance out the loss."

"Is Tim not a gain for all of us?" she asked.

I didn't know what to say to her. "Don't do it," I said, suddenly overcome by a fit of tears. "What if you guys changed your mind? Can you take it back?"

I'd never asked her not to do anything, even when her choices had ripped me out of schools and taken me to new towns full of strangers. But this time things were different. I'd lost childhood friends and comfortable beds and rooms that were cleaner than some others, but this time I'd lose everything. I worried I'd lose me, who I was, who I was becoming, who I could be.

She was crying as hard as I was, the two of us sobbing in the living room.

"It's not too late," I said. "There's still time to take it back."

She shook her head. "I don't want to take it back, Aurora. He's good to me. He's good to us."

"He has a family," I sobbed, my volume just below a yell. "I'll go to school with his daughter. Haven't you thought about that? About me? I see her at the pool, Mom. I see her at the bowling alley. I'll see her in the halls. She's everywhere."

Mom continued to cry. This felt like my last chance.

"Mom," I said, taking her face in my hands, like I could force her to hear me, "listen to me. This doesn't have to happen. Change your mind. Change *his* mind." I took in a deep breath. "Do it for me, please. I'm begging you."

"I just—" She took in a sharp breath. "I just can't."

I hated myself for having had hope. Hated myself for thinking she'd choose anyone other than herself. My disappointment was a direct result of expecting anything different. After fifteen years of being her daughter, you'd think I'd know better.

Now it was my turn to make a silent exit. I stood and steadied myself on the corner of the couch, worn out from all the crying.

"Aurora," she said, when my back was to her. The record screeched to a halt, letting her next words take center stage. "Please. Ask me for anything else."

I couldn't ask her for anything else because this was the one thing I wanted. And when my door shut behind me, I let myself cry even harder, loud enough so she could hear it through the walls.

I'd finally found a place to call home, and Mom didn't care.

26

The house returned to silence, and nobody did anything to fight it. Mom called out of her second shift in a row, and Gran turned the TV volume loud enough to drown out everything else. We were on speaking terms, though, Gran and I, whispering good mornings and goodbyes.

It was Wednesday, three days until Tim was supposed to show up. I was still hoping it wouldn't happen, and I lived like it wouldn't happen. Or I guess I lived like it would happen, cherishing the things I might not have cherished before. Bike rides in the August heat weren't as miserable as they used to be. I waved and smiled back at neighbors who might not be waving or smiling this time next week. Or maybe they would. So much could happen in three days.

Harry's curls were a direct inheritance from his mom. The gray spirals closest to her neck were soaked with sweat, flattening them against her skin.

"The wall unit went to crud," she said, wiping her forehead with a towel. "Harold Sr. is great at preaching, but not so great at fixing things. I'll have the junior look at it when he gets home."

I smiled at her name for him. "The junior."

"So, Harold told me your favorite meal—of the instant kind—is meat loaf and mashed potatoes. Is this true?"

I nodded. "It's a heck of a lot better than the pot pie. Not quite as good as the pot roast, though, but Gran always eats those."

She smiled at this. "Well, then tonight's menu is settled. I'm going to teach you the home-cooked version, and I guarantee it'll have Swanson's frozen foods beat. You up for some cooking?"

"Let's hope so," I said.

She passed me an apron from a hook on the wall beside the stove. It was one of many in varying prints and colors. I'd only ever seen aprons on TV, and the Clark home was as close to a TV home as I'd ever seen. It looked nothing like ours, and Mrs. Clark was nothing like Mom. Mom never taught me to bake cookies, never asked me to set the table. Come to think of it, we'd never had a home-cooked meal besides diner-style breakfast. There was no reason to own an apron.

"I sew these myself," she said, noticing me staring.

I didn't want to say that I'd only seen them on TV so I just smiled, tying the cherry print around my waist. "I like them," I said.

She began pulling things out of the fridge one by one, handing them to me to bring to the counter.

Everything about it was so utterly normal. Was this what it was like to be a daughter? Was this what it was like to cook with your mom? Had Lyla Jr. grown up with moments like this?

"The meat loaf takes the longest," she said.

I leaned around her to see what else the fridge held, but there were too many things to count. Vegetables in drawers and Tupperware containers I'd seen over at Rexall. In this house, nobody ate old bananas for breakfast, washed down with bad coffee. They had pancakes and eggs, and I thought I saw bacon, but I couldn't be sure.

"Here." She passed me the package of raw meat. "This part's easy. We're just going to mix all of this up." She pointed to the meat, an onion, an egg, milk, and some sort of cracker. "That's one bowl. And these all go in the other." On the other side of the counter there was ketchup, brown sugar, and mustard. "Which do you want to tackle?"

I pointed to the side with fewer ingredients.

"It just looks a lot more manageable," I confessed, and she laughed.

She chopped the onion with a knife that looked nothing like the butter knives in our drawers at home. I just watched. My eyes began to water, and I worried I might have started crying, but then Claire-Ann wiped her eyes with the bottom of her apron.

"It's the onions," she explained, laughing at whatever face I must have been making. "Chopping onions is a lesson for another day."

She told me how much of each I was supposed to pour in the bowl. We doubled the ketchup because that was both Harolds' favorite part. After she put her meat mixture in the pan, I poured my stuff over the top, and she called it a glaze.

"What next?" I asked.

"It cooks for about an hour," she said, twisting the knob on a timer shaped like a chicken. "We've got about thirty minutes before we need to start the potatoes." She fanned her face with a piece of mail. "I figure we sit in front of the fan and try and get to know each other a little better."

I followed her out of the kitchen and into the living room, wiping my palms on my apron. I hadn't pictured this part of the afternoon—the in-between. Sitting with an almost stranger, having to find more than two words to answer her questions. I hoped my face didn't betray my nerves. I took the seat opposite the one with the cross-stitch beside it.

"What are you working on?" I asked.

"Just some flower patterns for my pillows."

She set her hands in her lap, and I swear I could hear the tick of the timer from the next room. The silence spread between us, and I hoped she wouldn't ask about my family. Not yet. I didn't have enough energy to lie.

"How did you and Pastor Clark meet?" I asked, hoping to fill up the silence and steer the conversation away from anything having to do with me.

"Oh no," she said, laughing, "that story's so ancient. You sure you want to hear it?"

"Very much," I said, setting my hands in my lap to mirror hers.

She smiled. "Okay, then. Let's hope I can still remember it. It was high school, you see. I was about your age, and he was a year above. I was in the church choir and led the Sunday school, and I'm sure Harry's mentioned he's a part of a long line of preachers. Sound familiar?"

"Just a little."

"Well, Harold Sr.'s father was the preacher at the time, but Harold Sr. was not so keen on the church scene. He was a bit of a wayward son." She paused and shook her head, smiling. "A wild child, if you will. My parents always talked about him at dinner, how he was turning out to be a bad seed. Any other fifteen-year-old girl would have been intrigued, but not me. I was a bit of a prude then, and his whole reputation horrified me."

I couldn't picture Pastor Clark as a rebel, especially not in his ill-fitting suits and patterned neckties.

"And then it was summertime and a group of us had decided to go over to the lake, and no one told me Harold would be coming. Probably on purpose. I really don't know if I would've gone, which seems silly now. But I was so passionate in my hate for him, which in hindsight isn't a very Christian emotion. So there he was, swinging from a rope on the rocks into the lake, splashing us girls while we sunbathed on the shore. In a moment of bravery—or perhaps stupidity—I went up to tell him my mind."

She laughed a little and put a hand to her cheek, which was turning pink while she spoke.

"I still remember the water splashing up onto my dress with my determined steps. I was so irritated, and I was ready to tell him so, but then when I reached him, he smiled and stuck out his hand.

"'I'm Harry,' he said.

"And I think I said something like, 'I know who you are.'

"But I did take his hand when he offered it. And he had a nice smile and kind eyes, and he was so handsome, just like all my friends had been telling me. All of my fight left me then, and I was just smiling back. He must have asked if I had anything to say, and I said, 'No, just hello.' And then it was history. It was my turn to walk on the wild side, I guess, staying out late with the preacher's son and sassing my parents."

"When did you become so—" I started, and then stopped.

"So *not* wild?" she filled in.

I nodded.

"Well, that wouldn't be for a couple years at least. But the elder Pastor Clark got sick, and I think my Harold had it in him all along. He knew what he was supposed to do, but he just had to do it in his own time. It was the Prodigal Son all over again. No questions asked, they took him back. Took *us* back, because we were married by then, living just one town over. And I rejoined the choir of course. The hymns hadn't changed much. I still knew most by heart."

I asked questions about her church wedding and her parents, who had passed away before Harry was born. I kept up the questions, mostly because I wanted to know the answers, but also to keep myself from having to lie to this kind and honest woman. I think we were both a little relieved when the timer went off.

"Potato time," she said, walking toward the kitchen with me trailing close behind her. In the kitchen, she passed me a knife and a potato. "Okay, watch this," she said, scraping the skin off her own potato in long, steady strokes. "Be careful not to cut your thumb."

I didn't understand how she managed not to cut her thumb. I scraped the potato skins off in short, unsteady chunks, peeling one potato for every four Claire-Ann added to the boiling pot. In the end I got the hang of it, sort of. I could make it halfway toward my thumb, unsteady and slow, before breaking off the skin and tackling the second half.

"You don't have to get all of the skin off," she said.

We peeled ten potatoes in the time it took to cook an instant tray in our oven at home. By the time they were in the pot to boil, both Harold Sr. and Harold Jr. had joined us in the kitchen.

"How'd she do?" Harold Sr. asked, kissing Claire-Ann's cheek as a hello.

I looked at the chicken timer counting down for us. "We'll have a better idea in fifteen minutes," I said.

"Oh, shush." Claire-Ann placed a hand on my shoulder. "She was great. We've got to speed up her potato peeling, but that's a practiced skill. Now get out of the kitchen."

She shooed them out with a towel and turned to grab a bowl from the cabinet above the sink. Harry squeezed my hand before he left.

"Can you keep a secret?" she asked, stepping into her pantry and shuffling around a few items. When she emerged, she was holding a can of green beans. "I never cook green beans fresh. Or corn for that matter.

I just buy these cans and heat them up. They taste just as good, and no one's the wiser."

"Now this looks like my kind of cooking," I said.

Claire-Ann and I sat across from each other, waiting for the Harolds to give their verdict.

"Highest praises," Harold Sr. said after his last bite. "The ketchup in the glaze was the perfect amount."

We turned to Harold Jr., who was smiling, his plate now empty. "Having been lucky enough to have tried Aurora's usual meat loaf and potatoes, I can assure you all that this was much improved."

"Hey!" I said, laughing. "I will say making this is more work, but it's also more fun."

Spending the afternoon in the kitchen and the evening at the Clark's dinner table, I'd only thought of Tim once, and that was a miracle. Cooking, and this family, was my perfect distraction.

"What's next week's menu?" Harold Sr. asked.

Claire-Ann smiled. "I'll teach her a casserole. One of my mother's."

Harold Sr. patted his belly while he rose from his chair. "Put me down for a plate."

I smiled at the friendly faces turned toward me, and at Harry's hand on my knee during the meal, beneath the table. But there was no way I'd be here next Wednesday. I had plans, or rather, *we* had plans. We were taking in a houseguest and ruining lives. I guess I could have told Claire-Ann that, but instead I just smiled and said, "That sounds great. I'll be here."

Lying to a preacher and his wife. If Gran was right and sins were ranked, this one had to be one of my worst yet.

27

Gran always said I searched for fires before anyone else smelled smoke. I think I just felt like I was the only one fit to worry about the three of us. Gran and Mom waited until the fire was outside our door, trapping us inside. I was the proactive one.

But it was Thursday, and nobody needed warning. The fire was all around us, the smoke suffocating the little blue house. Mom was a mess, crying at the kitchen table and flipping through the same magazine she'd flipped through all morning. Maybe she was scared that he was coming so soon. Maybe she was scared he wouldn't come at all. I didn't ask.

"I'm going to the grocery store," I said, loud enough so Gran could hear me over the TV volume. "In case anyone wants to join."

Their silence was an answer. I left Mom at the kitchen table and Gran in her recliner. The Vega keys were on the side table by the door. I was risking Phil pulling me over, but at this point, I would've welcomed his company.

⁂

The cart I picked had a broken wheel that kept making me turn right, even when I didn't want to. I knocked over a display of potato chips and hurried onto the next aisle before anyone could notice. I kept wondering what Tim liked to eat, but we hadn't gotten that far in the getting-to-know-you process, and nobody knew how to make anything that wasn't instant.

The frozen aisle was usually one of our only stops in our short trips to IGA. Cereal, bananas, milk, and then enough frozen dinners to last us for a week—maybe two, just to be safe.

I picked more of the frozen variety than usual, stocking the cart with everything from meat loaf to chicken pot pie and some Italian dish too "spicy" for Gran. Tim hadn't been over at dinnertime enough for me to know his favorites. I don't know why I was concerned about his favorites.

Then I remembered the recipe Harry's mom had made and how simple it was. I decided to be a little brave and venture beyond the frozens. I knew the meat was somewhere near the back, so that's where my squeaky wheel and I headed.

There was a real live butcher in our grocery store, and his name was Brian. I'd seen him at the diner and a few nights at Paradise. He was meaty, and his face was a sweaty pink, like he'd been born for the role. I stood and stared at the glass case filled with raw meat.

"Can I help you, miss?" he asked.

I touched my finger to the glass. "Which of these is for meat loaf?"

"Ground beef," a woman's voice answered.

Brian passed a white, paper-wrapped package of meat to the woman standing beside me. *Harrison* was written across the package in a childlike scrawl. My stomach dropped, but I forced myself to look beside me. There stood Lyla Rae Sr. in all of her blonde-haired glory.

"Call me when the steak prices drop," she said, setting the package among a full cart of groceries.

"Will do, Mrs. Harrison."

I stared at her with wide eyes, unable to look away, and eventually she noticed.

"I promise," she said, nodding toward the glass, "beef is the right choice."

I couldn't even smile back at her or nod my head. Both Brian and I watched her go, and her cart, even full of groceries, didn't wobble a bit.

"You order it in pounds," Brian explained, mistaking my expression for confusion. "How many plates at your table?"

I walked away from Brian, leaving behind my cart full of thawing frozen food. I walked past the checkout where Lyla Rae Sr. unloaded food for her family onto a moving conveyor belt. I walked through the sliding glass doors and into the sunlight. It blinded me enough to make me sit down on the curb and wait until the spots disappeared from my vision and my eyes adjusted.

When I came home without groceries, I offered no excuses. I didn't have to. Nobody asked questions.

～

Mom was prettier than Lyla Rae Sr. by a mile. Her hair was fuller and her lashes were longer, even if it was with the help of mascara. Mom kept her hair long, and it made her look young. Lyla Rae Sr. had slipped into the role of motherhood seamlessly while Mom avoided it like a curse. Lyla Rae Sr. had more lines by her eyes too, and her hair had less shine. I couldn't stop thinking about her, comparing the two. Maybe Tim was doing the same thing, pitting the two against each other, making his list of pros and cons.

Lyla Rae won out on familiarity, but Mom was the new, shiny toy. Lyla Rae could cook a meal, just based on what I saw in that grocery cart, but Mom sometimes burned her instant stuff. But Mom made Tim laugh, hard, and she was always throwing her head back and laughing at her own jokes. She flirted with him and danced around the living room, slipping her hands into the back pockets of his Levi's while they swayed until the record needed flipping. He looked at her like she was the only one in the room.

Mom always talked about how the Harrisons had a bad marriage, but I didn't know much about marriage, and definitely not enough to tell the difference between a good and a bad one. I don't think Mom knew enough either. Lyla Rae seemed nice enough, though. She offered advice to strangers in grocery stores, which had to count for something.

In the TV shows we watched, women always found clues that the men were cheating. Earrings left behind in the car. Panties stuck in pockets. Makeup on his collar. I wonder if Lyla Rae had any suspicions, if she was kept up at night by the thought of where he was and who he was with, the unfamiliar scent on his skin. I knew the feeling. The panic.

Sunday was just a few days away. There was no point in wondering. She'd know soon enough.

Harry called our house in the early afternoon, and Mom beat me to the phone. She stood in the hallway with it cradled between her neck and ear. I was expecting a call, and I knew who it was. I motioned for her to hand me the phone, and she turned to face the wall.

"Oh, hi, Harry," she said. "I'm very well," she lied. "And how are you?"

"Mom," I hissed, "give me the phone."

"Oh, that's great to hear. Maybe she'll show off her talents around here some time." She laughed at the conversation I wasn't a part of. "You're funny. Well, I better pass you off to Aurora." Long pause. "I know you do. Okay, have a good night."

She passed me the phone, and her eyes looked watery, like maybe she was about to cry. I wanted to ask, but there wasn't any time.

"Hello?" I said, my voice an octave higher than normal.

"Can I pick you up?" he asked.

I smiled. "Straight to the point."

He laughed. "Is that a yes?"

"Yes."

After the afternoon at the grocery store and the hours I'd stared at the ceiling, thinking of Lyla Rae Sr., I was ready for a Harry distraction. Plus, it was Thursday, day four. I had to make the most of my limited time.

The end of summer was in sight now, and we'd done everything in town three times over. We were young, and we should have been bored, but things with Harry were never boring. We bickered about where to go, and Harry was laughing, hunched over the wheel in his usual driving style.

"I think I'm about ready for school to start up again," he said.

I didn't like to think that far ahead, because anything past Saturday filled me with instant panic. School halls filled with kids from town who knew what my mother had done that summer. What we had done. I wasn't ready to look past tonight.

He kept talking, making up for my silence. "I was thinking I could pick you up for school in the mornings. It's not too out of my way."

I swallowed the lump in my throat. "Charlotte said her mom can take us," I managed.

"Oh, I don't mind picking up Charlotte too." He smiled and glanced over at me. "Or at least I don't mind *that* much."

"Who do you sit with at lunch?"

"Probably my girlfriend," he said. His happiness was normally contagious, but no amount of Harry's blind optimism could stop the dread settling in my bones.

"I mean who do you usually sit with?"

"The usual suspects—Shane, Marie, Lyla Jr. You'll meet Joshua too. He's been gone for the summer, working at a summer camp, but I think you'll like him. And I know they won't mind Charlotte joining."

Before I could stop myself, I began to cry. It took Harry a minute to notice because he was so focused on the road, but when he did, he pulled over.

"Aurora," he said, his voice panicked. "What's happening? What's wrong?"

I couldn't speak, so I just kept shaking my head and crying. The truth was inside of me, trying to claw its way out. I couldn't do it, though. The words couldn't come. I wouldn't let them.

"Is it me?" Harry asked. "Is it us?"

That couldn't be further from the truth, and just him thinking it made me cry harder. I shook my head again.

"Is it Gran?" he asked.

Again, I shook my head. "What if we aren't together then?" I asked, trying to stop his guessing game from going any further. "We might not be together when school starts."

"What?" His question came out like a laugh. "Aurora, are you crazy?"

"I don't know," I said. "Maybe. So much can happen between now and then."

"But I love you." His voice was still almost a laugh, like us breaking up was as likely as aliens landing in Monroe. "Don't you love me too?"

I did. "I do," I said, wiping the snot from my nose with the back of my hand. "But what if I'm gone by then?"

He furrowed his brow. "You got plans to head out of town?"

"No," I said, "not really."

He adjusted so he was turned toward me and took my face between his hands. He pressed his forehead against mine, staring into my eyes until I closed them because looking at him hurt.

"What if you change your mind?" I asked, putting words to my lingering fears.

"I love you, Aurora. *Period*. I don't think that's gonna change."

"Okay," I said, choosing to believe him.

I didn't want to face reality tonight. Instead, I kissed him hard, leaning my whole body into his. He swore he loved me now, but that didn't mean he would love me then. If I'd learned anything about love from watching Mom's escapades and Gran's soaps, it was that love could come and go. I had to take advantage of it while it was here. I didn't know if he'd love me come Sunday, so I kissed him like Sunday didn't exist.

His hands clutched at the small of my back. We stayed kissing like that long enough to miss the first raindrop hitting the windshield, and the second. The sky had darkened with the suddenness of a summer storm.

"Wow," Harry said, pulling back and looking at me.

"We should go," I said, breathless. I nodded toward the droplets streaming down the windshield. "It'll only get worse."

Harry scooted back to his side of the car and started the engine. He drove back to town on the same road we'd used to escape it, retracing our steps. The rain was heavier now, and his hands were white on the steering wheel.

When he turned into our driveway, I told him to call me when he got home. The rain soaked through my clothes when I ran to the porch and watched his taillights disappear down the street. It was heavy enough I didn't notice the pickup parked in front of the little blue house.

When I stepped inside, the three of them were facing the door, like they'd been waiting. Tim on the couch with Mom beside him, Gran in her recliner, the TV volume so low it could have been muted.

I looked at Mom. "What's going on?"

Mom forced a smile. "Slight change of plans," she said, just as I noticed the suitcase against the wall.

"Surprise," Gran said, her voice deadpan.

For Karl, the summer storm brought rain for his flowers. For Indiana, the summer storm brought relief. For us, the summer storm brought us a houseguest who looked like he'd packed for a weeklong stay at a coastal resort. Maybe that's what we were. A vacation. There was just the one suitcase. I should have known it wasn't going to last. She should have known too.

I didn't say anything else that night, just walked to my room. And when the phone rang, loud and shrill, Gran answered it. She came in to give me Harry's message. He was home safe, and he promised he'd call me tomorrow.

And then tomorrow came, and the sun rose to take back the cloud-covered sky, making me feel like the storm had been some sort of strange dream. I waited by the phone all morning, but Harry never called.

* * *

The phone rang at half past one—a loud, shrill, earth-shattering ring. I ran to answer, leaving Tim behind on the couch, the smallest spark of hope fanning into flame.

"Hello?" I answered.

I hoped it was Harry. I was terrified it was Harry.

"Aurora? It's Al."

I pressed my palm against the wall. "Hi, Al," I said, unable to hide my disappointment.

"I'm looking at the schedule, and I have you down for tonight, but it looks like I double-booked. Jim is supposed to work the snack bar, and I know he's hard up for cash right now." His lines sounded forced, and I knew what he was saying, even though he wouldn't outright say it. "The good news is you're freed from the ball and chain of a Friday night shift."

"And tomorrow?" I asked, testing him.

Al let out a long sigh into the phone, and with his asthmatic breathing it almost sounded like static. "Let's give it a week or so, okay?" Stripped of the false cheer, he just sounded sad. "A week for things to blow over."

"Who else knows?" I asked, overwhelmed by the claustrophobia of the little blue house.

"For now, I think it's safe to assume everyone."

A giant lump settled in my throat. Harry hadn't called today, and he probably wouldn't call tomorrow. The fears I'd felt all summer would be confirmed with each passing day.

"Okay," I said, forcing the words out. "Goodbye, Al."

Before I could hang up the phone, he spoke quickly. "It's not about you," he said, his words tumbling out. "You're a good kid, and you've still got a job. I'm just trying to shelter you from the people who haven't figured that out yet. Rain eventually gives way to the sun."

"You sound like Gran," I said.

"She may be a cold bitch, but she's a wise woman," Al said. He barked out half a laugh. "You be good, okay? I'll call you when you're back on the schedule."

"Okay, bye Al."

I returned the phone to the receiver and leaned against the wall, sliding down to the tiled floor. The tears I tried to hold back slipped down my face.

Tim returned the TV to its normal volume, and Mom joined him in the living room. I could smell her perfume filling the house, and I didn't have to go out there to know her hair would be done up, even though there were no plans for them to leave. Not now, maybe not ever. The cartoon on the TV must have been funny. Mom and Tim joined in with the laugh track.

My world was collapsing around me, but they carried on as if everything wasn't burning to the ground.

⁂

Charlotte was our first visitor. I saw her through the blinds. I'd been watching the world passing by, tracking the clouds outside of the window and Karl's gardening. She was a flash of blonde hair on her bike, which was pink, with ribbons down the side and beads on the wheels. It was only brought out for emergencies. I opened the door before she could even knock.

"Holy shit," she said, her makeup-free skin pink from the sun. Loose strands of hair clung to her temples. She lowered her voice. "Is he here?"

I nodded. "We can go in my room."

She walked ahead of me, leading the way in my own home. When I shut my door behind me, she spun around.

"Um, what happened to Sunday?" she asked. "Laine had a very specific timeline, no?"

I shrugged. She hadn't given much of a reason, and he hadn't given much of a reason either. I'd been on a silent streak ever since.

"Is this for good?" she asked.

Again I shrugged. "Who told your mom?"

"Gran called me." She flopped across my bed. "She figured you'd need a friend."

I had no idea when Gran had managed to sneak in a call, but I was grateful. Tim and Mom had slept in the living room last night after Gran took her and Jay's room back for good. She'd locked the door behind her, and no one had seen her since.

"Al called and said everyone knows. I'm basically fired for the time being. Off the schedule."

"Al's such an exaggerator." Charlotte was staring up at the ceiling. "But the Lylas know, which means Harry probably knows. He was probably Lyla's first call. God, she was jealous of you from the start."

I couldn't imagine Lyla's first thought after her dad abandoned her family was to call her crush, but the seed was planted. Thoughts of Harry and Lyla played out in my mind, and I knew I'd never be able to shut them off.

Was his heart as broken as mine? I'd been so worried about my own that I'd forgotten about his. Yes, my insides felt shattered, but I'd lived all summer carrying this reality with me, the potential to lose it all. I hadn't been blindsided, but he had. This sudden realization—that I could have broken his heart—was too devastating to bear.

"So is he nice?" Charlotte asked, forcing me out of my trance.

"I don't know. I guess so. I'm not sure it matters." I climbed up in the bed beside her. "I just want to turn back time."

"I know." She took my hand. "But hon, that's impossible."

"School will be hell," I said.

"School's always hell. But I suppose the first month will be particularly hellish."

"They're going to be so mean to me."

A sad smile lifted a corner of her mouth. "They'll be mean to *us*."

"I can't ever see Harry again." Again, the images played out in my mind. Harry and Lyla hand in hand. Tragedies always bring people together. It's a plotline in every season of *General Hospital*. "I mean it. Like ever, ever."

And maybe I didn't deserve to see him again. More and more, my heartbreak was being replaced with a giant serving of guilt. I'd kept this from him, never giving him a choice. Never giving him a chance. I was the one who had spent all summer making promises I couldn't keep.

"I don't know how we'll manage that, but we can try."

"Okay," I said.

Charlotte, for all of her talking, was good at the silent parts of friendship too. We stayed in my bed well into the afternoon, side by side, staring up at my stucco ceiling. Eventually Mom knocked and offered Charlotte frozen meat loaf, which she politely declined. She promised she'd be back tomorrow, and I returned to the blinds to watch her go. The pink ribbons on her bike handles twisted and twirled in the wind.

Tim spent all of dinner ranking our frozen meals, and he managed to get us all laughing. Gran emerged for dinner, probably out of necessity. She joined us at the kitchen table, but she refused to crack a smile until he started in on the meat loaf. Every time he'd been over before, we'd given him the worst dish because he was too dumb to know the difference, but he was starting to catch on.

I hated being charmed by him, because it made me feel like her. I feared becoming my mother's daughter. Look at me long enough and make me laugh, and I'll throw away my whole life for you. It was sad and pathetic. But then again, here I was, laughing at his jokes and wondering if he'd actually stay. It was easier to become her than I'd thought.

We moved the party into the living room, and Gran turned up the TV. Mom settled in the spot beside him, and I took the space on the floor. Soon it would be twenty-four hours since I'd stepped foot outside of the little blue house. Monroe continued on without us, which was unnerving. The bowling alley was open. Jim was serving popcorn and drinks. Kids were kissing in the trees by the river. The pool was dark and empty. Claire-Ann was needlepointing a pillow with her favorite flowers. And Harry was somewhere in all of it too, not calling me.

And then there was the house across town, with three girls in it. They ate dinner at a kitchen table too, but with a fourth chair left empty. Maybe the mom in the house had set out a plate in case he came back. Did she hope he'd come back? I imagined her crying while she passed the peas and buttered the bread.

⁂

Charlotte came the next day with a bag full of groceries.

"Figured I'd spare you a trip to the gossipiest place in town." She set the paper bag on the kitchen table just as Tim stepped through the door.

"Oh, hi," he said, extending his hand. "You must be Charlotte."

"And you must be the mailman," she said, smirking.

He laughed. "Tim will be just fine." He reached into the bag on the table and lifted out a stack of frozen meals. "I don't mind putting these away."

"Thanks," I said.

He was studying the names of the meals. "But I get dibs on the pot roast."

"Good luck trying to swing that."

When we got to my room, Charlotte looked over at me with raised eyebrows.

"What?" I said, sitting cross-legged on my floor, holding a bottle of nail polish.

"You two seem polite, *almost* on the verge of friendly."

"*Friendly*'s a stretch." I could tell she didn't buy it. "But he does live in my house for now, which I'm sort of stuck in. So yes, I am making the best of it."

She threw up her hands. "No need to get defensive. It was just an observation."

"Any news from the outside?" I asked.

"Well, I did go to the pool this morning."

"What? And?"

"Calm down. He wasn't there, so I asked around. He called in sick."

"Sick? He's sick?"

She rolled her eyes. "Don't be dumb, Aurora. He's lovesick, maybe. Probably home with heartache."

"Should I call him?"

I'd gone back and forth all day. I mean, did the news really change things between us? But of course it changed things between us. It changed things for everyone. Still, I wanted to hear his voice. I wanted to give him the chance to say the right things and to see the differences between my mother and me. If enough people told me I wasn't like her, I might start to believe it.

"Do you think you should call?" Charlotte always asked questions in a tone that gave away the answer.

"No." I layered a second coat of purple on my toes. "Chances of him calling? Honestly?"

"I say we give it a few days. I'm not counting him out yet." After studying the two bottles of polish in her hand, she settled on the red she always selected. "I'm still not sure if good guys even exist, but if they do, Harry's one of them."

"Hey, Charlotte," I said. She looked over at me. "When my mom asks you if you want to stay for dinner, can you say yes?"

She smiled. "Sure. But only if I get that pot roast."

༄

At dinner, Tim offered Gran a glass of whiskey, but she refused it. Mom took the glass from his extended hand, softening the blow. I couldn't think of the last time I'd seen Gran drinking whiskey, and I tried my hardest to remember. For the past week, maybe longer, she'd kept a glass of water by her side, sipping it throughout the day. Charlotte watched the people at the table like they were characters in a TV show. Any hint of tension didn't go unnoticed.

After dinner, when our instant dinner trays were empty, Tim suggested a game of Pictionary. Whatever faces the four of us made had him laughing.

"We're not really family game people," Gran explained.

"But we can try," Mom said, placing her hand on top of his.

It was his second night here, and we were already eating at the kitchen table, and now we were about to have a family game night like the families they showed in the commercials on TV. I'd spent most of my life ignoring the part of me that wanted that life.

In first grade, the teacher had assigned us to make a family portrait. She wanted us to draw a picture of our home and the people in it. Kids came to school with crayon pictures of yellow houses with moms, dads, siblings, dogs, and cats. One kid even had a turtle. When it was my turn to present, there was a gray house, and beside it stood stick figures of me, Mom, and Mario, our roommate at the time.

"Who's Mario?" a kid asked.

I had no answer that made sense to my classmates. Honestly, before they'd presented their photos, I'd assumed everyone had a Mario, but it turns out it was just us. The teacher was more perceptive than the students, though, and she moved along my presentation rather quickly.

We gave in to the game night. It turned out none of us had played before, besides Tim. It also turned out he was terrible at explaining games and rules. It took ten minutes of him rambling before Charlotte cut him off.

"Two teams. We draw pictures. People on our team guess what we're drawing. They guess right, the team gets a point?"

Tim nodded. "Exactly."

"Let's get this show on the road then," Gran said, releasing the sigh she'd spent ten minutes holding in. I'm sure she regretted turning down the whiskey.

Tim was a terrible artist. It was movie-themed Pictionary, and he'd really managed to terrify us all with *The Young Frankenstein*. Charlotte, to her own surprise, was an amazing artist. Her drawings looked like the posters outside of the theater. Mom, Gran, and I—we were average and apathetic. It must have been genetics. Gran hollered wrong answers and heckled Tim while he struggled to draw a shark for *Jaws*. In the end we won, mostly because Charlotte was a ringer.

If I were assigned a family portrait, my crayon drawing of the little blue house would look normal to anyone who didn't know the truth. Unfortunately, in a town as small as Monroe, a person like that would be hard to find.

༺༻

Besides Charlotte, we had one other visitor. On our third day trapped in the little blue house, we were startled by a knock on the front door. Charlotte wasn't big on knocking—she preferred to barge right in. By the second knock, it was clear I was the only one brave enough to answer it. Tim's face was a violent shade of red, and I could see the sweat forming on his upper lip.

"Who is it?" I called, like they teach you to do in the afterschool PSAs.

"Karl!" he called back in his warm, familiar voice.

I opened the door and stepped to the side so he could come in. Except for the morning of Jay's funeral, I couldn't remember a time Karl had stepped foot in our home. He was mostly confined to his own yard. A trip across the street was startling.

"Come in," I said because he looked like he needed some prompting.

He had a single flower clenched in his wrinkled hand, and it wasn't a rose. It was pink with smaller petals all around. His roses were more friends to him than flowers.

"For you," he said, extending his hand.

"It's lovely," I said. "I'll put it in some water."

I wondered if it was his condolences.

"Hi there, Karl." Tim stood to shake his hand. "I'm sure you're not at all surprised to see me here. What with you keeping watch on the comings and goings, I mean."

Karl smiled. "Can't say that I am."

"Oh, Karl," Gran spoke up from her recliner, "you've seen too much of our little blue house. The good and the bad."

"Seen you for sixteen years now, Katherine. Carried you to the front door when you passed out on the lawn. And when the cops came that summer. Remember the big fight between you and—"

"Okay," Gran interrupted, raising her hand to silence him. "That's enough. We get it."

Karl winked at me. He loved reminding Gran of the times he'd carried her to the front door and all the places she'd passed out on the street.

"Anyway, I just came to say hello because it's been a few days since any of you've taken a stroll past my yard." He gestured to the flower in my hand. "Thought I'd bring the yard to you."

"That was thoughtful of you, Karl," Mom stepped forward to take his hand in hers.

"I must be going," he said, like he had plans beyond his lawn chair in the front yard. "I only have time for a short visit."

Before he left, he leaned over to Mom and whispered something I couldn't hear. Gran noticed too, and Mom nodded at Karl before releasing his hand. I eased the door shut behind him and hurried over to the spot by the window, because Karl walking across the street was the most action we'd had all day.

Sometime after three, the substitute mailman tugged on our rusted, creaky mailbox. The sound reminded me of Dorothy's Tin Man coming to life. Tim had decided to make things easier by taking a week off for "vacation." I don't know why he thought a week was long enough for things to blow over, but that's probably all he could afford.

Tim leaned closer to the blinds and squinted. "That's Mark," he said, hopping up in time to yank open the front door and step outside. "Mark!" he called.

Mark didn't look shocked to see him, but he did look frightened. His smile was strained, and for every step Tim took forward, Mark took two back. Karl seemed to watch the show too. Tim was talking animatedly, though I had no idea what about. His weekend wasn't the kind you tell your coworkers about. In the end, Tim clapped a strong hand on Mark's shoulder, and the three of us watched Mark hurry down the street toward his mail truck.

When Tim faced the house, he stopped and stared at it, like he was seeing it for the first time. He looked pained by his first interaction with the outside world, almost as pained as I felt witnessing it. His arms hung limp at his sides, and I watched him turn to look back toward the place where the mail truck used to be.

I don't know what he'd expected to happen.

Nobody ever said anything about us not leaving the house; I guess it was just understood. It wasn't a rule, just a choice. We'd all silently agreed to give the outside world a little more time to absorb the news. Which is why Gran emerging from her room dressed in something other than pajamas shocked everyone.

"Big plans?" Tim joked.

"Just a drive," she said.

"Really?" I was itching to get out of the house, but even after days of watching so little life pass the front window, I worried we'd be met by the firing squad. "Where to?"

"Not sure yet. Why? You looking to hitch a ride?"

I stood up from the kitchen table, where Mom, Tim, and I had been playing a halfhearted game of rummy. The desperation to see the world gave way to bravery.

"Let me change," I said, hurrying to my room.

By the time I'd slipped into denim shorts and a tank top, the whole crew had decided to join. Tim was driving.

"Shotgun!" Mom yelled.

"As if we'd want shotgun," Gran whispered to me, linking her arm in mine.

Tim stepped outside first, looking both ways. Karl was the only neighbor outside. He waved before turning back to his roses. We piled into our Vega, with Tim and Mom in the front, Gran and me in the back. I worried it'd stall from neglect, but after two tries, it rumbled its way back to life. By the time we were in motion, turning left out of the cul-de-sac, I was smiling with relief. It was contagious. Mom laughed out loud at nothing at all. I don't know what we'd been so afraid of.

"Where to, misses?" Tim asked, changing his voice to sound like a chauffeur.

"Dairy Queen?" I suggested. It was a town over, far enough to feel safe.

"Yes, please." Mom turned around to face me. "The perfect place."

I smiled at her, and for the first time in a long time it didn't feel fake.

Tim drove with one hand on the wheel and the other on Mom's bare leg. She rested her head against the window, and I watched him sneak looks at her. Looking at love was painful, though, and I made myself look away. By now, I was certain Harry wouldn't call. Our love would be confined to the summer, just a fleeting moment I couldn't hold on to.

Once we were outside of Monroe, Mom rolled down her window and reached her arm out into the golden world. Everything was washed in light from the disappearing sun.

"You're beautiful," Tim said to her, quietly enough to think we wouldn't hear.

She was beautiful. She took his hand from her leg and brought it to her lips. I hated her happiness for costing me my own. I looked to see if Gran was listening, but if she was, she didn't show it. Her poker face was almost a glare.

When we pulled into the parking lot, Tim parked with much less caution than Harry, and I was sick with the memory of that first night. I'd felt sick for days, really.

"I miss that boy of yours," Gran said, like she was reading my mind.

Mom glanced in our direction before plastering a smile on her face.

I ignored Gran because I wasn't ready to talk about him yet. Harry was a constant thought swirling in my mind, but to say my fears out loud, that things were really over—well, that would make them feel even more real.

Tim held the door open for all of us, and we hurried inside. Allan sighed when he noticed Gran and me.

"Three dipped cones," Mom ordered.

"One with peanuts," Gran chimed in.

"Tim?" Mom looked over at him. He was studying the menu.

"Amateur," Gran whispered.

"Maybe the Orange Julius? Any good?"

Mom made a face.

"What?" he asked.

"I just think fruit has no place in a dessert." It was one of her rules. Our rules. "Chocolate or bust."

"One bite of my wife's strawberry shortcake will get you to sing a different tu—" He caught himself, way too late to make a difference. "I'm sorry," he said.

Gran smiled but it was insincere—and a little frightening. "Hmm, Lyla's shortcake. Can't say I've had the pleasure."

"I'm sorry," he said again, this time to Mom more than the group.

Mom was a good sport about it, though. "It's fine," she said somewhat convincingly.

I pretended to study the menu posted on the wall, and Gran tapped her nails on the counter where Allan was waiting to take Tim's order.

Allan's interruption saved the day. "I can't start making your order until you pay."

"Oh, right. Sorry. I'll just join the girls." Tim reached into his back pocket for his wallet. "Dipped cone for me too, but hold the peanuts."

The shift in mood was palpable. Desperate to push through the awkwardness, Mom spent the entire outing explaining our love for Dairy Queen. Tim, to his credit, smiled at all the right parts, but even I could see he was miles away. She tried to include Gran and me too, prompting us to join her in the storytelling. We both sulked in our swivel chairs, halfheartedly licking our ice-cream cones.

I kept thinking Harry might pull into the lot, parking his car in the space farthest from the others, but he didn't.

Gran had said Jay was the one who kept things in control—that none of this would be happening if he was around. Maybe she wished we'd never come back after all. In one night, she'd lost her one true love and life as she once knew it. And then, Mom had hurried back to blow up whatever shreds were left.

When we stood to leave, there was a ding at the door. Marie walked in with a boy I didn't recognize. I held my breath.

"Hi, Marie," I said, when our eyes met.

She was silent, fixing her eyes on the menu to avoid mine.

I kept looking, waiting for her to say something, knowing she wouldn't. She was a brick wall. My body turned cold, a panicked feeling settling beneath the surface. I knew I should stop staring, stop waiting for something that would never come, but I couldn't look away.

Mom and Tim moved to make a quick exit. When the door dinged above them, she looked back at me.

"Aurora—we're leaving," she said, her voice soft.

I watched her follow him to the car. Gran linked arms with me, putting me out of my misery, making my concrete feet move, steering me toward the door.

Marie was just a preview of what was to come—the whispers I'd endure as I walked through the Monroe High halls, the desks people would cover with their books just to avoid sitting with me, the lunchroom tables where girls would shoot me their meanest glares. I'd spent the last fifteen years flying under the radar, but Mom had managed to put me on the map.

When we returned home, no one said a word. Gran plopped down in her recliner, leaving her room to Tim and Mom, who were probably happy to have it back. I went to my room, even though it was way too early for bed and even though that meant I'd miss *The Tonight Show*.

Tim said goodnight to me in the hall, squeezing my shoulder while he walked past. It made me happier than I cared to admit. There was still something so dad-like about him, and it was the thing I'd been noticing in men for most of my life. Only now it existed in the man saying goodnight to me before bed and sleeping in the room down the hall. Despite every circumstance telling me otherwise, it felt normal.

○○○

I wasn't asleep when he tapped on my window, and I wasn't startled by the sound. Maybe I knew he would come, a sixth sense I never knew I had. For the past few nights, it had been my only hope. A nighttime daydream. The thing I was waiting and wishing for.

I was a bundle of nerves and inexplicable optimism. Finally, after days of waiting, here was my chance.

I knelt beside my window and pushed it up with both hands. After about three inches, it stuck. Harry slipped his hands through the crack, accidently brushing mine in the process, and helped me push it further.

"Hey," he said.

My hands rested on the windowsill, but I slipped them back inside, into my lap. "Hi."

"Can you sneak out?" he asked.

My heartbeat was so loud I was sure he could hear it.

The crack in the window didn't seem big enough to squeeze through, but no one would notice if I used the front door.

"Meet me out front," I said. I looked down at my pajamas. An oversized T-shirt and ratty underwear. "Just give me a minute to change."

Before he disappeared from my bedroom window, I swear I saw him smirk.

I had no idea what to wear to a midnight rendezvous. I had no idea what he was here for. For all I knew, he could've come to break up with me. Did I really want to look cute for that? It'd been four days of the silent treatment, so a breakup seemed most likely. Still hopeful, with a touch of wishful thinking, I settled on the yellow dress I'd worn on our first date. I thought it might remind him of a time when things were less complicated.

After I dressed, I ran to the living room because I couldn't bear the thought of Gran checking in on me and finding an empty bed. She was awake in her recliner, of course, the TV volume turned down low.

Gran looked concerned. "What's wrong?"

"I'm sneaking out."

"Oh, honey, sneaking out doesn't include telling an adult where you're going. It's not very sneaky that way." She smiled. "Why can't you just be a normal teenager?"

"I just didn't want you to worry."

She looked me up and down, noticing the dress. "He came through, huh?"

"This is just me hoping." I gestured at my outfit. "It's still to be determined."

Gran reached out a hand for me. I went to her side and held it. "He'd be a fool to let you go, but a lot of men are fools. Just look at the man one room over." She winked. "But I've still got hope for that Harold Clark. When you sneak back in, come let me know."

"Okay, I will. Sorry I missed Johnny."

She smiled. "Johnny will be here tomorrow—it's the one thing we're guaranteed."

I left her in her recliner, washed blue by the light of the TV. I could picture the nights she spent with Jay perfectly—how she'd bark out a laugh at the crass parts of the monologue, the way he'd smile at her when she wasn't looking. I know she wished he were still here, and I wished he were too, because then I'd feel less bad leaving her behind.

Harry didn't say anything at first, but he did open my door, which I took as a good sign. Small victories were enough to turn my stomach inside out. I was a bundle of nerves. We drove down the street in silence. He turned right, and I knew where we were going. The pool. Three minutes into the silent drive, I realized that I too had a working voice box, and while it terrified me to use it, I made myself do it anyway.

"You didn't call," I said, which wasn't the best opening line.

"You didn't tell me about your mom."

"Who told you?"

I had become obsessed with Charlotte's theory and had dreams at night of Harry comforting Lyla in the places he'd once taken me. In the stir-crazy, heat-stroke daze of the little blue house, waking up glistening with sweat, these dreams seemed plausible. Her dad was charming. It could be genetic.

"Shane," he said. I felt an instant relief. "His mom is close with Lyla's mom. He said she called their house, hysterical." The relief gave way to dread. "He asked if I knew. I swore I didn't, but then I started to wonder why. Why didn't you tell me?"

"I don't know." I pressed my head against the glass and stared out the window because I didn't want to look at him. "I was scared."

"Of what?" he asked.

He parked across the street from the pool and turned off the engine.

"Of the things you're about to say," I said, finally turning to face him.

"But what if I don't say the things you assume I'll say?"

There was a chance he'd surprise me. He could take my hand and tell me it was only us that mattered. That the rest of it was bullshit. Although he wouldn't say *shit*, but the sentiment would be the same. But those were soap-opera lines, and I knew we weren't a plotline on some daytime TV drama. This was real life, and I couldn't risk real-life answers.

"But what if you do?" I asked.

He ran a hand through his hair, clearly frustrated. "Can you just give me a chance?"

"Hey, Harry," I said, my voice flat, "you know your ex-girlfriend Lyla Rae? You know her dad? Yeah, Tim, the mailman, the one who goes to your dad's church and shakes your hand after Sunday service? Well, he's actually sneaking around with my mom. Has been all summer, actually. Yep, might leave his family for ours."

I watched Harry chew the inside of his lip.

"Just say it," I said, and the venom in my voice reminded me of her. "Say what you'd have said then, what you'll say now."

I knew what was coming, and I'd decided in that moment to hate him for the four days of silence. To hate him for the things he was about to say. To hate him for the way he'd made this about him, as if the things that were destroying my life even touched the life he led in his perfect home, with his home-cooked meat loaf, a mother who spent her whole adult life praying him into existence, a father who set curfews to make sure he got home safe. In that moment, hate felt easier than love.

"You never even gave me a chance." His voice was as close to angry as I'd ever heard it. "I asked you, point blank, about your family. Said you could tell me anything. *Anything*, Aurora," he said, his voice pitching just slightly louder.

"If I'd told you, I knew it would end. I knew you would leave."

"No, you *thought* it would end," he corrected. "You thought I would leave."

"But didn't you? When you found out? It's been four days—" My voice caught on a sob. "Four days and you never called."

"I'm here now, though." His voice was softer, but he maintained the distance between us. I wanted him to close the gap. "Tell me the truth. See what I say."

"Harry, my mom is sleeping with Lyla Jr.'s dad. Like, I have to turn up the TV so I don't overhear them. It's been going on all summer long, and I've had to see Lyla Jr., at the alley, at the pool."

I was crying so hard I had to gulp for air.

"And then I'd spend time with you, and I could forget about it for a while. I was happy, and I could forget about it all. So the thought of losing it, losing you—I just—it wasn't a risk I was willing to take."

Harry reached for my hand. "If you'd have told me, I might have been a bit shocked, sure, but then I'd have said it sounds like you've really got no say in it." He tilted his head so I'd meet his eyes. "I mean, at least I think you don't. I know you, Aurora."

I was never sure where I ended up when it came to right and wrong. But I did feel guilty about the mess my mother had made and the people it affected. I had a weak stomach when it came to hurting others.

"I wanted them to stop. I asked her to." I looked over at the pool. The cement was washed blue, and the water was lit with lights beneath the surface. "Should we go in?" I asked, embarrassed by my tears.

I opened my door before Harry could reach me. He used the key to unlock the gate, and I walked in ahead of him. I sat on the edge, dangling my bare feet in the water. I'd forgotten shoes.

"I don't hate her," I said, because I thought I needed to make that clear to him. I stared straight ahead. "I hate what she's done, but I don't hate her. She's my mom."

He sat down on the cement beside me, keeping distance between us. "I know that."

"Do your parents know?" I already knew the answer, but I asked anyway.

"Yeah." Beneath the water's surface, his legs swayed back and forth.

"What'd they say?"

Now it was his turn to stare straight ahead. "Well, of course they're sad about it. But the Harrisons didn't have a perfect marriage on either side of things. Lyla was always complaining about them."

"That makes sense." I didn't know what else to say.

He turned to face me and took both my hands in his. "But you know what my mom said?"

"What?" I asked, terrified of his answer.

"She said the world is full of people, and no one is all good and no one is all bad." Gran's wisdom. "Said you were about as blameless as they come. And then she said I'd be stupid if I let something like this get between us."

He was all teeth. I couldn't help but smile back.

"Claire-Ann is a wise, wise woman," I said. "She'd kill you if she knew you snuck out, though."

He pushed himself to his feet, taking off his shirt in a single tug. "She caught me," he said, nonchalant.

"What? Harold Jr. you have got to be kidding me." I stood up too and tried not to get too distracted by his bare skin. He shimmied out of his shorts and stood before me in his boxers. "Tell me you're joking."

He shook his head. "No joke. She caught me sneaking out, and then she asked where I was going. I told her 'cause she's hard to lie to. But then she just let me go."

He cannonballed into the water, and the waves spilled over the sides of the pool, reaching the tips of my toes. When he surfaced, he shook out his hair, like a dog, and grinned.

"You didn't get into trouble?"

Harry bit his bottom lip. "I didn't say that. This is the last you'll see of me for two weeks." He dipped below the surface and buoyed back up. "I'm grounded."

I watched him swim in the deep end.

"Did you hear me?" Floating on his back, he cupped his hands around his mouth to create an echo in our concrete paradise. "This is the last you'll see of me for two weeks, so it'd be great if you jumped in and joined me."

"Shh," I said, thinking of the houses nearby. My reputation in Monroe was shot, but I worried about his.

"Aurora," he whispered. "Get in here."

I reached back to unzip my dress and let it fall to the floor by my feet. Harry didn't even pretend to look away. Before I could think too much, I jumped in the pool and swam to his side, hooking my arm around his neck. Under the water, his hands found my waist. I inched my face closer to his.

"So we're not breaking up?" I asked.

Then I kissed him before he could answer.

❧

Gran was still awake when I got home. She stood in my doorway, and I must have had a funny look on my face, because she smiled and said, "Ah, to be young and in love."

"Will you sleep in here tonight?" I asked. I couldn't bear to sleep alone. "Please?"

"Aurora, you're fifteen years old," she said, shaking her head. But then she stepped inside and climbed into my bed. "Next thing I know you'll be asking me for a nightlight."

We flipped on our sides to face each other, like two girls at a sleepover.

"So spill," she said. "What happened? What did he say about all this?" She threw her hands out as if to encompass the whole house.

She had scattered sunspots across her cheeks, and her barely thinning hair was tied back with a scarf. Her eyes looked clear, and I could tell she hadn't been drinking, not for a while now. Looking at my gran, I knew she'd always be my favorite person on this earth.

"Go on, missy," she said. "Don't spare the details."

I told her everything, and she listened and hung on every word. Gran always made me feel like every word I said aloud was worth hearing, like I was right to take up space in this world.

"He's about as good as I thought he was," she said when I finished.

"Mom seems happy."

Gran didn't look convinced. "Maybe. For now. If he stays."

"You think he'd be willing to ruin his reputation for a week vacation in our house?"

"No, I think he thought he was going to stay, but I think he might wake up tomorrow and wonder what the hell he's done. And if not tomorrow, the next day or the day after that. If he went back, they'd take him. Hell, the whole town would take him."

"Would they take us?" I asked, a new blossom of hope forming in my chest, as pink and bright as Karl's flower. I was excited by the idea of a clean slate. "What about Mom?"

My mind began to race before I could stop it. A do-over. A restart. Charlotte was wrong. We could turn back time. It was still possible. I'd serve popcorn to people who'd smile and tip me. Mom could return to Norma's and wipe down the counters and serve the coffee. Gran could be Gran. She would *always* be Gran, and the three of us could live the same life we'd lived before. The three of us and Monroe.

"I said they'd take *him*," Gran said, her voice turning soft. "Don't you go getting your hopes up."

Too late, I thought.

"Our world is easier on men." Gran sighed.

Another of Gran's life lessons, but this one was harder for me to swallow. I wanted to ask questions, but when she reached over to turn off the lamp, I knew she was done talking. It killed me to know time could turn back, but not for us. It made no sense to me. If we were going to burn at the stake, he should burn with us.

28

Tim offered to cook us dinner. He called Charlotte with a list of ingredients and promised her a crisp five-dollar bill if she'd deliver. She showed up, small beads of sweat on her temples, bike discarded on our lawn, and everyone began to laugh.

"Oh, screw off," she said, dropping the bags on the carpet. "This is the last time I deliver. All of you need to take a step outside, see the world. See the inside of the grocery store." We were in our TV living-room spots, staring at her with wide eyes. "And Tim?" she said, clearly not done yet. "I hope you know that delivery fee doesn't include a tip."

He rose from the couch, looking a little terrified. Gran looked over at me and winked.

"Here you go," he said, passing her bills from his wallet.

She counted them, nodded, and then tucked the money in her back pocket. Before she reached the door, she turned around to face us. "One more thing: I don't know what the hell he's cooking you, so you might want to preheat the oven for some instants."

Everyone laughed, and Charlotte, always aware of her audience, slammed the door behind her. She came and left with a bang.

⁂

The smell from the kitchen wasn't bad, just interesting. We listened to him search our cupboards for pots and pans none of us knew we had. When he hollered about a ladle, Gran asked what in the hell he was talking about. We weren't allowed to check up on him, and he refused to let us peek at the ingredients.

"I think it's going to be bad," Gran said, shaking her head.

Mom nodded, and it seemed like this was the first time they'd agreed in days. Weeks. "Even if it tastes like shit, you need to be nice," she said to the both of us. "It's really sweet he's doing this for us."

"Us," Gran mouthed at me and smiled.

"*Okay!*" Tim yelled from the kitchen. "*Come on in!*"

Gran covered her ears with her palms. "I hope his culinary skills are better than his manners."

"Shush," Mom hissed.

Tim, to his credit, had managed to set the table with dinnerware we never used. Mom preferred the plastic variety, preferably with cartoon faces and mismatched spoons. That or we ate straight from the instant trays. These were Jay's plates, wedding china he'd made Gran pick out despite her protests. Tim hadn't even been here a week, and he was already morphing us into *Leave It to Beaver*. Or maybe a twisted version of the family he'd left behind? The thought stung.

"Bon appétit," Tim said, gesturing at the table, where in the center a single candle was lit.

"The bone of a what?" Gran said, leaning forward to get a closer look at what appeared to be a casserole.

"No," he said, correcting her, "Bon appétit—it's French for 'enjoy your food.' I heard it on TV."

"If you say so," Gran said, taking a seat in her usual chair. "What's this called, then?"

Tim scooped a healthy helping on each plate, probably more than I would have asked for. I guess he was feeling confident. We sat down, and it still felt strange to have the fourth chair occupied.

"This," he said, shoveling a bite into his mouth, "is my famous White Trash Casserole."

Mom, who'd managed to eat the smallest forkful, choked on her food.

"It's called what now?" Gran said, leaning away from the plate.

"White Trash Casserole," he answered, his mouth full of another bite.

Gran pushed the plate toward the center. "Oh, Tim, sweet Tim, I don't know about that."

"What's in it?" I asked, stirring the slop on my plate.

Mom, to her credit, had managed to swallow a couple of tiny bites.

"Well, that's the fun of it." Tim raised his eyebrows. "It's a secret."

"Okay," I said, thinking I'd just ask Charlotte for the grocery list tomorrow. "I'll bite."

My forkful was bigger than Mom's but smaller than Tim's. "Gran, you going to join me?"

Her mouth was turned down at the sides while she brought the fork to her mouth.

"One . . . two . . ." Mom was counting, but before she could get to three, my forkful of White Trash Casserole clattered on the floor.

The house shook with the sound of shattering glass. Mom screamed. And then there was the sudden squeal of tires. The four of us stood up from the table and ran toward the sound, Mom leading the way. The brick was in the center of our carpet, and the blinds were bent in the center. The glass on the floor reflected the light from the lamp. Tim was already out the front door, running, ready to chase down whoever had thrown it.

"It was the girl!" Karl yelled from his rose garden. The sound carried through the broken window, and Gran and I exchanged looks.

The three of us stared at the brick in the middle of our living room like it was on fire. I'm surprised it wasn't.

Mom bent down to grab it. "There's a note."

Nobody noticed Tim until he took the brick from her, his small gut heaving with unsteady breaths. He untied the string that held the piece of folded white notebook paper. Mom read it over his shoulder. She left the room. Tim dropped the brick and the note on the floor and followed her. The note landed face up.

Dear Dad,

We miss you.

Love,

Lyla and Caroline

The writing had to be Lyla's. Large, loopy letters in a swirly script. Caroline's name was signed in a childlike scrawl.

"Nothing like a brick through the window to kill the honeymoon," Gran said, bent over and squinting. "If I'd known that, I might've thrown one myself."

She walked to the kitchen to pour herself a glass of water. I knew she was shaken up. We were all shaken up. Too scared to touch it, I leaned over and read the note a second time.

I couldn't imagine the conversation in the next room. I waited for yelling, but there was silence, which was harder to interpret. I wondered if Gran was right—would this be what ended it?

I walked to my room, our uneaten White Trash Casserole turning cold on the kitchen table. It was only seven thirty, but I felt as tired as if it had been midnight. I lay down in my bed, not bothering to change into pajamas, desperate to go to sleep and set the world right side up. Or maybe the world was upside down, and the brick was our reset. I wasn't sure I wanted a new day.

∽

I woke up to Mom's screams—loud, shrill, and animal-like.

My heart pumped in my chest while my room came into focus. The casserole. The brick. The note. The daughters. The night came back to me in fragments, as disorienting as if it'd been a dream.

The red numbers on my watch stared back at me. Three AM.

Her second scream was louder than the first. If I hadn't been fully awake before, I was now.

The hallway was still dark when I stepped out of my bedroom, Tim flying past me, certain of his direction. I could feel the rage coming off him in waves. I knew where he was going. He didn't look at me, the same way he didn't look at Mom in the Paradise parking lot. Mom was next, her anger carrying her through the hall. It looked like she was floating.

"Mom?" I said.

She grabbed a frame off the wall, one of Gran's only photos of us, pulling her arm back like a baseball pitcher before hurling it toward Tim.

She missed, the picture shattering on the entryway table. He didn't miss a beat, didn't even turn around.

Mom hurried toward him, but Tim was out the front door before she could catch up, slamming it behind him. I followed behind, something I'd done for most of my life. Mom reached for the doorknob, and I grabbed her elbow, knowing whatever she was about to do, she couldn't take it back.

"Don't do it," I said, but she shook me off, flinging open the door.

I ran to the living room to see if Gran was awake. Of course she was. Eyes wide open, her body remained sunken into her recliner.

"Aren't you going to do something?" I screamed.

She didn't look at me when she said, quietly, "What could I even do?"

The front door was still open. The sky was dark, freckled with bright stars. I followed the sound of Mom's voice down the driveway. Most of what she said was unintelligible until she screamed, *"You lied!"*

Tim spun around to face her, and I felt terrified.

The lights on the street winked on one by one, like summer fireflies. Karl was already in his front yard. The screams seemed to have woken up everyone in the neighborhood. Houses in the development side of town were packed tight, like sardines in a can. Everyone came out for the show.

Again, I tugged on Mom's elbow, but she shook me loose.

"*'Laine, we're gonna be a family.'*" She lowered her voice to imitate his. "*'Laine, I've never felt like this before. Laine, you don't know what she's like. Laine, I could fuck you forever.'*" The last words came out like a scream. "*'Laine, Laine, Laine!'*"

Tim reached for her arms and shook her while she chanted her own name. "This isn't real!" His voice was ragged.

She flinched at his words, like he'd spat on her.

"None of this is real," he said, letting go of her arms to gesture at our street, at our house, at me. "Don't you get that?"

"You said we would be a family," she yelled. I wished she'd lower her voice.

"I *have* a family!" He raised his voice to match hers. "I have *a wife*. I have *daughters*. What were we thinking? What was *I* thinking?"

Mom reached her hands up to his face. "We love each other," she said, her hardened voice turning soft, desperate, pleading. "That's what we were thinking. That this was where we were meant to end up. *Together*."

Tim reached for her wrists, forcing her hands to her sides.

"It's insane," he said. "You sound insane."

It was a painful scene, but that didn't keep the neighbors from watching.

She reached out and grabbed his arm, trying to pull him back inside.

"Just stay," she sobbed. "You said you would stay." The steady stream of tears stained her cheeks black. She looked terrifying. "I told her you would stay."

He shook her loose like she was an inconvenience, and in spite of myself, I waited for him to look my way. He didn't. I guess all summer had led to this. Maybe this was the end all along. He'd made promises he'd never keep, and she'd been stupid enough to believe him. Sometimes I'd been stupid enough to believe him. I felt foolish and angry and embarrassed—for her and myself.

"What was this, then?" she asked, her voice just above a whisper.

He lowered his voice like he was speaking to a child. "A mistake," he said. "Laine, you have to see it. This was a mistake."

Before she could respond, Tim walked down the driveway, leaving our life as quickly as he'd entered. Mom continued to scream while his truck roared to life. A few neighbors had gone inside, but most remained under the glow of their porch lights, watching her world fall apart.

I couldn't stop her from chasing down the street after Tim's disappearing headlights. Her hair flowed out from behind her. She was in only a T-shirt and underwear, barefoot and hysterical. By the time Tim turned left, a direction that made his destination all the clearer, Mom collapsed.

Some neighbors stood on the edge of their lawns, their toes edging the line where grass turned to cement.

I walked toward Mom, ashamed that she was mine. It was the first time I'd ever wished her dead, and the guilt of it weighed down my chest.

Karl came up beside me, hooking my arm in his, moving me toward her. I might not have made it without his gentle pull. When we reached her, he sat on the pavement beside her. I followed his lead.

"Mom," I said, "we should go back inside."

"No," she said, her voice like a child's.

"Listen to your girl," Karl said. He reached over to tuck Mom's hair behind her ear. "Let's get you home."

I held one elbow and Karl held the other. She didn't fight us when we pulled her to her feet. I pulled her shirt down to hide her underwear—the street had witnessed enough of a show. The walk to the little blue house was suddenly a mile long, a parade for the neighbors grimacing on their lawns. I wished Charlotte were there to wave at them like Miss America on a float in the Macy's Thanksgiving Day Parade. I kept my head down.

It wasn't a far drive to the house Tim shared with three other women. By the time we made it to our front door, he might've reached them. Maybe his homecoming was like that Prodigal Son story I'd heard on the TV. Perhaps less than a mile away there was a party, a renewal of vows. But on this side of Monroe, washed in our neighbors' front porch lights, we were planning another funeral.

When we got Mom inside, Karl helped her lie across the couch. Gran's face was stone, but she offered him a blanket for Mom. The breeze from the shattered front window chilled the room, letting the outside in.

Without a word, Karl kissed Mom's cheek. Before he left, he reached for my hand and squeezed it. I think he knew his voice would shatter our building silence.

"I'm going to bed," Gran said.

I was stunned, but I didn't say a word. I didn't ask her to stay. First Jay, now this. I wouldn't be surprised if she never came out of her room. Mom continued to cry, although the sobs were less of a wail now. These were silent tears.

"You should too," Gran said, squeezing my hand like Karl had.

But I didn't go to bed. I sat on the floor by Mom, holding her hand while she cried herself into a fitful sleep. I couldn't sleep. Maybe it was my penance for wishing her dead. Regardless, I remained by her side, watching her features turn into those of a sleeping child. When the morning light shone through our shattered window, the heat came with it. She shook off the blanket, and sometime after sunrise, Gran returned to her recliner. It didn't look like she'd slept either.

I waited for someone to say something, anything at all, and when neither of them did, I stood and walked to my room. I packed a bag. When I walked to the front door, I hesitated, giving them a chance to ask where I was going. No one said a word.

29

If Charlotte was at all stunned by my plan, she didn't show it. She just nodded her head and slid her feet into her flip-flops, following me outside. Her mom had heard about the night before, but I didn't ask how. There were enough phones on our street to spread the news through town.

"Are you sure about this?" she asked, placing a foot on each peg.

"I'm sure," I said, forcing down the pedals and urging the bike forward.

My backpack was heavy, making the bike ride even more of a strain. Luckily our destination wasn't far. Nothing in Monroe was far.

When we rounded the corner onto the street, the houses looked similar to ours. There was no glaring difference. His house was the third one in. I'd looked the address up in the phone book at the start of summer. I don't know why. I guess I wanted to see it for myself. Or maybe I knew this day was coming even before I really knew.

"I think it's this yellow one," I said, turning into the empty driveway, searching for the house numbers.

Most of the street had empty driveways. I guess the neighbors were all sweating in church. Harry would be there too.

"You should park the bike on the side of the house," Charlotte said. "Just in case."

I leaned the bike against the wall, and we unlatched the fence on the way to the backyard. There was a tire swing hanging from a tree, stilled by the warm, breezeless air. It looked unused.

The back door was open; just the screen was closed. Lyla Sr. seemed like the kind to keep the door open for a breeze. She had nothing to fear, nothing to hide. The man's voice carrying over into her neighbor's yard was her husband's. She was no secret.

I put a foot inside on her tiled floor before turning to Charlotte. "Are you coming?"

She shook her head. "I'll stand guard."

The house was eerily quiet. School pictures of Lyla Rae Jr. and Caroline lined the hallway beside the kitchen. I recognized the familiar backdrop of the portable photo studio brought to schools each year—a forest of blurred, green watercolor trees.

Lyla had braces two years in a row and then none the next. Her hair, normally up, was down in each photo, landing in soft curls on her shoulders. I pictured Lyla Sr. the night before picture day, painstakingly taking two-inch sections of her daughter's hair, burning her fingers on the hot rollers. I'm sure this was the kind of family that bought their kids new shoes each fall and new shirts each picture day.

Tim had told Mom their relationship wasn't real—that *we* weren't real. Walking down the hall, his words made more sense. This was a house with history—wedding photos, Caroline's art on the fridge, and a smell that was unfamiliar to me but to them must have smelled like home. How could she expect him to leave this?

The hallway led to the living room. It was painted pink, like a baby's room, with home decor magazines intentionally scattered across the coffee table. There was no ashtray in sight. No *National Enquirer*. No water stains from sweating glasses of whiskey.

Another hallway led to the bedrooms. The first was Caroline's, tiny shoes scattered across the floor and a rejected Sunday dress hung over a chair. I walked past it. The second, Lyla Rae Jr.'s, looked a lot like Charlotte's. David Cassidy and Donny Osmond were plastered on the walls. Her desk was littered with makeup, but I'm sure she paid for hers. I picked up a nail polish, bright blue, and tucked it in my pocket.

I sat at the foot of her bed, one she probably made every morning, and wondered if there was a version of my life where I ended up here. Not as an intruder, but as a guest. Would I ever have gotten an invitation? Maybe it was a sleepover she'd eventually have invited me to. We might've been friends in a world where my mom didn't sleep with her dad.

But that was fantasy, and this was reality. I got up off her bed and looked for any sign of me left behind. Just a small crease in the comforter. An empty spot on her full desk. I smoothed the crease with my palm.

A few feet down the hall, Tim and Lyla's room was open just a crack. I stepped inside, suddenly nervous he'd be there. What if he didn't go to church after all? Maybe he needed a week to repent before showing his face. But the room was empty, and he was nowhere to be found. Maybe church really was a place of acceptance if they were willing to welcome back someone like Tim.

The master bedroom had a big oak dresser. A stack of clean men's pajamas was folded next to a photo of their wedding. Lyla Sr. looked just like her daughter, with the same blonde hair falling in long curls. Tim had been even more handsome then, his smile crinkling the skin by his blue eyes. My body became soaked in a cold sweat, and I ran to the master bathroom, vomiting into their toilet. For a moment, I thought I might pass out.

I stood, my legs still shaky. The weight of my backpack reminded me of my mission. I let it drop to my side and unzipped it, removing the brick that had flown through our window less than twenty-four hours ago. When I held it in my palm, I realized what great aim she must have had.

I replaced Lyla's note with one of my own, tied with that same twine. There was no reason to break a window. We'd already shattered enough. Instead, I set the brick on the center of their shared bed.

Dear Lyla,
I'm sorry.
Aurora

Before I could change my mind, I ran through the house to the back door, where Charlotte stood waiting.

"Did you actually do it?" she asked.

I nodded. "For your time," I said, handing her the nail polish.

She threw her head back and laughed.

✦

We took the long way home, going up and down streets we didn't need to. I swerved the bike down the center, and I did my best not to worry about Mom's reality or Gran's silence. Instead, I tilted my face toward the sun and hoped it could heal me.

After I dropped off Charlotte, I unknowingly biked my way toward a war zone. I could hear Gran and Mom's yelling from three houses away. Phil was out front, and I biked a little faster. He was in his plain clothes, with a tool belt tied around his khakis. I watched him nail wood boards across our window.

"Glass won't be in at Tom's hardware for another week or so," he said. "This'll have to do for now." He dropped the hammer to his side and turned to look at me. "Aurora, as a cop, I've got to ask: You know who did this?"

"I don't." I lied like it was second nature. I guess I'd gotten used to it this summer.

He looked over at me and smiled with just the corner of his mouth. "You, your gran, your mom—you're all the same," he said. "That's exactly what they said."

"What we did was much worse," I said, not wanting him to dig any further.

"Aw hell, Aurora, it takes two to tango. What I'm saying is if that asshole threw a brick through your window, I want to get a chance to throw a punch or two."

"Oh no," I said. "It wasn't Tim. I swear."

He nodded like he didn't totally believe me. "Okay, but if you figure out who it was, you let me know."

He turned back to his project. I watched him nail the final board, turning down the volume on their escalating fight.

"Any idea what it's about?" I asked. I was dreading going inside.

"Now it's my turn to lie," Phil said, reaching over to ruffle my hair. "I don't know what it's about. But Aurora?" Phil put his arm around my shoulder.

"Yeah?" I said, looking up at him.

"You call me if you need anything. And I mean *anything*."

"Okay," I said.

He looked at his work. "I'll be back in a week or two to install the new window. Tell Katherine."

He walked down our driveway, and I wanted to chase after him like Mom chased after Tim, but I didn't. I let him go because, unlike Tim, Phil would come back. I guess you shouldn't have to force a person to stay.

Before I pulled open the front door, I took a deep breath. Their screaming was louder just before I went inside, but when they saw me, they both fell silent.

"What?" I said, terrified Tim had called and told them what I'd done.

"Aurora," Gran said, patting the spot by her feet. "Come sit a minute."

"*Mom*—no," Mom said. "Don't do this."

"Hush," Gran hissed. "The girl's almost grown. She's nearly sixteen. As old as you were when you had her. Let her have a say."

"She's my daughter," Mom said. "She's not yours."

"What is it?" I asked.

"Tell her," Gran said, nodding toward Mom, who by now had slits for eyes.

But when Mom looked at me, she changed her face, letting her strained smile take over.

"'Rora," she said, using the name reserved for conversations like the one that followed. "This town's small, and I know I've screwed things up here. I'm sorry. I hope you know how sorry I am. But there are things you can come back from, and some you—" Her voice caught but she stumbled forward. "Some you can't. I don't think I can come back from this."

I knew the next lines. I'd heard them eighteen times in my fifteen years. "So I was thinking you and I might hit the road. Head out West, even. Finally make it out of Indiana." Her smile looked unhinged and desperate. "Maybe see some palm trees? What do you think?"

The nausea I'd felt in Tim's bedroom came back in waves. I looked around at the house I'd learned to call a home. Sure, the fridge was always on the verge of empty. There weren't any school photos of me on the walls. And yes, it smelled like cigarette smoke with a tinge of something sour. None of that mattered to me, though. It was home. It was *my* home.

The life we'd lived before Monroe wasn't something I wanted to go back to. But then again, she hadn't just burned a bridge this time. She'd lit this town on fire, damaging me in the process. How many of her mistakes had left a mark on my life? Who would talk to me besides Gran, Charlotte, and Harry? I had Phil too. And Al maybe, once things blew over. And there had to be kids in town whose parents had done worse or, if not worse, something close.

The road with Mom and the men she'd pick up along the way seemed impossibly long, and I was tired. This summer had showed me what it was like to have a world of my own. And then there was Gran, sitting there with a glass of water, her cheeks stained from tears I knew she cried for me.

"I think I'll stay," I said, wiping tears from under my eyes that I hadn't noticed falling. "I'd like to stay here. In Monroe. With Gran."

I think I'd known this would be my answer all along. Maybe even before the affair had begun. Maybe as soon as we'd pulled into the driveway.

Gran exhaled and slid from her recliner to the floor beside me. She placed her hands on my cheeks and looked in my eyes. Mom began to cry, of course. Dramatic sobs. I crawled over to the spot by her legs and set my chin on her knees, looking up at her. I held Gran's hand too.

"I'm not choosing her over you," I said. "I'm choosing a home."

"But isn't a home the people in it?" she asked. "Isn't our home the two of us?"

I didn't know the answer to that question. I guess I thought it had to be some combination of both.

"It's not for forever," I said. "I bet you'll come back. Or who knows, I might hate this place as much as you do. Maybe I just need a little more time." But I didn't and wouldn't. I loved this town. I couldn't imagine that would change. It was home. But Mom had taught me to lie, and now seemed as good a time for one as ever.

She smiled through her tears. "Maybe you can come meet me wherever I end up."

"Sure," I said. "I'll come see you when you're a big Hollywood star."

And even though she cried and cried, eventually leaving us to cry in her bedroom, I had this strange suspicion that it was all for show. Because underneath the thick droplets streaming down her cheeks and the loud heaves and sobs, I thought she seemed a little relieved.

When she'd asked me if I'd go back on the road, there had been something strange about the way she'd asked it. I knew there was a right answer, and it was a right answer not only for myself but also for her. Maybe her tears were tears of guilt because she got exactly what she wanted.

※

Mom's sudden moves never required many arrangements. For years, she barely had to pack. I watched her slip back into her usual routine with little fanfare. She called Norma and quit without notice. If it was up to her, she would have left the day after he did. It was Gran who convinced her to wait a few days.

"Pack your things up properly," she said. "We'll get some more moving boxes. Say your goodbyes. It's about time you outgrow the disappearing act."

Mom rolled her eyes, but she didn't argue. I could tell she was itching to leave, going through the motions. I couldn't blame her—we were rip-the-Band-Aid-off kind of people.

Every now and then, I'd have to remind myself that I wasn't going with her. It went against years of muscle memory to stay behind.

I wondered who she'd be without me, what kind of life she'd make for herself without a full-grown person in tow.

The day before she left, Harry called.

"Hello?" I answered.

"What are you doing?" he asked.

"Nothing much."

I hadn't told him about Mom's big plans. It felt dishonest to keep it from him but saying it out loud would make it too real. Sometimes, the voices in the TV would put me in some sort of trance, and this whole summer would feel like a dream. Mom would rise from the couch and pop in the frozen dinners, and the world would seem normal again.

But then I'd see her cardboard boxes or a road map spread out across the kitchen table, and it'd come back to me all at once. My world wasn't normal—my life wasn't the same. I'd spend the rest of it living in the timeline of before and after. The one with Mom and the one without.

"Can I see you?" he asked. "Maybe I can come over?"

"I thought you were grounded."

"I'm off the hook. Got released early for good behavior."

This made me laugh. "Harry, you better not be lying to me. I'm not trying to get you in any more trouble."

"Honest truth," he said. "So, can I come over?"

I felt embarrassed by the wooden boards covering our window. Embarrassed for my mom, who would have to face a pastor's son in the wake of, well, everything. But Harry had forgiven me on one condition: that I be honest. This house, with shattered glass still embedded in our carpet, was about as honest as I could get.

"Yes," I said.

I could picture his smile. "See you in ten."

─ ⁂ ─

I didn't give anyone warning, so when Harry knocked, Gran spun around in her recliner. Mom walked out of her room, into the hallway.

"Who is it?" Mom whispered.

"It's Harry," I said, opening the door before she could protest.

He stepped inside with confidence, but I watched him run his eyes over the front window before meeting my gaze.

"Hey," he said, offering up a shy smile.

We hadn't seen each other since the night at the pool. So much had transpired since then.

Mom and Gran were paralyzed—I was surprised they hadn't made a quick retreat. Mom stepped forward and offered a quick, "Hi, Harry—it's good to see you," before heading to the kitchen like she had something important to do. Gran walked into the living room and turned the TV dial, which felt much more natural.

"Let's go to my room," I said, reaching for his hand.

"Better keep that door open," Gran teased.

Harry laughed. "Will do, Miss Katherine."

I walked down the hall with Harry behind me. We passed her moving boxes, and I wondered what was going through his mind. When I stepped inside, I tried to see my room through his eyes. Was it really that much different from the room of any other teenage girl? I had a dresser full of clothes, a nightstand cluttered with knickknacks. The walls weren't pink—they were yellow. But the comforter had florals on it.

I shut the door behind us. Harry raised his eyebrows.

"She's only joking," I said.

He seemed timid when he sat on my bed, his feet planted firmly on the carpet. I sat beside him, scooting back so I could cross my legs.

"I have to tell you something."

He angled his body to face mine. "Does this have to do with the boxes?"

I tucked my hair behind my ears. "She's leaving," I said.

Harry took in a sharp breath. "And you're . . . ?"

"Staying." He looked so relieved I wanted to cry. "I'm going to stay here with Gran." The next words came quickly, because if I didn't say them now, I didn't know if I ever would. "Harry, can I tell you something else?"

Harry scooted back and wrapped me in his arms. "Aurora, how many times do I have to tell you? You can tell me anything."

With my head on his chest, I began to tell my story. The apartments. The diners. The men. I told Harry about Sean and the bird—how desperate I felt to make these men my dad. I told him about the men who hurt her. I told him about how she had hurt me.

And then I told him the truth about Tim. How we might not have been real to him, but that sometimes he'd felt real to me. I wanted him to understand it all. I wanted him to understand me. In some ways, I wanted him to understand her.

At some point we became horizontal. I wanted to face him when I said these things. It would be easier to avoid his eyes, but honesty wasn't supposed to be easy.

Harry reached his hand, which somehow always smelled like sunblock and chlorine, to cup the side of my face. His thumb wiped away the tears that had begun to fall.

"So what made this time different?" he asked. "Why are you staying behind?"

"I don't want to up and leave when things get hard." I'd been thinking about this for days—what would possess me to say no to her. "And I've never really thought about what I want. What I want to happen next. Who I want to be."

"So what do you want?" he asked.

"I want to live in Monroe, Indiana, with my crazy grandmother. I want to hang out with Charlotte and listen to her stories that are almost always half-truths. And I want to be here with you."

Harry leaned in so our lips were almost touching. "Yeah?"

"Yeah," I whispered before closing the gap.

Harry left before dinnertime, and I didn't blame him. We were low on frozens, and when Gran offered him meat loaf, I told him leaving was probably for the best. Mom was holed up in her room—she said she wasn't hungry. It was just Gran and me and our friends on the TV. Our soon-to-be new normal.

"I haven't been drinking," she said without any lead-in. She wasn't looking at me. Her eyes stayed on the TV, like the Revlon commercial was absolutely riveting. "I just want you to know that. If you're done with a shift or you need a ride home from somewhere, I'll be good to go. Okay?"

"Okay," I said.

"And I think we ought to teach you how to drive. Properly. I'll give you lessons."

I got up from the couch and took my spot by her feet, resting my chin on her knee. I could tell she was fighting back tears.

"It'll be good," I said, hoping to ease whatever worries plagued her.

She finally met my eyes. "*I'm* going to be good," she said. "I can't promise I'll be all good, but I'm going to try my damnedest."

"I love you."

Gran wiped under her eyes. "I love you too, hon. Now do me a favor and turn up the TV." I let out a heavy sigh, which was just for show. Gran smirked. "And get me some water since you're already gonna be up."

30

The night before she left, Mom climbed into my bed like she had so many nights before. I wasn't asleep yet. Not even close. It had been four days since the brick, and we hadn't heard from Tim. Mark was the new mailman on our route, not that any of us had picked up the mail stacked in the rusted mailbox.

Her hand brushed the hair off my forehead. "Can I tell you something?" she asked.

I kept my eyes shut and nodded. If I opened them, I'd start crying. If I let myself start crying, I might never stop.

"When I gave birth, there wasn't a single familiar face. It was doctors and nurses and beeping machines, and I was terrified. I wasn't much older than you are now. It was so painful I kept screaming. I thought I was dying." She laughed. "I'm sure they thought I was crazy, and they weren't nice to me at all." Gran had told me once they're rarely nice to young mothers. "But I was stubborn too, and I couldn't call Gran. I think I worried she wouldn't come."

I opened my eyes and flipped on my side so I was facing her. She wasn't looking at me.

"But then there you were, pink and crying, and I didn't feel so alone anymore. All my life I'd felt alone, even in rooms full of people. And then I had a piece of me that I could have forever. You were my familiar face." She used her worn-out waitress hands to wipe the tears that streamed down the sides of my face, soaking the hair by my temples. "I knew then if I'd called my mom, she'd have driven straight to me. Hell, she might've hired a helicopter to get her there. It's the best and worst thing in the world, loving someone so much."

I waited for her to ask me to come with her, but she didn't.

"You're the best piece of me, and I wanted to be the best for you, but I was young. I'd like to think I'm still young."

"You are," I said, opening my eyes to look into hers.

"I just can't be here right now," she whispered, her voice thick with emotion.

I reached my hand out to wipe a stray tear making its way down her cheek. "I know."

We didn't have to say anything else. I didn't hate her for leaving, and she didn't hate me for staying. I turned so my back was to her, and she curved her body around mine. We'd shared plenty of twin beds before.

"My little spoon got so big," she whispered.

And when I closed my eyes, I breathed in her scent, hoping I could memorize it. Love was too complicated for me to think about, how you could love someone so much but still want them to leave. I was relieved at the thought of her driving miles and miles away, which felt wrong. And I think she was relieved too, at the thought of driving until she had to stop. Those were the complicated parts of us, the things we'd never say aloud. But other things were simple. The cigarettes mixed with the vanilla shampoo. The sound of her laugh. Our same eyes.

Epilogue

The Tuesday before school starts, I wake up to the sound of hammering, and I wonder if it's in my head. I have nightmares where I'm covered in glass, and when I stand up, the glass slides further into my skin. When I wake up, though, my skin is fine. I leave my room and walk down the hall. The door down the hall is shut. Our living room is flooded with morning light, and I can see Phil's head through the hole he's making in our boarded-up window.

"Good morning, Sunshine," he calls.

"You don't do afternoon installations?" I ask.

"Nope," Gran says, rising from her recliner. "Already asked."

"On duty in an hour, so I'm trying to be quick about it. You know what helps?" he starts to ask, but the both of us just shake our heads.

"Too early for manual labor," I say.

"They always say that." Harry pokes his head through the growing gap in the wood, and he's got all his teeth on full display. "Officer, you're looking at the laziest girls in all of Indiana."

"Okay, shoo," Gran says, pretending to cover herself up. "I'm in my pajamas. It's hardly decent."

The two of them laugh before he slips his head back through the wood boards. I hurry back into my room and throw on shorts and a T-shirt. The phone rings, shrill and startling. Mom's the only one who'd be calling. Most of my world is here.

"You get it," Gran says.

I round the corner and grab the phone before the fourth ring.

"Hello?" I answer.

"Aurora? That you? It's Al."

I twist the phone cord around my finger. My shifts were cut indefinitely, with the promise of things "blowing over eventually." I'm starting to think "eventually" is a pipe dream.

"Yeah, it's me," I answer.

Al clears his throat, and I brace myself for the worst. I've already lost my mom—what's my job at the bowling alley?

"I'm just in the office, trying to sort out the fall schedule." I can picture him perfectly. The red leather chair. The league photos on the wall. "What time can you get here after school?"

I think of Gran and the promise of proper driving lessons. Pretty soon, I'll have a license of my own. Until then, she can give me rides.

"I can get there by four," I say. "And I'd like to keep my weekend shifts if that's all right."

Weekends get you the best tips, and even though seeing the whole town sounds terrifying, I don't want to spend my life hiding.

"That sounds good on my end." There's a long sigh and then the shuffling of paper. "Yeah, let's just plan on you coming in Tuesday, Thursday, and Saturday. And Fridays when Jim flakes, which, you know, is often."

"All right," I say, keeping my voice even. It's a small victory, but I'll take it. "I'll be there Tuesday."

Al wishes me well and hangs up. I replace the phone on the hook and smile, smoothing my hair before joining Harry and Phil outside. Our lawn is only green because of Karl's recent upkeep. I sit cross-legged on the resurrected grass and watch them work.

"School starts Monday," I say.

Harry just nods, using the end of the hammer to loosen a nail.

I look up at the rising sun. Our world is washed orange. "So long, summer."

"It'll be fine," he says, like he's reading my mind. He turns to flash a confident smile.

I want to believe him. I want to believe things can "blow over," whatever that means. But everyone at school will know what happened this summer. Lyla knows what happened.

I keep reminding myself that the people I love will stay by my side, Charlotte on my left, Harry on my right. A new school hallway looks a little less terrifying when I picture them in it.

And Gran will keep time, watching the new clock above the TV, waiting for me to get home. She may not prepare after-school snacks, but she'll run her hands through my hair and fill me in on the soaps I miss. I'm trying my best to be brave.

Gran emerges from the living room in her pajama set, a plaid nightgown with lace trim and a matching robe. Karl is tending to his roses across the way, and his garden looks heavenly in the light of a new day. Gran sits beside me, and we watch Phil and Harry give us a new window, a second chance.

It's the end of August, almost the start of fall. I'll be sixteen tomorrow, but some days I feel sixty. There won't be a party, just a cake made by Mrs. Clark and candles bought from Rexall. I don't know what I'll wish for, because if I had the chance to turn back time, I'm not sure I would.

Somewhere near Nevada, I know she's driving until she has to stop. She might be terrified too. By the time she calls tomorrow, she should be in California. She'll wish me happy birthday, I'll say thank you, and neither of us will mention how this is my first birthday we'll be spending apart. We never say anything about how hard it is—the separation. I let her talk about the easy stuff—the towns she rolls through and the diners that aren't as good as Norma's. The world's largest fork in some Colorado town. The bright lights of Vegas. When we hang up, I refuse to cry.

Because even though my world looks different than it did in June, and even though I feel so far from the girl I was then, I wouldn't have it any other way.

END

Acknowledgments

To my agent, Ali Herring: thank you for loving Aurora and her story as much as I do. There's no better champion for this novel. Thank you for asking for more and for celebrating with me every step of the way. To my editor, Holly Ingraham: thank you for taking the time to meet with me when I was just a submission in your inbox. Your R&R was the greatest gift, and your timeline suggestion brought *End of August* to life. I'm so glad we were able to bring Aurora's story to the world. To the team at Alcove Press—from the copy editors to the social media managers, to Heather VenHuizen, who designed the most beautiful cover—thank you for your hard work in bringing this book to print.

To the girls who join me in the retail world day in, day out: thank you for being the best cheerleaders I could ever ask for. To Lew Lew: thank you for showing up to my readings all those years ago. Your support and our lifelong friendship mean the world to me. To my teacher and friend, Paul Buchanan, aka Buck: your classes changed the trajectory of my life. My pillars of writing were formed in those critique circles. Thank you for encouraging me beyond the classroom and for reading my work.

Mom, thank you for loving me so well and for telling me your stories. Dad, thank you for letting me major in English without questioning the job prospects post-grad. Heather, thank you for encouraging creativity in me. Noelle, you are the ultimate hype-woman and cheerleader, and your support means the world. Steven and Nik, as the youngest of four girls, I'm so glad my sisters found you and gave me brothers of my own. And to Peyton and Felicity, I love you more than you know, and I can't wait for you to be old enough to read this book.

I'd be remiss not to mention my furry companions, the best cats in the world. Ernest, being your spare human is my life's greatest joy. Marilynne, your constant need for a lap isn't always conducive to writing, but I wouldn't have it any other way.

And finally, to Hannah, my sister, best friend, and my absolute favorite person on earth, thank you for reading every iteration of this novel, for talking me out of what-if spirals, for turning my mountains into molehills, and for editing my work even when I'm not easy to edit. God knew I would need a sister and a best friend with your wisdom and capacity for love. Your heart is the best gift. I love you forever.